THE BIG FAMILY

Other books by Viña Delmar

THE MARCABOTH WOMEN

THE LAUGHING STRANGER

BELOVED

THE BREEZE FROM CAMELOT

VIÑA DELMAR

The Big Family

HARCOURT, BRACE AND COMPANY, NEW YORK

FOREWORD

A few minor characters in *The Big Family* are fictitious. Those who are pure invention are Anna, her sister, and their parents; René is also a creation of convenience.

Michael Kesson is a composite of several gay blades who were part of young John Slidell's New York.

In the case of Nell Winslow, only her name has been invented. John and Steve Price did fight their duel over an actress in Price's theatrical company. John and Charles Wilkes did come to blows because of this charmer. Diligent research has failed to reveal the name she actually bore.

On the subject of names—it is a nuisance that fact has produced so much duplication. In order to avoid absolute confusion, one of the Slidell daughters is here called Janie though she was named Jane, as her mother was.

I

The Progenitors

"There is a dead horse lying in the street," she said.

He turned and looked at her across the scarred and greasy counter of his shop. A white-skinned girl with scarlet cherries bobbing on her bonnet. She was no beauty. Her gray eyes protruded slightly, her jaw was ungirlishly firm and the white skin that should have been a dazzling asset was too thin. Veins showed bluely in her temples and her figure was so slim that he was aware of her bones. God, what death to romance, the awareness of a maiden's veins and bones.

"Yes," he said. "It is a nuisance—the dead horse. Did you wish to buy some fat candles? Bayberry, tallow-dip or beeswax? Some excellent soap? Soft or hard?"

"I did not come for candles or soap." Her tone was waspish. "Is it completely incomprehensible to you that a person might simply enter here to complain?"

"To complain of what?" he asked in puzzlement.

A pink rage tinted the white skin. Now he was aware of her blood. Nature had given her no protective devices with which to hide the sundry unattractive substances that form a human and cause him to operate satisfactorily.

"The dead horse, of course. It has been there two full days now." She was wrinkling her small nose in disgust. "Perhaps with your delightful occupation of soap-boiling, you have been unable to notice what is quite apparent to others."

"Most unbecoming of you to remark on my soap-boiling, miss. A man's method of earning his way is to be respected—providing his method is honest."

3

"Ridiculous," she said. "That's a story invented by men too stupid to improve their fortunes. But to return to the horse—"

"It wasn't my horse, you know."

"What difference does that make? He's lying in front of this place of business. What had you planned on doing? Letting him lie there for the hogs?"

He could scarcely believe his ears. The bonnet, the delicately worked shawl, the smooth white hands all testified to the fact that she was a lady. Yet as far as he knew, ladies never entered the shop, preferring to send servants for such homely items as soap and candles. And surely ladies never mentioned the hogs that roved the city streets.

She said, "Where is Slidell, the proprietor of this shop?"

"You must mean my father. He is dead many weeks now, miss."

"My sympathy, young man." Then continuing briskly, "Since you are evidently the new owner, I will speak plainly to you. The dead horse is an affront to the eyes, an assault on the nostrils and a menace to health. You will have it removed within the hour or else lose the patronage of every important house in the city."

He forbore to smile. He said, "You would ruin me if New York was composed of people all so sensitive as yourself."

"Many people are so sensitive. I can prove such to be the fact. Did you think me fool enough to make two trips? One to threaten and the other to show my threat not idle?" From beneath the shawl she drew forth a rolled paper. "Can you read, young man?"

"Oh, perhaps a little, miss."

"Then you will see exactly which houses are prepared to withdraw their patronage from you. Observe that Mrs. Alexander Hamilton of Number Fifty-eight Wall Street heads the list. Perhaps you have heard of her—or of her husband?"

Sarcasm, too, to complete the pretty picture.

He said, "Mrs. George Washington of Number Three Cherry Street did not sign?"

There was no trace of a smile. "I did not wish to trouble her, though I have no doubt she would have affixed her name to my petition. After Mrs. Hamilton's, you will see Mrs. Varick's, Mrs. Duane's, Mrs. Clinton's and a score of others who feel just as I do. My mother, Mrs. MacKenzie, has given me permission to say that

4

the custom of our house will also be lost to you unless the horse is immediately removed. I happen to know that our house uses four dollars and fifty cents' worth of candles every month."

He felt no wish to smile now. The little devil was both capable and determined.

He said, "Horses die every day in some part of the city, Miss MacKenzie. When the scavenger boys come, they are paid to—"

"The scavenger boys do not come often enough. Provision must be made to guarantee their constant attention. A regular fee must be paid by you merchants."

"Merchants! Dear miss, I run a poor and tiny business. Go to Water Street or Pearl if you would see the merchants."

"There is no dead horse lying on Water Street or Pearl. It is lying here on Broadway in front of your store. I assure you the ladies of New York are sick to death of the manner in which this city is mismanaged, young man. There is no thought given to cleanliness or comfort. The city is filthy—"

"I am not responsible for the entire city," he said and against his will he grinned at her, for it was amusing to be addressed as "young man" by this little scrap of a MacKenzie surely not a day over eighteen herself.

He was amazed that she did not challenge his remark forthwith. She was standing on the other side of the counter, eying him fixedly.

"No," she said at last and very slowly. "No, of course not. A city of thirty-three thousand people can not be any one man's responsibility."

She turned then toward the door and he was struck by the swiftness of her decision to leave, by the dazed look upon her face. It occurred to him that she might have been seized with illness or some strange shock of the system. He hurried from behind the counter.

"Miss MacKenzie, are you ill?"

"Ill? Of course not. I am in the best of health."

"May I take you to your carriage?"

"No. Please do not." She stood very still, her eyes raised to his face. "I never saw you before in the shop," she said surprisingly.

"Have you come often?"

5

"Perhaps three times. Where were you?"

Despite the curious urgency with which the question was put, he felt that it could not be answered on such short acquaintance. "Oh, various places."

"I understand," she said but she still looked dazed and her voice was suddenly as sweet and as weak as the bohea tea he drank of a morning in his room behind the shop. What freakish female thing had come over her?

"You will do something about the horse, Mr. Slidell?" And her tone now suggested that Mrs. Alexander Hamilton and Mrs. Richard Varick, the mayor's wife, notwithstanding, the matter was of no consequence.

"Yes, Miss MacKenzie. I certainly do not want my business ruined." He grinned at her again and she turned quickly toward the door and was gone.

He stepped away from the dimness of his shop and out into the sunlight of lower Broadway. Perhaps the little MacKenzie needed help.

With relief he saw her coachman coming toward her and he observed that the man's manner was not the offhand familiarity often meted out to employers' children. This was the special handling usually reserved for the master and mistress. Apparently the bony little creature was cherished by some.

He watched the carriage jolt its way toward the gambrel-roofed house in which the MacKenzies lived. He knew something of them. Scots originally. It would be this girl's grandfather who had been exiled from his own country. Highlanders who had fought against the English at Culloden Moor had needed to find other homelands. He pitied them their defeat. Standing there at the door of his own shop in New York City, the capital of this new nation, he gave a thought to unfortunates who had not won their freedom from England.

It was only a passing thought, for his mind was traveling with Miss MacKenzie in the carriage. His mind, as a matter of fact, had rushed ahead of her. It had already completed the trip to her home and had entered a clean and handsome room where a servant would relieve Miss MacKenzie of the bonnet with the scarlet cherries and of the dainty shawl. Then this servant—or perhaps another

6

—would prepare a delicious meal and present it on shining porcelain plates. He liked the idea that there would be pigeon and red Catalonia wine. At the table he imagined gentle conversation and— Gentle conversation! With that popeyed little girl? Lord, no. There would be argument and dissertation. Deliver him from such a female and all she stood for—always excepting the carriage, the clean and handsome house and the servants who would prepare the excellent meals.

Well, perhaps he would never have his own carriage or the luxury of servants but at his table there would be no skinny Scottish aristocrat to jaw at him. Anna would be at his table. Anna, black-eyed and ivory-skinned. Anna with the heavy, shining dark hair. She was the girl he would marry one day when he had succeeded in making himself acceptable to her. He sighed hugely. There was much to learn if one was to please Anna. Her sister had married a dancing master whom she had met through a flirtation at the Fly Market. The airs and graces of the man had become for Anna the standard of masculine desirability.

Miss MacKenzie's carriage had turned a corner and now that it was out of sight, John walked back into the shop. Something had to be done about the dead horse. That vixen with the scarlet cherries would rip his business to shreds. People were certainly becoming queasy. Didn't they realize that a city by natural process of being must always create filth? If the interiors of their homes were clean, wasn't that sufficient? And if people must consider the outdoors— well, taken by and large, it was a lovely city. It wasn't all swamps and refuse piles or gutters clogged with swill. Consciously now he called to mind the beauty spots of his city, ticking them off as he sometimes did for sober sailing men who wanted to see more than just the bedstead of a willing woman.

There was the tree-shaded Battery Promenade and the staid beauty of St. Paul's Church. The Presidential Mansion, four stories high and elegant indeed with its two graceful flights of stairs rising from the street. There was the Village of Greenwich and its songbirds. And just beyond the city lay Murray Hill and the breathtaking view of the house whose comforts had so seduced a British officer that history had been changed. Though John never called the attention of sailors to his own favorite prospect, he listed it now

7

among the most wonderful of all sights—the bright, wind-swept harbor.

Oh, it was a glorious city, holding within its own small self all that man could desire. The John Street Theatre, where one could look in upon the tremendous happenings of which Shakespeare had written, or laugh like a fool at *The Poor Soldier*. A cheery city that boasted of three hundred and thirty licensed drinking places, from grogshops to the luxurious tavern in which Mr. Aaron Burr drank his Spanish claret.

A city of shops that stocked a giddy array of finery and fripperies—brocaded waistcoats, black polished leather, cassimere breeches, white silk stockings, buttons of mother-of-pearl and hats of gleaming beaver. While for the ladies . . . ! Was there ever such a show of lace and gauze and taffeta and ribbons and flowers and plumes and furs and fringe? Such colors, such shimmer, such excitement!

Well, now for the dead horse.

There was a sign at 50 Broadway which read JOHN SLIDELL. SOAP-BOILER AND TALLOW CHANDLER. Behind the sign there was the store, which smelled evilly of the contents of the numerous vats. The store could not be expected to have the aroma of a spice shop, since candles frequently were made from bear grease, deer suet or mutton fat. And soap employed no daintier ingredients.

Behind the store there was the room in which John Slidell now lived alone. The pallet upon which his father had died had been removed and in its place had grown stacks of books. He could not think where the books had been before the removal of the other pallet, for surely there was no space from which they could have come. Books were everywhere.

Doubtless Anna would complain that there were far too many books. Being herself unable to read, she would regard them as useless and bothersome, but the books would stay. John loved them as his father had and he was grateful that he had discovered in his childhood the pleasure to be found in the printed page, grateful that his father had taught him the meaning of the odd little marks that were miraculously the key to a rare and joyful experience.

Perhaps he would teach Anna to read. He would suggest to her

8

this evening that she learn and if she accepted the idea with enthusiasm, he would reward her by paying the price for someone's indentured servant or slave to clean the room before the wedding night.

These thoughts possessed him as he washed his face and hands in preparation for his evening call upon Anna. With some anxiety, he glanced down at his garments and at the oxhide shoes that were muddy and splashed with something or other from the vats. There were grease spots on the linsey-woolsey shirt. Stains on the leather knee breeches. Anna so often pointed out that since he was too poor to own fine clothes, neatness became doubly important. Just this time she might not notice. He was not in a mood for fiddling with grease spots and stains. It had been quite enough to lug a pitcher of water from the cistern. When would Anna come to terms with reality? When would she reconcile herself to the fact that he was no dandy?

His mood, he thought, had been darkly tinged by the disagreeable surmise that Anna's sister and the dancing master would be in evidence this evening. John had not been invited to share the family meal so there was one slender chance that by the time he arrived at the house on Catherine Street, they would have taken themselves off to bed or for a walk around the pond. His resentment at the constant presence of Anna's relatives was not only that they prevented him from holding Anna in his arms. It was the never-ending reminders from the dancing master that this, that and the other thing was incorrect, obnoxious and thoroughly unacceptable behavior.

Well, there were places where his behavior was acceptable enough, where no one would remark on faults he might possess. Jauntily he stalked away from the vats and odors of his trade through the soft air of early evening toward the South Street dock. Since he was no visitor but a born-and-bred New Yorker, the crowds that filled the narrow streets, jostling and elbowing him, went unnoticed. It was usual to thread one's way through a fast-marching army of knife-grinders, orange girls, notion-hawkers, ragmen and wood-vendors. Ladies in slippers of celestial blue peered haughtily from sedan chairs as their servants bumped and prodded pedestrians into stepping aside. Honest seamen and pirates, merchants and slaves, milkmaids and harlots streamed through the streets, all bound for some unguessable destination which obviously must be reached in great haste. The daylight was passing and few regretted the twilit skies. The day was for sustaining life, the night for enjoying it.

John, with his cap cocked carelessly over one eye, strode on, dodging people, trees, pumps, hitching posts, stairs, stoops, open gates, refuse piles and low projecting bay windows. His spirits had risen as his mind had turned to thoughts of his evening meal. Where would he take it? He had a wide choice. The waterfront district was dotted with taverns any one of which served a good, hearty beefsteak and a pewter mug of beer. Perhaps he would go to the Madagascar tonight. But first a view of the sailing ships to make a man's heart leap with pleasure.

What a sight to behold! John stood transfixed at the familiar scene that never lost its excitement. There were the galleys from Fayal, the pink-sterns from Barbados, the proper, fully-rigged barks from Liverpool. Trim black vessels with long tapering masts and spars looking sinister and wicked as befitted slave-traders. Ships from Angola and the Azores, from Guinea and Algiers, from Brest and Ceylon. Tea and nutmegs, rich silks of China, woven fabrics of Cashmere, Indian sandalwood, perfumes, gems, spices, gums, gold and ivory. A world of wealth and adventure to make the pulses pound.

A stout, swarthy bearded man came walking on silent feet and John stared at the gold chain about his neck, at the jeweled rings upon his hands.

"Thinking of going to sea, my lad?"

"No, sir."

"And why not? A lad like you could make his fortune between winters." The man fingered the gold chain and looked sidewise at John. "This was wrought in an Arabian workshop. It would buy two lots on Wall Street. Yet I, too, was once a boy with nothing."

"Begging your pardon, sir, I am not a boy with nothing. I own a small but thriving business."

The man threw back his head and laughed, showing teeth so handsomely white and healthy that John was astounded. Surely the man was at least forty.

"A small but thriving business! What is that for a lad whose eyes fairly devour the ships, whose nostrils quiver at the smell of the sea? What would you say at the sight of green ocean, the fragrance of fresh wind as it rises newly born?"

"I would say, 'Who is taking care of my store?' " John said and the man laughed again and clapped him on the shoulder.

"You are no fool, are you, lad? For all that you are in love with the ships and the sea, you are no fool." And he went his way, moving swiftly and silently and, John thought, a little sadly.

John turned his steps toward the Madagascar. Here, too, there would be those to ask a question similar to that of the bejeweled stranger's. How has it come about, John Slidell, that never have you gone to sea? How *had* it come about? The sea was truly a natural career for him and while his father lived, he could have gone. He wished that behind him lay a voyage to the far islands so that he would at least have memories to enliven a dull day.

He shrugged and entered the Madagascar. Like all New York inns and taverns, it was poorly lighted and filled to capacity. The smoking oil lamps, though few in number, stank abominably. Candles—once they were made—gave forth, in John's estimation, a very friendly little scent, not unlike that of an affectionate animal, warm and pulsating.

The noise at the Madagascar was deafening. This was not a haunt of the gentry. It was a waterfront tavern filled with sailors and their girls and raffish elderly couples who liked their beer. Sprinkled between bar and table, a goodly assortment of common drunks added to the din.

There was a vacant seat beside old Peter Tare and John dropped into it. Tare, long-nosed, sharp-eyed, was a clerk in a shop at 18 Hanover Square. All day through, he worked very seriously, very soberly, selling Dutch linens, Marseilles quilting, Turk satin and Genoa silk velvet. Every evening, he drank himself into insensibility and was carried by courtesy of the tavern management to his room on Cedar Street. One-eyed Vic was to John's left at the long oak table. One-eyed Vic in the dirty striped shirt, his matted hair falling across the black-patched eye. None doubted that Vic had often responded to the wild cry of "Up, cutlasses, and board,"

11

but this was a small matter. Who was obligated to ask of another, "Are you quite sure you are not a pirate?"

John was greeted affably by all. The sailor across from him who was performing the difficult feat of eating his dinner with a plump brunette upon his lap called out, "Hold this for me, will you, Johnny boy?"

The brunette was willing enough but she had a squint and a poor complexion. John said, "My bride would object, I fear."

"Your bride!" Peter Tare dropped his knife and Hoxie, the tavern owner, who had come to take John's order, stared in open disbelief.

"Any day now," John said. "Maybe tomorrow. Maybe next day."

"If I was you," One-eyed Vic said earnestly, "I'd go to sea. She'll get somebody to marry her, never you fear. I see it like this: if you wanted to lie with her, someone else will want the same thing, so she'll nab her a husband. You're too much of a nice lad to get married just because some girl says you're the father."

"Before God, this is not my reason," John declared hotly. "I marry for love."

The brunette cooed softly. "Love is all," she murmured and fondled the gold hoop she had taken from her sailor's ear.

"Love!" Vic chewed noisily upon a morsel of mutton. "I had it once. It was in Java with a young Dutch widow. Before her, all women were conveniences. After her, they were all disappointments."

"Why didn't you marry her?"

"Because she would have smothered me in smug possessions, my lad. A house, a garden, chinaware, silver, churchly duties, children perhaps." Vic bent closely to his plate and added, "Besides, she would not have me."

The people in the smoking yellow lamplight roared with laughter and Vic gazed at them reproachfully. His story had not been intended to amuse.

Peter Tare said, "In thinking the matter over, I believe marriage is for you, Johnny. You are the man to settle down."

Somehow, the mild and friendly comment nettled John. He could not tell why, but it somehow smacked of insult. Far more

12

welcome would be the charge that so high-spirited and lusty a youth would make a poor husband indeed. He realized that he would have been pleased by a prediction that never would he be faithful or reliable. What nonsense was this? And yet he felt a sinking sensation at the thought that yes, he was undoubtedly a man made for marriage.

"Consider how industrious you are, how attached to your business," Peter continued. "You are a man of substance. Were you different, you would have been to sea by now."

"Bring me a beefsteak, Hoxie," John demanded. "I didn't come in here to have you goggle at me."

"I will stand a round of beers," Vic said, "in view of the fact that next time I touch this port, we will not have Johnny among us."

"Forget the round of beers," John said. "I will be here as often as I choose."

Again the table roared and it was John this time who gazed with reproach upon the diners. Like Vic, he had not intended to amuse. Amid the clatter of pewter mugs, he ate his dinner in hurt silence.

As he had dreaded, Anna's sister and her husband were at home that evening. The house, no more than a shanty, was clean and tidy and because the sisters affected gentility, the white sand on the floor had been artistically worked into a scalloped design at the borders. The girls had also prevailed upon their father to fashion rather good benches and a table for the room. Regrettably, on his carpenter's wage of fifty cents a day, paint for his creations was out of the question.

Anna's sister was called Miri and she was a tall, dark girl with a pronounced widow's peak. She was less beautiful than Anna but there was proof positive bulking largely beneath her dress that she was more generous. Miri had been married four months and the baby was due in a fortnight.

Miri's husband, the dancing master, was a Frenchman named René. He was not very young and in many ways so absurd that he could have been laughed out of one's consideration if it had not been for the esteem in which Anna held him. The man wore a

13

snuff-colored coat with silver buttons, a yellow-flowered waistcoat, black satin breeches, white silk stockings and upon his shoes, large, shiny buckles. John never had seen René wear anything else and for the first time, it came to him that René had nothing else to wear. Why, of course not. It was very clear now. The man had spent every last penny on this expensive outfit and had failed to impress a city whose devotion was given wholeheartedly to John Hulett's dancing school or to Andrew Picken, who conducted cotillion classes in the City Assembly Room.

How strange that it had never dawned upon him before that René was unsuccessful. Obviously he was. He would not have moved into this house otherwise. For festive occasions, the fare here was watery soup and a rabbit snared near MacDougal Marsh.

"Good evening," John said to Anna's parents and they responded coolly.

He took his place on the bench beside Anna and waited for conversation to begin. He was remembering that with elders present, it was manners to hold silence till they chose to break it. He glanced at the stolid, unsmiling faces of the carpenter and his wife. They were the elders and somehow it was a night for seeing things with remarkable clarity, for never till now had he realized that Anna's parents were not elderly. He studied the face beneath the mobcap. Had it ever been like Anna's? Or even like Miri's? Most unlikely. But it was not so much the absence of beauty that was depressing. It was the hard-held mouth, the cold glint in the busy, searching eyes. Life, the face said, was a nasty proposition made up of nothing but the business of fending off injury and spying out something to eat.

The silence continued. Ten minutes. Fifteen minutes. Once Miri's lips parted as though she dared from the eminence of her position as married woman to open conversation. But she changed her mind and amused herself in the stillness by reaching for René's hand and playing childishly with his fingers.

At last, Anna's mother spoke. "Louise has gone to Chelsea," she said. "She will, if she shows promise, be took for close maid to the Widow Clarke."

"Personal maid," Miri corrected. "They do not say close maid any more."

"I do. I say close maid. She's close, is she not, when she combs the widow's hair and helps her dress and even scrubs the lady in her tub?"

Miri laughed. "Very well. Close maid." She glanced nervously at René. "Louise is a distant relative of ours," she explained.

"Distant?" The carpenter suddenly came to life. "She is the daughter of my sister."

"And a good girl," his wife added. The cold eyes darted from Miri to Anna. "Had I used sense, you would both be close maids now, but I was witless. Because you were such well-featured girls, I let you idle and backed the chance that you would make good marriages."

Miri said, "My marriage pleases me."

Her mother spat contemptuously upon the clean white sand. "Your marriage had better please you. Without it, you would have a bastard to rear or to dump on the rubbish heap in Canvas Town."

René shuddered delicately and fixed his glazed eyes on a faraway point beyond the wall. Anna tittered and John thought her reaction to Miri's embarrassment, to René's hurt feelings and to her mother's downright hatefulness extremely objectionable. He frowned at her thoughtfully. How could she be amused?

Floundering for some remark to fling into the uncomfortable pause, he said, "The Widow Clarke was a famous British sympathizer."

"A great pity," said the carpenter's wife sneeringly. "Do you think Louise will sicken and die from the food, the bed and the good two dollars a month she will receive?"

"No, but I would think it finer to work for the wife of a patriot."

"Why? Are her petticoats easier to wash? I could puke at all this talk of Tories and patriots and new nations and freedom. What is freedom to the likes of us? I never had enough food or fire with England's king calling the tune, it is true, but neither has Mr. Washington come by to give me a fish or a load of wood. To the poor, John Slidell, it is all one. Freedom is for the fancy people."

"I do not agree," John said.

The carpenter rose and stretched himself wearily. "It is late." He walked from the room, his wife following after one more chilling glance at her daughters and the men they had chosen.

15

René had jumped to his feet, giving John the false hope that he, too, was retiring, but then the convention came to mind. Oh, yes, one stood when the elders did. What foolishment.

The four left behind let a few minutes pass without a word. Then René spoke. He spoke sadly. He said, "John, I am sorry to observe that you did not clean your fingernails this evening."

"What? Oh."

"I try very hard, you know, John, to give you the benefit of my advantages whenever I can. I have told you that clean fingernails are the fashion. If I were not your friend, I would keep quiet."

John repressed the easy reply. He pitied René and had a strange thought that the carpenter's wife made it necessary for the man to seek out ways in which he could affirm his superiority.

"It is only, you know," René continued, "for Anna's sake that I make a nuisance of myself. A beautiful girl has the right to demand a rather special kind of husband." Here he paused to bestow a congratulatory smile upon Miri. Then turning again to John, "You must not think it is enough to be extraordinarily handsome."

"Oh, for the love of God, René, I do not think of myself as handsome."

René's eyes narrowed in disbelief. "You mean to say you take no pleasure in that mop of curly black hair?"

"Pleasure in my hair? What rubbish is this now? I am a soap-boiler, not a mermaid." The thought of a man delighting in the color, texture or quantity of his hair was so hilarious that John burst into loud laughter.

Miri said, "What a liar you are. Of course you know you are handsome. Surely Anna has told you so."

John felt himself blushing. "I was more comfortable when the subject was my dirty fingernails," he said, but he looked questioningly at Anna. No, she had never said he was handsome. Was he? And if so, should she not have mentioned the fact? Had she, now that he thought of it, ever addressed a word to him that had been praise or tenderness?

"John." Miri bent toward him, smiling mischievously. "Seeing that I have a handsome husband of my own and am large with child, nothing ill will be thought of me if I say that you are truly the prettiest boy in New York." She was enjoying herself. It was

16

plain that John was disconcerted by the turn of conversation and Miri had few opportunities nowadays to tease a man. She babbled on. "Has no girl told you that when you grin, you are so glorious to look upon that we grow weak and wish to throw ourselves at you?"

"Oh, Miri," Anna cried, "that is a betrayal. You promised that never would you tell him that. You promised that he'd never know that if he would but grin in that funny way of his—" She fell suddenly still, chagrined and sullen.

And John sat quiet, too, remembering the white-skinned Mac-Kenzie at whom he had grinned that day. Surely she had behaved peculiarly. The determination had drained from her. The matter of the dead horse had become unimportant. She had departed in a daze. What sport! It was like having a magic weapon that reduced one's enemies to limp amiability. A pity he had paid to have the animal carted away.

René took Miri's hand and pulled her to her feet. "What would you think, my little one, of a walk? The evening is splendid. The air most bracing." He winked meaningfully at John.

So there would be a chance to hold Anna in his arms, to entreat her to name the wedding day. How brotherly of René. Did he really fear he had overstepped himself tonight, thus courting the hazard of losing the pupil whose inferiority so heartened him?

When she and John were alone, Anna said, "That talk of your handsome face . . ."

"I know. Not true. A silly game. It is not of my face I wish to speak."

"But I wish to speak of it. Now that the matter has been mentioned, I must tell you that you are very handsome indeed."

"Very well. I am handsome. When do we marry?" He reached for her but she turned from him, leaving his arms empty.

"I am still on the subject of your good looks. It is because of them that I have tolerated you but I must warn you that my patience is growing thin. Before René chose to speak, I had noticed your fingernails and the spots on your clothes and the condition of your shoes and you did not rise when my parents left the room nor just now when Miri rose and you—"

"Dearheart, enough. I will try. I will try."

17

"When?"

"Name the day of our marriage. Name a day and from this moment on, I will be as ridiculously clean and gentlemanly as René."

"No. First you must prove to me that I will be able to take pride in you. First you must listen well to René, then you must do as he says."

"Be quiet, Anna. We are alone. Give me a kiss."

"There will be no kisses for you tonight or any night until you are ready to learn from René and—"

He caught her in his arms but she fought against him, tossing her head, withholding her lips. In the end, he let her struggle away, for he had no wish to hurt her.

"Anna, I am a common man."

"Still you can act like a gentleman, can't you?"

"For what purpose? So that I may be unable to mingle easily with men of my own kind and equally unable to enter the front door of any fine house in the city? Did I tell you that you are a fool? If not, I shall tell you now."

She shook back the thick black hair that had come unbound in their small struggle. "You may call me fool, John Slidell, but you want me. You want me more than anything on earth and for that reason you will do as I say. You will do it or you will never have me." She searched his face, measuring her power, his desire. "Tomorrow evening you will call here as you have done in the past but I shall not be here."

"What?"

"I shall not be here. You will spend the time with René, listening to him, learning your lessons. Each night for seven nights you will meet with him and hear how things are done by the gentry. On the eighth evening, you may present yourself to me—in clean clothes—and if René reports well, then you shall have your kiss."

"You hold yourself in high esteem, miss."

She smiled but made no reply.

"And simply for information, milady, I would like to ask this; do you believe that a gentleman is created in seven evenings by giving diligent attention to the mouthings of a dancing teacher?"

18

She said, "You would learn much—enough, I should think, to bring your manners far above their present level."

"Indeed? Interesting. This, too, may be of interest. I shall not be here tomorrow evening."

Anna laughed. "Who is the fool now? You are talking to hear your own stupid words. If you are not here, you will lose me, John Slidell."

"Anna, do not say that. Anna." He reached for her again but she ran outdoors and when he followed, he saw her in the moonlight under the dark trees, streaking toward the Bowery, her black hair flying behind her like a witch's cloak.

He turned homeward, walking slowly, asking himself which grogshop to favor with his troubles. He considered returning to the Madagascar and, for the first time in his life, drinking himself unconscious along with Peter Tare. But the idea when analyzed lost its appeal. He kept walking and at length found himself at his own doorway with all the grogshops of the city behind him. Well, he was here now and he would sleep. But sleep did not come swiftly. There was so much to ponder upon.

What was with this girl Anna? Would it be a mistake to comply with her daft whims? Or would it be a mistake to risk losing her? Would he one day regret that he had not humored her or would he one day regret that he had? It was difficult for a man to know. He loved her, of course, but— And that was another difficult thing to know for sure. John remembered that only a year ago this time, there had been a barmaid with ginger-colored hair. He had believed himself in love with her, had thought seriously of marrying her and then one night, she had melted in his arms. Within a week, he had suddenly, mysteriously become a very clear-thinking young man, able to recognize that the barmaid was not really as important to his happiness as he had thought. Anna was not likely to give him the opportunity for making a similar test. She was a girl of lofty principles—or was she only clever? Again, a man was at a loss to distinguish one from the other.

If only Anna had not made so much of the art of elegant deportment. They would be married now. They would be comfortably settled and he would be peacefully sleeping upon his pallet instead of tossing. Would he really? Might there not be other things

19

to trouble him? Was not life a series of torments and vexations? What man would tell another that all worries ended with marriage? More probably would he say that marriage was but the signal for worries to gather.

Yet John knew himself destined for marriage. He did not hold as precious this freedom to come and go as he chose. Such freedom was a lonely, unrewarding thing valued only by those who had it not. With honesty, he admitted to himself that, more than all, he wanted to have someday a good house filled with good children.

"I will sit at the head of the table and gaze proudly at my big family," he thought, and though the idea amused him, he knew that that was the way he was. And he knew now why he had stood at the docks and watched others sail away to the golden islands. At heart he was not the man for a rousing adventure. He was not the man to buy a wondrous trinket in a Persian market place and be buried at sea. He was a man to buy a substantial house on Manhattan Island and be buried sedately with a marker on his grave.

All right, then; these things admitted and accepted. What about Anna? He would go to her tomorrow and he would tell her that here must end the absurdities. "We marry now or never," he would say. And he would warn her that he expected an industrious wife and many children.

Very roughly, with full intention of bruising her feelings, he would say, "You are placing too high a value on yourself, my girl. You are making it as difficult for me to marry you as it would be for me to marry a lady of quality."

He smiled to himself in the darkness. An effective comparison though an outrageous exaggeration. If Anna expected the manners of gentry, what would a lady of quality expect? Why, she would expect—she would expect the manners of gentry. Then the charge was sound, the argument valid. A lady of quality would expect no more than—

John suddenly leaped from the pallet and lighted a candle. If a man could not sleep, must he lie in darkness? He was still awake when the dawn laid its gray fingers on the dirty windows of the room in back of the candle shop.

. . .

"Now, René, I believe I have the greeting quite correct. The advance into the room, the expressed hope that the lady's health is fine and all that rubbish about one's joy in being admitted. Show me the bow again. Oh, it is deeper than I had thought. Why don't the old fellows creak as they do it?"

"You have it splendidly, John. Let me congratulate you on your ability to learn so swiftly now that you have decided to apply yourself. May I remark that your nails look quite the same as any gentleman's tonight? Now, as for the bow—it is used in the same form at the beginning of the dance, you know, but then, to be cruelly candid, you and Anna will be restricted to the ordinary jig or hornpipe or reel."

"Even so, I wish to learn how the gentry go about the performance of the rigadoon or *contredanse.*"

"Dear me, now that you have made up your mind, you are really determined, aren't you?"

"I am, indeed. Tell me about the important dinners."

"Alas, you and Anna shall be invited to none but I agree that the etiquette of these affairs is pleasant to know. First, a person receives a written invitation—this year it is terribly fashionable for them to be scribbled upon playing cards. You reply in writing but not on a playing card this time. That would be extremely poor taste. Let us assume you accept. Dinner will begin at three or four in the afternoon."

"But that is during working hours!"

"You are a humorous boy, John. For the purpose of instruction, we are dreaming. These dinners are not for you and Anna. They are for the wealthy. The food you will not be able to imagine. There would be soup and there would be fish both roasted and boiled, followed by meats and fowl of all known sorts. Then truffles and game. Lobsters and warm side dishes. Afterward pies, puddings, jellies, fruits, nuts and coffee."

"Who can eat so much? And must one try?"

"Oh, absolutely. A hostess who stops offering is ungracious. A guest who refuses to accept is rude."

"But a man could die at table from a complication of good manners."

"I will teach you the form by which a man saves his life at a

21

fashionable dinner. One has only to cross one's knife and fork upon the plate in this manner, John. You see? That little gesture entreats your hostess to offer no more. A true lady will cease to importune you further."

"I see. That is worth knowing."

"It is the same at a tea party, John. A hostess is required to keep your cup filled. When you feel yourself drowning in tea, you may place your spoon across the top of your cup as a signal to your hostess that you wish no further attention. But to return to the dinner—there will be toasts drunk. Thirteen of them. One for each state, you understand. These gentlemen of the upper world never become tipsy."

"Don't they?"

"No. It is part of their training to remain sober even after volunteers have been called for."

"Volunteers?"

"Yes. Those are toasts beyond the customary thirteen."

"René, I must have some clothes but I haven't a fortune to spend. Advise me, please."

"With great delight, dear future brother-in-law. I will go with you to assist in selecting the wardrobe. We can go to Daniel Campion's across from the Coffee House. His terms are moderate."

"Can we go tomorrow?"

"Of course we can. Now once again let us pretend I am a lady who has remarked on the coolness of the evening. How do you fetch her shawl, John? How do you wrap it about her shoulders with just the proper touch of flattery yet maintaining always your gentlemanliness? And let us repeat the exercise which concerns the presentation of flowers or any other gift, and I have forgotten tonight to guard you against your habit of slurring words. I must be more vigilant if I am to warrant the faith placed in me by our dear Anna. More vigilant, indeed."

Seven evenings of concentrated instruction. Perhaps it was true that one could not become a gentleman in seven evenings, but it was astonishing how much one could learn. It was impossible to suppress the suspicion that this talk of its taking many generations to produce a gentleman was only British-manufactured sirup which Americans were still innocently importing. The rules of etiquette

22

could be learned by any willing child and as for the deep, significant traits of character which were supposed to animate gentlemen —well, John had seen proof that cruelty and cowardice could exist under the skin of a nobleman.

It was on the seventh evening of his education—his graduation, so to speak—that René asked, "You, in your new clothes, are you not excited?"

"I am excited."

"You wear the clothes dashingly and you have learned beyond my wildest hopes, dear boy. Tomorrow evening when you see Anna, she will weep with happiness. Be sure you forget nothing of what I have told you. The jumping to your feet, the seating of the lady, the small compliments."

"I will forget nothing, René. And I would like to say that I thank you for all the trouble you have taken with me."

"It is nothing. Nothing at all. We are almost brothers, aren't we?"

"Remember only that I am grateful to you, René."

And on the eighth evening, John dressed carefully in his new buff-colored breeches of broadcloth, his French-blue coat with its high collar and broad lapels. He wore well-polished pumps and a good white shirt with modest ruffles. True, his buttons were steel instead of silver, his cravat muslin rather than silk and in the interests of further economy, he had chosen to go bareheaded. But he felt that his appearance was thoroughly acceptable and with confidence he picked up the long, slim package that had been awaiting this moment. Then he went out of the shop and walked thoughtfully in the opposite direction from Catherine Street.

The house was three stories tall and of fine brickwork. It had regularly spaced windows and classical doors in what was known as "the London taste." This house, John realized, had not been merely built. First it had been designed by an artist.

Boldly he seized the knocker and made it known that a visitor stood upon the doorstep. A servingmaid in cap and apron flung wide the door and said, "Good evening, sir."

Sir? Well, so much for the idle talk that a servant knew upon sight who was a gentleman and who was not.

"I wish to see Miss MacKenzie," he said in a matter-of-fact tone.

"Be so good as to enter. I will inquire as to whether or not she is at home. Your name, please, sir?"

"Tell her that Mr. Slidell awaits her pleasure."

"Yes, sir."

He followed the maid through the hall past high-backed Windsor chairs and two square silver-gilt lanterns. He had expected to be directed to wait here but she indicated that he was to enter the parlor. Thanks to the new clothes, no doubt. He would not have minded a few minutes in the hall. Its walls were covered with ornamental paper, of which he had heard but which he had never before glimpsed. This, in the MacKenzie hall, had a pattern of flowers and shepherdesses and he would have enjoyed a moment to inspect it.

However, the parlor was interesting, too. Never had he been in a parlor and never had he known the quaking nervousness that beset him now. What would happen in the next few moments? Would she simply decline to see him? Or would a pair of serving-boys be sent to assist him to the street? New clothes, new manners were, after all, of small matter when she knew well that he was only John Slidell, soap-boiler and candlemaker.

He looked about the parlor and noted that it was completely furnished in mahogany. To quiet his nerves, he counted the chairs. Eight of them. All with cabriole legs and claw-and-ball feet. Crimson silk for seats. Beautiful. A bookcase with glass doors. He longed to read the titles of the books but this was perhaps obnoxious behavior, tantamount to reading another's letters.

How mad the MacKenzies were for tables! Card tables, tea tables, writing tables. A table for chess and another with a drop leaf whose purpose he could only guess.

By God, the house was silent. Had the servingmaid been struck dead simply for having announced him? He tried to count the articles on the tea table. Lamp, kettle, tea tongs, sugar-cleaver, spoons, urn . . .

There was a large, gilt-framed pier glass. He wandered toward it to examine his cravat but drew back hastily. Suppose he were surprised in what could be interpreted only as self-admiration? Was that his heart pounding? Dismiss all thought of it. Regard the

24

portraits and the collection of carved crystal. There were so many things at which to gape—the impressive fireplace with its deep hearth, the marble mantel, the luxuriance of carpeted floors. He wished to bend and touch the rich material but contented himself with feeling the softness of it underfoot.

He knew he was not privileged to sit till invited to do so, but there was a piece of furniture that caught his attention. It was a backed sofa that looked as though its cushions had been stuffed with clouds. The inviting thing was covered in the same material of which the draperies were made—pearl-colored damask.

Ah, this was a lovely world in which the little MacKenzie lived. One could only imagine the glories of silver chest, china closet and linen cabinet. And one could not even begin to dream of the delights of larder, cellar and cupboard.

"Miss MacKenzie will be down in a moment, sir."

The voice of the servingmaid startled him, but no more than the import of her words. His brazenness was about to be tested. Miss MacKenzie would be down in a moment. What in blazes had René said about the bow? Oh, yes, arrange arms gracefully at sides. And the speech that went with the presentation of a gift? Spoken with a small, deprecating smile implying the gift to be unworthy of notice.

She came into the room all perfume and curls. The dress was a gray-striped silk with white satin petticoat. A large gauze handkerchief was about her shoulders and upon her hair a gauze cap decorated with artificial rosebuds.

"Good evening, Mr. Slidell."

He advanced a step or two toward her and bowed deeply. "So heavenly to be admitted to your home, Miss MacKenzie. It is my most cherished wish that I find you in the glowing good health your charming appearance suggests."

A wildly extravagant outpouring, but René had sworn that thus spoke the gentry. He must have been right for now Miss MacKenzie was curtseying and saying, "Our home is brighter for your presence, Mr. Slidell. My everlasting gratitude to you for having thought of us."

All this for the soap-boiler? Was she laughing at him? A glance reassured him.

25

"I have brought to you, Miss MacKenzie, something that might strike your fancy if you are in an indulgent mood. It is nothing, a whimsy, but it was thought that it might create a moment's diversion." He offered her the long, slim box.

"Why, I thank you, Mr. Slidell. Will you be kind enough to seat yourself?" And the amiable creature indicated the cloud-stuffed sofa.

"After you, Miss MacKenzie."

So they sat together with the properly approved distance of ten inches between them and she opened her present and gasped delightedly.

"They are exquisite, Mr. Slidell!"

He could not hide a craftsman's pleasure. The candles were indeed exquisite. More delicate and slender than usual, designed for beauty rather than practicality. The rose-pink coloring had set just as he had hoped. It would have been a mistake to have used one more measure of cochineal.

"How is it done? How are candles induced to forsake the tedious whiteness with which we are familiar?"

"It is a simple process but pretty, I think. May I explain to you, Miss MacKenzie, why I have come here?"

She turned to him, an appealing smile upon the small white face. He was still aware of the protruding eyes, the blue veins, but this was, by heaven, a beguiling personality when one met it in a parlor rather than across a counter.

"All this week I have thought of you, Miss MacKenzie." No lie, that. "And I have thought that I was very rude to you when you came to my store."

"Not so, Mr. Slidell. I came knowing I would be a trouble to you. I expected no fine reception."

"But you should not have met with argument, for you were right and I was wrong. I come with apologies and regrets."

"And the most elegant candles I have ever seen."

"I am enraptured that they please you. May I rest easily now, knowing myself to be forgiven for my uncouth behavior?"

"Your behavior was reasonable under the circumstances. I will not let you mark it as uncouth." She studied him for a moment, her

26

head tilted, her eyes bright with interest. "You are a man of excellent manners, Mr. Slidell."

"Thank you, Miss MacKenzie."

"And of excellent style and taste."

"Thank you again."

Her question came blunt and disconcerting. "Why is that, Mr. Slidell?"

He blinked. "What do you mean?"

"I mean a simple enough thing. We both know that you are a soap-boiler and candlemaker, do we not?" And even now she was not laughing at him but looking at him earnestly, seeking answers that he did not care to give.

He sought escape in hinting blandly that here was a mystery. "Someday perhaps I will tell you quite a lot about myself."

She nodded. "Perhaps you will, Mr. Slidell, but in the meanwhile, I will tell you that on the few occasions I spoke to your father, I found him a well-informed man but he was certainly not . . ." She hesitated only a second before ripping his flimsy veil of mystery to shreds. "Let me say he seemed quite at home with his soap-boiling."

René had failed to mention that even in the parlors of gentry, the simple truth was sometimes uttered. Having no defense against it, John met it head on.

He said, "And so he was. I will tell you with honesty that I had forgotten you knew my father."

"I thought you had," she said and continued to stare in puzzlement.

"You have been very kind, Miss MacKenzie. You have accepted my trifling gift, you have forgiven former boorishness. Now, carrying with me the memory of your kindness, I shall depart." Making as though to rise, he turned and grinned at her.

She lowered her eyes and said, "If no other duty spurs you on, you are welcome to remain yet awhile. Would you care for some rum? Or brandy?"

They were drinking a delicious rum concoction flavored with cream and dried pumpkin when her parents entered the conversation.

27

"Would you wish to be presented to them?"

"Who would not wish such an honor?"

She walked out of the parlor, returning in a moment to beckon to him.

"Will you come upstairs, Mr. Slidell? My parents are not well and keep to their apartment but their attendant tells me they are very fit this evening."

He followed her up the stairs past a tall clock on the landing, the face of which was embellished with the changes of the moon. He wanted to pause and study its cunning workmanship but now was not quite the proper instant to display his interest in clocks. Miss MacKenzie walked ahead of him down the corridor, disappeared through a doorway and then reappeared, beckoning once more.

The room which he entered was large and candlelit. It was dominated by an enormous bed draped in green silk. Again there were many chairs and tables. At one of the tables sat Mr. and Mrs. MacKenzie, playing cribbage. They smiled pleasantly, abandoned the game and turned their attention to John.

They were both elaborately dressed, the lady in yellow satin with coffee-colored petticoat, the gentleman in black satin save for a velvet waistcoat with tiny strawberries embroidered upon it. The couple was surprisingly advanced in years to have so young a daughter.

John was invited to seat himself and discovered that this room, too, had its stuffed sofa—more ornate, being Turkey red and strung with gold cords and tassels. Miss MacKenzie joined him there, bringing with her a small silver bowl of burnt almonds she had taken from the top of a delicately carved escritoire.

Mr. MacKenzie said, "Well, Mr. Slidell, you are a very tall, very strong young man. Were you in Mr. Washington's army?"

"No, sir. I was but fourteen when the war ended."

"How old are you now?"

"Twenty."

"Impossible. It cannot be six years since the fighting ceased."

Miss MacKenzie turned upon John a glance gone suddenly cool and challenging. "My father raises an interesting question. Since those who remained in Manhattan were well known to be in sympathy with that fat pig of a King—well, even considering

28

that at war's end you were only a boy, tell us something of yourself."

He was aware once more of the stillness of the house as the three MacKenzies bent toward him, intent upon his reply.

Oh, the smugness of these moneyed patriots who had been able to flee the city, who had had the luck to spend the war openly toasting Mr. Washington and offering him and his officers their warmest hospitality.

"Manhattan was a Tory city," Miss MacKenzie persisted. "So perhaps you would like to tell us . . ."

"By God, I intend to," he said.

He had forgotten now that there was a rule of proper posture. A gentleman sat upright, hands resting lightly on knees. He had forgotten that a gentleman's answer even to the most serious of questions must be witty and gay, that he must strive to be remembered for the amusing quality of his conversation. He reached for a handful of burnt almonds and sprawled against the sofa cushions. Chewing vigorously, he addressed Mr. MacKenzie.

"Let me tell you, sir, something of what it was like. I remember the day the news came that the redcoats had fired upon the men of Lexington. I was only six years old but I remember. It was a Sunday morning."

Mr. MacKenzie nodded. "It was a Sunday morning," he agreed. "That evening I met with others who hated Britain's treatment of her colonies as much as I. We gentlemen talked far into the night."

John's father, too, had hated Britain's treatment of her colonies and he also had been busy far into the night. After the news came, he fed his small son well and said to him, "Stay here, Johnny. Do not venture out upon the streets until I give permission." Then he had locked up the store and like Mr. MacKenzie had met with men whose thoughts ran with his own. But there had been no judicial palaver, no scholarly exchange of opinions. These men had no time for talk.

At one of the wharves, there were two sloops laden with provisions for the British troops at Boston. Short work was made of the cargoes. Patriots or only a mob? What mattered the appellation? Here were shipments the British troops would damn well

29

never receive. What was there to turn a hand to now? The Armory Room? Yes, yes, but let us make a request first. We have always been law-abiding men. Let us ask for the key. If it is refused, we can then decide. . . .

The key was refused and the law-abiding men made their decision. Shouting the name "Lexington," they battered down the door of the Armory Room and departed with more than five hundred muskets and bayonets.

After that, most of them scattered to taverns and grogshops, but Slidell had to go home. There was a frightened child crouched on a pallet awaiting his return. They ate some fruit together and with burning excitement in his eyes, the man told the boy all that had occurred on that day.

"You must not be frightened by the noise in the streets. It is the sound of wonderful happenings. Only do not go abroad without me. There are those so stupid that the business of just living on such a day is not intoxicating enough for them."

The boy thought the noise, the excitement and the absence of his father but this day's oddity. He was wrong. Every day after that was filled with danger and incomprehensible doings. The shop was open for business. People still bought soap and candles but they lingered longer in conversation and most of it was in whispers.

When the boy walked upon the streets, he held fast to his father's hand and he heard the rattle of drums and the commands of drill sergeants. Sometimes they walked at night and by the flicker of yellow street lamps watched the clerks and butchers and apothecaries and barbers learning how to be soldiers, and the child saw in his father's eyes a queer expression that could have been loneliness.

Many men came to the room in back of the store. At nights, they sat and talked while the boy on the pallet pretended to sleep lest they clear the room, taking with them their arguments that thrilled him though remaining incomprehensible.

"I cannot," his father would say over and over. "I have the child to consider. I will do what is possible but the boy comes first."

"We all have children, Slidell."

"Yes, and your children all have mothers. Count on me for

some things but count on me to fail you, too. I will always consider the child above all else."

And the child stood with his father in a crowd of cheering New Yorkers and saw a man, calm-faced and strong, wearing a purple sash, step from a ferryboat.

"Cheer, Johnny, that is George Washington."

The boy cheered, for it was good fun to be permitted to open one's mouth wide and to scream at the top of one's lungs. But George Washington looked singularly grave among all the shouting, laughing people and he did not stay in New York. He was on his way to Massachusetts. It seemed a strange thing to the boy that though the man with the purple sash had gone far away, his father and those who talked in the room behind the store never seemed to forget him. They spoke his name constantly and mentioned unfamiliar places where he rode.

The summer came and went its way; winter, too, and now the lightning-charged atmosphere had become normal. A small boy no longer remembered when there had not been British warships in the harbor, threatening the city, when there had not been the rumble of munition carts and when his father had been preoccupied only with the manufacture of soap and candles.

Now the store was neglected for hours on end as his father joined crews of men who called his name from the cobblestones outside.

"Eat your food, Johnny, and be a good boy. You know how to sell a candle as well as I do. If I am not home, go to sleep when the sky darkens."

In reply to the child's question, he spoke of moving cannon from the Battery, of loading wagons and dragging guns and stores through the city streets. Later, there was the need to dig trenches, cut down trees and erect redoubts. Barricades were thrown across Broad, Wall and Cortlandt.

"Every man of us has to help." And to the child's plea, "Not yet, Johnny boy. When you're a little bigger, perhaps. Not today, son." And he would be gone.

But the boy was on the streets with his father the day the Declaration was read. No one could remain indoors nor could a soul sleep that night. The city vibrated and rocked deliriously.

There was dancing and singing and drunkenness and there were thoughtful people who tried to recall the beautiful phrasing of the great document and there were those who prayed. Mostly the city streets teemed with ordinary everyday people who were not very drunk, very intelligent or very pious. And because such ordinary ones had to do something special in honor of this date, they joined in a curious, spontaneous mass descent upon Bowling Green and they pulled down the gilt statue of George the Third.

The child saw the gleaming horse and rider come crashing to the ground and he shrieked exultantly, for he had learned to hate the King though he knew not the who, what or where of the man. And he laughed as the mob cut the head from the statue and ran with it through the streets.

After that, he fell asleep, for his father had hoisted him to his shoulder, saying, "You have lived through a remarkable day, my boy. Now it is time to go home." And he had been carried to his pallet behind the store.

But that summer saw the end of high excitement and exultant shouts, for now came a time when men crept quietly to the store and spoke in tones of fear. And there was a night in August when they and countless others went out and manned a sorry fleet of rowboats, flatboats, wheelboats, canoes and sloops and shoved toward Long Island on the inky black waters of the river. Back from the threat of annihilation they brought their soldiers to the dubious safety of little Manhattan. The man in the purple sash had suffered a cruel defeat. The merry tones of drum and fife had ceased.

John and his father saw the young American flag pulled down and trampled underfoot by happy loyalists. They saw the King's colors rise again over the city and they saw the redcoats march into town with proud and swinging step. Then they went back to the store and the man spoke solemnly to the child.

"What we have here is our home and our living. It must not be taken from us nor must we be separated. I have to feed you and I have to stay close to you, so listen carefully. If you disobey me, you may never see me again."

The boy began to cry and the man took him on his knee and spoke kindly but unsmilingly. "You do not know the name of any man who has ever entered the shop. All, all were customers un-known to you. You have no knowledge of where I have gone or what I have done when we have not been together. You have heard nothing and been taught only that we are subjects of His Majesty, King George the Third. You understand, Johnny?"

The child scarcely knew the reason for his sorrow but the tears continued.

"On the other hand, Johnny, you are not to lick any redcoat boots or render service to them which can be avoided. You are not to— But, no, you would not understand. I will keep it simple. Do as other lads do, my boy. Cheer the British soldiers if you feel the wish. Admire the pretty red uniforms if you like. None of this was of your making."

That night for the last time, the whispering men assembled in the room behind the store.

"We are not staying, Slidell. We are going to Harlem Heights to become part of the army. Come with us."

"I cannot. What of the child?"

"Will you stay here and let the British rule you?"

"I will let the devil rule me if that is best for Johnny."

"But it is not best for Johnny."

The child heard his father's short, bitter note of laughter. "You speak of ideals, of principles, of the dignity of man. I speak of porridge for Johnny's breakfast, my friend."

"The King's troops will—"

"The King's troops will not interfere with my small son's break-fast."

"Don't you want to go with us, Slidell?"

"Of course I want to go with you but above all things in life must come the boy, his protection and welfare. Let me say that I did not cause the revolution to exist. Johnny is another matter."

The men went away and the child saw them no more.

God save the King. And every day Slidell placed before his growing boy three plain and solid meals and went about his business with face expressionless. A victory for the King? You don't say so, sir? A victory for Washington? You don't say so, sir? The French have joined with the revolutionists? You don't say so, sir? If there were moments when Slidell's eyes met another's with something more than glassy blankness, the moments were few. This was His Majesty's loyal city. Again God save the King.

Seven long years. Johnny was a husky boy of thirteen who knew all there was to know of soap and candles. He knew how to read and to figure. He dreamed of joining Washington's army but he said no word to his father of all he remembered of the early days, the days when there had been whispers of freedom in the room behind the store. What would the redcoats do to a man whose son ran away to the revolutionists? And the question was a terrible one to contemplate, for the boy well knew that it was for him that his father had abandoned his own wish to march with Washington. Perhaps the store could be sold and together they could slip away. . . .

Suddenly it was over. It was over. The war that had seemed like a permanent part of life had at last come to an end. On a chilly November morning, the boy and his father, both conscious now of witnessing history in the making, saw the redcoats form their columns and march to the East River wharves, where they were rowed out to the waiting British fleet.

And the boy and his father saw George Washington re-enter New York City. With tears streaming down his cheeks, the man turned to his son.

"Cheer, Johnny. That is George Washington," he said.

"You don't say so, sir?" Johnny queried flippantly. Then, drawing closer to his father, he added, "Thanks to you, there was never a moment when I had forgotten him."

And together they stood there on Broadway, laughing and crying and shattering with their shouts the silence of seven secret years.

When John had finished his story, there was a long, quiet moment. Then Miss MacKenzie spoke. She said, "I wish I had known all this when your father lived. I now think him a remarkable man."

"Remarkable, Miss MacKenzie?"

She looked at John with her steady gray gaze. "I enormously respect his conduct. Any romantic fool can join an army. It re-

34

quires more self-discipline to stay home and attend to the dull business of administering to the needs of a little boy."

John smiled at her. "I think so, too," he said. "It makes me happy that you approve my father's decision."

Mr. MacKenzie was staring thoughtfully into space, weighing the evidence, so to speak. John was amazed to see that Mrs. Mac-Kenzie was weeping softly.

"Such a touching story," she said, patting her eyes with a lacy handkerchief. She turned to John, her expression tear-bright but nonetheless penetrating. "You say this man was your father? How extraordinary. How did he become a soap-boiler?"

John shook his head. "Truth to tell, I do not know, madam."

"And what do you do, Mr. Slidell?"

John said, "I am a soap-boiler."

"You are? Really?" She sighed. "I do not understand the world any more. Soap-boilers used to be quite common fellows and now they are charming boys who are entertained in one's home, where they tell wonderful stories—and the heroes of those stories are other soap-boilers."

Mr. MacKenzie was at last ready to speak. He said, "You vouch, young man, for your father's activities in the days before British occupation? That he assisted in the rescue of our army after the Battle of Long Island? That he helped haul cannon from the Battery under the guns of the British warships? That he was one of the men who destroyed cargoes intended for the King's army?"

"I do indeed, sir."

"Then I take your word," Mr. MacKenzie said and he sounded somewhat surprised at his willingness to do so. "Yes, I take your word." The broad brow was wrinkled in perplexity, the greenish eyes filled with dismay. "I will tell you, too, that your father did more than I. This man who sits before you never contributed anything save talk and money."

"Talk can be inspiring and no war is won without money," John said.

"I could have done things that your father did. Yet I sat in this room wondering, like a woman, what I could do to help. The rabble—your pardon, young man—had more initiative than I."

In a clear, firm voice Miss MacKenzie said, "The rabble—and there is no need to beg pardon for the word—always has more initiative. The rabble is a wonderful creation of nature's that supplies the world with vitality and ingenuity."

"Yes, yes, daughter, you are right." The black satin coat and the waistcoat with the embroidered strawberries seemed to sag sorrowfully. "Never did I do more than talk and give money."

Later, when they were once more alone in the parlor, Miss MacKenzie told John a little of her parents and perhaps without meaning to do so, a great deal of what her life had been.

"Mother never knew good health and did not intend to marry. She was already a woman nearing forty when my father, a childless widower, persuaded her to become his wife. Fancy their astonishment, a year later, when they discovered they were parents."

"How fortunate they were."

Miss MacKenzie lifted the rum pitcher and poured generously. "Yes. I have been helpful to them. By the time I was fourteen, I had taken over the burden of household accounts and the management of the servants and related matters. My father was found to have a weak heart and any duties are really too much for him."

"I am sure you are very capable."

"Yes, I am capable. You wondered no doubt about my father's talk of war. It is rather an obsession with him. He equipped two regiments and has never understood why he was not invited to command either one. It is very plain to me. He is a dear man and I love him but he is not the material of which leaders are made. How can I tell him that?"

"It is not your obligation to tell him."

"Isn't it? He broods so terribly on the possibility that he was not liked or not trusted. But enough of my family history. Yours was more interesting."

"Not so, and mine, I fear, was very lengthy." John rose from the sofa after finishing his drink. "You have been exceedingly cordial. I trust I have not overstayed."

She walked with him from the mahogany parlor into the hall with its Windsor chairs and fascinating wallpaper.

"Mr. Slidell, will you come again?"

He said, "On what evening?"

There had been no one to instruct her in the art of coquetry. "Tomorrow evening," she said.

Upon his second visit to the MacKenzie home, he dared flattery.

"Did you know that you have the loveliest gray eyes in the world?"

"I am quite popeyed," she said pleasantly. "I don't particularly mind but there it is; I am popeyed."

He laughed. "Your eyes suit me. They are adorable. And your pretty red mouth—"

"Yes, that is not unattractive," she agreed. Briskly she rose and went to a small cabinet that stood beside the harpsichord. From within she drew a package which she handed to him. "Open it."

He looked at her questioningly, then obeyed. He found a book. Volume One, *The Decline and Fall of the Roman Empire*.

"What is this?"

"It is a book. You told me at our first meeting that you could read."

"Well, I can, you know, and I have read this. Why did you buy it?"

"Because if you had not called on me, I intended to call on you. I planned to enter your shop and present you with this book, saying that it was a reward for having removed the dead horse. But you came, bringing the rose-colored candles and— Great heavens, what will you think of a girl as brazen as I?"

"Small sweet lady, I can but think of you as completely charming."

On the third visit, she studied him contemplatively. "I am curious to know," she said unexpectedly, "whether or not you are a Jew."

"Satisfy first my curiosity, then we will return to yours. How does it happen that you raise the question?"

"I was informed by a servant this afternoon that a carpenter awaited my pleasure at the garden door. Since I had summoned no carpenter, I declined to see the fellow. Twice he returned the girl with entreaties that I give him a moment. In the end, when I continued to refuse, he sent a message which she delivered with understandable reluctance. He had instructed her to say that he felt it his duty to warn me that John Slidell was a Jew. Now, sir, who is this carpenter? And are you a Jew?"

"The carpenter is the father of Anna. Anna is a girl I courted."

Jane MacKenzie's gray eyes burned anxiously. "How ardently did you court her? Have you left her in desperate circumstances?"

"Indeed I have not."

"Then I take it that the carpenter is but full of spite."

"It is his wife who would have prompted this act of his. Not that she was pining to have me for Anna. It is only that to cause discomfort comes naturally to her. As to the other matter—you may not believe this, but I do not know whether or not I am a Jew. Mark you, it is highly probable, for when my father died, a man came to me from the synagogue on Mill Street and asked if I wished space in the burial ground."

Jane raised her eyebrows quizzically. "I do not understand."

"No more did I. My father told me once that with the death of my mother, he had lost faith in everything and that was the closest we ever came to discussing religion. It never occurred to me that the faith he had abandoned could have been Judaism. The man from Shearith Israel, seeing my surprise, asked, 'Was Slidell not a Jew?' And I asked back, 'Was he?' The man shrugged and disappeared. My father is buried in common soil and I do not know the land from which his ancestors came or what beliefs they held. I am equally ignorant concerning my mother."

Jane said, "How fortunate you are. You dare have no prejudice. Tell me, does the Episcopal Church not strike you as a solid fortress of dignity, good sense and lofty ideals?"

"Oh, yes," he said. "I have never passed St. Paul's without thinking exactly that. It is your church, I assume."

"It is my church, yes." She fixed her eyes upon the lace rosettes of her velvet slippers. "I would recommend it to you."

After the fourth visit, he dined every evening with Jane, enjoying the glitter of silver, the flash of crystal and the wonderful foods that were carried to the long table. On one occasion, their dinner was brought upstairs so that, as John knew, her parents might take a longer look at him.

"There was a gentleman in my shop today who spoke of you, sir," John said.

38

"Of me?" Henry MacKenzie ceased toying delicately with his roast partridge. "He spoke of me?"

"Yes, sir. We had been conversing of one thing and another and I mentioned—rather boastfully, I am afraid—that I have been welcomed to this house. 'Oh, I knew the MacKenzie family well in bygone years,' the gentleman said. And I, of course—"

"What was his name, Mr. Slidell? Who was he?"

"That I know not. Shopkeepers may not inquire, but he was a gentleman of importance. Upon his hand was a golden ring and his clothes were very fine. He said, 'We needed Henry'—pardon, sir, but it is his familiarity, not mine—he said, 'We needed Henry in the war. He had much to give us in solid thinking and brave action but, alas, Henry's health was not equal to the effort.'" John paused to bite into an apple that had been treated deliciously with cinnamon and brown sugar. "I remarked, sir, that I was not aware of poor health having come upon you so long ago and he said, 'Oh, yes, it was known to all that though Henry stoutly denied it, he was suffering. It was thought in high places that it would be an imposition to ask Henry to give of himself when he had already done so much for the cause.'"

Tears gathered in Henry MacKenzie's eyes. "God bless this stranger," he said fervently. "He has unknowingly sent me a message to brighten all the rest of my life."

"Really, sir?" asked John innocently. "Then I am indeed glad it did not slip my mind to tell you."

The candles shone softly on the bright satin of Jane's gown and their tiny flames were reflected in her gray glance as she considered him. "Mr. Slidell," she said, "it is difficult to believe that anything has ever slipped your mind. You are far too clever."

But he had the feeling that she approved.

Mrs. MacKenzie, who had eaten only a sugar bun for dinner, leaned across the table to pat her husband's cheek. "Dry your eyes, my love, and get on with the partridge. If you tarry so, we will not have our cribbage game at all this evening."

"And such may truly be the case," he warned her. "For I have long wished to converse with Mr. Slidell on the subject of his shop." He blew his nose, blinked his eyes and turned to John.

39

"Actually, my dear boy, do you stand all day at the beck and call of customers? What is the hope in such work as yours?"

John laughed. "Why, sir, all shopkeepers stand at the beck and call of customers and our hope is that there will be more and more customers all the time."

"Yes, but a lad like you . . ." His voice trailed off and he sat silently, thoughtfully gazing upon his young guest.

"In truth," John said gravely, "I do have a plan. May I speak of it?"

"Please do. We are very interested."

"Do you recall, Miss MacKenzie, that on your visit to the store, you asked why I had been seldom there? I will tell you now where I had been. There is money, you know, in getting contracts to out-fit ships for their long voyages. There are those who sell them food and grog, for instance. I had thought to get contracts for the furnishing of soap and candles."

"I see." She pursed her lips reflectively. "All this is rather an exercise in hard work for small return, is it not? Outfitting ships with soap and candles—this is, in Mr. Shakespeare's words, much ado about nothing. Why does one not own the ships oneself and forget all about small returns?"

His heart began to pound. "Very large sums of money are needed for such activities." He turned smilingly to Mr. MacKenzie. "Your daughter has little knowledge of what it is like to be poor."

"I pray that she may never know," breathed Mrs. MacKenzie, but her husband said nothing.

He looked from John to Jane with a curious light in his green eyes and John's heart pounded harder than ever. "If I had money, I would own ships as you suggest, Miss MacKenzie. Of course, I would have to be very cautious indeed until I had learned all the tricks of the trade. At first, I would hire proper advisers. Even-tually, I would not need them. I believe I could develop a talent for the shipping business. But I talk nonsense. What is it you would care to know about my modest little shop, Mr. MacKenzie?"

It was customary in the glittering circles of wealth to be married in the evening at the home of the bride's father, so Jane and John

40

were married in the brick house. It was a small and simple wedding, for John had no friends whom he was anxious to present to the MacKenzies. The MacKenzies, for their part, had spent years in discouraging any social life. A few doctors, a few lawyers, along with their wives and grown children, an ancient couple and an Anglican nun made up the wedding party. The guests were dull but the feast that followed the ceremony was elegant and everybody drank a great deal of golden French wine that sparkled spectacularly in crystal glasses.

The guests eyed John with open curiosity. It rather surprised him that the gentry was less subtle than the clientele of the Madagascar when it came to gathering facts on a new arrival in their midst.

It had been stated in the *Daily Gazette* that "Mr. John Slidell of this city, merchant, will marry on Saturday night Miss Jane MacKenzie, daughter of the Hon. Henry MacKenzie, Esq., also of this city, a very amiable young lady with a handsome fortune."

By this time, the lawyers knew all about Mr. John Slidell, merchant, but their wives and the others still had not the information they seemed to think rightfully theirs.

"Slidell? The name is not known to me. Exactly what branch of merchandising do your endeavors follow?"

"Oh, I have heard the name but it belonged to a peculiar fellow who made candles. Were you born in this city, Mr. Slidell?"

"How long have you known Jane? How did you meet?"

"Our paths have not crossed before but I may have known your mother. What was her name prior to her marriage?"

"You are perhaps acquainted with my son—that is, if you attended King's College."

"You must not say King's College. It is now called Columbia. Mr. Slidell, have you purchased property yet above Murray Street? They say that it will yield a profit in time."

John would not have minded; indeed, he thought he might have enjoyed facing these people with a bland look upon his countenance and answering all their questions with disarming frankness. But he had no wish to embarrass the MacKenzies, whose kindness to him had been beyond all belief.

He looked lovingly at the dear couple who were downstairs to-

41

night for this grand occasion. They appeared well and contented. God bless them, he thought, my wonderful golden geese.

At last the evening was at an end. The company departed and servants carried Mr. MacKenzie, in an armchair, to his room. Mrs. MacKenzie followed him slowly, leaning heavily on John.

"Now I have a son," she said happily and shed tears of pleasure when he replied in the only possible way.

Upon his return to the parlor, he found Jane busily snuffing out the candles.

"The servants will do that," he said, and though he spoke the words for the first time in his life they did not feel strange upon his tongue. "Come with me."

Together they climbed the handsomely carved staircase. Unbidden, a sudden vision of Anna danced through his mind. He would not be able to walk so sedately if at the top of the stairs a night with her awaited him. He knew well that right now, at this very moment, he was in grave danger of establishing Anna as a tormenting memory that could hound all the days of his life. She had not been that wonderful. She must not be permitted to assume the importance of the One True Love. She must not become a sad, sweet symbol of youth's mistakes. Full well he knew what life with Anna would be like. He even knew what she would make of a wedding night. She would parade her charms, promise much and then take joy in provoking a quarrel in order to frustrate him. It would not be so with the small MacKenzie. Whatever she had to give, she would give. Whatever she possessed was his and as he paused on the landing to smile at her, his eyes swept the mahogany parlor below with its fine paintings and rich carpets.

Any regrets concerning Anna went from his mind forever.

II

The Children

"I remember the day the news came that the redcoats had fired upon the men of Lexington. I was only six years old but I remember. It was a Sunday morning."

John Slidell, age seventeen, tore his eyes away from contemplation of a lovely equestrienne in black velvet habit to observe what had prompted his father's train of thought. Oh, yes, the colonial City Hall. The newspapers had only that morning given the information that it was to be demolished.

"The Stamp Act Congress met there in 1765 and the Continental Congress twenty years later. Seems a shame to destroy the old landmarks."

John did not reply. His father's memories of the past had been sufficiently stirred. Now, if one was not very careful there would follow a lesson in history, personal anecdotes and a lengthy declaration that no Slidell and no MacKenzie had ever buckled down to the British. John hoped to avoid it all. He knew well that his father had been but six years old on that long-ago Sunday and that he had stayed alone in back of the old candle shop while *his* father had gone forth to do something or other terribly patriotic. He knew all that but he did not know the name of the pretty thing in the black velvet habit. High-strung animal she was riding. He wished that he, on a devilish black stallion, were at her side instead of sitting like an old man here in his father's richly polished carriage. Who was that girl? Too flashy to be a lady and yet too elegant and haughty to be an advertisement for a business venture.

"Right over there, son, Marinus Willett, a militiaman, seized muskets from the British and with them he armed . . ."

And, John thought wearily, the little boy waited in back of the

45

candle shop while his father ran with a mob tearing up the King's cargoes and probably getting roaring drunk in the process. Who was that black-eyed creature in the velvet habit?

"Not much interested in the Revolution, are you, John?" his father asked abruptly.

"Well, sir, it's a very long time ago."

"A very long time ago? Little more than a quarter of a century. Yet to a boy who has but graduated from Columbia College, I suppose it is ancient history. Very well. We will talk of the things that belong to your world. They are not so different from the things that belonged to mine since the possibility of trouble with England is again occupying everyone's mind."

John said, "It is not occupying my mind, Father. It will all be settled peacefully."

"Really, boy? Glad to hear you say that." The tone was sardonic. "I had been worried till this very moment."

Striking sparks on the cobbles, the fascinating horse and rider turned at the corner and flew toward Pearl Street and out of sight. With the comforting thought that a description would easily establish identity, John turned his attention back to his father and found, still hanging in air, his father's last words and the tone in which they had been spoken. Now that he captured the meaning and flavor, he was stung by the jeering rejection of his opinion. He kept a sullen silence as the carriage rolled unhurriedly through Exchange and on to Broadway.

Why, at Columbia no one had received his views with anything but interest and respect. The instructors had discussed and sometimes even had agreed with ideas set forth by him. Yet his father would not. . . . John's resentful thoughts weakened here. The instructors, he suddenly remembered, were not shipping magnates and were not in contact with men who knew how the international winds blew. Strange how often he forgot that without benefit of a college education, this father of his, shipowner, bank president and head of an insurance company, was sometimes in a position to know more than the most brilliant instructor. John swallowed hard. He hoped his father would understand that a question meekly put was by way of being an apology.

"Are we going to fight England again, Father?"

"I do not know. I refuse to make predictions. I do know that Napoleon has ruled that no American ship may unload in Europe if she's been to a British port first. And I know that England has ruled that American ships have to clear from a British port before touching Europe. Now, what do you make of that? Do you want to reconsider your own prediction?"

"I guess I wasn't thinking."

"I guess you weren't. My God, the harbor is a forest of spars, and an army of unemployed march the waterfront. Four times a week we open soup kitchens but what are the men supposed to do in between? No wonder they are going into British service."

"Are our ships idle, Father?"

"*Our* ships? Oh, you're a partner, are you? In that case, I think you'd better come down and have a look for yourself. The time has come for you to know what is going on."

"Yes, sir, you are quite right."

They smiled at each other. The small moment of mutual dissatisfaction had passed—for now. Say what one would, the older man thought, the young were one way and the old— The old? But I am little past forty. Still, you are father to this tall young man and father to his older sister, who is a married woman, and if forty plus is not really old, then you should have been more diverted by that vision in black velvet that just passed the carriage.

John Slidell, the older, sighed, knowing well the root of his depression. On this day, he had concluded arrangements for the family vault at the Church of St. Mark's in-the-Bouwerie. A necessary piece of business to be sure for a substantial, sensible man but the new possession was not calculated to fill one with a sense of youth or gaiety. Vault number ninety-five, he thought, and even the number had a melancholy ring. Ninety-five. On winter nights, the wind would moan the number as it passed his window and— Well, if he was really a substantial, sensible man, why didn't he think of something else?

"Who will be with us this evening, John? Do you know?"

"Mr. Livingston is coming. Had you forgotten?"

"Yes, I had for the moment. Nice having him in the city again— if only for a visit."

47

"Ellen and Richard are coming, too, and they are bringing Richard's friend, Oliver Perry. He is a naval lieutenant."

"Good. Good. Anyone else?"

"Well, Perry is bringing his young brother and there will be little Charlie Wilkes but of course they'll be at the children's table with Tom and Alexander and Janie."

"Doesn't sound like much of a gathering. I thought your mother would plan something more elaborate for Mr. Livingston."

John nodded. The whole thing sounded extremely dull and Michael Kesson had pleaded with him to remain at his house. The senior Kessons were away and Michael had sent a message to the Quarle sisters over on Beaver Street that he and a friend were very lonely. Only John's admiration for Mr. Livingston, a leftover loyalty from nursery days, had given him the strength to part from Michael.

"I guess Edward is doing very well in New Orleans," his father said.

"Could he become mayor there?"

"No reason why not but it is difficult to imagine that a man who has been mayor of New York would condescend to accept such a position in a lesser place. I hear great things of New Orleans but wouldn't every city be less than New York?"

"Yes, sir." John knew that one careless remark now would precipitate a tirade on the folly and villainy that had resulted in the nation's capital being moved; first to ugly, sprawling Philadelphia and then to that dreary, undeveloped mudbank on the Potomac. Gratefully he saw that his father was not thinking of that now. His eyes were filled with satisfaction and pride as he surveyed the city that was his, the street that was his and, as the team of bays turned the corner, the house that was his.

Before the coachman had prepared his old body for the formalities expected of it, John sprang from the carriage and offered his hand to his father.

"Not quite yet, Johnny. The day will come but this isn't it."

Ten-year-old Alexander ran to meet them on the doorstep. "I have been watching for you, Papa. I have something to ask you. May I go in the Navy? May I? Charlie Wilkes has decided to go, so may I?"

To John's mind, the red-haired Alexander was not especially huggable. He was always amazed at his father's enthusiasm for the boy. Now there was the hug, of course, the loving smiles and a great amount of importance placed on Alexander's preposterous notion.

"The Navy? Well, perhaps the Navy's for you, Alec boy. We'll talk about it. What brought the matter up? Oh, I see. Lieutenant Perry is here. Is that it?"

"Yes. He is in the small sitting room with Ellen and Richard and his brother is there, too, and—"

John walked past them and on into the house. There was a great fire roaring on the hearth and before it sat his mother puzzling over some needlework. Within his memory, she had never completed a single piece of embroidery or lace and he suspected that she was rather inexpert at this dainty pastime. He kissed her and dropped to her side on the sofa.

"How are you, dear?" she asked. "Did you and your father meet by accident or design?"

"Design. I went to his office and asked for a ride home. I had been at a friend's house."

She said, "I trust you enjoyed yourself."

"Thank you, Mother, yes." He had a silly impulse to kiss her again. Most mothers would have asked, "What friend? What did you do?" Not his mother.

"Don't you want to join Richard and Ellen, dear? They have the Perry brothers with them."

"Both Perry brothers? Isn't one of them a child?"

"He is sixteen." She was kind enough to make no point of John's being only a year older. "A slight problem arose. I can scarcely place him at the children's table or expect him to romp with them while awaiting dinner. He's by way of being a naval officer, too."

"What? At sixteen?"

"He's a genius, I suppose. He's a midshipman. Richard tells me that at fourteen he had finished all the Navy's courses, the youngest graduate they have ever had. Such a sweet child, too." She paused to consider a tangle of green and yellow skeins. Then, "Janie has gone upstairs to change into a more becoming frock."

49

John rose from the sofa as his father entered the room with Alexander still hanging to his arm.

"We have had a talk about the coach house, Jane, and Alexander has convinced me that there is definitely room there to raise a family of terriers."

"Is there really? So you are to become a dog fancier, Alec?" She bent her sober attention upon him. "It was my impression that you were seeking your father's permission to enter the Navy."

Her husband cleared his throat and looked as grave as she. "The dogs are to take the place of a naval career while we are all thinking things over."

"Oh, I see. Very wise. Very. Do go get ready for dinner, dear. Mr. Livingston will be along soon. Perhaps you had better go meet the Perry boys first and then—"

There was a sudden scampering on the stairs, a few sharp yells, and two youngsters came bounding into the parlor. Charlie Wilkes, the imp of Vesey Street, followed by Tom Slidell, John's twelve-year-old brother, whom he rather liked.

"Charlie has my penknife. He won't give it to me," Tom cried. "Make him give me my penknife."

"I'm a guest here," Charlie protested. "If I want his knife, he has to be polite about it, doesn't he, Mrs. Slidell?"

"No," she said thoughtfully. "I don't see why."

"But I'm a guest!"

"True, Charlie, and if you simply hate the way you're treated, you can leave. Give Tom his knife."

Stunned, Charlie handed the knife back to Tom, meanwhile casting wondering looks at Tom's mother. This was not the way he had expected things to go. Always, in his experience, he had found that if you grabbed something and allowed yourself to be pursued into the presence of the owner's mother, she would wearily give orders to "let your little guest have it." The Slidells were very odd people.

"Now go upstairs and stay there till you're called for dinner. And Alec, you go with them."

The youngsters climbed the stairs reluctantly, pausing on the landing before the moon clock, examining its fascinating face, then going on their way.

John and his father went to the small sitting room to meet the Perry brothers. Jane MacKenzie Slidell dropped her tangled silks and sat gazing into the flames. Oh, if everybody would just stay where they were for a while. What joy it would be to forget that young John had no plans for the future beyond amusing himself and that Ellen had not yet conceived and had an angry, disappointed husband to face at dinner every evening.

How wonderful if she could journey to some place far away. What bliss to say, "Good-by until I feel like seeing all of you again."

Would she actually go alone if the opportunity presented itself? She knew that she would not. Gleefully she would leave the children. That would be no sacrifice at all but their father . . . She would not willingly be separated from him past nightfall, for it had become her habit to sleep upon his shoulder and his habit to awaken her with a kiss. How strange that he had finally learned to love her. Poor sweet, the first few years must have been horrid for him with all the pretending. But he had been so good about it, never failing once in the role of attentive husband.

And at last he loved me, she thought. And she remembered a morning when she had awakened to find John propped up on his elbow, staring at her. "Damned if I can see that you're popeyed," he had said soberly. She had drawn him down against the pillows and screamed with laughter and looking into the flames, she laughed now, remembering.

Yes, he loved her. And Jane MacKenzie Slidell knew that there were as many kinds of love as there were kinds of people. She saw very clearly that her husband's love for her had developed naturally and inevitably because she was the source of all earthly comforts and pleasures. He could have no more withheld his love than he could have failed to enjoy the rich and spacious MacKenzie house. Men never knew what made for love. They did not recognize its various faces. To them love was love. It amused her to think that many a poet in his male innocence had sung of his adored not realizing that his soul was hers because she had thoughtfully thrown an extra blanket over him on a cold night.

The knocker sounded. That would be Edward Livingston. The moment of quiet was over. Jane rose from the sofa, prepared to

51

meet her guest. From the small sitting room came her husband and John, Richard and Ellen and the Perry boys. Down the stairs flocked Charlie Wilkes and Janie and Alexander and Tom.

"Good heavens," she thought, looking about her. "The stage is set. But for what? It is only an old friend coming to dinner."

Edward Livingston, forty-six and attractive, was a figure out of a storybook, a storybook given to a child by his parents in hope that the child would set his standards by those of the hero. Son of the Livingston who had been judge of the Admiralty Court and the Supreme Court of the Colonies, brother to the Livingston who had administered the oath of office to George Washington and who had conducted the negotiations which had resulted in the Louisiana Purchase, Edward was also an outstanding legal mind. None doubted that he, too, would bring fame to the great name. None believed that voluntary exile to New Orleans could change Edward's destiny one whit. He was clearly marked for great things and there were those who said that his service as congressman and later mayor of New York would be noted as but inconsequential stages of his career when his final biography was written.

That was an exaggeration, for one action of Edward's while mayor of New York would long be remembered and discussed. An employee of his office had been discovered to have misappropriated city funds and Edward had instantly proclaimed himself responsible for the crime.

"It is my judgment that places a man in a position of trust. If I am mistaken as to the man's character, then surely the blame is mine, for I chose the man." Ignoring arguments that freed him of any obligation, he had straightway sold his possessions, reimbursed the city for its loss and at the end of his term, with very little money, had gone to New Orleans to begin life anew.

"And how does it go in New Orleans?" Jane asked him. He was to her right at the table. To her left was Lieutenant Perry, but she kept forgetting him. "It was to give full attention to your description of the place that I made this dinner a small, almost family affair."

"Things go well for me in that wonderful city, my dear, but it is good to be here just the same." He glanced around the table with

52

an affectionate look for each of the Slidells. "You have so exceptional a family. Beautiful Ellen and handsome young John." Then gazing beyond to the table at which the younger children sat, "How did you all happen to be fortunate enough to look like your mother?"

His voice brightened a room already bright with crystal, silver and snowy linen. Smooth and soft yet commanding, that voice of Edward's would sound the note of authority anywhere on earth, young John thought. And such gallantry. It was true enough, a well-known fact indeed, that they were all extraordinarily well favored but not one of them resembled Mother except poor little Tom, whose eyes protruded quite shockingly.

"Who is the guest at your table, Janie dear?" Edward asked.

"He is Charlie Wilkes, sir," Janie responded.

"A friend of yours?"

Janie threw a dagger of a glance at the distinguished Mr. Livingston. "I should say not, sir. He is Tom's friend and only twelve years old. I don't even like him." Her eyes went to the dashing midshipman at Ellen's side who was quietly giving his whole attention to a huge slice of roast lamb. "Please don't think Charlie Wilkes is my friend," she said plaintively.

Edward's glance followed hers to the young Perry. "No, no," he said quickly. "Charlie Wilkes is here because Tom invited him. He is not your friend at all, Janie. We understand that now." But his eyes had not returned to Janie. They had stayed with the midshipman in sad contemplation of the long lashes of the lad as they lay on the smooth cheek. Only a baby, in God's truth. It was touching to Edward that here was a boy who had never known boyhood. At what age had they sent him to sea to learn mathematics and astronomy from a chaplain, navigation from a captain and seamanship from a rough, tough crew? Already years of study lay behind him and ahead the crushing burden of responsibility and decisions and a need to perpetually replenish the sources of courage and energy.

"What's your brother's name?" he asked the lieutenant.

"Matthew. He is never called that, though. His middle name is Calbraith. He is called Cal."

"Must be a clever little chap."

53

"Yes," the lieutenant said. He twirled his wineglass and looked down the table at his brother. "Cal's worth ten of me, or had you already guessed that, sir?"

"No, I had not guessed it nor do I believe it. You brothers seem much alike to me—two fine gentlemen of whom our Navy can be very proud."

Oliver Perry gazed at him with a sullen burn in his eyes. "You are very kind, sir, but I am twenty-five years old and I am known to a rather large circle as Cal Perry's brother, so when I tell you he is worth ten of me, I know what I am talking about."

Edward was a pleasant man but he knew the futility of trying to heal a wound that delighted in bleeding. He said, "Forgive me, Lieutenant, for seeking to impose my opinion upon you."

Oliver Perry raised his goblet and drank deeply. Edward turned his attention to young John.

"What will you do now that you are out of school? You must tell me, my friend, what you have planned for the future."

Young John stared at Edward Livingston whom he had idolized in childhood and certainly respected now. Future? What future? Had he not intended to use his education as a gentleman should? Fine books and paintings, travel, a worthy circle of intellectual friends. Had his parents really intended that he should make his way in the world? With the help of Grandfather MacKenzie's money, John, Senior, had made a huge success of his life. So wasn't the way already made for all the Slidells? What was this talk of the future? The future would be—well, good living, gentlemanly diversion.

With this in mind, John found it difficult to take pleasure in a confection of spun sugar which happened to be his favorite dessert.

John, Senior, also took little pleasure in the confection. Other aspects of the dinner, too, had left him unsatisfied. It was splendid seeing Edward again and there was no doubt that uniforms graced a table magnificently. Still, since Jane had not chosen to honor Edward with an important assemblage, he wished she had done nothing at all. It was an evening when the family should have been alone. He would have liked to speak to his wife and older children about vault ninety-five. The purchase of it was so serious a matter,

54

so in the forefront of his mind, that even under existing conditions he had considered mentioning it.

Just after the fish course, there had been a moment when he had thought of saying in a light, matter-of-fact tone, "Today I invested in some property. I bought a piece of a churchyard. . . ."

But as he had weighed the propriety of making such an announcement, his eyes had chanced to meet those of the young midshipman. The boy had smiled at him, a bashful smile but friendly, and his host had thought, "He is young and he is happy. Only a very self-centered bore would force him to listen to talk of where the Slidells will lie in death. Why should he have to hear of anything so dismal? What can vault ninety-five mean to him?"

He had smiled back at the boy, had urged him to accept another pickled peach.

Almost the moment that dinner ended, a servant called to walk Charlie Wilkes home. Soon after, Ellen and Richard left, taking the Perry boys with them. Not having spoken a word all evening to the little girl who had sat at the children's table, young Cal was understandably perplexed by the importance she placed upon his departure. He could not think why a gift was in order but on the doorstep the child handed him a small and beautiful Bible bound in pale-blue leather. He could only murmur his bewildered thanks and hurry after his brother, conscious that this Janie Slidell was watching as he scrambled into Richard's carriage.

"What was the meaning of that?" her mother asked.

"Sailors have a cruel life," Janie said, her eyes piously raised to heaven. "The Bible could be a comfort and a guide."

"True, but I might wish you had given him your own Bible to comfort and guide him. That one was mine, presented to me by my grandmother on my tenth birthday."

"I know, but it is of a color to cheer a lonely boy."

And of a color to remind him of Janie's frock and Janie's eyes. Remembering the nonsense that had gone through her mind when she had been alone at the fireside, the thought came to Jane: If I did go away from my children and even if I stayed away from them, here is one who would get on splendidly without me.

And when the moment came for her three youngest to say their

55

good nights to Mr. Livingston, she felt pride in their good manners and relief in their departure.

"Now, Edward," she said. "Tell us about New Orleans."

Edward Livingston settled himself comfortably and obliged her. He was in partnership with a prominent lawyer named Grymes. The city was fascinating. Very French, very gay, excelled by none in the art of elegance.

There was much to tell and Edward told it well. He described the magnificent live oaks, the fabulous splendor of the plantation houses, the culinary skill of even the poorest Louisianan. He spoke of Congo Square and the slave dances and the incredible luxury in which the wealthy lived. The older Slidells listened spellbound. Young John with delight.

He was suddenly relaxed and happy. His problem had vanished. He knew now what he would say to Mr. Livingston and what he would say to his parents when they finally turned their attention to him. Oh, this was an inspiration over which he and Michael Kesson would laugh for days. He would claim that a tremendous excitement had gripped him, a call that could not be denied. He would say that above all else in life, he desired to study law and move to New Orleans. It would of course be essential to perfect himself in French and perhaps Spanish, too. By God, it would take years to learn law, French and Spanish.

Doubtless it would be wise to interject here an intelligent question concerning New Orleans but, no, it was too late. Mr. Livingston was changing the subject.

"Well, enough of me and my pursuits, dear friends. How does business go?"

John, Senior, frowned. "The shipping business? Damn badly. If I depended on that alone, I would soon be back boiling soap."

"And there are days when responsibilities press so heavily that you think wistfully of such a simple enterprise. Is that not true?"

"Very true. Would you believe it, Edward, only a month ago on sudden impulse I walked into a soapmaking shop just to breathe again the vile, dreadful, soothing odors of my youth. I am certain the young man who owned the shop thought me quite mad."

"I will wager he understood."

"No, he is a young Englishman not very tolerant of American

nonsense. His name is Colgate and he told me earnestly that I had made a mistake in forsaking the business of making soap. When I consider the plight of our shipping, I think he was right. Edward, I tell you many will face ruin before this is over. Coming on top of Jefferson's long embargo, it cannot be ridden out. Do you realize that there was not one crossing from the Port of New York last year? One hundred and twenty bankruptcies! Think of it."

"But the embargo has been repealed, John."

"Yes, and now the British have thought of a way to starve us. They are treating us like colonial vassals. Edward, it is not to be endured."

"Then," said Edward Livingston calmly, "America will not endure it. There will be war. But, pardon me, Jane, for introducing such a grim possibility into your pretty parlor. Tell me something of what interests you, my dear. I had really no opportunity to speak to Ellen. Would you like to tell me a great deal of her and her new happiness?"

Jane picked up her needlework and stared at a daisy which she had absent-mindedly embroidered scarlet. "Oh, Ellen is divinely happy, Edward. Her life is a song from noon till night."

"I am happy to hear it. Very happy." He waited expectantly for further details and none came. He was ready now for young John. "And you, my dear boy. At the table we were speaking of your future." The smooth courtroom voice rolled mellowly in the mahogany parlor. "Please believe I am as interested in you as your parents are. If I am able to assist in any way with advice or guidance, I stand ready. But then you know that."

"Yes, sir," John said. "And truth to tell, you have already advised and guided me." His eyes met Edward Livingston's. "Sir, I know now what I want to do with my future."

His father said, "I have always known what you *want* to do with your future. Just tell us how you think you can earn an honest dollar."

John told them and they listened attentively. Law. French. Spanish. New Orleans.

Edward Livingston was impressed and a slight mistiness appeared in his eyes as John said that he would ask no more of life than the chance to follow in Mr. Livingston's footsteps. John noted

57

the mistiness and it was at that moment that another innocence fell from him. Suddenly his admiration for Edward Livingston was a part of the past, like milk teeth or baby fat. For John Slidell, age seventeen, had seen that simply by sounding a note of sincerity, he had fooled this man. He had looked straight into his eyes and had spoken falsely and he had been believed. So much for Edward Livingston.

But wait, the thought must be followed through. There was more to it. Much more. A thousand exciting possibilities lay pleading to be explored. Most men were less experienced than Edward Livingston, less knowing.

If Edward Livingston could be fooled . . . The conclusion was astonishing but very clear. If Edward Livingston could be fooled, then there were probably few men on earth who could not be.

As young John Slidell—and his father, too—had noted, the dinner for Edward Livingston had been far from an elaborate affair. Yet it was strange how often the evening was mentioned in later years and how vividly it was remembered.

Commander Alexander Slidell MacKenzie who, upon entering the Navy, had taken his mother's maiden name, had been heard to remark, "It was the sight of Cal Perry in uniform that made me want the sea. I was but ten years old when he first came to the home of my parents and he influenced my life."

Secretary of State Edward Livingston recalled, "Till that night, I had not seen John Slidell, Junior, since his childhood. I liked him. But is it not a singular misjudgment that I made? I thought him to be without ambition."

Captain Charles Wilkes was to tell newspapermen, "I remember dining at the Slidells' house one evening when I was a boy. Yes, it is interesting, isn't it, in the light of what has just occurred?"

Commodore Matthew Calbraith Perry would of course speak with a sailing man's sentimentality of a little blue Bible and of the angel who had given it to him. "Her eyes were just the color of the binding."

For one reason or another, there were those who remembered for all the years of their lives the evening that Edward Livingston dined with the Slidells. Perhaps some forgot in time but there was

58

an autumn in which they were remembering. And they were remembering because the children in the streets sang only one song. Laborers at their work whistled only one tune and bands never neglected to play everybody's favorite, for it brought cheers and shouts from the listeners.

> Perry, Perry, Oliver Hazard Perry.
> He met the enemy, they are his.
> The bravest hero existing is
> Perry, Perry, Oliver Hazard Perry.
> Perry, Perry, Oliver Hazard Perry.
> He fought with courage on the Lakes.
> To beat the British what it takes
> Is Perry, Perry, Oliver Hazard Perry.
> Perry, Perry—

Young John Slidell sat in the public parlor of the hotel in which Nell Winslow lived. He disliked the room and the tone of the entire establishment. He had no sympathy for Nell's willingness to endure any and all discomforts simply because the Park Theatre was conveniently close to the dreary little hotel. He turned toward the window and frowned at a group of small boys gathered outside. "Are they going to sing it again?"

"Why not?" she asked. "It was a great victory."

"But we know about it now and I am awfully tired of those screechy little voices."

Nell said, "Children have screechy little voices, to be sure, but they have a right to play in the street and to sing of Perry if they wish. His achievement was wonderful. He must be wonderful, too."

"Do you really think so? What a child you are."

"No nicer compliment was ever presented to an aging lady," Nell said, laughing. "Child indeed!"

He wished to heaven she would pretend a little. He had heard that women were arch about their age. Not this one. Though she looked eighteen, she never missed an opportunity to remind him that she was twenty-five. Her candor disquieted him. It placed him in the position of a foolish, worshiping boy. Also, he had a painful suspicion that if she cared for him, she would have hesitated before admitting her five-year seniority. Oh, how lovely she was.

Even the "Josephine" gown she wore was lovely, though unfashionable ever since the Empress had been banished from the royal bed. Nell belonged to a group of loyal and lively ladies who had vowed to honor the unfortunate creature by having their dressmakers continue to copy the design that Josephine had favored. The fact that each and every member of the group had just the bosom for the style seemed to no one a curious coincidence.

Perry, Perry, Oliver Hazard Perry—

John sprang to his feet, causing the dusty little rocker to agitate furiously. "Let's get out of here, Nell."

"Now, you know I cannot. I told you Mr. Price is coming with the manuscript of the new play."

"He will leave it with the clerk."

"I don't want that. I want to be here so I can begin studying immediately. This is going to be a very difficult role."

"Not for you, Nell. No role is difficult for you."

"Oh, John, how you exaggerate." She smiled at him and he suffered because the flashing smile represented only an actress's joy in hearing herself praised. There was nothing personal about the smile.

"Let us go upstairs and sit in your private parlor. It is perfectly proper. We could leave the door open—"

"How sweet you are, how thoughtful, but I am afraid we will have to stay here. I told Mr. Price that—"

"To hell with Mr. Price," John muttered.

"Such talk! Please remember that I work for a living and cannot afford to have successful managers sent to hell just now, thank you."

"I had hoped to take you for a walk or a ride today."

"I know, John. Think how disappointed I must be."

Her black eyes really did seem quite sad, he thought. There was no doubt she enjoyed being with him. She certainly gave him a lot of time—considering how busy she was. There were always rehearsals and performances and the hours in which she must study. It was true, though, that she allowed him to tour the shops with her in the mornings and very often she accepted his invitations to after-theatre suppers. No one in the city was more familiar than he with the Park Theatre stage entrance in that narrow little lane known as Theatre Alley that connected Ann and Beekman Streets. There was satisfaction to be found in the envious glances that followed him wherever he walked with her. It was the only satisfaction. As he ruefully admitted to Michael Kesson, he was still waiting for kiss number one.

"What!" Michael had been dumfounded. "You mean that you spend all that time with her and— Oh, I don't believe it. You're not that patient. Are you spending money on her, too?"

"She will not accept a present, Mike. Flowers, of course, and maybe an occasional book or a bottle of perfume."

John could never bring himself to tell Michael that, oh, years ago, when he had been only a boy of seventeen, he had first looked upon Nell Winslow and had found her the most alluring thing he had ever seen—a vision in a black velvet riding habit who had caused his heart to sing a hopeful song. He had made inquiries and discovered her name and occupation. Nell Winslow, actress. Like a little boy prolonging the thrill before opening a Christmas package, John had delayed presenting himself at the Leonard Street Theatre. When he had done so, it had been too late. Miss Winslow, he had been informed, was not a regular member of the company. She had been appearing but briefly in New York and now had departed.

Sensibly he had put Nell Winslow out of his thoughts and when he had almost forgotten her completely, he had seen her name on handbills distributed by the Park Theatre. He had sent flowers and a note in which he had told the lady that she had filled his dreams for three long years. She had consented to receive him in her dressing room that very evening and he had gone to the rendez-vous with sweet expectations. Well, there was nothing to complain about, he reflected. He still had those sweet expectations, had he not?

"Nell," he said, sitting down again in the uncomfortable rocker. "Sometimes I think nothing is important to you but the stage."

"That is exactly what I think sometimes, too," she said pensively. "You know there are people who live only for their work. How are your law studies, by the way?"

"I am doing very well but there is nothing in the law books that tells me how I am to gain your love."

"Hush. This is a public place, John." And as though to illustrate the truth of her remark, a stout lady in bronze-colored bombazine came through the faded green portieres and deposited herself on a settee not far from Nell.

John's pleading eyes flashed the message "Please let us go to your parlor," but Nell turned her flawless profile to him and said, "As we were saying, it is indeed a very great victory and Perry is the man of the moment. Such a war god as he is, such a—"

The portieres stirred again and Steve Price, manager of the Park Theatre, entered the parlor. He was a tall, gaunt man, more electric and attractive, many thought, than the actors he hired. Always perfectly correct in his attitude toward each and every person who touched his life, Steve Price had not an enemy in the city. New Yorkers expressed surprise that so well-mannered a person could be associated with the stage. Price's smile was irresistible but disciplined. For subscribers to his theatre, it beamed affably but without a trace of familiarity. For others, it was the warmest and friendliest in the world.

"Good afternoon, Miss Winslow, Mr. Slidell. Beautiful day, is it not?"

They agreed and Nell invited him to seat himself but he declined. "I would like nothing better but I have an appointment and I must run." He handed a manuscript to Nell. "Please read it at once. There have been some changes and I would like you at the theatre early this evening so we may discuss them." The smile, a jaunty wave and he was gone.

Nell rose with a sigh. The Josephine gown, wide-skirted at the ankles, moved sensuously. "I fear I must get to work, John. It has been so pleasant."

He stood looking down at the dazzling view which the gown generously provided. If only once he dared draw her to him and take those lips he so hungrily desired. It was not the stout lady in bombazine that deterred him. It was the almost certain knowledge that never again would Nell Winslow suffer him as escort. To part from him forever would not cause her a single pang, he thought miserably.

"Tonight after the performance?"

"No. Tonight I will work with this." She fluttered the pages of the manuscript and smiled bewitchingly. "Good-by, John. It was nice to have seen you." And—something to dream about for the rest of the day—she paused at the portieres to throw him a kiss from her slim, lovely fingers. Then she was gone.

Well, perhaps tomorrow she would have more time.

Perry, Perry, Oliver Hazard Perry—

Janie Slidell thought it hilarious that her mother, who had always been able to tame the most rebellious of servingmaids, had been completely helpless in the matter of that wonderful song. The servants sang it on the stairs, in the kitchen and while dusting the parlor. Janie thought she had even heard humming while platters were being passed at dinner.

Perry, Perry, Oliver Hazard Perry—

Janie laughed aloud and threw herself over backwards upon the candlewick bedspread to lie dreaming up at the ceiling. Oliver Hazard Perry, the hero of the Battle of Lake Erie. This man would be her brother-in-law. He did not know it yet. Even Cal did not know it. Cal with his dear polite little letters. If that brother of his could be a hero, she reasoned, there was no limit to the dramatic successes Cal might achieve. Had Oliver been the youngest man in history to complete the naval course? Certainly not. Yet his name was on everyone's lips today. Oh, Cal would be more famous, more—more everything.

She pulled herself to a sitting position on the edge of her bed and took Cal's latest letter from the lacy bosom of her second-best frock. Before rereading it, she crossed the room to examine her face in the mirror. Why, she was lovelier than she had imagined! The flushed cheeks, the sparkling eyes held her earnest attention. Would mother permit her just a dab from the rouge pot in case she happened to be pale on the day that Cal visited? And what would she do with her hair? Wear it all tumbled and beautiful as it was now or restrain it primly beneath a cap to indicate that she was a grown lady? This had to be carefully considered.

The letter now.

Dear Miss Slidell:

Thank you very much for the fine words you wrote describing my brother. He is indeed all that you said. Think how I glory in the fact that I always knew he needed only the circumstances to prove himself one of the ablest and bravest men alive. Now that the entire country is literally singing his praise, I fear I have a rather smug I-could-have-told-you-so attitude.

In answer to your question, I must confess that I have contributed nothing to the winning of the war. The only excitement I have seen was prior to actual declaration of hostilities. When I was aide to Commodore Rodgers on the "President," we did defeat H.M.S. "Little Belt." That was a peacetime action although the "Little Belt" was guilty of impressment of seamen from American ships.

Yes, indeed, I will call upon your father and mother if I am ever able to leave New London. They are very kind to "look forward to seeing" me. I have never forgotten their hospitality. Please give them my fond regards. And thank you very much for your letters.

Respectfully,
M. C. Perry

Hardly a love letter, yet Janie was content with it. Shrewdly she had assessed the character of this Rhode Island boy. Serious-minded, pure of heart, conscientious. There was nothing of the irresponsible trifler in his nature. He would choose the discourtesy of leaving a letter unanswered in preference to the sin of encouraging a young lady to think him interested if he were not.

So perhaps any letter from M. C. Perry was a love letter. When she wrote again, she would mention that she joined her parents in hoping he would soon be in New York. Or was that too forward?

She remembered how Ellen had looked floating down the staircase in white satin and lace. And she was so much prettier than Ellen. How surprised Cal would be when they met. At thirteen, she had been a mere child, skinny and unpromising.

Dear Mr. Perry:

It was with pleasure that I received your letter. The weather here is very fine—

"Perry Hazard Oliver, Perry, Perry.
His are they, enemy the met he."

64

Alexander Slidell, lying on the floor stomach down, raised his eyes from a book to say, "Did you hear? I can sing it backwards."

His brother Tom said, "Well, don't sing it that way. It's disrespectful to Captain Perry."

"Oh, it is not. What does he care about the song? How can it possibly be disrespectful to him? How can it be? Answer me."

"Read your book and quit singing."

"I can do both."

"No, you can't. I won't let you," Tom said.

He was playing chess with his friend Charlie Wilkes, and had no patience with the nonsense of a thirteen-year-old brother. Not now. Not at any time. Alexander knew that Tom had requested a room of his own.

"It is a very large room," Mother had said. "Ample space for you both."

The case had been decided against Tom. Alexander had been secretly delighted though he had pretended disappointment. As Mother had said, it was a very large room. Moreover, it had the best fireplace in the house and was close to the staircase. A person could make a stealthy raid upon the kitchen at night without having to walk past his parents' room. Location and accommodation were of the most desirable but it was the room in which both Grandfather and Grandmother MacKenzie had died and Alexander did not want to sleep in it alone. Even with the protection of Tom beside him, there were nights full of unexplained noises. Strange sounds came from the wardrobe, and the china pitcher standing in its china bowl on the washstand looked all too white in the dark hours of morning.

Once, on a bright summer afternoon, exploring an island of intimate conversation with his father, he had spoken of those strange sounds, had told something of his fears.

His father had smiled, not in the way that made a boy regret a confidence but in recollection of something pleasant.

"Alec boy, you are going to ask me if there is such a thing as a ghost. I will tell you candidly that I do not know. But here is the thing: with ghosts I have had no contact but the MacKenzies I knew well. They were the sweetest, gentlest people who ever lived and perhaps the most polite. If they are ghosts, their first thought would be that they must not frighten anybody. Their second thought, that the room no longer belongs to them and they would not think of entering."

That had comforted Alexander till he had read somewhere that death ruined a person's disposition and that ghosts were usually quite ill-natured and enjoyed terrorizing the living.

Charlie Wilkes looked up from the chessboard. "Stop that whistling," he said. "I can't concentrate."

"Who do you think you are, Charlie Wilkes? This is my room as much as Tom's. I'll whistle all I like."

"Mind your manners," Tom said. "Or get out."

"What! Out of a room I own half of? You just try to put me out."

Tom shot him a scathing glance. Alexander knew he deserved it. Tom could easily whip him. He was older and bigger. Besides, Charlie Wilkes would probably give him some slight assistance. Alexander's only hope would be to shout for his mother. But he had not done that in over a year now, he thought proudly. He was training himself to do without her support. Once he was in the Navy, she would not be available.

A sudden thought struck him. "Hey, Charlie."

It surprised him when Charlie replied.

"What do you want?"

"Weren't you going in the Navy? I thought—"

"Of course I am going in the Navy. Next year, probably."

"Next year! You will be sixteen by then. Look how old you will be before you are anything at all. Nobody is going to catch me waiting till I'm any old sixteen."

Tom said, "You are not going in the Navy at all."

"Yes I am."

"Then you will go when Father says you may."

"That will be when I am fourteen."

"All right. Shut up now."

"I will not shut up." But he could think of nothing he cared to add. Suppose the Navy would not take him? Suppose the Navy did take him and he was unable to distinguish himself? Suppose he never proved worthy of being a comrade to the Perry brothers?

The dream-filled gray eyes narrowed as an idea occurred to him. A hateful idea but one that must be examined. Could he not in-

66

sure against failure by never entering the Navy at all? Would it not be clever to put from his mind all thought of a Navy career? True, he thus forfeited the opportunity to stand on equal footing with the Perry boys but there was a consolation: he protected himself against the danger of discovering that though handed their tools, he could not match their achievements.

Sternly reminding himself that he had not as yet agreed to relinquish a naval career, he let his mind wander to other possibilities. There was writing, of course. He thought he might find pleasure in being an author. At this very moment, hidden beneath his stockings and woolens, there lay the first twenty pages of what he hoped would grow into a splendid novel of life among the Indians. Now, suppose it did? Suppose it was an enormous success? Would such a triumph satisfy him? Would it be a thoroughly acceptable substitute for the Navy? He thought about Matthew Calbraith Perry. Could Perry take for a friend a person who had made a life's work of sitting at a desk and merely *inventing* perilous situations? Oh, no, Perry would laugh at such a man. He would laugh scornfully.

"I had better go in the Navy," Alexander thought hastily.

Maybe he would write a few books just for fun. He would give one—suitably inscribed—to Matthew Calbraith Perry and then his writing would count for something. Perry's attitude could only be deeply admiring in the presence of someone who was a great and courageous naval officer and also an excellent writer.

"I don't know how you do it, Alec," he would say wonderingly.

"Oh, it is nothing, my friend. Nothing."

Tom said, "Run down to the kitchen and fetch us a few cookies, lad."

Alexander stared at him. Who was this insane stripling? Kitchen? Cookies? Lad? The dreaming eyes cleared. Oh, it was Tom who had spoken. His brother Tom. And if he did not obey the order, the older boys would make him wish he had. He scrambled to his feet and made for the kitchen. At least he could get on their nerves a little.

"Perry Hazard Oliver, Perry, Perry.
His are they, enemy the met he—"

67

John Slidell, Senior, came home early from the office solely to be with Jane. She was feeling so wretched, poor little thing. Though common sense told him that it was foolish to blame himself, he could not dismiss a feeling of guilt. There was no denying that the situation could be dangerous. Jane was forty-one. Not the ideal age for childbearing. Besides, there was more than physical discomfort troubling her. She had been embarrassed by her condition, reluctant to leave her room, to have family or friends know the reason for her illness.

"Dearest Jane, there should be no embarrassment. Recall that at your birth, your mother had reached her forties."

"But she was still a bride!"

"By female logic, your condition is deplorable and hers was not?"

"Of course. *This* is just a cruel joke. We should be grandparents now. If only Ellen were producing a child, how happy we would all be. But since it is I instead of—"

"I am still happy, my dearest, except for the indisposition you experience."

"Happy? How can you be happy? We will appear ridiculous. We are elderly people, John."

"Doesn't that now become debatable?" he had asked dryly.

As he approached the bedroom, he walked on tiptoe and opened the door quietly. She was lying in bed but not sleeping. Her gray eyes sparked with surprise to see him on the threshold.

"I am glad you are here," she said. "I have had the most horrible day."

He went to her and kissed her fondly, then drew a chair to the bedside. How curiously this pregnancy had changed her. There had been a whining note in her voice as she had greeted him.

"Horrible day, dearheart? I am sorry."

"Oh, really horrible."

She gave him the details and he was appalled at this further evidence of the way in which Jane had somehow become another person. In the past, she had made a veritable crusade of concealing from him any inkling that childbearing was more than so much sewing and knitting. Sympathetically he listened, murmuring appropriate words though he realized now that he was not alone in considering himself a monster who had imposed his will upon her. Only her wish to punish him could have prompted this deluge of unpleasant revelations.

When she had concluded the sorry list of all the day had brought, she turned her face from him and wept quietly. He patted her shoulder and tried to think of something diverting.

"I had a letter today from Edward Livingston," he said.

"Did you?" The question came blurrily through tears and sniffles.

"Shall I read it to you?"

"If you like."

He pretended that his offer had been met with wild enthusiasm. "You will really enjoy it. It is very interesting and of course concerns our John in part." He reached into his pocket and brought forth the letter, unfolded it importantly and began to read.

Dear Friend:

I trust you have not become angered at what may have seemed indifference from this quarter. My thoughts have been with you though your letter has remained unanswered on my desk. I have been excessively occupied. New Orleans, I may tell you, is war-conscious to a very great and feverish degree and I have been swept into the warm current of events. At this time, I am chairman of the committee on Public Defense and confidential military secretary to General Andrew Jackson.

Today I am resting at the home of friends. It is a large plantation house with eight Doric columns and a three-storied spiral staircase. The rooms would dwarf any furniture we put in New York houses. This family who is entertaining me has a private park for the strangely colored birds indigenous to this region. All very startling.

It may interest you to know that even here, in what may be considered the backwoods, everyone is agog at the exploits of Oliver Hazard Perry. The young man has certainly made a name for himself.

It was with delight I noted in your letter that young John is doing well with his law and language studies. I am impatiently awaiting his arrival here one bright day in the future. I know I can help him enormously. Even socially I will be of help. With your boy in mind, I am courting the young as well as the older people. John will need someone livelier than I when he comes south. I have made a friend of one André Deslonde, who is a handsome young man of a fine family. He and his lovely little wife are about John's age and in a few months they will be parents. This, however, will not curtail their social activi-

69

ties one iota. The Creoles pass their children over to capable black girls and go on with the dance. Nothing interrupts the Creoles' enjoyment of life. My point is aptly illustrated by the following: the Théâtre d'Orléans opened here this month. It has grilled loges for people in mourning!

With deepest affection for you and yours, dear friend, I bring this letter to a close.

Edward Livingston

John refolded the letter and glanced toward what he could see of his wife—the delicate lace panel at the back of her night robe, the tangled yellow hair falling uncombed across the pillow. He was astonished to observe that she was sobbing wildly.

"Jane! Jane, my love, what is it?" He bent over her and still failing to see her face, rushed around to the other side of the bed. "Are you in pain?"

She shook her head.

"Did something in Edward's letter—" He did not complete the ridiculous question. What could possibly have been in Edward's letter to distress her?

Surprisingly she nodded. "That girl," Jane wailed.

He knelt beside her. "What girl, dearest?"

Her face was squeezed into a tight little knot of misery, her voice choked and low. "That Creole girl who is having a baby, too."

He felt himself an absolute idiot for not grasping at once where lay the cause for tears. "Yes, dear, the Creole girl. Why does she trouble you?"

Jane flung herself about impatiently. "It is what I have been telling you. She is young John's age. Now do you see why I am ashamed? What will Edward think when he hears that I and a childish acquaintance of his both have had babies?"

John said, "I am very fond of Edward Livingston but I do not really give a damn what he will think when told that you have been delivered of a child. I care only what you will think. Come, Jane, try to be the sensible little woman you always have been. God decided—"

"*God* decided!" She glared at him and her mouth worked as if there was something she might add.

And he knew that if she died in childbirth, he would never forgive himself for what he was about to say. But in the event that Jane survived her ordeal, there were still years of marriage ahead. He did not wish to live those years with a madwoman or with one who had discovered that he would spinelessly accept female bullying.

"Listen to me," he said flatly. "You and I have lain together many times and I have had no complaints that these encounters have been less rewarding for one than the other. Nothing you have said or done in twenty-three years has led me to believe that you were a helpless creature, cruelly victimized. God made the decision that the experience of a certain night should result in a child. So that is how it is and now let us have an end to this nonsense."

Jane pulled herself bolt upright in the bed and then turned to cling weakly to the silk canopy curtain. He was frightened and penitent as he saw the whiteness of her face. He was ready to apologize, to ask forgiveness for his harshness, when she spoke.

She said, "Get out of the room. I am going to be sick."

He went into the upstairs hall, closing the door behind him. Ought he send a servant to her? Ought he re-enter? He turned the doorknob purposefully and she screamed.

"Stay out!"

He stayed out. For three days and nights, he stayed out because she sent messages to him which the servants shyly delivered. "The mistress says please she wishes to be alone."

On the fourth night, Jane came downstairs for dinner. She had brushed her hair till it glistened and, he suspected, she had made use of the rouge pot. A small black Pompadour patch had been stuck impishly on her cheek and she wore her newest gown. John's throat tightened in terror lest this be a symptom of the madness he had feared.

He drew her to the sofa and asked timorously, "How are you, darling?"

"I am pregnant. Had you not heard?"

"I had heard, my love. How does all go with you?"

"Very well. I have turned the corner and am able to contemplate with delight the thought of dinner. Now, more important are my questions. Are you able to contemplate with delight the thought

71

of me? Am I to be forgiven for having acted like a raped kitchen wench?"

He laughed. "Oh, Jane, never have I loved you more than at this moment."

"How fortunate, for I feel the same toward you, my dear husband."

His heart swelled with happiness and it was a world of great beauty filled with understanding and love and fine, strong children and good fragrances from the dining room and everything wonderful and pure. But as he had known when a boy in the candleshop, life was a thing that offered only brief glimpses of bliss. Already his happiness had faded in the terrible remembering that babies do not come easily to women past forty.

Julia Slidell was a good baby and she did her mother no harm at all. She was born in the year that Americans suffered the embarrassment of having the White House, the Capitol and the Library of Congress burned by the British. People more clear-thinking than the group of disgruntled New Englanders who convened in Hartford to discuss secession and a separate peace knew that the burning of a few buildings—even buildings nationally revered—was not going to win the war for Britain.

The Slidell family spoke little of the war. It was the year that Alexander left home to join the Navy and the year that Janie, in a manner of speaking, did the same thing. She became the bride of Matthew Calbraith Perry.

Sitting quietly beside the cradle of her new baby, Jane had moments in which she felt very young. The baby was Ellen, not Julia. She herself, though a mother, was still a pampered daughter with her parents playing cribbage in the front bedroom, adoring the two strangers—big John and little Ellen—who had come to live with them. Yes, it was a lovely world. This was then, not now. This was Ellen, not Julia. This was— But she could never hold the mood.

She would think of Alexander and grow uneasy. Was the Navy really for him? Despite the fact that for four years he had strongly declared for the Navy, Jane still had her doubts. He was so sensitive, so full of dreams. And what a strange thing he had done about his name.

"Why, dear?" she had asked.

He had looked away from her. "My reason will sound foolish."

"I am sure it will not."

"Well, then, it is this way, Mother. Brother John is very smart. He is certain to be important one day and he will bear Father's name. Tom I am not sure about but it may be that he will distinguish himself and again Slidell will be the name he will carry. Now, for myself, I know positively that I will become famous and it seems unfair that your side of the family will have no share in any success of ours unless I take your name."

"Yes, dear, but—"

"Please show your faith in me by letting me be known as a MacKenzie."

"When you put it that way—"

"I do put it that way. If you refuse, I shall think you do not believe I can bring credit to the name."

"Alec! It is your father of whom I am thinking. It may be that he will be hurt by your choice. Have you considered that?"

"I have and I say again: he has brother John."

Jane had studied him closely. She had not liked the note in his voice when he had mentioned his brother. Nor did she like now what she saw in his eyes. A cool contempt for brother John.

A captain who was a friend of John, Senior's, had attended to the forms and ceremonies that had entered Alexander into the Navy. This captain had personally taken the boy upon his ship and into his care.

"We will make a midshipman of your red-haired lad," he had promised.

Jane did not now know where Alec was. Somewhere, poor child, living the rigorous life of an apprentice. His father had passed but one remark concerning Alec's odd request, and that she had not understood completely.

"By God," he had murmured with some bitterness, "I cannot even send my name to sea."

And Jane, sitting beside Julia's cradle, would think of her grown daughters. The childless one, whose husband refused to un-

73

derstand that her disappointment was as deeply galling as his own. And she thought of Janie, who had placed herself under the protection of a knight in shining armor. How characteristic of the child to have chosen someone with the strength and wisdom to guide her safely through life. Headstrong and willful she was but with instincts so sound that she wanted no man who would permit her to lead the way.

Jane would bend above the cradle to rearrange a bow or smooth a blanket and her mind would turn to young John. Young John, who enjoyed his courses so much that he might be sixty and the world's greatest authority on French and Spanish before he considered himself ready to face the world. It amused her that Tom, when his school work was done, was reading law on his own and that already he could confound his older brother with his learning.

Jane still sometimes had moments of rebellion, moments when she wished she could run from the children. But she knew the truth now. It had taken her years to learn it. No woman is ever free of her children. It would be diverting to embroider those words in neat cross-stitching and surround them with buttercups or perhaps forget-me-nots. One could frame the finished work and hang it in the upstairs sitting room and people would nod and approve the sentiment. But what flowers would one use, what sort of stitch to convey the tone in which Jane thought the words? No woman is ever free of her children. A worthy thought, a touching thought, a depressing thought. Never free of them? Good God, never? Was there no hope for a time when one could gaze upon one's children and see that they were sensible, careful, clear-thinking individuals over whom there was no cause to worry? No, there was no hope for such a time. No woman is ever free of her children.

"I shall embroider it," Jane thought, "and have it framed, too. My husband will think it very sweet. Poor darling, I wonder if any of these children he wanted are any pleasure to him."

There were times now when there were only three Slidells at the long table. Tom had become a popular boy and was much wanted at all manner of levees and dancing parties. More conventional than his older brother, he had accepted as natural an active association with the children of his parents' friends.

It was on an evening that had slipped almost unnoticed into the new year that Jane, her husband and young John sat lingering over their coffee. Peace had returned to the country and John, Senior, read aloud a letter from Edward Livingston concerning the Battle of New Orleans, which had been fought before the news of the treaty had arrived.

"At the end," John, Senior, said, turning to Jane, "after Edward has told all about the battle, he adds some chatty remarks. He says" —his eyes went back to the letter—" 'I was happy to hear about baby Julia and to know that she and Jane are flourishing so magnificently. You may remember my mentioning Mr. and Mrs. André Deslonde, the young couple whose friendship I am keeping warm for young John. They, too, had a little daughter. They have named her Mathilde. Have I mentioned that André is also on the General's staff? What assistance he has given in so many ways! For instance, he brought his slaves to create ramparts out of cotton bales. Marvelous inventiveness. I wish you could have seen the ceremonies here honoring General Jackson. Young Mrs. Deslonde was selected to place a crown of laurel leaves upon his brow. I regret the scene was not captured in marble so that I might often gaze upon it. Her sweetness and loveliness, the General's strength and humility—' "

Young John laughed. "Humility! That is not what I have heard is Jackson's outstanding characteristic."

His father frowned. "Let us take Edward's word," he said. "Edward knows the General intimately. Can the same be said of those who have described Jackson to you?"

"Oh, Father, do not be so stiff-necked. Jackson's no angel. Everybody knows that. Mr. Livingston is just so noble himself that he thinks it evil not to look for virtue in others."

"I do not like your attitude," John, Senior, said. "You sound as though you held Edward's Christian spirit in contempt."

His son made a gesture of impatience. "I do not hold it in contempt. I just feel that it is not realistic to blind oneself to facts. You know it could prove dangerous. A man might at last be unable to recognize a scoundrel when he saw one."

"By God, sir, General Jackson is no scoundrel."

"That is not the point. The point is this: if he were, do you suppose Edward Livingston would know it?"

John, Senior, looked helplessly at Jane. "Did you know the boy

75

was taking a course in iconoclasm? No respect for General Jackson, none for Edward Livingston—do you respect President Madison, sir?"

"I respect his office. The man fills me with no awe or reverence."

"Such talk sickens me. At your age, there should be—nay, *must* be—an admiration for men of honor and integrity. To what size and form will you adapt your character if there is no pattern to follow?"

"More coffee?" Jane asked.

"No, thank you, my dear."

"No, thank you, Mother. If you will pardon me, I must be on my way."

They murmured politely and young John left them. Outside, there was a fine, powdery snow drifting down upon the city. He drew his cloak more closely about him and walked swiftly toward the Park Theatre. He had seen Nell Winslow but three times since her return from Philadelphia. She had had a triumphant season there duplicating her Baltimore success, which had immediately preceded it. Now she would remain at the Park at least until the heat of summer began.

As he walked with the snowflakes swirling about him, he experienced a sudden presentiment. It was not in the nature of things to continue changelessly. He felt that something significant would occur and very soon. Surely Nell must realize by now that he was faithfully adoring and that she could trust her love to him. Perhaps in Philadelphia or Baltimore, she had met other men and had come to know that none would give the unswerving devotion he had given. Could it be that her heart was calling out to his, saying that at last she was ready to surrender?

He had no engagement with her this evening but his spirits, gladdened by the interpretation he had placed upon his presentiment, were very high. It seemed to him that after the final curtain, he would walk backstage and find Nell waiting as patiently as though an appointment had been arranged. The more he considered the matter, the more natural it seemed that she would be watching for him and in just the right mood. She would be alone, a little melancholy. His arrival would awaken her to the fact that pensiveness and loneliness were symptoms that she was in love. Before she

76

was aware of what she was doing, she would run to his arms. . . .

Despite the snow, there was a large and lively audience at the Park. It was a beautifully appointed theatre, the finest in the city, and it never lacked patrons. John, gazing about, saw many people with whom he was acquainted. Why, there was Charlie Wilkes entering the theatre. Little Charlie, the imp of Vesey Street. Not so little any more. Damn near six feet tall, John estimated. Charlie was alone. No girl. Well, he was pretty young for girls. No, he was not, come to think of it. Charlie was seventeen. When I was seventeen . . . John's current of thought was diverted by Charlie's gaze suddenly meeting his. Charlie, instead of taking his seat, hurried down the aisle toward him.

"How are you, John?"

"Very well, thank you. And you?"

"Fine." Charlie's bright blue eyes had a devilishly merry glint and he wore a halo of snowflakes upon his curly brown hair. "I am in the Navy, you know."

"Really? So is Alec."

"I heard that. How is Tom?"

"The same Tom."

"I always liked him. I must try to find time for the boy," said Charlie, the Navy man.

"Where is your uniform?"

"There is no need to wear it in peacetime."

"No?" John asked in surprise. "The Perry brothers always—"

"They have no other clothes. I think they were born in uniform. You know what I found out? There are four Perry brothers. All of them are in the Navy and there are three Perry sisters all married to naval officers."

"My, how good of you to tell me."

Charlie snapped his fingers in self-annoyance. "I swear to God I forgot that they are part of your family now. I forgot about Janie marrying Cal."

John raised his brows. "Cal? Charlie, do you actually know him that well?"

Charlie reddened. "What the hell? I can call him Cal when I'm talking to you, can't I?"

"No," John said. "You make yourself ridiculous."

77

Charlie went sulkily to his seat and soon after, the play began. John's mind wandered away from Charlie. Nell was beautiful and so superb in her role. To watch her play a scene of wild gaiety, no one would ever guess that tonight she was pensive and lonely, with an unexplained longing within her heart.

At the final curtain, he rushed down Theatre Alley and threw open the stage door. The first person he saw was Charlie Wilkes. The first thing he heard was Charlie saying to the doorman, "Will you tell Miss Winslow I am here?"

John could not control his laughter. "What a big boy you are, Charlie. Calling lieutenants by their first name and trying to become acquainted with lovely actresses."

Charlie said, "I am acquainted with Miss Winslow."

"Really? Do you know her as well as you know Cal?"

John laughed again and Charlie hit him. The blow came unexpectedly and with a force that staggered John. There was a crashing pain in his eyeball and he saw Charlie through a red mist but he managed to land a powerful fist and felt the skin of his knuckles break against Charlie's teeth.

He was aware of the commotion they were causing. Stagehands and actors were running about, shouting and gesticulating. A few pulled cautiously at the antagonists and John dealt one a mighty swipe with the back of his hand lest the fellow in his rage for peace pin his arms and leave him a helpless target for Charlie. Charlie was no easy mark. He acknowledged the roughest body blows with only a gasp, his efficiency undiminished. John knew that Charlie's bloody face was a mirror of his own. How absurd they must look, still in their cloaks, grappling, grunting and bleeding. He heard a woman scream as Charlie fell. He knew it was not Nell but he had no time to guess who it might be, for Charlie was up again, crazy with anger. So strong and painful was the punch he delivered that John thought as he dropped to his knees that Charlie had hit him with some heavy metallic substance.

"It is even now, my boys," someone yelled. "Quit!"

John pulled himself up and struck again. To his surprise, Charlie's flailing arms were suddenly still. For an instant, he stood seemingly undecided, then he collapsed on the floor and lay quiet.

At once there was bedlam. Everyone had a suggestion on the

subject of what to do with and for Charlie. The entire company with the exception of Nell, the entire stage crew and a few visitors clustered around the unconscious boy.

John slipped out through the stage door unnoticed. He could not present himself to Nell in this condition. What an ending to an evening that had promised so much. He walked homeward in the snow, thinking that at least he had given that insufferable little pup a whipping he would never forget.

In answer to a note he had received—delivered by an usher from the Park Theatre—John waited in Steve Price's office. He had been told politely that the manager would be there presently. The office was just off the lobby, a small, interesting room decorated with posters, programs and handbills. It struck John that it was not sentiment that led theatre personalities to collect such memorabilia but only a wish to remind those who had excluded show people from respected society that the theatre enjoyed an incontestable exclusiveness of its own.

Here was the first program printed for the Walnut Street Theatre, evidently a newish show place in Philadelphia. All members of the cast had signed their names to a poem in praise of their friend Steve Price. Over the desk, an amusing letter from William Dunlap, the country's leading playwright. Beside it, an announcement from the Mount Vernon Gardens, proclaiming itself to be a regularly organized summer theatre, whatever that was. Framed pages from a theatrical magazine called *The Thespian Mirror* had a place in the office and of course much wall space was given to Price's personal triumphs. Reviews and advertisements were everywhere for the spectacular *Forty Thieves,* in which the Park Theatre had starred John Howard Payne. The following year, the theatre had apparently surpassed this success by presenting *The Pandean Band,* from Drury Lane. "Mr. Price," said a news item over the bookcase, "is a gentleman of taste and genius."

John found himself tiring of the manager's bouquets and turned to gaze out at the melting snow. The winter sunshine was surprisingly warm this morning. What did Steve Price want? Of course, the matter concerned that ridiculous brawl with Charlie Wilkes but would Price have the nerve to invite him over simply to chat about a matter that was certainly none of his business?

Or perhaps it was Price's business. Possibly during the fight, something backstage had been damaged and Price wanted him to pay for it. Damned if he would. Let Charlie Wilkes pay. He had struck the first blow.

Steve Price entered the office, a frown upon his gaunt face, the celebrated smile not part of the morning's work. By God, the fellow wore his clothes well. He had an inspired tailor but no tailor could fashion careless grace.

"Sit down, Mr. Slidell."

John wished he had already been seated at Price's arrival. He was annoyed that the theatre manager had kept him waiting and had not felt it necessary to produce an apology or a smile. He regretted now that he had responded to Price's summons, for summons it had really been. What cheek!

He sat down and looked superciliously at the other man. "What have we to discuss, Price?"

The manager dropped into a chair at his desk. Beautiful desk. Probably a leftover from some stage set.

"Mr. Slidell, I wanted to tell you here, privately, where you would be spared embarrassment, that you will no longer be welcome at the Park Theatre."

"What!"

"I could have told you in my note but you would have come here immediately with questions just the same. I may tell you that I am very displeased with what has happened. I—"

John found words at last. "Are you serious? Are you addressing me? You must be out of your senses. That stupid young man punched me. What was I supposed to do?"

Steve Price tilted his chair back and gazed steadily at John. "One might ask what was he supposed to do after your sneering remark. You gave him provocation, Mr. Slidell. I was told that you took the attitude that his calling for Miss Winslow was somehow comical and—"

"And indeed it was. This boy is a friend of my brother's. I know his age."

"What does his age matter? If he behaves like a gentleman, I

80

would think him capable of escorting Miss Winslow to a restaurant. In any case, sir, I trust you will understand my position. We have never had anything of this kind happen at the Park Theatre before and I shall not have it happen again."

John said coldly, "Needless to say, your ordering me from the Park Theatre is a waste of words. I shall return when and as I choose."

"Really? The Park Theatre is private property, Mr. Slidell."

"And you will have to offer proof that I am an undesirable patron. Good God, no man is going to agree with you that I conducted myself disreputably by thrashing someone who attacked me."

Steve Price was silent. He picked up a small silver-gilt clock and wound it thoughtfully. He had said all he wished to say but was sensitive that his visitor still would have questions and arguments. He was willing to give him as many minutes as seemed necessary.

"Listen to me, Price, and give me the truth. Does Miss Winslow know that you are requesting me to stay away from here?"

"She does. She respects my judgment and accepts that fist fights do not in any way further her career or enhance the prestige of this theatre."

"When I explain to her—"

"Mr. Slidell, you are not going to see Miss Winslow."

John jumped to his feet. "You mean you have sent her away?"

Now a flicker of a smile lighted the manager's face but quickly disappeared. "No, she is still here and will remain. Did you think it impossible that she would simply decide it unwise to see you again?"

"Yes. She and I have enjoyed each other's company."

"True," Price agreed. "But she enjoys the company of others as well. Your behavior suggests to her that you have developed a possessiveness which she gave you no license to feel. When you fight over her, then—"

"Fight over her! The boy hit me!"

"Yes, yes, but you resented his calling for her. She had a right to go out with him. She goes out with you, doesn't she?"

"That is different."

"In what way?"

"I am deeply fond of Miss Winslow."

81

The theatre manager did not reply. He shifted his attention from the contents of his desk to the dripping icicles outside his office window.

And John saw a look in the other man's eyes that astonished him. There was pity in those eyes. Pity! And when Steve Price spoke again, his voice was quiet. Quiet and gentle. "Mr. Slidell, please do not make this more painful than it has to be. Surely you can find someone else of whom to be fond."

"That is not your concern."

"If you were older, this would be easy. We would have a laugh and a drink together. Mr. Slidell"—and now the voice was pleading—"clear out of my theatre and forget Nell. She is my girl. She has been for years."

For ten seconds, John stood dazed and uncomprehending. Then he exploded. "Why, you son of a bitch! You dare to sit there and tell me that you have taken advantage of— By God, sir, you will marry her."

Steve Price looked into the livid face and said coolly, "I am not obligated to explain to you our reasons for preferring things the way they are. And now that you know there is no room for your jealousy in our lives, perhaps you will get to hell out of here and stay out."

"It will not be that easy for you," John shouted, feeling a sickening hatred rising within him. "I am going to kill you." He knew that he was shaking, that his voice had cracked like a schoolboy's. "Notify your friends, sir. You are going to pay for this!"

Steve Price sat back wearily in his chair. "Yes," he said. "I am going to pay for having told you the truth. You have no stomach for it."

John, white to his trembling lips, rasped, "Send your second to Michael Kesson." He flung himself from the office then, choking with fury.

Steve Price sat alone for a long time, lost in thought. Life had been so busy that years had passed since he had had the opportunity or the wish to talk intimately with this fellow who was Steve Price. And what kind of fellow had he turned out to be? What was he like today?

Well, he was a fellow who knew that fighting a duel was a pretty

82

silly way to die, especially when the opponent was a hotheaded, spoiled youngster eager to prove himself a man. There were many ways to prevent the duel from taking place. Slidell had a father, who might talk some sense into him. Dueling, moreover, was against the law and the authorities, if notified, would step in. The simplest way of all was open to him. He could apologize. He could confess himself to be a cad and a coward.

The only drawback to each of these sensible plans was that this fellow Steve Price, when consulted, would accept none of them. Slidell had a valid complaint. Certainly he had been used as a cover for the affair between Nell Winslow and her manager. It had been thought that her appearance in public places with one admirer or another would still any gossip that might rise involving the Park Theatre. Well, the Park Theatre had retained its high reputation and John Slidell had suffered. He had grown too fond of Nell. Had he known from the beginning— But it was too late for that now. He had not known. He had believed it possible that at some time Nell might be his. He had believed it possible because the whole city had been encouraged to believe that she belonged to no man.

And after a while, Steve Price left his office and went backstage, where a rehearsal was in progress. He looked at all the actors thoughtfully, then smiling wryly, he called aside the comedian and asked him to be his second. It seemed appropriate.

On the New Jersey side of the river, the bare, winter-whipped trees stood stark and black against the cold sky. The air, heavy with the promise of snow, lay moistly upon the pallid faces of the men who had met to play out the drama that had begun in the Park Theatre. The clearing in the woods, a respectful distance from any habitation, was startlingly ugly by the light of dawn. In April, there would be a soft green carpet and colonies of small purple violets to gladden the eye. Now there were only streaks of snow caught by a freezing blast midway in the process of melting. The earth, rigid with cold, seemed dead of a disease that had marked it with terrible deformities.

The five men gathered in the clearing knew what they were about. The doctor, seedy and slightly drunk, was much in demand at these affairs.

83

Steve Price, solemn-eyed, advanced into the dawn's bleak business. At his side walked a stout little man with tears in his eyes.

"Steve, go back to the coach. Let me try to talk to these bastards. There must be some way—"

"Forget it. We are in for it, friend."

A few feet away, John Slidell waited with Michael Kesson.

"Is there anything you want me to say to the others, John?" Michael asked.

"You have inspected the pistols. That is all I want you to do. Are you worried for me, Mike?"

Michael shivered and stared down at the ground. "No."

"The formalities of this business have really undone you, boy. You are not your sunny self."

"Perhaps not," Michael admitted.

"The formalities of this subdue everyone." John gazed upon the two coaches standing at the roadside. "Do you observe that even the hackmen are solemn and thoughtful? They can be such rollicking fellows, but now—" He broke off. "Here comes another coach. Who in hell can that be?"

"The authorities, perhaps," Michael said. He sprang forward, then fell back dejectedly. "No."

"No, indeed. In the style of the worst melodramas, it is she, the heroine," John said sourly. "Here she comes in a cloud of plumes, flowers and scented, tear-wet handkerchiefs to plead for her lover."

Michael Kesson averted his glance as Nell Winslow leaped from the coach and ran to Steve. John watched, feeling a trifle disappointed that after all there were no plumes or flowers. She had obviously flung her sealskin coat over her night robe. Her hair was uncombed and her face unpainted. What a way to remember her!

He could not hear the conversation taking place between the theatre people but it was clear that Price was angry at her for having come. John waited for the end of the colloquy, a bored expression upon his face. In keeping with the drama, Nell must next approach him. The role would call for her to implore heartbreakingly, to plead that in the name of pity, he must forget his bitterness. When all this had failed, she was obligated then to offer herself to him in payment for Steve Price's life. What cutting, sardonic thing could he say in refusal? Could he say, "Madam, you must

84

forgive me. When I asked to spend the night with you, I had no idea you would look like this in the morning"? Would that be a good thing to say? It would have to do, for here she was. He bowed mockingly to the slim girl with the wind-blown hair, noting as he did so that it would be absurd to pretend that she needed cosmetics or a fancy coiffure.

"Good morning, madam," he said. "Did you wish to speak to me?"

"Yes. I wish to tell you that you are without a doubt the most contemptible specimen of animal life I have ever seen. You want to kill Steve because I preferred him to you."

"A gentleman must have satisfaction for wrongs inflicted—"

She flung her head back and stared up into his face, smiling coldly. "Now, just how would you know what a gentleman must have? You, you overbearing ass, are the son of a soap-boiler. Do you think you ever fooled anybody?"

She turned then and ran back to Steve Price. Wildly she threw her arms around him and kissed him upon the lips, then retreated quietly to her coach.

"Have the histrionics been taken care of?" John demanded. "May we proceed now?"

Whispers between Michael Kesson and the stout little comedian. The word was given and the antagonists grimly marched off the paces as directed. John, as he stepped across the frozen earth, was aware of many things. The numbing cold whipping through his white silk shirt. The rather splendid courage of Nell in not having alerted the New Jersey constabulary. The curious loneliness of this short walk . . .

"Turn! Fire!"

In the hushed cold, John heard the crack of the pistols. Even as he saw Steve Price fall upon a patch of gray snow, he knew himself to be unharmed. He heard the high-pitched, agonized scream of Nell as she darted toward the wounded man. On the stage of the Park Theatre, he had often heard Nell scream. This time, it had sounded different and he thought he might remember forever how different it had sounded.

He turned to find his cloak and became aware of the fact that Michael was not there to help him into it, to inquire how he felt or to congratulate him. Michael, he observed, was kneeling on the ground beside Steve Price, apparently steadying the hand of the doctor. Very decent of Michael, considering that both Nell and the silly little second Price had chosen were useless. Still, Michael should have considered his duty to his principal. Well, his defection did not relieve John of honoring the rules of etiquette.

With correctly sober bearing, he approached the group and put the proper questions to them. "What is the condition of my opponent?"

The doctor did not raise his eyes and John turned his from the operation that was in progress there on the frozen ground.

"His condition is very serious, my dear sir."

"Is the wound mortal?"

"It will be hours before we know."

"Can I be of some assistance?"

"Thank you. You cannot."

Michael said, "Go on home, John."

John scowled at such uncouth blundering in contrast to his own courtliness. Go on home? This had not been a street brawl. There were niceties to observe. He had imagined that Michael knew these niceties well.

He said, "I will wait for you in the coach. My dear second, we return home together."

"No, we do not. I will ride with the doctor and Mr. Price. I can be of help. Go on, John. Go home."

A strange way to leave the field of honor, ordered from it in the manner of a stray dog who has wandered upon the scene. He gathered about him what dignity the stupid Michael had left to the encounter.

"Will you call upon me after I have rested? Will you bring me word of Mr. Price's condition?"

Michael sighed in exasperation. "For the love of God, go away, will you? This is a nervous business. The doctor is probing—"

"Very well," John said. He turned from them and walked toward his coach, passing the sobbing Nell Winslow and the stout comedian, who in angry frustration was beating a tree trunk with his fists.

86

There was a bottle of whisky in the coach. John took a drink and on impulse offered the bottle to the hackman.

"Too early in the day for me, sir."

John took another swallow of whisky and walked fifty feet down the road to the man who had driven Steve Price.

"Drink, old fellow?"

"Never touch it."

"What? Not even on an icy morning?"

"Not even on an icy morning."

The driver of the third coach also felt no need for a drink of whisky and John drank alone, standing at the fellow's side, suddenly finding it necessary to explain that a duel was an honorable affair and that it might have been him instead of Steve Price and that for centuries gentlemen had settled arguments in this fashion. The hackman said nothing to all this, so John took another drink. When he looked up, he saw Michael and the doctor carrying Price from the field. Behind them walked Nell and the comedian, dry-eyed now and stony of face.

John hurried back to his hackman and said, "I am ready to leave."

The hackman said, "You will have to wait till I find out if I can help."

John stepped into the coach and waited. He thought of Nell screaming and he drank some more whisky and reminded himself that duels were very ancient and honorable affairs. And he cursed Michael for abandoning him and he cursed the hackmen, who had not been willing to drink with him. He heard Steve Price groan as he was lifted into the other coach and it was as dreadful a sound as Nell's scream had been. And John Slidell knew that he was very drunk but he knew, too, that though duels were as ancient and honorable as he had claimed, still somehow, this one had been a terrible mistake.

Suddenly nothing in the life of John Slidell was as it had been. Naturally he would not have cared to go to the Park Theatre to watch that deceitful Winslow woman perform but it was outrageous to discover that he could not buy his way into any other theatre, either.

87

"Sorry, sir. Not a seat left."

"Now look here, my good man. You told me that five minutes ago and I stepped aside and watched others enter. I demand that you accept my money and seat me in the auditorium."

"Take my advice. Do not demand anything. Leave while you have no broken bones."

It was then that John had noticed the bully boy standing on the sidewalk taking in the conversation and nonchalantly twirling a ridiculously heavy walking stick. John understood. Oh, he could gain admittance to the play if he persisted, if he made some sort of demonstration, but then on the way home, he would be clubbed to death by one of those unprincipled hoodlums in the pay of Price's friends. Show people! What a joke it was to pretend they could ever behave like gentlefolk.

So John gave up the idea of going to the theatre. Theatre! Good God, he could not even get in to see John Scudder's Wax Works. The restaurants and coffeehouses offered some diversion but there childishly emotional people had taken to cutting him dead. At first, he had been unable to credit such idiotic behavior and had inclined to the belief that a series of odd coincidences had produced the effect of his being ostracized. After a time, he was forced to accept that he was alone at a table as a result of concerted effort.

When he was quite certain that such was the case, he never again risked loneliness. He went nowhere without a girl upon his arm. Only now he missed the envious glances that had followed him when he had escorted Nell Winslow. Well, she was not the one beautiful girl in the city. There were others. Of course, they were not actresses. Actresses were all occupied in shedding tears for Steve Price. There was only one place for John to find his companions and there he found them. Though many were startlingly fair, no man was envious, for John's companion tonight could be any man's tomorrow. So in due course, he drifted away from the restaurants.

Sometimes on an evening when he could no longer bear either solitude or the company of his family, he sat in a tavern taproom and bought a drink or two for Pierre de Landais. Senile or demented it was difficult to tell but, no matter, the old man spoke eloquently enough on the harsh manner in which he had been used by life and by the United States of America. His short, stout figure, clad in a faded Continental uniform—cocked hat, small sword, knee breeches—was familiar to all New York. He claimed the rank of American admiral and made nothing of the fact that he had been born a French count. In 1777, he had given up his commission in the French navy to join his fortunes with the struggling American revolutionists.

"Now, Mr. Slidell, you are a lawyer—"

"Not yet."

"Perhaps when you are established, you will represent me in Washington."

John would signal a waiter and the Admiral would bow in gracious acceptance of "perhaps a glass of wine."

"Now, as you know, Mr. Slidell, every year at the sitting of Congress I travel to Washington and this is not an easy matter in those lumbering old coaches. I suffer on the journey but this is not your concern. I am approaching you professionally, seeking to engage your future services. I literally haunt the lobbies and galleries, pursuing fair play. The country owes me back pay and an apology. For forty years, they have owed me—"

"Yes, yes, Admiral. Everyone knows. Would you like a slice of that red beef upon the cart?"

To conceal his eagerness, the Admiral would draw a veil of blankness across his eyes. "Beef? I sometimes fancy it. Perhaps a sliver to keep you company." And he would ignore the fact that he ate alone. "Now, Mr. Slidell, you know I directed the building of American ships at Portsmouth and Salisbury. The admirable frigate *Alliance,* with thirty-six guns, was conceived and created out of the naval knowledge of this Pierre de Landais who sits at your table. And who was her commander? The same Pierre de Landais, honored by all as one of the great men of the American Navy."

Difficult to believe, but true nevertheless. This grotesque wreck of another century had once been styled in the restrained language of Congress as "an excellent sea officer and skilled in the construction of ships of war."

"My life was happy and useful until I encountered John Paul Jones. Sir, you may take my word, this man was haughty, imperious, quarrelsome and a martinet."

John, only half listening, would grin across the table. "In short, your twin brother, eh, Admiral?"

"I, sir, was always reasonable."

"Of course."

"This man Jones was jealous of me. So jealous that he bore false witness against me. He accused me of cowardice, claimed that the *Alliance* held aloof in that famous engagement against the British fleet. Then he accused me of treachery, saying that when the *Alliance* finally joined the action, she fired not upon the British *Serapis* but upon Jones's own *Bonhomme Richard*. He charged that I endeavored to sink him in order to win all glory for myself. God damn it, sir, when I demanded a trial, when I demanded to confront my accuser, why did the United States refuse to grant me this right which was mine?"

"I do not know. Have another glass of wine."

"I challenged Jones. I would have run him through but he had no wish to pay for the work of his evil, lying tongue. Fourteen officers of the *Alliance* declared in writing that I was brave and capable and that unless I was restored to command, they would resign. But I was dismissed from the service, stained in reputation and broken in spirit."

"Yes, yes. Deplorable." John would toss a handful of coins upon the table. "Continue to be my guest though I must leave you now."

Always in the past when there had been an hour or a week that seemed to stretch yawningly ahead, it had been his habit to join forces with Michael Kesson. Together they had been able to invent excitement and laughter. Boredom had been defeated by whisky-drinking contests or the search for a new food, a new tailor or a new brothel. But Michael was no longer a part of John's life. He had slipped away like the Park Theatre and Nell Winslow and the comfortable relationship he had enjoyed with shopkeepers. They had never hounded him in other days. Now several had threatened to inform his father that a year of unpaid bills awaited settlement.

On the day of the duel, John had slept through the sunlit hours. Once his rest had been broken by a maid hoping to be permitted to make up his room. He had shouted her away from the door and had returned to sleep only to be reawakened by his mother. She had come to his bedside and looked at him with worried eyes.

90

"No, Mother, there is nothing really wrong. During the night, I was slightly ill but I am fine now. I need only the sleep I missed."

She had not been satisfied but she had left the room, her eyes still worried. As he had sunk back to sleep, he had congratulated himself on having got out of the house and into it once more without his absence being noted. And then his mother had been there at the foot of the bed again. He had been so annoyed with her. Why, only a moment before he had told her— But it could not have been a moment before. That was dusk pressing against the windows of his room.

"John, Michael Kesson is here to see you." She had lighted a lamp and holding it high, had stood staring silently at him.

"What is the matter?" he had asked.

"That I am unable to determine," she had replied and setting the lamp down, had walked out of the room.

The next minute, Michael had entered, closing the door behind him. His eyes had been glazed, his legs none too steady, but he had spoken clearly enough.

"It was a very near thing but Steve Price will live."

"Oh, you decided to discharge the office of second properly, after all? I thank you for bringing me the news."

"I bring you other news as well. You and I are no longer friends. I was damn well ready to ditch you when you asked me to be your second but I realized you had no one else to ask."

"What do you mean, I had no one else to ask?"

"Well, you had not. Let us be honest. Nobody has ever liked you very much."

"Congratulations. You were the one with the discriminating taste."

"How could you have challenged that man to a duel? How could you have done it? This was a sober, earnest businessman who knew nothing of dueling. And instead of pinking him, you tried to kill him!"

"It was coming to him."

"Coming to him? Why, you bastard. I cannot stand the sight of you another instant." And Michael had flung himself from the room and out of John's life.

There was no point in pretending that the loss of Michael's

friendship was inconsequential. It had been a great loss. Had Michael stood by him, he could have borne his banishment from the theatres, the snubs in the restaurants. He and Michael and a few pretty girls could have ridden out the storm. They could have made tables of such jollity that others would have wished to join them. And eventually, the unfortunate Steve Price matter would have passed from memory. Oh, to go back, to go back to that night when he had walked through the soft snowflakes to the Park Theatre. He thought of it now as the night upon which he had lost New York.

He sought his father out in the busy, untidy office at the Mechanic's Bank and when John, Senior, glanced up almost impatiently from a document on his desk, young John looked him straight in the eye and said, "Father, I am now extremely proficient in both French and Spanish and I believe I could pass legal examinations. All that I have worked for, all that you have paid for, is now ready to be put to the test. It is time for me to go to New Orleans."

"It was time a year ago," his father said bluntly. "God damn it, sir, I resent being treated as though I were half-witted. I live in New York, too, you know. I hear all the same things other people hear."

"You are speaking of Steve Price so I will say that I regret deeply what happened to him. I—"

"Of course you regret deeply what happened to him. It ruined your sport. I blame myself for what you are. I was a bad father to you. You had too much spending money, too much time for deviltry and too little discipline. Do you know why these things were as they were? It was because, God help me, I was a soap-boiler and you were the grandson of Henry MacKenzie. Soap-boilers clout their sons to make them behave but they do not usually have sons with aristocratic blood in their veins. I was afraid of you, if the truth be known. I was afraid." John, Senior, got to his feet and walked back and forth with downcast eyes, his hands folded behind him. "I felt myself less than you because in your line was noble blood." He paused in his pacing to stare at his son. "Was I not a fool? When you were a child, I hesitated to give you the thumping you damn well needed because I thought you so sensitive, so fine, that you would hate me for a soap-boiling brute. It is all to laugh at now, my boy. Here am I a respected, prosperous citizen and high in the council of Grace Episcopal Church, and the only shame upon me is not that I lack aristocratic blood but that my eldest son is a scoundrel."

Young John dropped his eyes before the chilling light that flashed from his father's. "Father, when I first planned to go to New Orleans—"

"For the love of God, quit insulting my intelligence! You never planned to go there." John, Senior, sat down at his desk, opened a drawer and tossed to his son an envelope that looked pleasantly fat. "Control your excitement, boy. It is a ticket on a boat bound for New Orleans and a modest amount to keep you housed and fed for a reasonable time. I have settled all your bills here including one from a lady who says you broke some furniture in her rather public parlor."

"I did not. I was not even in the fight. It was—"

"But you recall the incident clearly, I see. Well, I paid her. She seemed determined to have either her money or the importance of a day in the law courts. Your boat, by the way, leaves tomorrow morning."

John held out his hand. "Good-by, sir. Thank you for enduring me all these years."

His father clasped his hand. "Good luck to you. And if, by any chance, you *are* grateful for anything, do me one small favor. Build yourself a good life for, God help me, I love you well."

III

The Fortunes and Misfortunes

When the news came that Oliver Hazard Perry was dead of yellow fever, Janie Slidell Perry, still in mourning for her first-born son, fell upon her mother's bed and screamed. Her mother knew that Janie screamed not because her brother-in-law was dead but because her child was. Janie had accepted that terrible blow with dry-eyed calm, with the admirable Christian fortitude expected of Mrs. Matthew Calbraith Perry. Now she screamed. Quietly Jane sat down beside her daughter to bathe her brow with violet water, to give her what comfort she could take from another's presence.

"It will kill Cal, Mother. Oh, it will kill him."

"No. Cal is strong. It will not kill him." How absurd to think that a man who had survived the death of small John Slidell Perry would be felled by the loss of a brother. "Cal's eyes will fill with tears, darling, and he will pray for Oliver. Then he will vow that in his brother's memory he will be a better Navy man than ever and that will be all. Do not worry for Cal."

"But he was so devoted to him."

"I know, dear. See if you can keep your eyes closed. A little nap would be such a good thing."

Janie shuddered. "I am afraid to sleep. I will dream that it is Cal who died. Oh, Mother, I will not be able to stand it if he is sent again to the Caribbean after what happened to Oliver."

"Cal has been many times to the Caribbean and has come back safely. His constitution is not the same as his brother's was."

Nor his appetites. Cal was a moderate drinker. Oliver would never have grown famous for abstemiousness. Poor boy, his thunderous success at Lake Erie had established him as the greatest

97

Perry but he had then discovered a new reason for self-loathing. "I drink too much," he often confessed. And Jane, sitting beside her daughter, wondered idly if there were people who always replaced one problem with another. And if so, how dangerous to cure them of the first.

Janie's eyes, closed for only seconds, opened wide again. "Surely they will not expect Cal to ever look at the Caribbean after this."

"Now, do not worry about it, dear."

Jane smiled soothingly at her pretty daughter, wondering how salubrious the child thought the climate of the Ivory Coast. Cal, as executive officer on the *Cyane,* was cruising African waters in pursuit of outlaw slave ships.

"Mother, I keep thinking of how the news will pain Cal."

"Keep thinking of the other news you have to tell him, Janie."

"Yes. If the child is a boy, I think I would like to name him for Oliver."

"Do that and, Janie . . ."

"What is it?"

"When Ellen comes this afternoon, do not mention that you are pregnant again. For a while you can keep the secret from her."

Ellen, who had mad weeping spells whenever word reached her of another woman's pregnancy. Ellen, who bitterly resented that her baby sister, Julia, had not been given to her to raise. Ellen, who —now that her husband had ceased to reproach her—tortured herself with the suspicion that he had consoled himself by fathering children away from her.

Janie said, "If she were sensible, she would see that we all have heartaches."

"But some can bear them and some cannot. That is the way things are."

And Jane thought herself insufferably smug to be wise and informative on the subject of heartaches. Long ago, she had lost two children but today they were only misty shadows that caused no grief. Someday Janie, too, would recall only infrequently the yellow-haired toddler who had been John Slidell Perry. That is, if God granted her other children and the continued love of a good husband.

Jane had a feeling that God would do His best for Janie Perry. Everybody always did.

In the comparative cool of Maspero's Exchange on St. Louis Street, gentlemen gathered to argue politics, discuss business or simply to order a drink or a bowl of gumbo. The first story of Maspero's was given over to the café and the kitchens. A bar ran the full length of the room and a great number of small tables were scattered invitingly upon the sanded floor. At one of them sat John Slidell and André Deslonde talking languidly of this and that. Outside, the city steamed and stank in the summer sun but John by neither word nor act suggested that New Orleans was not heavenly. The people here were not like New Yorkers. They did not grumble about their city and they certainly did not expect outsiders to do so. A slighting comment on the climate, the design or the management of New Orleans would be as unpardonable as a criticism of a man's home. Why, it was said that some silly son of a bitch had recently challenged a visitor who had remarked that the Mississippi River was dirty. A curious place but fascinating.

André and John conversed in French and sipped their coffee.

"I am so happy that you now have your first client, my friend. From here you will go on to great things."

John smiled. "I believe I will. A young man under the aegis of Edward Livingston must succeed, unless, of course, he is stupid, lazy or dishonest."

"And such a young man would not be under the aegis of Edward Livingston."

"How true."

The conversation rested there for a few moments. The heat was so oppressive that even talk was too much effort, but everyone pretended that the long silences were graceful evidences of the manner *Louisianne,* so different from the constant prattle of *les Américains.*

John kept the silence. André would indicate when it was time to speak again. Best to study André and his ways if one were to learn how to get on in this place.

Such a pleasant fellow, this André. Handsome, witty, good-tempered. Not much of a companion, unfortunately. Young married men were always rather dull, anxious to get home to their wives.

André was faithful to his pretty little woman, too. If he were not, the city would be livelier for John. He felt that Edward Livingston might close his eyes to escapades organized by André Deslonde, but André organized none. New Orleans throbbed with exciting promise but John acquired no unauthorized acquaintances. Edward Livingston was too powerful a friend to lose.

"Your family is doubtless desolate at the death of Commodore Oliver Hazard Perry," André said at last.

"Yes, indeed. A very great loss."

"You personally have been deeply grieved?"

"I have been torn apart."

"I am sorry."

"Thank you, André."

They both lowered their eyes solemnly because Commodore Oliver Hazard Perry was dead and John had been torn apart. And it was time to rest again from conversation. How in hell did these Creoles stay so fresh and dry in this abominable climate? Did they all share a secret that saved them from perspiring through their clothes? And how could they drink hot coffee in such weather? John thought longingly of a tall glass filled with rum and cold fruit juice but André drank alcoholic beverages only in the evening.

"More coffee, John?"

"Thank you. I should relish it."

Was it safe to speak to André on the subject of women? And if it was not, why was it not? Certainly before his marriage, such a dashing young man must have known a few addresses. He could not possibly have forgotten them. What was the harm of passing them on? And surely Edward Livingston expected no more than common ordinary discretion.

John waited till the fresh coffee had arrived. "André," he said, choosing his words carefully, for after all, Creoles were not entirely predictable, "I wish to consult with you on the subject of female companionship."

André smiled. "The air of our lovely city is so gentle, so romantic. Already you think of finding a wife."

John shook his head. "No, André, not a wife."

"Oh, not yet a wife. Only someone to dance attention upon for a time without seriousness, to escort to the opera, to—"

100

"No? What then?" André looked at him, his brows raised in innocent questioning, but John saw amusement lurking in the dark Creole eyes.

"It was not quite that, either, André."

He thought, "Oh, you are going to have fun with me, are you? Very well." He reached across the small table and laid his hand on André's arm. He said, "André, my apologies. I have committed an error, have I not? I pray that you will forgive my ignorance of regional etiquette, dear friend." He removed his hand and smiled charmingly at André. "As I was about to say, do you happen to know a barber who can shave a man without cutting his face to ribbons?"

André exploded in laughter. "You Americans are wonderful. So full of surprises and mirth-provoking sayings. Yes, it is true. You are wonderful."

But though John waited in happy expectancy, there were no addresses forthcoming and it was time for another silence. This one was broken by a joyful cry from André.

"My friend Jacques Toutant-Beauregard from St. Bernard Parish," he explained to John. "Pardon me while I go invite him to our table."

John turned to watch the meeting of the two friends. He saw André fondly embracing a slim, somber-faced young man. Another husband who had piously forgotten the old addresses, no doubt. This one had a haughty bearing to match André's but he was less handsome.

As they approached the table, the two Creoles were chattering not like *les Américains* but like boarding-school girls reunited after summer vacation.

"My great friend Jacques Toutant-Beauregard of Contreras Plantation, John. Jacques, Mr. John Slidell of New York City, protégé of Edward Livingston. He has been a New Orleanian for less than three months and is already a practicing lawyer with his first case."

Jacques and John shook hands with extravagant assurances of the great delight this introduction had brought. In imperfect English, Jacques began to tell the news of St. Bernard Parish.

101

"Mr. Slidell's French is perfect, Jacques. Proceed as is natural to you. How goes the sugar this year?"

"It flourishes," said Jacques gloomily. "At Contreras, all is well. I have a son."

"A son!" André sprang from his chair to throw his arms about his friend and kiss him upon the cheek. "Why did you not shout the news as you entered? A son! Tell us of him."

"He is beautiful and healthy and eleven months old."

"Is it that long since I have seen you?"

"It is fourteen months to the day."

"Too long, Jacques. What have you named the boy?"

"Pierre Gustave Toutant-Beauregard."

"I hear no mention of De Reggio. Surely the family of his mother—"

Jacques shrugged. "I have convinced her that though illustrious, her family is still but Italian. The boy, I told her, must know the full glory of being thoroughly French."

John Slidell had great difficulty in holding his tongue. Thoroughly French! What hogwash. Who in hell did these people think owned Louisiana? He gazed wonderingly at André Deslonde, who had fought for the United States. He was stunned to see that André was nodding in agreement. The baby must certainly know the full glory of being thoroughly French. Louisianans, he decided, were rather fuzzy in their thinking.

"A son!" André was saying again in wondering admiration. "My dear wife produces nothing but girls. First Mathilde, now Henriette. Would you care to reserve one of them for Pierre Gustave?"

In New York, this would be a lighthearted remark, calling for a smile. Here everything was different. Jacques Toutant-Beauregard shook his head regretfully. "Oh, my friend, I am downcast. I have already had discussion with Jules Villère concerning his daughter, Marie Laure, born last week."

And André, a little tight-lipped, was assuring Jacques that it was quite all right, perfectly understandable, though of course, as the world knew, the Deslonde family was no less than the Villères.

"Mr. Slidell, we tire you with talk of our babies," Jacques said. "Is there any service I may render you here in the city?"

John said, "Thank you, no. André has anticipated my every desire and has been a devoted cicerone, having shown me everything I could possibly wish to see—the Cabildo, the Presbytere and of course, the French Market."

"I plan to take him to the new chapel of the Ursuline Convent one of these days," André said. "Its architecture is pure poetry. It will be such an experience for him."

Jacques said, "And a newcomer to New Orleans must not miss a drive through crocodile country."

There was more coffee and a great deal of talk about sugar and cotton. As a matter of fact, there was more talk of sugar and cotton than John was of a mind to hear. During one of the pauses, he excused himself.

"My regrets, gentlemen. Deep though my reluctance to leave you, I feel I must work a little in behalf of my lone client."

John left the coffeehouse, bracing himself for the damp heat of the narrow little streets. Slowly he picked his way along the filthy plank sidewalk, or banquette as it was elegantly called. He turned his eyes from the Negro convicts in iron collars and heavy ankle chains, who were clearing the wooden drains of refuse. He forced himself to look back at them.

"I must become so accustomed to them that I do not notice them," he thought. "This is my city and the sights, sounds and smells are all to be accepted."

In his office, he flung himself upon a leather couch and straightway fell asleep. He was awakened by a small black boy who handed him an envelope. Inside, there was a single sheet of paper with four names written upon it.

> *Belle Bazin*
> *Blanche Marque*
> *Véronique Le Clerc*
> *Marguerita da Rosa*

Each name was followed by an address and John could hear the Creole laughter that must have accompanied the penning of this tiny directory. He knew that nothing would be more objectionable to André or Jacques than an acknowledgment of this sheet of paper.

John Slidell grinned. "How very Creole of me to sense that," he thought. "I wonder how I did it."

At Cape Mesurado, the word was waiting for Lieutenant Matthew Calbraith Perry. He read the letter and dazedly gave the news to a fellow officer at his side.

"Good God, Cal. I am sorry. What a loss to you and to the Navy. Come, boy, we need a drink."

"I need no drink," Cal said. He was conscious of a feeling of weakness and fright. A sudden lonely terror swept over him and the question "What shall I do now?" sprang to his mind as though in that moment he had learned that the Navy was no more. "I guess I want to take a walk," he said.

"All right, Cal. Where shall we walk?"

"Please—I—"

"I understand. Go ahead. If there is anything I can do . . ."

After all, the Navy had not disappeared with the numbing news and Cal knew what his first duty was. Since Oliver Hazard Perry had belonged at least as much to the Navy as to the Perry family, he sought out the skipper of the *Cyane*.

"I have word, sir, of the death of Commodore Oliver Hazard Perry."

The skipper gazed up into eyes wet with tears. He saw a trembling young mouth and knew the burden of grief in the heart of his executive officer. He said the only proper thing there was to say to a naval man of the stamp of Matthew Calbraith Perry. He said, "Thank you for reporting."

In a warm jungle rain, down a narrow road bordered with wild, evil-looking greenery, Cal walked, thinking of Rhode Island. He thought of Rhode Island for Oliver. He thought of the rambling old house where the Perry family had lived, of Ma and Pa and the girls and of his brothers, Nathaniel and Raymond. Where were they? At what ports had they received the news? He thought of the *Chippewa,* the brig that had been built under Oliver's command this time last year. They had all been together then. Raymond and Nathaniel had been Oliver's aides and he, Cal, had been recruiting officer for the *Chippewa.*

At the end of the road, there was a church built in the style of New England, but it was something from a fevered dream. White clapboard, cruelly blistered by African sun. A door open in sweet welcome to the heavyhearted, but upon the threshold a dead green viper. A cross leaning dizzily in the churchyard, with a woman's red shift thrown across one of its arms. A Negro minister greeted him.

"Good morning. You wish to pray?"

"I wish to pray. I have lost my brother."

"Then I have lost mine. I grieve with you."

Cal prayed in the stifling little box of a church, then returned to the *Cyane*. He took his Bible bound in pale-blue leather and read for an hour or more. He thought of the time he and Janie had lost the child and he made the discovery that sorrow wears diverse faces. Just as he had loved his son in a way that differed from his love for his brother, so did his mourning differ. The child was gone. Oliver was gone. That much was the same but the losses could not stab in the same way. John Slidell Perry had been part of him and dearly loved but he had not been confidant or friend. Cal knew what his losses had been. There would never again be a child to take the place of the one he had lost. Never again a friend to take the place of his brother Oliver. And he knew that he could suffer and weep for his little yellow-haired boy but there were no memories of him that went back through the years, woven tenderly into the pattern of living. It was loss that caused the sharp and terrible agony but it was memory that made for a constant ache one carried all the days of one's life.

And Cal prayed again for the repose of Oliver's soul and made up his mind to keep the name of Perry bright in naval history. That much he could do for Oliver. All that he could do for the child was to be a good husband to the girl who had been the child's mother. And as Cal saw it, it all added up to the same thing in the long run. If one was a good naval officer, one could not fail as a man.

In the city of Alzey in the Grand Duchy of Hesse, Herr Simon Belmont read aloud to his wife, Frederika, a letter which had come to him from America. Frederika pretended interest. Actually, she was interested in nothing for she knew that in a few weeks or a

105

few months, she would be dead. She knew, too, that her husband insisted upon reading news of busy, far-flung places to her in a superstitious belief that if he kept her in touch with the world, she could not slip away from it. His many interests brought letters weekly from all over the globe. To Frederika, the ones from America were the most trying. She was acquainted with no one in America and the activities of people personally unknown to her, no matter how famous, could be nothing but a bore. If Simon would speak of their vineyards beyond the city or tell her stories of the days when his grandfather had been ambassador to Spain, she could make a show of being entertained, but the news from America . . .

"Oliver Hazard Perry has died," she heard him say. "Were you listening, Frederika? Oliver Hazard Perry—"

"Who was he, Simon?"

"Who was he! Why, he was a great American naval hero."

"Really?"

Simon smiled at her. "Yes, but we do not really care, do we? What do we care about, Frederika, my love?"

"The children. Especially Aaron. He is only a baby. What will you do with him?"

"What will we do with him?"

"You, Simon. Be brave enough to accept—"

"I am not a brave man, Frederika."

She turned her dark gaze to a small yellow bird in a golden cage. She detested birds but Simon had brought it this morning as his daily token of love. "In all decency I must die soon," she thought. "This business of producing a surprise every day is beginning to be hard work and he is running short of ideas."

She said, "You are a brave man. Never think differently. Tell Aaron that he is descended from generations of brave men. Tell him of Don Luis de Belmonte, who fought side by side with Don Sancho of Navarre against the Mohammedans."

"That was in the thirteenth century, Frederika. I doubt Aaron will care."

"He will care."

Simon's mouth twisted in a small secretive smile. "Shall I mention that for many years after Don Luis, our name was Schonenberg?"

"Of course. Mention, too, that my name was Elsass. I do not want Aaron deceived. I want him informed."

"Then I must tell him that the De Belmontes may not actually have been ancestors of mine."

"Oh, but they were, Simon. I feel they were. I know they were. You will tell Aaron?"

"You will tell him, sweetheart."

"No." She stroked the pink velvet counterpane with a hand that was all but transparent. "You will have to rear Aaron. I pray you, do not let the servants do it. They have taught him to walk and they have taught him his first words. You must soon let him know that he is yours, not theirs. Educate him, Simon. Teach him all the languages we know. Read him your wonderful letters from America. Tell him the news from the world outside of Hesse. Tell him —who was it you said had died?"

"Oliver Hazard Perry."

"Oh, yes. Tell Aaron that his mother knew nothing of this great hero but that she knew much of fashion, music and love."

Simon lowered his head and wept. Frederika sighed. She was forcing him to face her death a hundred times instead of once. Still, what could a woman do when she wished so passionately for her son to think of her in a certain way? Simon, dear good Simon, if not instructed, would tell Aaron that his mother had been an angel, selfless, honest, pure. Frederika, dying while still in her twenties, had no wish to be easily forgotten, as all good mothers were.

"Tell him I was beautiful and gay and often tempestuous."

Ah, that was a message from the grave that a boy would never forget. "My mother," he would say to ladies of the future, "was a romantic figure. She had great beauty and wit and a rather stormy temper."

What man in an elegant drawing room bothers to say that his mother had been self-sacrificing, faithful and a really excellent cook?

Simon was still weeping. She ran her hand through his hair. "My darling," she said playfully, "control yourself. After all, you did not even know this Oliver Hazard Perry."

* * *

107

Midshipman Alexander MacKenzie was so silent a lad that often the chaplain of the frigate *Macedonian* had a feeling that he was unhappy and that something should be done for him. The chaplain had tried. Conversation with MacKenzie never flourished. The dreaming gray eyes were always fixed upon the sea rather than upon the chaplain. This was a polite young man but one with whom it was impossible to communicate.

The chaplain had been moved to make inquiries and had discovered that MacKenzie's duties were performed with an almost fanatical exactitude. No officer had anything but praise for him. The common seamen found him "fair and square." Among MacKenzie's fellow midshipmen, the response was enthusiastic. The chaplain met none aboard the brig who disliked MacKenzie but he met no friend of MacKenzie's, either.

In the end, the chaplain concluded that no man could gain the friendship of Midshipman MacKenzie. It was by Midshipman MacKenzie's wish and direction that somehow the moment was never right for the sudden confidence, the unguarded smile that breaks down barriers. Still, the lad could not be happy living in such isolation. It was the chaplain's duty to see what could be done about this lamentable situation. Certainly if he were worth his salt as spiritual guide, he could make Midshipman MacKenzie lower his defenses.

Off the west coast of Mexico one balmy midnight, the chaplain again attacked the problem. MacKenzie off duty, at liberty to study or sleep, was leaning against a bulkhead, dreaming up at the stars.

"Good evening, MacKenzie. Beautiful night."

"Yes, sir."

"God is good to His children. He gives us the beauty of the night and the glory of the day. Are you right with our bountiful God, MacKenzie?"

"Sir?"

"I say, are you right with our—" Too late the chaplain became aware that MacKenzie's question had not indicated failure to hear. Instead, it had represented shock and surprise, as though the lad did not believe that a gentleman had actually been asked how he stood with God. And the chaplain realized that the hearty, simple technique often very good was no good at all here. This youngster was from New York City and probably worshiped in one of the more pretentious churches of one of the more pretentious religions. The chaplain himself was a small-town Virginian and an admirer of the meek and lowly Jesus. He was in the habit of regarding The Man as a mutual friend of his own and of those he encountered, someone for whom everyone felt a neighborly warmth.

The chaplain knew well, however, that there were others who considered it downright bad form to mention Him save on certain specified occasions. Midshipman MacKenzie was now figuratively running from him. The chaplain could see him disappearing in the distance. Yet it was still his obligation to pursue.

"I am afraid the tranquillity of the night made me feel very near to God," he said. "I am usually sensitive to the fact that laymen suffer embarrassment when a clergyman grows effusive."

The midshipman turned and gazed at him. By starshine, the boy's eyes were singularly luminous and yet cold. His continued silence was almost unbearable but the chaplain was committed.

"Let us talk. What interests you?"

"Obviously the sea," Midshipman MacKenzie said. "That is why I have made it my career."

"Well, the same can be said of me."

MacKenzie shook his head. "Your career is searching for souls, sir. You belittle your call if you say that you are here because you are interested in the sea. I should think the land would be as acceptable to you since salvation is needed everywhere."

"True, true. Note, lad, that this time you have given the conversation a theological turn. I meant only to discuss generalities which would be diverting to us both."

"It is only fair to warn you that I shall not easily be diverted, sir. I am in a somber mood."

The chaplain's heart leaped with pleasure. He was about to receive a cry for help and because advice and consolation were what the church had to offer, this time he would not fail to win the lad.

"Care to say what caused it?" he asked with cautious indifference.

"The death of someone I greatly admired," MacKenzie replied.

Ah, a death. This was even better than he had hoped. He was very good on deaths.

109

"I may have a message for you. Old, yet ever new. Poetic, yet as common sense as a good slice of bread." He paused to remind himself of the pretentious church in New York City. Better forget references to homely things. This boy's religion was costly stained-glass windows, ladies at Easter service in Paris bonnets and a minister who was a prosperous professional man. "May I ask when the death occurred?"

"The date I did not hear, if indeed it was mentioned. The news must have been waiting at Mazatlán. When the Captain announced that he was dead—"

"Oh," said the chaplain. He felt a sharp pang of disappointment. Only a publicly mourned death, nothing cozy and personal, with which a churchman could really do his best work. "We all share your somber mood. We all admired Oliver Hazard Perry. I had the honor of once seeing him. Did you ever see him?"

"Yes, sir. His brother, Matthew Calbraith Perry, is married to my sister."

The chaplain suffered a little of the painful self-consciousness he always experienced when he discovered himself in conversation with someone of importance. No doubt this boy's family had wealth and position. To the best of the chaplain's knowledge, promising young naval officers did not seek out the poorest, most obscure young ladies to marry. Still, the matter at hand had taken on a brighter glow. Oliver Hazard Perry's death had now been revealed as a personal loss, after all. The chaplain knew many things that could be said on the subject of personal loss, though with this boy, it would be clever to introduce the solace in subtle ways.

He said, "Let us talk a little of Commodore Perry."

The luminous eyes fixed themselves upon him for a brief moment, then turned away, rejecting him. "No. I hope you will not mind but I do not really care to talk of him. I plan to write his biography and I fear to stale my excitement with too much discussion."

"Oh. Oh, I see. Well, if you ever feel you want to talk to me . . ."

The chaplain was not a particularly knowing man but there was a point at which even he could tell when a job was too big for him.

110

He walked away, leaving the boy to dream up at the stars. He sensed that he was in no real danger of having all his spare time taken up by Midshipman MacKenzie's wanting to talk to him.

Edward Livingston was going back to Washington, back to Congress. For a year or more, he had seen little of his young friend John Slidell, but in his thoughtful, kindly way he had saved one of his last evenings in New Orleans to dine alone with him. Now, after an elaborate dinner, they lingered over their brandy.

"I feel no guilt in deserting you, John," Edward said. "You are a popular New Orleanian and a busy young lawyer with a few rich clients. You are perfectly at home here and have no further need of me."

"I am perfectly at home, sir, because you have opened all doors for me both professionally and socially. As to having need of you —there will never be a time in my life when I do not need your friendship."

They smiled at each other and sat for a time in comfortable silence. John thought back to the night Edward had dined in New York at the Slidell house and how innocently all the Slidells had accepted Edward's modest assertions that he was doing well in New Orleans, that he was even beginning to have friends among the Creoles. What understatements, what a pose in humility!

"I am in partnership with a prominent lawyer named Grymes," Edward had said simply that night in New York.

Well, indeed he was, and it had sounded like a nice, promising little partnership. He had failed to mention that Grymes and Livingston were the most powerful and high-priced members of the Louisiana bar. He had also neglected to say that though Creoles did, as a rule, keep a safe social distance from the American invader, this rule had never applied to Edward Livingston. John had been astounded upon his arrival in New Orleans to discover that he was being launched into law and society by a gentleman whom New Orleans esteemed as highly as though he had been born a Creole.

He had written to his father, drawing a clear picture of Edward's actual standing, realizing even as he wrote that the law firm of Grymes and Livingston was going to puzzle his father somewhat. It

111

had rather puzzled young John until he had grown accustomed to the fact that New Orleans loved a masquerade. In the matter of the partnership of Grymes and Livingston, it was still difficult, however, to determine which man was the mask. Was it Livingston, so that the firm could go to the party as a dignified barrister? Or was it Grymes, so that the characterization could be a lighthearted, laughing charmer more concerned with the gambling table than the courtroom?

Both lawyers had great minds, electrifying talents, but while Edward Livingston busied himself preparing a new code of laws and criminal procedure for the State of Louisiana, a work of such spectacular legal perception that it brought international attention, John Grymes occupied himself in a different way. He, for a fee of forty thousand dollars to the firm, applied himself to the case of the brothers Lafitte, pirates. New Orleans adored every moment of the show and approved as each partner performed his role as expected. Grymes fought a duel with the District Attorney, who said in open court that he, Grymes, had been seduced by the bloodstained gold of pirates. Livingston politely declined to be entertained at Grand Terre, the luxurious stronghold of the Lafittes. Grymes gaily accepted the invitation, spent a week with his pirate hosts and was escorted back to New Orleans by bearded, scowling men with gold hoops in their ears. In the interval, he had lost his twenty-thousand-dollar share of the fee in a card game. Solemnly he delivered Livingston's half. Livingston had accepted it, banked it and had continued with his code of laws for the State of Louisiana. Young John did not think his father would understand any of this.

"Mr. Grymes is going to miss you, sir," John said.

Edward looked up from contemplation of his brandy. His expression was expectant, questioning. It almost said, "Who is Mr. Grymes?" Edward himself said nothing for a moment. He sat quietly absorbed in study of the deceptively plain little restaurant where one might, in all good sense, count upon a decently prepared commonplace dish. What affectation it was to present these temples of culinary art as though they were intended for the hurried man with an unsophisticated palate.

"John, I hope you will soon marry and settle down in a fine home of your own," Edward said at last.

"I have not yet met the lady, sir, with whom I would spend my life."

"Too bad, but I approve your waiting till you are quite certain. Still, you should have a home where you can offer good dinners, evenings of music, stimulating conversation."

John nodded. "You are quite right, sir. The rooms I have are comfortable but—"

"Two rooms of rented furniture may be sufficient for the average bachelor, and inviting gentlemen to dine with you in restaurants is acceptable procedure. I must tell you, though, that their wives will be potent factors in building your future. When you do not entertain the ladies, you are weakening your position."

"I had not thought of that. Thank you, sir, for this useful though expensive hint. How much do you suppose an excellent cook would cost?"

Edward considered the matter. "Around a thousand dollars, I would say. If she is old—and of course they are often the very best cooks—you can probably do better on the price. A capable butler will run as much, too. For a third thousand, you can get two other servants less skilled. A cook's helper and a sort of all-round boy."

It would be their last meeting for some time. There was still much to say. Please tell my father how devoted I am to my work. Tell my mother how well fed I look. With all your friends here, sir, it is almost impudent to offer but if there is anything I can ever do for you in New Orleans—

Edward Livingston, too, had his parting words, affectionate and platitudinous. They shook hands and went their different ways, John speculating on what it would be like to live in Washington, to serve in Congress, Edward doubting that ever again would he see New Orleans. Once he turned and looked back at the tall, handsome figure of his youthful friend. His regret at parting with this well-loved, warmhearted city was somewhat assuaged by the thought that he would remain in spirit in the person of young lawyer John Slidell. He liked to think that John was as he had been at the age of twenty-nine.

John, too, looked back and watched Edward Livingston's carriage move slowly through the narrow, muddy street. He stood beneath the restaurant lamp post, realizing for the first time that for

113

all his show of simplicity, Mr. Livingston kept a remarkable silence concerning himself.

"Was I so interested in Slidell throughout dinner that I never thought of questioning Livingston? Or was he so adroit that I never got the chance?"

For here, in a way, was a perplexing thing. Why did Edward Livingston want to be a congressman? He did not need the experience. He had had that earlier in his life. Why should he give up the prestige he enjoyed in New Orleans? Had he plans that could only be advanced by settling himself in Washington? John wished that he had asked. In his role of seeking understanding of the great big world, it could have been done so guilelessly. Now only time would tell what had prompted Edward's move to the capital.

"I may go there myself someday," John thought. "It would do me a lot of good. Damned if I can see from here what it will do for him."

He turned toward his rooms at the Widow Didot's and began to think about an establishment of his own. The idea was exciting and since he knew that André was at present in residence at the town house on St. Anne Street, he had an impulse to drop in on him. Then a most pleasing thought struck him and he dismissed the notion of asking for André's suggestions and advice. In keeping with Edward's counsel that the ladies could be of great assistance in furthering a young lawyer's career, why not let them have a hand in creating his small ménage. Their feeling of responsibility, of personal interest, could do him no harm and might even, if he was lucky, relieve him of many tedious details. To hell with André. Madame Deslonde was the person he needed. Madame Deslonde and as many of her friends whose kind offices he could enlist. He would see them all on the weekend at the Toutant-Beauregard anniversary party in St. Bernard Parish.

At that party, he thought, he would even turn an appraising eye upon some of the young ladies. Sooner or later, he must really get down to business. He wanted a Creole wife, of course. None other would do. Yet what Creole father was going to turn his daughter over to an American, even to an American who rejoiced in Edward Livingston's sponsorship? These people were damnably unyielding in the matter of blood lines.

114

All this returned to his mind on Saturday as he mingled with the New Orleans aristocracy in Contreras, the plantation house at St. Bernard Parish. He thought these people too impressed by their heritage and importance but since that was the way the game was played, it must be played seriously. Only a fool would question the rules. Madame Toutant-Beauregard, a calm-faced brunette with startling black eyes, a descendant of the House of Este, was in the habit of mentioning the De Reggio splendor in the days when they had lived in Milan. It had been a year before John had realized that she was speaking of the sixteenth-century De Reggios and that she herself had never been outside Louisiana—nor her parents before her.

The house was lavishly decorated, doorways garlanded with roses, mantels ablaze with the exotic blooms of the fer-de-lance country. Crystal chandeliers bathed the parlors and dining room with golden light. An orchestra had been brought from New Orleans. Ladies gowned in silk and lace sparkled with jewels and flowers in their hair. In Louisiana, a country party did not mean the same thing as in New York.

John made a great point of inquiring as to the health and progress of small Pierre Gustave.

"Do not speak of him to me. He ignores me, caring for nothing but drums and horses." But Madame Toutant-Beauregard could not conceal that she was touched by her visitor's interest and she became the first lady to listen with profound attention to John's plans for his home.

"Permit me, Mr. Slidell, to be of help. I have some tiny knowledge of furniture. Oh, those rosewood armoires of Mallard's! Exquisitely carved. And please do nothing about your cook for a month or so. I just may be able . . ."

Supper was served at midnight. Upon the huge oak table covered with lace and silver and upon the sideboards were turkeys, hams, cheeses and salads. The desserts were dazzling. Cakes in richly iced pyramids, *nougats pièces montées,* sherbets and ice creams in baskets carved from orange peel and decorated with candied rose petals and violets. There would be dancing till dawn. John made good use of his time. He found seven young matrons—all with important husbands—who apparently had always yearned to be of assistance in the furnishing and staffing of a bachelor establishment. He danced with three shy, velvet-eyed creatures and one not so shy who smiled at him and whispered, "I have heard André speak of you." André? Why not Monsieur Deslonde? He forgot the question because he had noticed that her face was heart-shaped and her eyes a warm, smoky gray. Any one of these darlings would have made a splendid Mrs. John Slidell but he must wait till he could laugh in Papa's face if Papa were ill-advised enough to ask, "And who were your father's people?"

Meanwhile, he was certain to receive invitations to dinners and parties. He could see the older women beaming cordially on the sidelines. Cordially enough for invitations, at any rate.

On the gallery, he stood in the warm breeze with André and spoke idly of his plans for his house.

"Will you buy or rent?"

"When I find the house I fancy, I will do as the owner wishes."

John knew how the Creole mind worked. André would think, "So money is no problem with you." But André would say, "The important thing is that the house and you must like each other."

"You are right," John replied. "The house and I must be friends."

André took a glass of wine from a silver tray that flashed by in the darkness. "Are you quite certain that this is to be a bachelor ménage?"

John laughed. "Do you not think that if I had a betrothed in the background, she might pout a little at Madame Deslonde selecting the curtain fabrics? She has promised to do so, you know."

"Has she? I am delighted. It will be for me the most painless way she has ever indulged her passion for expensive brocades." He paused, then drawing closer to John, he said, "I saw Madame Toutant-Beauregard present you to my wife's cousin." Oh, that was the explanation for the informal "André." "What impression did she make upon you?"

"She is enchanting," John said.

"She is an orphan. Beautiful, as you saw, also rich, sweet-tempered, intelligent and a month from her eighteenth birthday."

John slowly lighted a cigar and studied the small pink fire. Why need André beat the drums for his lovely kinswoman? Why was

116

she being called to the special attention of an outlander? Well, André was his friend. André loved him. André wanted him in the family. An answer to his questions, an answer so simple that it would take a simpleton to believe it. Creoles wanted no one in the family save other Creoles.

John said, "This young relative of yours must have dozens of gentlemen besieging her guardian for her hand."

"Dozens," André said, "but she has not yet made a decision. Did you look at her well?"

John remembered the smoky gray eyes, the cloud of soft black hair. A willowy, small-waisted girl with a sweet womanly bosom.

"I did not stare at her, my friend, but I marked her for a relative of your wife's. The resemblance is delightfully strong." Madame Deslonde would die of joy when that outrageous untruth was repeated to her.

"The young lady's father," said André, "was brother to my wife's mother. He was a man of great character, integrity, devotion and generosity."

"This is easily believed, since his blood is the blood of your wife."

"Her father," André said, "had a remarkable brain and was a gentleman of culture extraordinary. He painted exquisite portraits and composed poetry, profound and of rare excellence. Her father was the most magnetic personality imaginable. He—"

"Forgive the interruption, dear André, but my interest is piqued to the point where I must ask how this amazing person, so far above the usual dull specimens of mankind, found a lady worthy of being his bride."

How is that for Creole talk, my friend? I think I have played a ticklish card rather gracefully. Come on now. Speak up.

"I do not wonder that you ask, John, and it was certainly a miracle that he was able to find a lovely girl whose accomplishments almost matched his own."

A lovely girl. Not a lovely lady. Note the shading, John warned himself.

"She also painted—landscapes, I believe. She wrote verses, too, and was an inspired musician."

John permitted a silence to fall. He stared out toward the cane

117

fields of the Toutant-Beauregard plantation. From the slave cabins came the screech of a fiddle. Because the sedate young owners of this plantation had been married seven years tonight, their field hands were rejoicing. They were dancing and singing and eating holiday fare, happy in the knowledge that they were safe. With prosperous young owners, the danger of being sold was practically nonexistent. A roar of laughter came from the cabins, rolled through the night across the rich earth and the elegantly tended lawns right up to the gallery where stood John Slidell, thoughtfully puffing his cigar. This laughter was loud and honest. There was another kind. The quiet Creole laughter. Charming when it was with you.

"A truly fabulous couple produced your wife's cousin, André," he said at length. "The young lady herself will not find it easy to marry. Where is her equal? I should think a man would hesitate long before risking the disdain she would feel for one who dared aim so high."

André said, "If you found her ravishingly attractive, John, would you hesitate?"

John laughed lightly. "Great heavens, yes. How could I possibly aspire to such a goddess?"

André's voice though low-pitched was eager in his ear. "A young gentleman of good looks and much promise need have no reason to despair."

"And why not, friend?"

André flung an arm affectionately about John. "Let us carry a glass of punch to the lady."

"Dear André, a question first. Whom did the young lady's father finally marry?"

"But I have told you."

"No, you have not exactly done so. Your charming story is un-finished. I am left in suspense."

André withdrew his arm from John's shoulder. He said, "I am happy to tell you that there is no chapter in this story that is not beautiful and romantic. As in Perrault's fairy tale, the lovely girl was discovered in incredible circumstances. Domestic tragedy had forced her to work as a seamstress. She was employed in a great

118

house where she attracted the attention of the gentleman who became her husband."

"I see," John said. "A beautiful, romantic story, as you say. New to me, of course, though all the other gentlemen in New Orleans must be very familiar with it."

"It is possible," André said evenly, "for the storybook quality of this pretty courtship and marriage would appeal to anyone's imagination and often be retold. Shall we go inside now and talk to my wife's cousin?"

John had an almost overpowering desire to say, "You mean the dressmaker's daughter?" But he contained himself. He had a suspicion that André's boiling point would be reached right there. No use losing New Orleans, the charmed circle of gay companions and perhaps life itself for the sake of a bitter quip.

He thought, "Will this man not be amazed at how demanding I shall be in the matter of a wife when the moment comes? Not less demanding than he himself was."

He said, "I do not think I am going to talk to her, my friend. Forgive me but I can scarcely keep my eyes open. This country air . . . I will see you at breakfast."

"They are serving black coffee now, John. Have a cup and you will be a new man."

John smiled and walked slowly along the gallery toward the *garçonnière* where he had been quartered for the night with the other bachelor guests. "No, dear friend," he said. "Black coffee will not make of me a new man. I shall still be the one who insists upon good food, good sleep and the very best of all that life has to offer. Only the very best, you understand."

He walked on, thinking of the smoky gray eyes and of how the soft pink mouth had smiled at him.

"God damn it," he thought savagely. "I am a reasonable man. I would be willing to wed with a dressmaker's daughter if only my father had not been a soap-boiler."

John Slidell, Senior, had been saying for a month, "I am refurnishing the house from top to bottom for my wife and family," before it came to him sadly that the family was only twelve-year-old Julia. What other family had he? Ellen, God ease her broken heart, was in her grave. Young John, it seemed, had settled permanently in New Orleans. Tom led a curious, haphazard existence in a house which he shared with three other young lawyers. Janie and her batch of children were Rhode Islanders. Alexander's home was on the sea. John made the most of every day with Julia, knowing her to be a visitor in his house.

He thought that when a man begins a family, he looks upon it as a life's work, yet the work is finished and out of his hands before it has been properly organized. In a twinkling, the children are men and women and the family to which all living was geared turns out to have been a most temporary and fleeting condition. Instead of having laid up for oneself a treasure in everlasting companionship, one has arranged for the middle years to be filled with longing for the days when the children were at home. It was probably one of those sly tricks of nature that made it impossible for a man to gaze upon a new baby and coolly estimate that his close contact with it would, at the most, last for twenty years. If parents were permitted to see that clearly, they might conclude that there was little sense in growing fond of the creature.

Jane had had the fancy to sell all of Grandmother MacKenzie's belongings, so they had refurnished and redecorated the house with everything brand new and shining bright. Painted ceilings, gilded moldings, rich satin ottomans, curtains in Parisian style and splendid mirrors great and small. Venetian carpets were all the rage and chests of drawers with brass handles. Crimson was no longer a fashionable color. Pale shades of amethyst and topaz for sofas and chairs. Beds without canopies . . .

"A hell of a time to break in a new bed," he had said to Jane.

"Braggart!"

"Braggart? I am only fifty-five."

"I know. Fifty-five and your grin still captivates me."

"Madame, are you implying that only my grin remains unchanged?"

It was good to have a new dining-room table. This slender-legged one had never seated a circle of children. It had no memories. John tried not to associate Julia with any particular chair or corner of any room. By his swift calendar, soon she would be walking out that newly painted door upon the arm of some young man. God bless her, she had the lucky look of Janie about her. Poor Ellen; he remembered that even as a child, her laughter had been infrequent and Henry MacKenzie had called her his quiet little angel.

And as soon as the house was refurnished and almost as bare of memories as a grain of sugar, the children began drifting in.

"Tell them we are not entertaining this season," John said when the letter came from Commander and Mrs. M. C. Perry.

"Oh, you will be delighted to see them."

"What? With all that raft of children?"

"There are only seven now," Jane said and they thought of little Susan, who had died the preceding summer. "Though of course Janie is pregnant again. Janie is always pregnant." And they thought of Ellen, who might have lived if only once . . . "Let us give Cal a really splendid visit. The poor boy has had his heartaches. Imagine, of all that strapping collection of Perry brothers, he is the lone survivor, and they were all so young."

John nodded. "Very well. Tell them they may come."

They all came that autumn, the Perry family—big, soft-spoken Cal, wearing his sorrows and his commandership with dignity; Janie, who had forgotten to pack enough clothes for the children but had brought gloves and slippers to match each of her own costumes; the children, all blue-eyed blonds, enormously respectful of Papa, slightly uncertain as to what was the use of Mama.

"Just scatter pallets and cots wherever you can," Janie said. "We will make out wonderfully well. I may need a little more space for my frocks but—"

"Janie, how can you care so much for clothes when your middle is bulging like a flour barrel?"

"Mother, this is the very time to care about clothes. Would you have me look like a frump just because I am whelping? I make it a rule to look lovely for Cal."

"Lovely for Cal! That makes a nice excuse for the sin of vanity, does it not? I happen to know that you would primp and posture if you were alone on a desert isle."

Janie laughed. "If I were, my figure would be better."

Whimsically she had outfitted Matthew Calbraith, Junior, and

121

Oliver Hazard, the Second, in sailor suits. Little Jane, who seemed to be her favorite, was always dressed in the same color that she wore herself. Isabella, Sarah and Anna put on whatever they found at hand and there was as yet no problem as to what William, the baby, would wear.

Twelve-year-old Julia looked at her nieces and nephews and delivered an ultimatum. None would sleep in her room.

"Darling," Jane protested, "you must take Isabella and Sarah in with you. It is only for a little while and—"

"I did not invite them. I consider them loathsome. The room is mine."

Jane said, "You are not being generous or helpful but you have a right to your opinion and incontestably the room is yours."

There was, of course, Alexander's room, standing always in readiness in case he came ashore. And come ashore he did, just when his room had been converted into a female dormitory.

"Leave two of the cots," he directed, grinning at the little tow-heads in their sailor suits. "I will take the commodore and the commander in with me. Just get rid of the females."

"We Perrys are a terrible nuisance," Cal said. "Truly I did not imagine how we would upset the entire household."

"How could you imagine it?" his father-in-law asked. "After all, there are only nine of you."

Alexander said, "Cal, I am very glad you are here. Had you not been, I would have journeyed to Bristol to see you."

Cal's glance went anxiously to his young brother-in-law. For a reason he had never been able to explain to himself, he felt responsible for Alec's having embraced the Navy as a career. And for a reason equally inexplicable, Alec, though a lieutenant now, did not seem to Cal the stuff of which Navy men were made. For one thing, he was too sensitive. Witness, Cal thought, how at this very moment he is instantly divining my thoughts and fears.

"No, I am not in trouble, Cal. I have still not destroyed the American Navy."

Cal laughed uncomfortably. "As a matter of fact, I hear you are doing fine," he said and though he had heard nothing at all of Alec, it seemed a pleasant thing to say. "What did you want to see me about?"

122

Alec said, "Well, it is rather exciting to me and I think it will be to my father and mother, also. To you, Cal, I hope it will bring satisfaction." He turned and unstrapped his bag, withdrawing a package wrapped in brown paper. "It has taken me a long time to do this, but I finally succeeded."

In puzzlement, Cal unwrapped the package. A book. Well, since Alec had selected it, undoubtedly it would be good reading.

"Why, thank you, Alec," Cal said politely and then he saw what it was. *Life of Oliver Hazard Perry* by Alexander Slidell Mac-Kenzie, U.S.N. "Alec! Oh, Alec!" Cal's eyes brimmed over as he embraced his brother-in-law. "How did you do it? How did you get time? How did you keep the secret that it was being published? This is the most wonderful thing I ever heard of! Alec, my heart is bursting with pride and gratitude." Lovingly he turned back to the book, fingering the pages, opening it at random to devour a phrase or to read a chapter heading. "I do not know how you did it, Alec."

At last, he was ready to let the book pass from his hands so that the author's parents, too, might glow with pride.

John, Senior, opened the book and read the first paragraph. He looked up to say, "A labor of love, of course, but is this to be your entire literary output?"

"No, I have another book half finished and the outline of one in my mind. It needs research just as this one did."

Before the Perry family had begun to think of returning home, before Alexander's leave had expired, there came a letter in a familiar hand but it was postmarked Philadelphia.

"Philadelphia?"

"Yes. What is he doing there?"

The letter did not say. It only said that in a few days or perhaps a week, he would be along for a short visit. John and Jane looked at each other, trying to hide their excitement.

"Do you suppose he has a wife? Could he be on a honeymoon?"

"In Philadelphia?"

"I wish Janie and the naval squadron would up anchor."

"Oh, well, it will be a good thing for him to see his whole family at once. It has been years."

Julia did not remember her eldest brother at all. She expected him to be like Alexander or perhaps like Tom. He was like neither. He was amusing, and attentive when one spoke to him. She had never before known a brother who would bother to tell her that she was pretty.

"And I know pretty when I see it," he assured her. "Where I live, they raise sugar, cotton and pretty girls."

"You can have my room," she said. "I will move in with the children."

He smiled at her. "You keep your room, sweetheart. Never establish an awkward precedent."

"Some of the girls at school speak like you do. Soft and slow. You have a Southern accent."

"Bless you, Julia. I have been trying for years. Where do you go to school?"

"Madame Chégaray's. I do not board. I come home every night. Some girls board."

"Is it nice there?"

She wrinkled her nose. "It is ladylike."

"I should hope so. Are you learning French?"

"Learning? I have learned."

"Then why are we using English?"

"Do you speak French?"

"Better than most Frenchmen."

"Does everybody in Louisiana speak French?"

"No, but they won't quit trying."

She laughed and said, "Oh, please take my room."

"Thank you, no, dear. I will be at the City Hotel."

"I am going to tell Mother that you must stay here." She scampered away in a whirl of pink petticoats that she had not yet learned to manage gracefully.

Tom looked across the room at this stranger with the almost too elegant air. He had to keep reminding himself that this was only John, his brother John. Say what one would, there was something impressive about success. A man could sit over a drink or a cup of coffee all night long agreeing with his fellow failures that success meant nothing, that it was no indication of ability, that it was not even desirable, but in the morning, when he met success face to face, it was damned difficult not to feel inferior. Tom knew of only one way to show his brother that he was every bit his equal. It was by being critical and rude.

"Why be such a pill?" he demanded. "City Hotel! Are you too good to flop on a pallet in Alec's room?"

"Yes," said John.

"I'll tell you what, then. Come down to my place. One of the fellows just moved out. We can give you a room all to yourself."

"Really? A *clean* room, Tom?"

"The bed is soft. I live in the house. You could, too."

"Yes, I could if I had to. I do not have to, Tom."

"Well, I do not have to, either. I could live here."

John smiled and said softly, "Oh, no, you could not possibly live here. You Yale men always have to keep proving something to yourselves."

John, Senior, studied his eldest son and thought that this boy, always too arrogant, had learned at last to carry himself with the grace of a gentleman. No small achievement for a man whose family tree was woefully lopsided. He has learned the trick and it is a trick, his father thought. A man must know how to say to himself, "I am a gentleman," and then learn not to wear the knowledge awkwardly, as though it were an ill-fitting suit which is binding him in many places.

"What are you doing with your money, son?"

"Spending it."

"All you earn?"

"Every penny."

"You are not investing in anything at all?"

"I did not say that, Father. I am investing in my future. I cannot have a modest office or an economically managed home if I aim to reach the top in New Orleans. There one entertains lavishly. For instance—" John hesitated as though weighing the advisability of giving his father an example of New Orleans hospitality.

"For instance?"

"Well, I travel a great deal now in company with John Grymes, Edward Livingston's former partner. He married the beautiful lady who was Governor Claiborne's widow."

"Is not Grymes a little on in years to be a companion of yours?"

John shrugged. "It is a matter of similar tastes rather than similar birth dates. At any rate, I was going to tell you something of a recent dinner party. The Duke of Saxe-Weimar-Eisenach came to town on his American tour and Grymes entertained him at his home. Picture the scene: The dinner was arranged in huge double dining rooms at Grymes's gorgeous Royal Street house. During courses, the folding doors were kept shut. At the end of each course, the servants opened the doors and we proceeded to the other dining room, where we sat ourselves in the same order at a table where crystal, silver, linen and lace were in exact duplication of the table which we had just left. This continued through nine courses. Needless to say, the food and wine were equal to anything the Duke had ever been offered anywhere. You see, do you not, that there is no place in that world for a thrifty young man?"

John, Senior, looked sharply at his son. "And that is the world you want?"

"It is. I want no other."

"Julia reports that you own four slaves."

"Her reporting is quite accurate. Did she tell you what I was doing in Philadelphia?"

"No. Perhaps she was afraid I would be shocked. What *were* you doing in Philadelphia?"

"I was there buying a carriage."

"What?"

"Yes. The best carriages are manufactured in Philadelphia. Most people simply write their specifications, but this being my very first—call it foolish but I wanted the pleasure of seeing the bodies, the wheels, the appointments, having the carriage assembled to my personal taste, even selecting the color of the lining. Next time, I shall be more casual."

"The horses? You have them?"

John nodded. "They are magnificent. I won them in a card game. Should I be lying to you about all this? Should I present a picture of a sedate and cautious young man who—"

"No. Tell me the truth."

"Very well, but you may not always like it."

"But I shall always guess it."

They laughed together and the older man thought, "If I never see the boy again, we will have laughed together."

126

Janie, who wanted desperately to see the inside of the City Hotel, asked her brother why she and Cal were not invited to tea. She was amused at the astonishment and embarrassment upon John's face.

"I know Southern ladies stay home when they are in a delicate condition but I am not Southern and no condition could be less delicate than mine. Good grief, if I hid myself when I was blooming, by this time I would have spent about seven years of my life in seclusion."

She only managed a promenade through the main hall, for John had ordered tea served in his suite. Stuffy old stick! And she had worn her tangerine merino. But she was impressed by the way her brother lived at the hotel. Two tremendous rooms all to himself and trays and trays of delicate pastries and a waiter stationed in the parlor who kept bowing and saying, "Yes, Mr. Slidell."

To Alec, the suite in the City Hotel was not at all impressive, for he noticed neither furnishings nor spaciousness. He dropped in on his brother at nine o'clock one morning and suffered confusion and bewilderment to discover John still in bed.

He supposed an apology was due but he gave it grudgingly, feeling that John really should have been up and about at that hour. Actually, he had considered calling earlier lest he miss the chance to catch John in the quiet of the hotel.

"I am writing a book about John Paul Jones," he said, staring dreamily out the bedroom window.

"Well, three cheers for you. Would you not still have been writing it at noon? Since I am awake, I must have coffee. Ring the bell for the waiter."

"The bell? Oh, yes, of course." Alec rang, wondering if John intended to drink his coffee in bed. A slovenly habit. "I wanted to ask you about Pierre de Landais."

"About whom? You must remember I am scarcely awake. Is he a Louisianan?"

"A Louisianan? For God's sake, what is the matter with you? There were French names before there was Louisiana, you know."

"Really? Do close the window. It is cold in here."

Alec closed the window, not regretting that he had come but

wishing that his brother had disciplined himself to awakening in full possession of his senses.

"I hear that you often spoke to Pierre de Landais, John. You must help me. I need your opinion, your impressions. Tell me what you thought of him."

"You tell me something first. Who the hell is he? And where is the waiter?"

"Of course, he is dead now," Alec said.

"No wonder then that he moves so slowly. Open the door and shout for him."

With the first swallow of coffee, John's wits began to gather. "I know the man you mean—the old lunatic who called himself Admiral de Landais."

Alexander leaned forward eagerly. "You knew him well, I understand."

"Now, how could I have known him well? There were sixty years between us and he was more than a little deranged."

"But he spoke to you of John Paul Jones."

"Of nothing else."

"Tell me what he said."

"Oh, really now, Alec. You can read anywhere what he said. He said Jones was a son of a bitch."

"And did you believe him?"

"Of course. I am always inclined to believe anyone is a son of a bitch. The odds favor such a conclusion."

Alec set his cup down and told himself that he must not grow angry. How could he convince this idle, self-centered dandy that the words De Landais had used and the tone in which he had spoken them were of the utmost importance? He kept a silence for a time, studying with distaste the way his brother lounged back against the propped pillows. He remembered that Janie and Cal had visited here and he hoped fervently they had witnessed nothing like this. God, what would Cal think of a man who took breakfast in bed? And Alec's own brother, too.

"John, there is a great argument to this day as to whether or not Jones's charges against De Landais were valid. I hope in my book to tell the truth."

"Why?"

128

"Why!" Alec sprang to his feet and paced the bedroom nervously. "Is it impossible for you to see my responsibility? I must learn all I can before I express the opinion that yes, Jones lied about De Landais or yes, De Landais was a coward and a scoundrel."

"Oh, sit down," John said. "You are only writing a book. You are not deciding whether or not to lower the lifeboats."

Alec said, "I take things seriously."

"You do, indeed. Take them seriously somewhere else, will you? All this bombast and pacing of the deck is too much for me the first thing in the morning. In Louisiana, we never mention honesty or responsibilities or obligations or truth or any of those high-flown things till at least four o'clock in the afternoon."

Alec said, "I am sorry but I live with these 'high-flown' things every hour of every day. It is my intention never to forget them even for a moment. I hoped that you would help me with my book. Is there nothing at all regarding De Landais that you wish to tell me?"

John leaned over and placed his cup upon the floor. He rearranged the pillows, placing them flat again as though he intended to return to sleep. He lay back, eying Alec gravely.

He said, "Yes, there is something I wish to tell you. I wish to tell you that De Landais was a coward, a scoundrel and a God-damned liar. I wish to tell you that no purer soul ever walked the earth or sailed the sea than John Paul Jones."

Alec's astonishment sent him swiftly to John's side, to stare into the suddenly earnest face of his brother. There were no humorous overtones to the words, no amusement in the eyes.

"Why do you say that, John?" Alec asked excitedly.

"I say it because you are in the American Navy. Are you going to be fool enough to keep digging till you find out that Jones crucified De Landais? And then are you going to be crazy enough to put it all in a book? Let me tell you something—De Landais was a hell of a good officer but the American Navy managed to do without him. They could manage to do without you, too, Lieutenant MacKenzie."

Alec was disappointed. For a brief moment, he had believed that an unsuspected depth had been reached in his brother, a secret

129

underground river of idealism. Annoyed at himself for having credited John with any warmth of feeling, he spoke priggishly. "Your approach to this is thoroughly cynical. I will always do what I believe is right even if I suffer for having done it."

John sighed. "You are that kind of person, aren't you? I have heard of them. If I were you, though, I would do what the American Navy did. I would avoid bringing De Landais to trial. The Navy is smarter than you. They handled the situation brilliantly."

"I am searching for justice."

"An overrated item. Is there any more coffee in that pitcher?"

John stayed in New York a week. He had seen his family and they had seen him. New Orleans was very far away. The seven seas were vast and perilous. It was unlikely that ever again would they all be together. Each thought that perhaps the impression made at this meeting was the one that would be carried throughout the remaining years of life.

His parents wanted to drive with John to the dock but he insisted upon saying his good-bys to them in the little upstairs sitting room that had been the day nursery. It was furnished now with soft, comfortable chairs and reading lamps. On one wall, in a frame of a particularly poisonous shade of green, was a sampler that Jane had worked in cross-stitching. The words were sweet. No woman is ever free of her children. John thought it very characteristic of Mother to have paid little attention to her skeins. The sweet words were formed in steely gray silk and the flowers surrounding the sentiment were the same poisonous green as the frame.

"I am going to be a personage in Louisiana," he promised his parents. "It will keep me occupied. God knows when I can return here."

They said that they understood and kissed him fondly. He had arranged for Tom to drive with him to the *Southern Star*.

Tom sat beside him in hostile silence, waiting for the matter that John had said he wished to discuss with him. John let him wait. He was busy examining his father's carriage, comparing it to the sparkling beauty he had just purchased in Philadelphia. This one was dull and rather shabby. John thought it must be a fine thing to stand so well in one's city, to be so certain of one's social position, that one could afford to be seen in such a comfortable old monster as this. Even the horses seemed to have the distinguished dowdiness of elderly society leaders. Alas, the coachman was young, an incongruous touch.

"And now, Tom." He turned suddenly to his brother. "The time is short, so do not give me a long, tiresome dissertation on how happy you are and how bright your prospects. I think you know a lot of law but for some reason, you have been unable to make it work for you. I can use you in New Orleans."

Tom raised his head and looked coolly at his brother. "What use for me had you in mind?"

"I have not the slightest notion at the moment. Maybe you would run errands. I do not know. I am sure you would prove useful in some capacity or other."

"I'll be God-damned if I am going to run errands."

"Suit yourself. It is a wonderful city and you might amount to something there."

"I will think the matter over."

"Oh, do not be pompous, I beg of you. Come if you like or forget the whole thing. And do not write me any long letters full of 'ifs' and 'maybes.' It was just a passing thought of mine and not worth anyone's spending time on it. Ah, there is the *Southern Star* awaiting me. Lovely as a bird, is she not? The sight of her thrills me. I feel quite as seafaring as our dear brother Lieutenant MacKenzie." John slapped Tom on the back and leaped from the carriage. "Good-by, boy," he called. He slipped a few dollars into the hand of the coachman and jauntily followed his luggage as it was carried by a boatman to the *Southern Star*.

The coachman said, "Such a wonderful gentleman—Mr. John. But is it really true that he owns four—four *people?*"

Tom shook his head. "Five," he said.

In his suite at the Indian Queen Hotel in Washington, Senator Edward Livingston sat writing a letter. A bright fire blazed in his comfortable parlor and at his elbow on the desk a bottle of Madeira awaited his pleasure. Often as he wrote, he paused to stare into the fire and once he debated the advisability of sampling the generous gift from his landlord. He decided against it. He was of

131

two minds regarding the letter, as it was, and thought it risky to give the Madeira any voice in the decision.

Should the letter be written at all? Why not? He needed whatever assistance could be mustered and certainly the young man's discretion and loyalty were to be trusted. Still, was it not always an error to do anything in life that depended on someone else's possession of these excellent qualities? Well, there was a way of writing the letter that would render it innocuous and he felt now that the letter had to be written. He tossed into the fire the pages already completed and began again.

Dear Young Friend:

I was so pleased at the news that you are running for Congress. I take it as an accomplished fact that you will soon join me here. We will dine together at my very good hotel and at the famous Union Tavern in Georgetown, and when in a mood for exertion, we will haunt the tenpin alleys, which are very popular. It is a damnable lie that since becoming a Senator I associate with no Congressmen. Just join me here and you will see.

The extreme pleasure was mine last month of entertaining your father. He came here on a complicated business matter. I am glad to say I was able to be of service. He is in perfect health and reports the same of your entire family. Alexander's *A Year in Spain* is very successful. It has been highly praised and is selling remarkably well. Your father says that Alec contemplates writing a biography of John Paul Jones. I doubt not that it would have an impressive sale, for on the strength of this latest book, Alec's name has become known to all.

I myself have been tremendously occupied. Like all men who have the country's interest at heart, I want to see Andrew Jackson elected President. Naturally, this is what you want, too, so I trust that as you go about your personal campaigning, you will keep reminding the people of Jackson's many virtues. He is a very brilliant and great-hearted man but, I fear, he has often been misunderstood. For instance, after the Battle of New Orleans, he suffered the loss of Creole affection simply because he did not furlough and disband troops quickly enough. I would appreciate your calling to attention wherever you can the nobility of Jackson's nature and the power of his intellect. I hope that you will read a book on him by Senator Eaton. This book will supply you with answers to questions, rebuttals to anti-Jackson arguments and an overwhelming assemblage of reasons why this great candidate should be our next President. Of course, the reasons are very obvious but, sad to say, there are opportunists who confuse issues and distort facts.

Eaton's book will prepare you for the type of challenge you can expect from men who have not the welfare of our country in mind. I rest easy knowing that you will do all that is possible to further the fame of a man whom America desperately needs.

I wish I were in New Orleans so I could take future pleasure in recalling that I had been of some use to you in your race for Congress.

With sincere fondness and the hope of having you in Washington very soon—

Edward sat back in his cushioned chair and wondered, as he often did, how long was the memory of the voter. Would it be remembered that Jackson had been an undistinguished Congressman or that his hotheaded handling of the Seminole trouble had almost plunged the United States into serious trouble with both Spain and Great Britain? Would it be recalled that as first American governor of Florida, he had been hated? Would the people be enthralled or repelled by the man with the lightning-flash temper? And always, of course, there was the problem of Mrs. Jackson. A hard-working President-maker could learn to detest that earthy, pipe-smoking woman, the love of Jackson's life. In many ways, she was a greater peril to her husband's ambitions than all the stories, true and false, that were told of him.

Experimentally Edward drew a fresh piece of stationery toward him and scribbled a postscript.

Also, John, dear friend, if questions are asked concerning Mrs. Jackson, do make quite certain that your questioner departs knowing that she truly believed herself legally divorced from Mr. Robards before she formed even the most innocent of friendships with Andrew Jackson. I realize that a divorce is, under no circumstances, acceptable to Louisianans but—

He crumpled the postscript and dropped it into the fire. What could be said in Louisiana that would make a divorced woman eligible for the position of First Lady? Young John would just have to do his best with that difficulty if it arose, and arise it certainly would.

Edward thought back to the night when they had last seen each other and John had promised that if ever there was anything he could do for Edward in New Orleans . . . There was something he could do now. He could produce a magical formula that would render Rachel Jackson acceptable to Roman Catholic New Orleans and that would cause Creoles to forget that more of their men had died of illness than had been killed in battle. If only, Edward thought now, if only Jackson had not kept them stationed on wet and marshy grounds, if only he had discontinued martial law at a reasonable time.

Gazing sleepily into the fire, Edward reflected that few actions are performed for the reasons one imagines. He had believed that the contacts he had established for young John Slidell had been no more than an evidence of the high regard in which the boy's father was held. The Fates had no doubt laughed at such simplicity. Actually, he had been busily though unknowingly laying the groundwork for a day when Andrew Jackson would have need to carry the State of Louisiana.

On the gallery at the Deslonde plantation house, John, with half-closed eyes, watched André's youngest children as they tumbled on the bright grass. André had nine children now. Nine. Mathilde, Henriette, Juliette, Adrien—or was Adrien the new baby boy? Had the first son been named—been named— John caught himself as his head drooped suddenly upon his chest. This lovely, lazy air. Anxiously he glanced to see if André had observed his drowsiness. André had not. His eyes were fixed adoringly on the little ones. John made a second attempt to call the Deslonde roll. Mathilde, Henriette, Juliette— No, it was useless. These toddlers on the lawn were nameless to him.

The black girl in charge of the youngsters suddenly raised her head in its scarlet *tignon*. Swiftly she herded her flock off the lawn, away from the gallery and out of sight.

André laughed. "My wife must be approaching," he said. "The lawn is only permitted as a playground when there is no guest on the gallery."

"Oh, is that it? And how did the girl know that Madame Deslonde is approaching?"

André shrugged and turned to smile at his wife, who had just appeared on the threshold, the cool dimness of the house making a pretty background to her pink cotton frock. "Join us, my dear."

"I am not interrupting? You are speaking English, so perhaps—"

"For the delight of your presence," John said, "we will be happy to speak your language."

Madame Deslonde seated herself and said, "You know I have always thought it rather selfish of the gentlemen to have only their sons instructed in English."

"For what reason does a daughter need it?" André asked. "She will not engage in business or travel without her father or husband."

Madame Deslonde frowned slightly. "Even so, there are times when I have wished . . . And now the world is changing so rapidly. For example, imagine a theatre in New Orleans where no French at all is spoken, and you cannot deny that every year more Americans settle among us. I would like my daughters as well as my sons to learn English. I would begin with Mathilde, since she is the eldest. I would like to send her to school in the North."

André stared in displeasure at his wife but John pretended not to notice. "There is an excellent school in New York City," he said. "Madame Chégaray's. My sister attends classes there. If you are serious, I will write my mother for full information."

"How kind you are, Mr. Slidell. Madame Chégaray's."

"Yes. If Mathilde were there, it would give you comfort to know that she had friends close by. My mother would sponsor her in the school and act as a Northern godmother to your little girl. Also, the home of my childhood would be hers to use when she wished."

If Mathilde learned English, John thought, it would be from some bony Bostonian tutor who would settle down in the luxury of the plantation house and secretly write a book on the evils of slavery. He had mentioned Madame Chégaray's and had hospitably opened the doors of his father's house to Mathilde only because it was an opportunity to apprise these Creoles that his own background was not humble. Madame Deslonde's wish for her daughter to speak English had provided him with a splendid chance to say that his sister attended an exclusive school, that he relished the idea of his childhood home being viewed and that his mother was a lady of some consequence. All this at absolutely no cost.

André said, "My dear, please order us some coffee."

"It has been ordered. André, would you entertain the notion of Mathilde going to school in New York City?"

"Not for a moment. Do you realize, madame, that we have four daughters? I did not hear Mr. Slidell mention that in this New York school the tuition and board are free of charge. It would be to assume an endless burden, a burden that—" He broke off as he became aware of John's cool eyes thoughtfully studying him. He smiled and said in English, "A woman is deflected from her purpose only if she is told that money is unavailable. By no other argument is she swayed."

The coffee arrived and they drank it slowly, gossiping a little, repeating the news of city and country, speaking of mutual friends.

"Oh, by the way," John said, for here was the perfect place to say it. "I had a letter from Edward Livingston."

"Really? How is he?"

"In good health, I am happy to report. He wrote to tell me that a book which was written by my brother Alexander is a huge success in Washington."

"I am very happy for your brother."

"Thank you. Naturally, Edward also wished me well on my attempt at winning a Congressional seat."

"We all wish you well."

"Thank you again, dear André. The slate will be filled with names of your friends, will it not? I hopefully call myself your friend, and then, of course, in the high place, at the very top will be the name of your old chief, Andrew Jackson."

The corners of André's mouth tightened. John saw Madame Deslonde veil her eyes as though she had never before heard the name. She who had placed a wreath of laurel leaves on Jackson, the victor.

"My old chief," André said, "is likely to drive me to voting for Mr. John Q. Adams."

"Adams, the hater of Roman Catholics?" John asked in surprise. The surprise was genuine. He had not known till that very moment how he would promote Jackson's cause with André. From what secret source had come this wonderful inspiration to accuse Adams of anti-Catholicism? He saw at once that he had struck a note that could be sounded again and again. Not alone on this gallery but on every gallery in Louisiana. André's eyes had darkened at news of this unguessed danger.

Madame Deslonde said, "Mr. Adams has been President for four years and no Catholic has suffered."

John smiled gently. "No, not *suffered*," he agreed. "There have been only the small straws in the wind that make one fear the activities of a second term. But I have not come here to talk politics." He glanced at André and saw the Creole eyes still clouded with concern. Well, so much for John Q. Adams. "Tell me, Madame Deslonde, how old is Adrien now?"

Tom was waiting when he entered his house late that evening. It annoyed John that his brother insisted upon unpacking his work case in the sitting room and scattering pages of contracts, figures and memoranda over tables and chairs.

"Damn it, Tom, I have told you a hundred times this is a home, not an office. I do not want you working here."

"Sorry. I had to see you and there were things to verify and reread."

Tom was chewing on an apple and John looked at him with distaste. This brother of his had no instincts for the refinements of life. He had a habit of snatching food and sleep as the opportunity presented itself. Of course, all this was a result of that disordered existence he had led after leaving college. If it were not for the imaginative mind behind those bulging eyes, one might say there was nothing left of the Tom who, as a boy, had been so popular socially and so certain that success was meted out in direct ratio to competence.

"Did you not have any dinner, Tom?"

"No, as a matter of fact, I did not. I have been busy. I have assembled all the material from the Eaton book for you. Also, I have here several extracts from a sour little pamphlet entitled *General Jackson's Youthful Indiscretions Between the Age of Twenty-Three and Sixty*. There are, among other things, charges of unjust executions in the Florida campaign. You had better read these charges and devise some refutations."

John nodded. "I will read them."

"The Eaton book is, of course, absolute proof that Jackson is purer than pure. I investigated and found that the 'facts' in it were obtained from Jackson himself and the charming Rachel. It makes some very pretty claims but still offers no really enticing reasons why Creoles should vote for Andrew Jackson."

John said, "I am attending to that. Pack up this stuff and go home, will you?"

Tom made no move to comply. Thoughtfully chewing the apple, he said, "You are to talk on Thursday in behalf of your candidacy for the Congress of the United States. Your speech awaits you over there under the fruit bowl."

"Thank you. Good night."

Tom still did not rise. Deliberately he dropped the apple core into an empty nut dish and turned his eyes away from his brother. "I have confirmation now," he said, "of something I have drearily suspected."

"Yes? What is that?"

"It is that you are not going to be elected to Congress."

John stiffened. "What in hell do you mean?"

"Is there a clearer way to say what I have said? You just simply are not going to get enough votes to be sent to Washington. Instead, your opponent is going. Now do you understand?"

John blinked his eyes in puzzlement and sat down. "No, I do not understand. You are going to have to do a little explaining. How could you possibly know—"

"I asked questions," Tom said. "A great many questions. Naturally, I did not undertake the task alone. I had help. I am rather good at gathering and organizing people for a project. You would be surprised at the assistance you can get in exchange for a few drinks. By the way, you paid for the drinks. I am sorry to say that your guests brought back no happy tidings. You are going to be licked, John."

John sat in silence, tasting of the bitter cup of defeat well in advance of its having been poured. What absurdity was this, counting votes before they had been cast? How could it be done? This blasted popeyed Yale man had been given general orders: Make work for yourself. And this is what he had done. He had got the election returns before the election. A sudden heartening thought occurred.

"I have not as yet talked to the people. They have not heard how I stand on—"

"Regrettably, it does not matter. Your opponent's birthplace has a more sentimental appeal."

"But I cannot afford to be licked."

"Nobody can ever afford it, John."

"I least of all. The Americans who come here and hang onto the habits and customs of their old homes have excuse for failure. But I have embraced this land with both arms and all my heart. Defeat will be a reflection on me personally, a great big well-advertised defeat!" He bent toward Tom anxiously. "Assuming that your officious activities have resulted in a true forecast, will I be licked badly?"

Tom responded with a brief nod and John circled the room, nervously biting at his thumbnail.

"What in hell will I do?"

"Why do you not withdraw, claiming sudden illness?"

"A magnificent idea! It would fill my clients with warm faith in my strength to wage battle for them, would it not? You must think of something better than that."

Tom said, "Not tonight. I am going home."

"Home? What is the need to go home? There is work to do. I must find a way—"

"You will not say you are ill?"

"No, I will not. Good God, I cannot imperil my practice."

"I suppose you would not care to state that on second thought, you feel it your obligation to your clients to remain in New Orleans and therefore—"

"Certainly not. Someday I will be a Congressman and later a Senator. Mark my word."

"Very well. Your word is marked but find something that will serve as a hedge right now. You are not going to be a Congressman on this shake of the dice."

"Tell me the exact details of how this trick of yours was performed. Who? Where? How many?" John walked the floor fretfully but listened with intense concentration throughout Tom's de-

139

scription of how the operation had been conducted. At the end of the account, he stopped his pacing and stood at the window, suddenly motionless and calm.

"Have you thought of something?" Tom asked.

John gave no answer. Silently he stared at an oil lamp swinging in front of the house across the street. He wondered if this neighbor had decided to vote against him. And if so, was it because he had installed a gaslight at his door?

Tom began packing his work case. "Do you want me to leave this material from Eaton's book? And the extracts from the opposition pamphlet?"

"Yes."

"What about the speech?" Tom asked, walking toward the fruit bowl. "Do you want it here or in the office?"

"I want it in the office—torn up into very small pieces."

"Are you not going to address that meeting on Thursday?"

"Yes, I am going to address that meeting on Thursday and many other meetings right up to Election Day."

"As you please, John."

"Of course, as I please. And since you are so superlative at getting and organizing people, I want you to make quite certain that on Thursday, the hall is filled. See that the newspapers are represented. Notify *L'Abeille* and the *Courrier*."

"The speech of a Congressional candidate is not very exciting to them," Tom said.

John turned from the window and faced his brother. "You are developing an uncommonly irritating habit," he said. "You are finding reasons for having failed me before you have even tried to succeed. I shall speak on Thursday and I expect the hall filled and I expect men from the newspapers to be present."

"I will do what is possible."

"I could hire a ten-year-old black boy to do what is possible," John said.

"Then, God damn it, do so. I have had enough of you and your self-importance."

With face flaming hot and tears of fury stinging his eyes, Tom bent above the work case. Disjointed, incompleted thoughts rushed through his mind. "If I had any pride, I would not— Never will he find anyone to work for him as I—" He finished fumbling with the buckles and leather straps and walked toward the door.

"Did you say good night to me?" John asked.

"Oh, go to hell."

From the window, John watched his brother disappear into the darkness. An uncomfortably moody fellow. No question, though—he had earned another raise in salary.

Now as to the important thing—defeat. So he was not going to Washington? He was not going to be a Congressman. Not this time. Well, some other time, then. That other time would be taken care of when it rolled around. This was *this* time. Thursday, when he addressed the meeting . . .

Thursday, when he addressed the meeting, the auditorium was crowded. The newspapers were represented. The men from *L'Abeille* and the *Courrier* were there. Even one from *Le Journal de Commerce*. The New Orleanians gathered in the hall gazed with admiration upon the young man with the curly, chestnut-colored hair and the steady gray eyes. Here was a handsome young man of large stature with strong, broad shoulders, the chiseled features of a patrician and the poise of one who has matured through fearless acceptance of himself and the world around him. And how faultless his attire. None missed the tailored perfection of the swallowtail coat and the tight gray trousers, the high choker collar and the flowered white stock—surely a fashion designed for such a firm chin, such dignified carriage.

He spoke beautifully, his diction and accent a joy to the ears of the educated. He began by telling them what they already knew, that New Orleans was the loveliest, the most heavenly place on earth.

"And because I feel as I do about my adopted city, I yearned to be one of the men to watch over her and protect her at the seat of government. But, my dear friends, I realize that someone else can do that as well as I. I am not even going to say to you what my Congressional policies would have been. I am not going to tell you what I would have stood for and what I would have stood against. Do you know why? I will tell you why.

"Last night, as I lay in my bed thinking of the pleasure I would take in being your representative, the thought suddenly struck me

141

that I was thinking of myself, of John Slidell, of my own wishes and dreams. Quite honestly then I told myself what I have just told you—New Orleans has no dearth of sons to represent her with integrity and brilliance. You can rest easy about New Orleans, John, I told myself. Whichever man goes to Congress, he will love New Orleans well and defend her righteously. But, John, can you rest easy about New Orleans when you view her future as seen through the eyes of a man who does not love her? And, my friends, the answer was of course no. And I asked myself what is to become of this great city of ours and, indeed, the entire South, if the country remains in the hands of a stiff-necked New Englander who knows nothing of our needs, our beliefs, our traditions? And lying in my bed, I trembled with terror as I envisioned what four more years of this man's influence would do to the South, to Louisiana, to our own dear city. And I said, John, since you know that in any case a worthy man will go to Congress, why do you not use the kind attention of your fellow citizens for a wider, broader purpose than simply to impress them with the importance of John Slidell's going to Congress? That is not important at all. New Orleans does not need John Slidell in Congress. New Orleans needs Andrew Jackson in the White House!

"Dear friends, do not ask me for what I would have stood in Washington. I will say no word of myself. From this day on, I shall devote all my time to speaking of the one really great issue. I beseech you to listen while I tell you why we must elect the magnificent Southerner Andrew Jackson President of the United States!"

The audience was electrified. The newspapermen were stunned. No one had ever heard of such selflessness in a political campaign. Naturally, it was expected that a word or two would be said for Jackson, but this young man had literally submerged his own interests. How deep and earnest his convictions must be. How noble his soul.

Jacques Toutant-Beauregard said, "John, you threw away your chances."

"Threw them away? Jacques, I offered them up to a cause more worthy."

"How can you so adore Jackson?"

"He is a man of fire and steel, Jacques. A man of determination."

"Yes. His determination to play king of Louisiana was so strong that he killed off five hundred Creoles."

"You put it badly, Jacques. The epidemic was the hand of Fate. In maintaining martial law, Jackson was only doing what he thought right for Louisiana. Luck ran against him, but give me a man who does what he thinks right for Louisiana. And give me a man who neither whines nor makes excuses. Never once did Jackson point out that he was not responsible for the wet, fever-ridden ground of this lovely parish."

"And that woman he calls his wife!"

"Dear Jacques, she is an abomination but you know and I know that to elect a candidate because his wife is respectable and ladylike would be rather foolish. Your vote should not be influenced by a candidate's taste in women."

"I have heard," said Jacques unexpectedly, "that Adams is anti-Catholic."

John responded with a shrug.

"It is true, John?"

"And if it is? That, too, should influence no man's vote. If you think he has been a fine President, you must vote for him. It may simply be gossip that he intends to declare the churches and convents as property under foreign control."

John made a dozen public speeches for Andrew Jackson, a hundred unscheduled ones in parlors and dining rooms. Of course, his opponent went to Congress, but the newspapers gave more admiring space to the loser of the contest.

Andrew Jackson, as a small token of his esteem, honored John Slidell with the position of United States District Attorney at New Orleans. In Washington, over countless drinks and cigars, it was noted that a clever young fellow down in Louisiana might prove very useful to the party for many a year to come.

The city lay smothered in a pall of acrid black smoke. Tar and pitch burned on every corner and filled the air with vile fumes. Asiatic cholera had joined with yellow fever to bring panic upon New Orleans. Corpses lay unburied at the cemetery gates and drays

143

dragged more and more dead down the muddy streets or dumped them secretly in the dark of night. Entire families lay unattended, dying behind ornate black ironwork balconies. Priests gave words of consolation to the grieving, then staggered away to fall lifeless on a staircase or in a courtyard. There were those in the city who did not doubt that it was the plan of the Almighty to erase from the face of the earth the population of New Orleans.

"All my life," said John Grymes, opening another bottle of champagne, "I have been a gambler. I have learned that one's luck is in or it is out. There is no defense against a feeble-minded jury, the wrong card or death from the plague. I shall not leave New Orleans."

"It was not my suggestion that you leave," John Slidell said. "I feel as you do. Death cannot be outwitted. I only wanted you to drive with me to look at the property on Bayou St. John. It is my hope that you will like it."

"Do you really wish," asked Grymes, pouring the champagne, "to celebrate my birthday so expensively?"

"Frankly, I was thinking of a few nice white handkerchiefs for your birthday. The property on Bayou St. John— Well, Grymes, to put it bluntly, do you not think too many merchants are getting into our clubs?"

"Perhaps the fever will remedy that situation," Grymes said brightly.

"What would you say to founding a club ourselves? Initiation ridiculously high. Dues astronomical. I would think membership limited to successful professional men and gentlemen of leisure."

"Splendid," said Grymes. "You do not suppose, do you, that anyone will think us undemocratic?"

"How could they possibly think such a thing? We will throw the club doors wide open to anyone at all who qualifies."

Mrs. Grymes, who had been sitting quietly in the small mauve-and-silver room, picked up her champagne glass and rose to her feet. "You are insufferable," she said. "Both of you. Here you sit planning an exclusive club while all over the city, people are dying."

Her husband said, "My dear, they are not dying for me."

"I can stand the company of such callous beasts no longer," she

144

said, extending her glass. "Pour me a little more champagne and I will leave."

"I think," John Slidell said when she had gone, "that you should tell her what truly great souls we are. I, personally, contributed five thousand dollars to the relief of the stricken poor and I know you did even better than that."

"Yes, I am one of the stricken rich. I gave ten thousand."

They laughed and poured more champagne and after a while, they drove out the shell road in John's carriage to look at a piece of land that could be bought at a reasonable price. And on that day when New Orleans recorded as dead one-sixth of the population, the Elkin Club was born.

Grymes and John celebrated the purchase of the property with a large and elegant dinner in the course of which they signed five charter members. Four others to whom they had intended to offer membership had died during the afternoon.

Grymes was startled at the news. "That knocks my theory into an Indian canoe," he said. "I will tell you confidentially that I believed the illness was a result of unclean living conditions."

John said, "Your theory may still have merit. All four of our sainted friends were frequenters of a certain house not noted for its trimness."

"Good God, I would have thought them more fastidious." Grymes shuddered. "I never have understood gentlemen going to such places. It is rather like renting one's clothes, don't you think? So common. Did you ever—"

"Yes, as a boy in New York I did. But I will tell you that as a boy in New York, I did many things I would not do now. Would you believe that in those days I was quite impossible?"

"Very easily, Slidell, very easily."

"Kind of you to take my word without hesitation, old friend."

Grymes laughed. "You were a boy who sought vulgar company because you thought it a smart and worldly thing to do. All boys think that. Now that you are a man, you reserve one pretty little kitten all for yourself. Is she a quadroon?"

John said, "If you were sober, you would not ask that question, Grymes."

145

"Like hell I wouldn't. There are no secrets between friends. You can ask me anything you like."

"I will remember that one day in court."

"All bets are off there, Mr. United States District Attorney. In court we only snarl at each other."

"You can stop snarling. I am going to resign. I weary myself to death over that picayune job they handed me. Jackson must have thought I was a starving young lawyer for pickpockets. They had better find me a brighter reward or I shall be extremely busy next time they need me."

Grymes said, "Don't be a fool. Let them use you and someday you will grow up to be a President-maker, too."

John studied his friend with interest. "Maybe. Would you like to be President?"

"I am not your man. I am too old, too smart and too tired. And remember, I was once seduced by the bloodstained gold of pirates."

"I will stump for you and prove that you gave the fee to the Ursuline Convent."

"Blockhead! You have lost me the Protestant vote."

"Not at all. I took pains to make it clear that you accepted the case only with the solemn understanding that Livingston would distribute his half among the Methodists, Baptists and Episcopals. By the way, he is going to be Secretary of State. Did you know that?"

Grymes nodded. "He deserves the position. He has written the best God-damned speeches for Jackson that—"

"What talk is this, Grymes? Presidents write their own speeches."

"To be sure. Shall we go home now? I am worried about you. You are beginning to look very fuzzy."

John took Grymes home, placing him in the loving hands of the valet, who never retired until he had seen Grymes safely to bed. John himself was virtually immune to the effects of alcohol. To-night he would work for an hour or more before sleeping and in the morning, providing he was not dead of the plague, he would be fresh and ready for a large breakfast and a busy day.

His personal mail lay on a silver card tray in the foyer. Three invitations, a few notes expressing pleasure in his most recent dinner party and a letter from his mother.

Dear Son:

It is a long time since you have written but Tom reports you to be in good health. He also mentioned that you are very busy so we accept that as an excuse for your silence. I assume you are still interested in news of your family and shall proceed as though you have indicated as much.

Your father and I are well and can find nothing to discuss with people our age for we remain unacquainted with lumbago, palpitation or loss of appetite. We hope to find a subject in common with our contemporaries when the misery of winter sets in. One little twinge of rheumatism would renew our popularity, I feel sure, and would relieve us of the boredom we suffer when forced to listen to the symptoms that enrich the lives of our friends.

Janie had her twelfth child last week and is wonderfully well. The family is now living over at the Navy Yard in Brooklyn, so we see them quite frequently. Cal was assigned a lovely house with three floors and encircling porches.

Julia, as one might expect, has become very fond of Mathilde Deslonde, finding her the most fascinating friend she ever had. I like Mathilde very much myself. She comes to us most Sundays and her study of English is really progressing miraculously. Madame Chégaray thinks the child extremely bright and of course her behavior is exemplary. No wonder! Good grief, son, do you know what your friends, the Creoles, do to their daughters to train them for high society? They force them to sit on chairs that have no backs—this for ladylike posture—and the girls are dragged from bed no matter how ill (unless there is a fever, Mathilde informs me) to make charming conversation at table.

Do tell Madame Deslonde, or perhaps the father (I do not know who is chief of the budget in a Creole household and this is a delicate matter in any case), that Mathilde has not enough dress-up frocks. From the talk of land, slaves and food, I gather they are frightfully rich. Are they stingy or is it part of their stern discipline that young ladies learn to live with only a few expensive things in the wardrobe? Julia would scream on Mathilde's clothes allowance and Janie would have died. I would not have Mathilde hurt for the world nor her family embarrassed, so be very smooth about this, if you bother at all.

Alexander is engaged to marry Miss Catherine Robinson. We have known the family for years and are delighted with the prospect of having Catherine for a daughter-in-law. All this merry business will take place in six months or so. In the meanwhile, Alexander is writing a book to be entitled *Popular Essays on Naval Subjects*. Is he not optimistic? Can naval subjects ever really be popular? He had better make a great deal of money. His future father-in-law is truly a Croesus. Alec is, at present, over in Brooklyn with Cal. Cal has consented to be

147

best man at the wedding if he has not been sent to sea by that time. Catherine is very amusing. She said, "Alec is more concerned about Cal's presence at the wedding than he is about mine."

At the Hones's house last week, we encountered Richard for the first time in the five years since Ellen's funeral. His meeting with us was very touching and no doubt slightly disconcerting to his second wife. He has been married to her almost four years. No children.

Now I do believe in return for this letter you should write to us. I do not regard myself as overly sentimental but the wistful look upon your father's face when your silence is prolonged is almost more than I can bear. Please write in time for his birthday.

Your fond mother,
Jane M. Slidell

John folded the letter and placed it among the papers that he would carry to his office in the morning. Tom might take it badly if the news was not shared with him.

As it turned out, Tom already knew of Alec's engagement.

"He wrote to me," Tom said.

"The hell he did! And not a word to me?" Then transferring his annoyance from one brother to the other, John demanded, "Why did you not tell me that Alec was engaged?"

"I hadn't the faintest notion that you would be interested. I told you when Janie's eleventh child was born and you only grunted, not even bothering to look up from two woolen swatches that your tailor had sent—"

"Oh, that reminds me. I have a fitting at three o'clock. Would you mind calling my attention to it?" And when Tom did not immediately reply, "Have I somehow managed to hurt your feelings again?"

Tom's mouth twisted grimly. "If so, let it not disturb you any more than usual. I was really pondering if this is the moment to call your attention to something other than your tailor's appointment. I wonder if it is the moment to tell you that I am not a faithful servant, a hunting dog or even a clerk—I am a lawyer."

"That you are, Tom," said John, smiling pleasantly. The nervous, restless fellow in the rather shiny black coat had this day reached the end of his endurance. It was there in the hardness of his eyes, in the deepening scowl, in the senseless drumming of his fingers upon the arm of his chair.

148

"I want desperately to work at my profession, John. I have a chance now to do some very interesting work in another office. It—"

"Another office? What other office?"

"You have never heard of it. It is very small, very new, but—"

Tom paused and drew a handkerchief from his pocket. John watched him narrowly as he wiped his eyes. Tears? This was incomprehensible. And upon Tom's forehead a gathering moisture. Good God, was the boy coming down with the plague? Surely a pallor had spread across his face.

"Tom, are you all right?"

Tom nodded. "I am all right. I am only— You would not understand. I have finally done it, John. I have summoned the courage to tell you that I am leaving you."

John's eyebrows rose. "You needed courage for this? God save you, boy, if ever you face a moment that places a genuine demand upon you."

"I told you that you would not understand. Please do not try." Tom's nervous fingers moved along the smooth glass sides of the inkwell as he leaned upon John's desk. "I am going to assist in legal research and the assembling of a very important piece of work. I am going to—"

"Yes?" John interrupted. "For whom are you going to do all this?"

"He is a very young lawyer. Very brilliant. Very—"

"Very brilliant, eh? Tell me all about him." John lay back in his chair, his long legs comfortably outstretched. By God, he had never realized how unstable Tom was. This was a boy—no, not a boy at all—a man of thirty-two so emotionally undisciplined that he could weep and pale like a woman. The thing to do was to maintain the conversation at matter-of-fact level till Tom had himself well in hand. "I should like to meet the young man. Who is he? What is his name?"

"Judah Benjamin."

"Oh? Is he a Jew?"

"He is, but do not be haughty about that. Father has never been certain that—"

"I was not being haughty. Jews are very interesting people. But

149

that is a foolish remark, is it not? I dare say that somewhere there is a dull Jew or two. What is this important piece of work Benjamin is doing?"

"He is writing a digest on decisions of the Louisiana Superior Courts and I could do the plodding for him, the gathering of material and the tedious chores of sorting and separating." Tom's wet eyes shone with excitement. "John, this boy is twenty-one years old and his knowledge of law is so massive, so profound, that one is spellbound when he speaks."

John stared at a pile of papers weighted down by a small gilded statue of Napoleon Bonaparte. So a twenty-one-year-old upstart was going to take conscientious, hard-working Tom from him, was he? Careful now, or he would take him and keep him forever.

"You make me eager indeed to meet Benjamin. For all that I appear to be very commercial in my approach to law, I am as idealistically drawn to it as any man who lives. Nothing is more thrilling to me than a legal point propounded by genius. Tell me, is the boy doing well?"

"Not yet. He has just passed his examinations and opened the office."

"He has, I trust, enough money to survive."

"He will manage."

John looked worried. "Nothing is going to interfere with this important digest of his, is it, Tom? Such a work is sadly needed. My God, how I would like to be part of such a monumental undertaking! How I would love— I wonder if Benjamin would consent to—but, no, of course he would not—though perhaps—" Tom was watching him warily. "I do not mean that I could actually contribute time to the work. You know that I am too busy for that but, oh, how I would like to feel myself even remotely connected with— Tom, I am going to risk being rejected. I am going to tell you what I had in mind. Would Benjamin accept you on leave of absence from this office? Would he accept your services as a gift from someone who sincerely wishes to see this work of his completed?"

Tom made no secret of his surprise. "You would pay me while I worked for Benjamin?"

"What is startling about that? I really am interested in law, you

150

know. Young fellows lose sight of the fact that we older boys are lawyers because from the very beginning we also loved law. God, Tom, it is not necessary or even kind for you to cut me out of your life just because you want to do a serious job elsewhere. Let me have a small share in your excitement."

Tom stood up, looking slightly bewildered. How badly he wore his clothes, the collar not firmly laid to the back of his neck, the garment itself so carelessly flung on the scrawny frame that it hung unevenly.

"I will talk to Benjamin," he said. "Frankly, a living wage for me has been a problem. If we could look upon this as a manifestation of your deep interest in the digest—"

"Well, what in hell do you think it is? I do not even know the boy. Why should I do him a personal favor?"

Tom said, "I have another thought but I will not speak it. Being Tom Slidell has done miserable things to me."

"In what way?"

"In what way! Good God, John, how would you like to be in the middle between a brother who is a famous writer and a brother who is a famous lawyer?"

John laughed and came from behind the desk to pull Tom into a warm and bearlike embrace. "God bless you, you fool, you have more brains than either of us. Now, go work like a son of a bitch for Benjamin and do not bother me unless I can be of some help."

Tom stood in the doorway for a long moment, his eyes fixed searchingly upon his brother's face. The worst thing about being clever, he thought, was the tendency to be oversuspicious. It was no comfort to reflect that that was also the worst thing about being stupid.

Even Philip Hone, who had once been mayor of New York—and believed in the future of the city as much as anyone—was aghast at the idea of people buying property so far from what must always be the heart of the metropolis. The Robert Rays had built a palatial residence at the corner of Twenty-eighth Street and Ninth Avenue. One might say that they had moved out of New York. And now John and Jane Slidell had actually gone to live on Thirty-second

151

Street. It was, of course, a beautiful section, with soft, silver-green maples and stately gardens. But such an inconvenient place to live, so far from all old, close friends.

The Honorable Mr. Hone, calling on the widow of Alexander Hamilton, had found her chuckling over a note from Jane Slidell.

"I am too old to make a journey of such distance," she said, "but Jane has been kind enough to invite me to see her new house. She is most amusing, Mr. Hone. You must listen. 'Our house is Number Forty and our lawn has an address, too. It is Thirty-four, Thirty-six and Thirty-eight. Did you ever hear of such nonsense? It is John Slidell's lawn and that is what any sensible person would call it but the city has gone slightly lunatic on orderliness. I just thought I would tell you, in case you ever wish to write a letter to our lawn.' " The widow laughed again and added, "You must visit them, Mr. Hone, and tell me what manner of house is being built away out there."

It was a small house that the Slidells had built. Only five bedrooms and space for no more than three servants. The parlor, dining room and kitchen were half the size of those in the old house. Now that John had retired, there would be less entertaining. Alexander and his Catherine had a house in the Brooklyn Navy Yard and Julia most certainly would soon marry if the soft glances she and naval lieutenant Raymond Rogers exchanged had any meaning at all.

It was a delightful house, Jane thought, for two elderly people very much in love. Here was serenity, compact and civilized. The veranda for a summer evening, and for a winter night, the library, with its cozy fire and all of John's favorite books. It was a good-natured house, flooded with sunshine and offering dozens of little unexpected places for well-loved tables and small cushioned chairs. For the first week she lived there, Jane found herself wandering, like a child in a toy shop, from one bright corner to the next. The multihued fanlight cast such a heavenly glow upon the cream-colored bishop's clock in the foyer. The magnificent fourteenth-century chart of seas known to man—a gift from young John on his father's birthday—melted mellowly into the background of the library. The portrait of little Caroline Slidell Perry in a white dress, her eyes brimming with suppressed laughter, gave the parlor a lighthearted touch. In due course, the bedroom would have small climbing roses peering through its windows, admiring the furniture shipped from France by Alec on his last voyage. Jane loved the house, every inch of it. And she had not the slightest warning that within six months, she would live in it alone.

Standing between Commander Alexander Slidell MacKenzie and Captain Matthew Calbraith Perry at vault ninety-five, she was very still. Very still and very polite to these two strangers who had been so kind. Behind her, their wives and a young girl named Julia were sobbing hysterically. She wanted to be away from all this dismal ceremony. She wanted to get home to her cheerful house, throw herself in John's arms and say, "Oh, it was perfectly awful but of course I had to go. It was, after all, the funeral of—of—" And for a moment she pretended that she could not remember whose funeral it was. And she pretended that he was waiting for her in the foyer by the bishop's clock and that he would grin at her childish horror of attending funerals.

The kindly naval men somehow let her know when it was time to leave. They led her away and she was surprised to see that hundreds of people had gathered here at the church. Many of them came to her saying, "Jane dear, if there is anything—" and "Please, Mrs. Slidell, call on us if—" She did not answer. She could not bring herself to talk to them. She was angry at them for being alive.

She was driven home and the house was suddenly filled with Perrys and Robinsons and MacKenzies and other strangers who thought their lives had been touched by sorrow. How little they knew of sorrow, these foolishly sad-faced people who stood with their loves beside them.

"He was the best father anybody ever had," Janie wept.

Jane studied her with interest. Why, yes, of course. He had had another entity. He had been a father. He had been important to this stylish young matron and to the dreamy-eyed man who was a commander in the Navy and to the weeping girl who looked so odd in black. With them he had lived in a world apart from the one she and he had shared. To them he had been a solid, unexciting fixture of life, fondly regarded, reasonably respected—a father. They had never been acquainted with the man who had been buried today. Or

153

would they, remembering his skill with a kite or his coldness when disobeyed, say that it was she who had never known him?

"Catherine and I will stay here tonight," Alec said. "Cal and Janie, too, if you want them. They are going to ask you to live with them but I think you had better decide on coming to Catherine and me."

Later, there were letters from New Orleans. The invitations were characteristic. From Tom:

I have three small rooms, not very clean, not very comfortable. I have the same sense of the ridiculous that you have. I am not going to ask, "Why do you not come live with me?" However, this I will say: You could like New Orleans. You have the means to purchase a type of elegant living unknown in the North. The Navy makes Alexander an uncertain factor in your life. Moreover, he has Catherine now. If you feel the need of attention from a bachelor son who would dash in and out and do his best to be agreeable and helpful, do consider New Orleans.

And from John:

You and I need homes of our own, I do believe, and I could find you a very nice one. Do not worry about breaking ties with old friends. I can supply you with dozens of the most charming new friends you can imagine. I think life in New Orleans could be for you a rather enchanting proposition.

Jane smiled at both letters. She did not need Tom dashing in and out. And life would never again be an enchanting proposition.

She raised her eyes from the letters and said to Julia, "We are moving to New Orleans."

There was a cruel, twisted kind of comfort in seeing the stricken look on Julia's face. For a moment she had company, someone else understood pain. Julia was very young and Raymond Rogers was replaceable, but this Julia did not know. She could not guess that till a man had fathered your children, scolded you for your nonsense and held you close in time of trouble, that any one of them was as good as another. And so Julia suffered at the thought of losing the slim, shy lieutenant and her mother watched her suffering. But when the tears came, the game was over.

154

"No, Julia, do not cry. I was wicked. We will stay here. We will stay."

Julia said, "I think *you* should go. I could live with Alec or Janie. Someday you will be here all alone."

Did the child think she was not alone now?

Edward Livingston, before assuming his duties as United States Minister to France, intended to visit England, so he had chosen to sail on the *British Queen.*

"You need not tell anyone but I am not feeling my very best. I am saying good-by to New York and London now—just in case."

Alexander, sitting beside him in the closed carriage, was startled. "But you look very fit, sir."

"I do not feel so, Alec, and I am older than your father was when suddenly one day—" His voice trailed off and he gazed thoughtfully out the carriage window at a group of French and American dignitaries who had come to see him off. "I did not want to ride with any of them," he said. "These last few minutes on American soil I wished to spend with someone who had been a part of my personal life. I always loved your family, Alec."

"My family has always loved you, sir. I am greatly concerned for your health. Could you not have declined this appointment?"

"No. I will give the President whatever is left of me. And now let us speak no more of that. Soon I will have to go to my stateroom and listen to flowery compliments and of course offer a few myself. Tell me about the new book."

Alec accepted the change of subject, recognizing that Edward regretted the weakness that had led him to mention his failing health. "It is called *The American in England*. I wish it had been printed in time for your departure. I will send you a copy."

"Do, I beg of you. What has become of your *John Paul Jones?* It was years ago that I first heard—"

Alexander said, "It is not an easy book to write." His eyes clouded and Edward observed that it was no easier to discuss. It occurred to him that this red-haired Slidell brother might be a more complicated fellow than he had thought. Curious how Alexander never seemed to take pleasure from the large sales his books enjoyed. Neither was he all Navy man in the way that Cal was. In looking at him now, Edward saw clearly for the first time that Alexander was not at peace with himself.

"Are you happy when you are at work on a book, Alec?"

Alec turned his eyes to the huge two-hundred-and-seventy-five-foot liner in her berth at the foot of Clinton Street. In a shouting, bustling whirl of activity, she was readying for her voyage. Live cows and poultry were being hurried aboard, boxes and barrels of stores, great lumps of ice, mountains of coal sinking into the crater of the lower hold.

"I write because I must," he answered.

"Then you are happier at sea?"

Alexander smiled palely. "You are pinning me down to the admission that I am a thoroughly ungrateful wretch. I am not satisfied with things as they turned out. You see, I wanted to make an adequate showing with my books and a lusty success of my naval career. My guardian angel reversed my orders."

"But your naval career is flourishing magnificently. It is—"

"It is standard for any intelligent, conscientious officer," Alexander said.

"And you wish to distinguish yourself?"

"Yes. Is that childish?"

"If so, then few of us have mature minds, Alec." He studied the lean, wind-burned face with its troubled expression. "Do you feel yourself living in the shadow of John?" he asked anxiously.

Alec laughed. "Does my brother cast a shadow, sir?"

"Yes, he does," said Edward swiftly and a little sharply. "Lawyers and politicians sometimes grow as tall as Navy men, my boy."

"I did not mean to belittle your profession, sir. It is only that, to my mind, John is not one of your giants."

"Perhaps you have been too occupied to measure him lately. He is a very able lawyer and the political leader of New Orleans. With a little more age on him, he will be the biggest man in Louisiana."

"He will enjoy that," Alec said.

"Yes," Edward agreed. "Few men would not. I am very glad that you do not envy John but I am sorry there is not a closer tie between you. I am very fond of John. I wish I could have seen him again before I—before I went to France." He extended his hand. "Send me that new book of yours."

The coachman opened the door and Alexander watched as Edward was immediately surrounded and hurried away. His two secretaries, carrying leather cases too precious to be heaped with the other luggage, followed him to the *British Queen*. Alexander wondered about the young men. Was the position of secretary to the United States Minister to France a piece of good fortune beyond a wildest dream? Or did these young men regard with sullenness the fate that had not made them naval officers or well-known authors?

Alexander shook his head. He did not know very much about happiness. Was it like a good cake, the result of having mixed and baked all the right ingredients? Or was it instead the prize awarded for the mixing and baking? Difficult to tell. He thought of Catherine. Certainly she should represent happiness to any man. At least to any sensible man. Did she know, did she feel how deeply he loved her, how anxiously he strained to give her the lighthearted companionship her joyous spirit needed? It was not in him to give. He had not the booming laughter of Cal Perry nor Cal's wonderful talent for loving life and meeting all that it offered with calm faith and clear vision. He, himself, was a restless brooding man, dissatisfied, worrisome. Why? Good God, poor Catherine.

He signaled the coachman that he was ready to leave the dock. He would return the carriage to his mother's house and have tea with her. Perhaps he would prepare her somewhat for the day when there would be bad news of Edward Livingston.

He looked back once more at the *British Queen*. What a monster she was. He judged her to outweigh two thousand tons. Steamships. They had no grace or romance but he was not one who thought them a dangerous novelty doomed to failure. He knew that they would eventually drive the beautiful sailing ships right out of existence.

"And steam will drive me right out of the Navy," he thought. But he knew that was not true. He could not live without the Navy. Into Alexander's mind drifted a memory from the past. He saw himself as a boy in the old house, lying on the floor in that room that he had shared with Tom. Tom had been playing chess with Charlie Wilkes and Alec remembered how he had thought that day of giving up all idea of the Navy, of concentrating on a literary career. How would it have been with him had he done so? "You would have regretted it. That is how it would have been. Well, you are in the Navy so there is nothing to regret. For the love of God, man, you weary me with your cold and joyless acceptance of all you have in life. Is it that you are truly an ingrate or is it"—Alec shivered suddenly—"or is it that you have feared to count your blessings, knowing full well that what lies ahead will make them all add up to nothing?"

It was the custom for gentlemen who had remained all night to breakfast together at noon. John sat with six other members in a shady corner of the dining room at the Elkin Club. He ate his fricasseed tripe à la Bertrand and took no part in the conversation, which mostly concerned last night's whist losses. He had no interest in hands that had already been played. His mind was on something his mother had written: "Philip Hone says Jackson is not a second Washington but that Washington was only a first Jackson. Of course, Mr. Hone said it sarcastically—"

Of course Mr. Hone said it sarcastically but could it be adapted to use, made to sound a warm, genuine appraisal of Jackson by his admirer, John Slidell? It was really a very good line. John became aware that a question had been directed toward him. The topic was evidently no longer cards. He had been asked what he thought of property on Esplanade.

"I think very highly of it. Are you buying some?"

"Perhaps. There is quite a large piece for sale."

John made a few routine inquiries for the sake of politeness and was rewarded with a full description of the property and its exact location. Though no names were mentioned, John knew to whom it belonged. It belonged to André Deslonde. So circumstances still had not improved. Last year, André had sold his town house on St. Anne Street, saying that he no longer enjoyed spending time in New Orleans.

It was a long while since fortune had favored André. Or perhaps he was a very poor businessman. John had at times suspected this to be the case. He ordered a pot of fresh coffee and again removed himself from the conversation. But now he thought no more of Philip Hone's remark and how it could be pirated. He thought of André Deslonde.

158

It was a Sunday afternoon in late summer and it was a pleasant drive out to the Deslonde plantation. Along the road, one listened to the sweet-throated songbirds and allowed the heavenly blaze of wild mallow to dazzle one's eyes and dizzy one's senses. John felt within himself a stirring of excitement. Louisiana was beautiful and generous. She had withheld only one important gift. Only one, and he had not grown impatient. He had waited.

"I would like to speak to you in private," he said to André when they met. "The gallery, I fear, is not quite the correct setting for us today."

André, smiling but puzzled, led the way to his office, a large, airy room with a stone floor and a doorway giving direct access to the working land behind the bright gardens.

"A most unattractive place to receive you, John. It was intended for men with mud on their boots." He sat down behind his desk and faced John with the same smiling puzzlement. "What is it, my friend?"

John said, "No amenities? No polite circumlocutions? Well, you are quite within your rights. I set the tone for a business meeting, did I not? To business, then. André, I would like to buy the property on Esplanade."

André's smile vanished. "Is it general talk that it is for sale?"

"Not at all. I heard of it in a curious way. Some time I will give you the details. It is my thought that I would like to own the property. Will you sell it to me?"

"There is no reason why I should not. What difference does it make to whom I sell it?"

John said, "It makes this difference, André: If I buy it, I shall hold it in trust for you. You are my friend and at any time you wish the property back, it is yours at the price I paid for it."

"In other words, you propose to lend me money."

"That does not tell the whole story. I propose to lend you money, yes. Between us there should be no absurdity such as your signing the property over to me but you are a proud man and so—"

"And so your friendly impulse is reduced to a thing of signatures and clauses, is it not? Please believe I appreciate your kindness, John, but if you wish to buy the property, then buy it without thought of returning it to me. I see no prospect of ever—"

"Are things so bad for you?"

"Things are so bad for me."

"I want to help."

André reached across the desk and touched John's hand affectionately. "Do not worry. With the sale of the property I shall manage. If you had a plantation, I would ask you to take twenty or so field hands to feed and clothe. By God, I cannot sell people. Who knows how they would be treated? I have asked Jacques. He cannot take them. I have asked—"

John said, "Strange that you should mention it, since I am now in the market for a plantation."

"You are?"

"I would take a few inside servants, too, if you care to lend them. I am also buying a bigger town house."

"How well things go for you. I am delighted but of course not surprised."

"You always thought me promising. I remember that you once dropped the flattering hint that you would not protest my becoming the husband of your wife's cousin. Do you remember?"

A crumpled piece of paper on the stone floor engaged André's interest. He stooped to pick it up and returned to his position with a flushed face.

"It was kind of you, André, I have never forgotten. There would have been quite a dowry, too. By the way, did you not once tell me that your town house was to be Mathilde's dowry and the Esplanade property Henriette's?"

"I may have said that," André admitted, turning his eyes away.

"Well, that makes for domestic complications, does it not? Are either of the girls betrothed?"

"Oh, no. They are too young."

"Too young? Why, Mathilde is the same age as my sister Julia, who was married a few weeks ago." He paused, permitting a dawning wonderment to appear in his eyes. "Dear, good friend André, surely you do not mean to say that your lovely daughters are being passed over for lesser girls simply because—"

André shrugged. "I realize that to you our customs must seem cruel and senseless. They are not. They have deep meaning. Good blood and good land are the backbone of our marriages. I de-

160

manded it myself so I cannot now despise a man who expects my daughter to bring—"

"Would you despise a man who expected her to bring only herself?" John asked quietly.

"I would not despise him but among Creoles—"

"Her husband *must* be a Creole, André?"

"Oh, I suppose it is not imperative. However, it is only natural for her mother and me to think no other union suitable. Still, if upon the scene there stepped a—"

"What qualifications would he need?"

"The usual. Fine family and proper religious affiliations."

"A great deal of money and considerable prestige are desirable factors, too, André, are they not?"

"I do not ignore them but they could never substitute for—"

"Could they not?"

"No. And of course I value Mathilde's happiness. I want her to love the man she marries."

John said, "Now you are growing fanciful. I have been in Louisiana more than fifteen years and have yet to hear of a Creole girl being consulted on the subject of love. Good blood. Good land. You said it yourself. That is what your marriages are made of and, by God, they are fine marriages. If a man and woman are kind to each other, then love comes." John caught André's eye and leaned toward him across the desk. "And, André, I am prepared to be very kind to Mathilde."

André stared dully at John for a long moment. "You are prepared to be— Oh, no, you cannot mean it. You are my age."

"I am three months older, André. Next objection."

André shook his head in unhappy bewilderment. "John, it is an impossible idea."

"No, it is not impossible at all. It is only new to you. That is all. As it loses its novelty, it will become quite easy to discuss. True, I am not a Creole and I am not a Catholic but since I am a sensible man, I would gladly permit my children to be raised in the ways that seemed good to their mother."

André sighed sadly. "I do not know what to say to you. I do not know what to think."

"You could think what I have to offer your daughter. I have told

161

you that I intend to buy a plantation and a larger town house. Also, André, as time passes, I will be increasingly prominent in politics. I will go to Congress and the Senate. Mathilde will be a proud wife and I shall fondly cherish her."

André fixed his gaze on the stone floor. He said, "We have lived in certain ways here. We have set certain standards. For generations, families have known each other and—"

"And still subordinate this ancient friendship to the importance of a dowry." John jumped to his feet. "I will tell you this, my friend: I do not value money that highly but I will show you how highly I value the happiness of yourself and Mathilde. If she is sighing over some Creole boy who has turned from her because she no longer has the house on St. Anne Street to bring to the marriage, you may promise him that it will be delivered as a wedding present."

André said, "I have not challenged your financial standing, John." He sighed again. "You interrupted me a moment ago when I was explaining that certain standards have been set. Family means much to us. We seldom have to ask, 'Who were your father's people?' for our grandfathers were boys together." He sat quietly for a time and then he asked, "John, who *were* your father's people?"

"Oh, for the love of God, André, what a question! If we were not such friends, I would become annoyed."

"I am confused and incapable of clear thought. I would like to discuss with my wife this very serious matter—"

"Why, of course you must discuss it with her and if she is not opposed to a marriage between myself and Mathilde, then there is something else you must do. You must discuss it with Mathilde. If she finds me unattractive and weeps at the thought of marrying me, please make no effort to change her mind. She must be a contented bride."

Tears sprang suddenly to André's eyes. "John, that is a very nice thing you have said. No matter how things are concluded, I will always remember that you considered Mathilde's feelings."

Without lingering on the Deslonde gallery for coffee, John drove back to the Elkin Club. It would be days before he heard from André. By this time Madame Deslonde would already have

162

said, "He did say that the children could be raised in the Church? And he did say he was buying plantation land? André, this is magnificent, is it not?"

Still, they might give him no reply for at least two weeks. A Creole bride. A Deslonde. A wife who had been trained to entertain in the grand manner. A woman to give the blood of French nobles to his children. He tried to remember what the girl, Mathilde, was like. He had never particularly noticed her. She had been André's daughter, Julia's friend, a quiet, pretty little thing. Hair rather a light shade of brown. Eyes? Dark, no doubt. He recalled that she, too, spoke Spanish. They could bore each other in three languages. Most couples had only one at their disposal.

This would be a good marriage, he determined. God knows he had had enough of affairs, enough of playing at love. He would be faithful to Mathilde. He would be kind. He would buy her houses and dresses and jewels. She would bring her Creole elegance to his entertaining. She would bear his children. She would be Madame Slidell, living proof of his gentility. A Creole wife.

In ten days' time, he heard from André. A courteous little note. Please spend next weekend with us.

It was the first time John and Mathilde had ever really looked at each other. She was taller than he had thought and prettier. Her eyes were a *café au lait* color and there was no silliness about her. Gravely and graciously, her manner acknowledged the occasion for what it was—the making of a lifelong decision.

They were married in November. The Reverend Abbé Mina performed the ceremony at the Deslonde plantation house. The reception which followed was, Madame Deslonde said, very simple. It could not be that. The Creole flair for arranging flowers, for preparing food, for wearing clothes with the grace of royalty placed upon the smallest gathering the touch of dramatic splendor. Still, had he been a Catholic . . .

"I am sorry," he whispered to his bride, "that you have been robbed of a wedding in St. Louis Cathedral. You would have had the Swiss Guards and an impressive procession. But I will tell you the kind of man I am—"

Mathilde smiled. "Let me find out for myself," she said.

. . . .

163

Jane, fanning herself languidly, listened without the slightest pleasure to the music that filled the ballroom. It was a distinguished orchestra the Robinsons had hired for the evening but she resented having been settled against a wall of foliage and forgotten. Her host had led her there, remarking that he wanted her to have a comfortable location from which to view the festivities. Jane's lips twisted in wry amusement. She had been acquainted with Mr. Robinson for many years and knew him to be five years older than herself. His attitude toward her had suggested that she was a contemporary of his grandmother's. He, like a happy peasant, was now leaping about, dancing the polka with a red-cheeked young lady. Jane bore him no malice for his choice in partners. The young made captivating companions. Undoubtedly, Mr. Robinson was as tired as she of old people. But she disliked the way he had deposited her here and gone smugly about enjoying himself, satisfied that he had prettily discharged his duty to an elderly guest.

What a bore it was to be elderly. Her health was perfect and her interest in gossip, clothes and world affairs undiminished. Neither her hearing nor her vision had failed and her little feet still carried her as speedily and reliably as ever. Rather sulkily, she stared out at the dancers, her black lace fan suddenly accelerating its tempo. It had occurred to her that the Robinsons probably thought she was enjoying herself tremendously, that it was quite a privilege for an old lady to be here midst all the glitter and gaiety. Damn the Robinsons, anyhow. She was not enjoying herself tremendously. Oh, it was agreeable to be invited to a ball, but no one seemed to understand the manner in which it was agreeable. Everyone who had spoken to her this evening had said, "How wonderful for you! So much of your family is present tonight."

Well, yes, that was nice, she supposed. However, the really exciting thing about a ball was the gown one wore, the gowns the other women wore and the reaffirmation that one's waist was still the tiniest, that one's skin was still white enough to do honor to a black lace extravagance imported from Paris.

The music was now in waltz time. She felt herself becoming hypnotized by the swirling circles of color and motion. Lovely and so much more suitable than the polka to a ballroom decked in golden leaves and great cascades of hothouse roses. A pity about

164

the lighting, she thought. Only candles could create an atmosphere of true elegance. The Robinsons, by installing shell reflectors on their chandeliers, had softened the innate vulgarity of gaslight, still nothing did as much for a ballroom as a few hundred slim pink candles. Slim pink candles. How exquisite they were. She thought of the first time she had ever seen them. "I have brought you, Miss MacKenzie, something that might strike your fancy—"

She became aware that someone stood at her side. She turned and saw a very young man gazing at her, respectfully awaiting her attention.

"Madame, is the chair beside you occupied?"

"It is not. Please use it, if you wish."

"Thank you for your kind permission. May I introduce myself? My name is August Belmont."

She inclined her head politely. "I am Mrs. John Slidell, Senior."

"An honor, madame." He bowed and sat down.

He spoke with a European accent which she could not place nor could she imagine from which circle of the many Robinson contacts he had come. He was attractive and distinguished looking, in the way American men never were till middle age had come upon them. A dark young man with intelligent eyes that looked capable of both easy laughter and fierce storm.

She said, "You have tired of dancing?"

"No. I have but arrived. My hostess very kindly offered to present me to some young ladies but she seemed vastly relieved when I asked permission to just watch for a time. She had just received the shocking news that the Spanish Consul does not care for Spanish wine."

"You are a stranger here, Mr. Belmont?"

"Completely. I have been two years in the United States but most of my time has been spent in Philadelphia. My company sent me on an errand to your country. I fell in love with it and informed them that it was my desire to remain—but in New York."

"Where are you from originally?"

"Alzey in Hesse. That is Germany, madame."

"Yes." She looked at him thoughtfully. "Why do people always expect Germans to be blue-eyed blonds?"

"I do not know. Do you expect that?"

165

"I suppose I must, for I was surprised to hear you are German."

"My father told me that long ago the family was Navarese, that we are descendants of Don Luis de Belmonte, who fought against the Mohammedans in the battle of Las Navas de Tolosa, July sixteenth, twelve twelve, a date which of course is familiar to all New Yorkers." He grinned suddenly and unexpectedly. "Is this not a charming evening? What is the reason for the ball?"

"Mrs. Robinson's passion for entertaining."

"Oh. And Mr. Robinson—does he approve of all this?"

"Of course. Do you not observe the enthusiasm with which he is punishing his old heart and his young partner?"

"Which is he? The gentleman in white satin waistcoat?"

"Yes. You are not acquainted with him?"

"No. You see, the situation is this: Poor August Belmont, the little foreign fellow, has met no important New Yorkers, so the next time you entertain, do send him an invitation. Such is the gist of what my company wrote to Mr. Robinson."

Jane said, "Your company seems uncommonly anxious to make you happy."

"Yes. They are very nice people."

"Do these nice people have a name?"

"Rothschild. You have perhaps heard of the House of Rothschild?"

"Oh, yes. That is your company?"

"It is, madame. I am learning how to be an international banker."

"I have an idea the lessons are going splendidly."

"My company and I are pleased with each other." He tilted his head to one side and gazed at her earnestly. "You are, I take it, one of the important New Yorkers it is my delightful duty to meet."

"No. I am an old widow and nothing in the world, I assure you, is less important."

"You would not be here unless you were—"

"Yes, I would. I have a son who is married to the Robinsons' daughter Catherine. They had to invite me."

"But the Robinsons' daughter Catherine could not have married your son unless the Robinsons thought him and his family extremely desirable. Is your son here? Be so kind as to indicate to me which gentleman he is."

Jane looked back at the dancers. "The man with reddish hair in naval uniform whirling with the girl in white is my son Alexander."

"And is the girl in white the Robinsons' daughter Catherine?"

"No, she is the Wadsworths' daughter Elizabeth."

He shrugged. "I am not now interested in Wadsworths. Tell me only about Slidells. Your son is very handsome. Is the other man in naval uniform also your son?"

"No, but he is my son-in-law. That is Commodore Matthew Calbraith Perry. His brother was the great naval hero Oliver Hazard Perry, but I dare say his fame did not extend to Alzey in Hesse. This commodore has just returned from consultations with the French and British navies on the subject of steam vessels for use in—"

August Belmont laughed. "Must I tell my company I learned tonight the efficacy of steam vessels? Madame, this Perry must be married to a Slidell. Tell me of her."

Jane gazed in surprise at the young man. Such impertinence. He had interrupted her and he had dared to state what lines he wished the conversation to follow. How satisfying it was to meet someone who did not know she was to be revered and respected like any other fine antique. Why, one might actually be able to *talk* to this young man.

She said, "He—this Perry—is married to my daughter Janie."

"Where is she?"

"She is wearing the Nile-green velvet. You see her? She is dancing with the small man who has a white goatee."

"He is from the Italian consulate. Your daughter is very appealing. So fresh looking, so slender."

"She has had twelve children."

"What!" He turned and looked appraisingly at Jane. "Of course, her slimness is an inherited charm."

"What a nice young man you are. Are you still interested in having Slidells pointed out to you?"

"Very."

"Well, you are in luck, for we just happen to have with us to-

167

night the prize specimens of the collection. Do you see the young lady with the incredibly wide diamond collar? That is Mrs. John Slidell, Junior."

"But she is a young queen, madame."

"Indeed." Jane's eyes lingered on the fabulous ball gown Mathilde was wearing. How many days had it taken how many women to cover that voluminous skirt with its pattern of tiny pearls? It seemed only yesterday that the child had stood in need of a nice dressy muslin. "She is a Louisianan."

"That is special, madame?"

"Yes. She is a Creole. Do you know what that is?" He shook his head and Jane raised her fan to whisper behind it. "Creoles are Louisiana-born descendants of French and/or Spanish blood. They are here because their illustrious progenitors were tough enough to survive plagues, snakes, mud, insects, crocodiles, pirates and Indians. In Louisiana, if your ancestors endured all and faltered not, you are automatically an aristocrat."

August Belmont's eyes filled with laughter. "Why, you are very naughty to say that."

"I am. Truthfully, the Deslondes have honest claim to aristocracy but I am at the age where nothing has a sweet taste upon my tongue save bitterness."

"Really?" he asked with interest. "Does it get that way in time?" He arranged himself more comfortably in his chair as though he had just decided to remain. "A fascinating notion, but you do not look bitter. You are very sweet to the eye. That may be because you are so beautifully fitted into that magnificent black lace gown. I am terribly aware of clothes. A shallow person, I. Your gloves are remarkable, madame. Did you know that?"

She nodded happily. "Same glovemaker for forty years."

"Yes, one would not part from him. He is an artist. The fit at the upper arm is as perfect as at the small finger. Did you know that few glovemakers do well on the small finger? It is a challenge they rarely meet with courage."

"I have seen examples of their cowardice," she said. She raised her fan again and added, "Some of my friends have glovemakers who can acceptably create a thumb but when it comes to the small finger . . . A scandal, sir, that these ladies appear in public."

He sighed. "There is chaos everywhere."

They looked at each other and roared with laughter.

"You may go now," she said when she had patted her eyes with a tiny lace handkerchief. "You have made of my evening something memorable. It is long since I have laughed. Find a pretty girl, Mr. Belmont, and dance."

"Madame, I am being dismissed? For what reason? Permit me to stay, I beg of you." He leaned toward her eagerly. "Do you realize you have not revealed to me which gentleman is John Slidell, Junior?"

"That is so. Let me see . . . He is not dancing. Oh, there he is. Look in the far corner near the entrance. Do you see a tall gentleman surrounded by other gentlemen? That is John, Junior."

August Belmont regarded the group with knowing eyes. "They are talking politics, madame."

"How did you guess?"

"There are two subjects that gentlemen discuss with such animation. Your son is a politician?"

"Yes, a lawyer of some note with high political aspirations. His mentor was the recently deceased United States Minister to France, Edward Livingston."

"Ah, yes, a vastly respected statesman," he said absently. "How I adore the ruffles on your son's shirt. They are exquisite beyond words. Truly a laundress's nightmare. And the cut of his trousers, madame! His barber is no blunderer, either. Such people, the Slidells, all beautiful, slim bodies and gold-trimmed uniforms and diamond-collared necks and wonderful ruffles. I am in awe of each and every one of you. How did you all become so extraordinary?"

"We married well," Jane said demurely.

"Very clever of you." The dark glance studied her approvingly. "When I thank my company for wangling this invitation for me, I shall tell them about you. I shall say I met the most entrancing lady with curly hair and bright eyes."

Jane said, "I am popeyed." And it pleased her to say it, for it reminded her of long ago and another young man. August Belmont looked away from her, sensing that it was not to him she had spoken. She was startled at this evidence of his deep perceptiveness.

"You are an exceptional person, Mr. Belmont," she said. "How old are you?"

"A few months from twenty-five. You, too, are exceptional, Mrs. Slidell, Senior. How old are you?"

Oh, his darling impertinence.

"A few months from sixty-five," she said.

He rose and held out his hand to her. "In that case, let us dance."

And so Jane danced that night. She danced with August Belmont and her children looked, then looked again, but she did not appear to notice them. Within her she was filled with silent laughter, for her partner was the youngest man at the ball and certainly one of the most attractive.

"Have you other daughters, madame?" he whispered as they waltzed past the Nile-green velvet that represented the wife of Commodore Perry.

"A young one who is also married to the Navy."

"Shame on you for not saving her for me. Now we are lost. There can be nothing but good-by."

"Perhaps our paths will cross again sometime."

"It will not be the same. You will be laughing with some other man and I will have only my memories. I will never forget you."

"Nor I you, August Belmont. If ever you are in desperate need, do not hesitate. Let me know and I will send my glovemaker's address."

"You would do that for me?"

"If your need proved great enough."

"Oh, you are wonderful."

"I am plain but sincere. By the way, would you care to meet John Slidell, Junior?"

"In some other ballroom, some other night."

"No. The Creole branch of the family is in New York but briefly. They came North so my son could confer with certain gentlemen in Washington. Then he will return to Louisiana and the bayou mists will conceal him from the outside world. This is your chance to find out who irons his shirts."

"And cuts his trousers."

"And his hair."

August Belmont said, "When the dance ends, we will have some

170

refreshments, and then I should love being presented to your family. Would you be so kind?"

"It would be my pleasure and there are also many others here whom you should meet."

"When I have met them, may we dance again?"

She looked up at him. "August Belmont, what is wrong with you? The room is filled with beautiful young women."

He smiled. "What is unusual about beautiful young women? I have seen hundreds of them."

She was willing to believe that he had. A curious young man. An unforgettable young man. August Belmont.

"Have you other sons, madame?"

"I have Thomas."

"Thomas? Tell me of him."

"He is Chief Justice of the Louisiana Supreme Court."

August Belmont blinked his eyes. "They are all so thunderous, your children."

"Well, my husband wanted a big family."

The music stopped. He led her from the floor and they drank champagne at a prominently placed table for two.

"Tell me," he said, "what was their father like?"

"Their father? You saw the very stunning Alexander? You saw my Creole son, John? You have heard of the eminent Thomas? Sir, they are all very dull Slidells compared to their father."

He nodded his satisfaction. "Of that I was sure, madame."

They spoke of many things. August's accent. A mélange, he explained, for his father had taught him five languages before he was twelve years old.

They spoke of the manner in which John and Mathilde lived in Louisiana. The plantation house, Belle-Point, with its many slaves. The town house on Royal Street with its staff of excellent servants. Well, yes, of course they were slaves, too, but when they worked indoors, it was the custom to refer to them as servants.

August Belmont asked shrewdly, "Is that because indoors they can hear what they are called?"

She said, "I have a feeling you do not approve of slavery."

"Madame, until I am an American, I am not entitled to an opinion on that subject."

The homes of Commodore Perry were of interest, too. One in the Brooklyn Navy Yard. One in New York City and the heavenly hundred acres near Tarrytown which was called Moorings. It adjoined Washington Irving's estate. Alexander had a home there, also. Washington Irving was an intimate friend, had, in fact, done a foreword to one of Alexander's books. Oh, yes, Alexander was an author. Not profound but talented. August would find him worth while and as for the Commodore—August must become well acquainted with him. He was brilliant, his conversation absorbing. He had known Negro kings, buccaneers and slave-traders. He had dined with the Czar of Russia, the Khedive of Egypt, the Emperor of Austria, the Bey of Tunis.

"The United States must value your son-in-law very highly." August Belmont's eyes wandered to the table where Perry sat. The Commodore had a glass of champagne in his hand and was laughing boyishly with a group of adoring young ladies. Still, for all the informality of the moment, Perry's imposing, authoritative presence could not be denied. "Strange, madame, that the country has not yet found a truly historical use for him."

"There has been no war," Jane said. "Peace is a tragedy for men like my son-in-law."

"Not so. Consider the American commander Charles Wilkes, who has explored the Antarctic. He will be remembered though his was an accomplishment of peace."

Jane said, "Yes, they named a frozen lump of earth Wilkesland, did they not?" She smiled. "I used to know little Charlie very well. I was astonished when I read that he had explored Fiji without breaking it."

They spoke of Alzey in Hesse. The elder Belmont had owned vineyards and had dabbled somewhat in world commerce. He was now dead. Oh, yes, both parents dead. The mother when very young.

"I never really knew her. I know about her, of course. I hear that she was bewitching, that she had enormous charm and an unpredictable temper. A lady of fashion and great wit."

"You speak of her as though you had known her and had loved her very much. How nice."

"My father kept her alive in memory, madame. Often he said

172

to me, 'Aaron, dear boy' "—August Belmont paused and looked at Jane with eyes quizzical and challenging—"I was named Aaron."

"Were you? And you did not care for it? Well, the Commander did not like the name Slidell. He is Alexander MacKenzie."

"We were Schonenbergs for a few centuries," Belmont told her.

"Well, Belmont is merely a literal translation and it is more euphonious. I hope you are quite ready to meet my children. They are more than ready to meet you. Approaching us are Nile-green velvet, diamond collar and forty fathoms of gold braid."

August Belmont got to his feet for the introductions and Jane sighed. It had been such fun. Now the children would move in and take over. As the thought came to her, he flashed her a rueful smile, exactly as though she had voiced her regret. What an amazing boy he was and she thought resentfully of Julia's haste in marrying Raymond Rogers.

A few minutes later, when August Belmont led Mathilde to the dance floor, Jane glanced toward the chandeliers in startled surprise. She had had the illusion that the lights had suddenly been dimmed.

Stepping aboard the brig *Somers* on a bright September day, Commander Alexander Slidell MacKenzie was smartly saluted and, he realized, warily scrutinized by his men. Though the brig was a boiling mass of human activity under Lieutenant Gansevoort's trumpeted orders, there was always time to take a quick squint at "the old man" and evaluate from the look of him what the months ahead might bring.

Alexander made it a point to present for inspection a smile and a brisk, cheerful manner. This would not impress Warrant Officer Wales but it might encourage a lowly sailor wrestling with rope and canvas. Wales, Alexander observed from the corner of his eye, was not giving a good performance. The last time they had sailed together, he had earned Wales's dislike and the expression on the man's face now clearly revealed that nothing had occurred in the interval to lessen his animosity. The matter must be dealt with promptly. That same lowly sailor involved with rope and canvas was seeing what Alexander saw—Wales's open dislike.

"Beautiful vessel, Captain," said the doctor. His name was

Leecock. He was less than thirty years old but a recent illness had left him scrawny and chalk-faced. Alexander wished he had seen him before accepting him.

"Beautiful, indeed." Alexander seized the moment to widen his smile and direct it toward Wales. "Come, Mr. Wales. Let us look the lady over. Carry on, Lieutenant."

Gansevoort raised the speaking trumpet once more and resumed his bellowed commands. The men noticed a certain dullness in his style since the skipper had come aboard.

The *Somers* was a brig which Cal had designed. She was the fastest thing under sail, a lovely slender vessel, a joy to the eye and the heart of a sailing man. Beneath Alexander's feet the deck seemed to quiver impatiently. Let us be off to the Sierra Leone coast, the brig whispered. Let us be off.

With Wales walking behind him, Alexander moved methodically over the *Somers*. From the berth deck to the wardroom. From the steerage to the cabin. Very limited space, he thought, and the frailty of the partitions surprised him. Still, were not such departures from custom exactly what made the *Somers* so slim and swift? He glanced but briefly at his cabin and returned to the berth deck and for a long while, stood quietly studying its proportions. Each man, he judged, would have less than an eight-foot length for hammock space and perhaps twenty inches in width.

He was aware that Wales's eyes were upon him, awaiting his comments. Alexander said, "Best and most economical use of space I have ever seen."

Wales turned his eyes away. "Commodore Perry certainly was economical. Truth is, we are crowded."

"Truth is, you are unacquainted with vessels that have been cleverly designed. This one is a masterpiece."

There was no answer to that and Wales gave none. Silently he followed Alexander to the hold. It was packed as neatly and completely as a sausage, without an inch of extra room. Ballast, water tanks, ammunition, stores, each and every necessity had the appearance of having been measured, weighed and fitted on the draftsman's drawing board. No wonder Cal had said, "This first time she'll be stowed by the boys who worked on her. You just go aboard when you are ready and you'll find everything in

174

order." Yes, if one had not seen the puzzle solved, one might be tricked into declaring that it had no solution. Rather embarrassing. Cal had saved him that. He felt Wales's eyes resting questioningly upon him once more.

"Perfect," he said and again Wales's glance slid away from him.

Slowly Alexander turned to continue his inspection but thought better of it. There was no time like the present. Why was it that the present always held an unpleasant duty?

"Mr. Wales, I am remembering—as you are—that on a former voyage there was little harmony between us. However, the fact that you did not protest sailing again with me and that I did not refuse to have you indicates that we both feel agreement is possible."

"Yes, sir."

"I will admit that I am in temperament curt and dogmatic. Though neither of these traits is likable, I submit that you have failings of your own. Let me say that on that other voyage, you exhibited an unfortunate proclivity to procrastinate and to accept reproof in very poor grace. Now, Mr. Wales, may I hope for better things from you this time?"

"Yes, sir," Wales said but there was nothing in his manner that suggested he welcomed a truce. It occurred to Alexander that Wales had not protested sailing with him because it was doubtless the man's conviction that one captain was as great a bastard as the next. Perhaps it had been a mistake to accept Wales but now it was done and they had each other's company for the voyage. Common sense dictated that even a mild feud must be discouraged or ignored.

Chattily Alexander turned to the man. "Had you noticed that four of our young men are rather special cargo?"

Wales raised his eyebrows, "Four, sir? Two, I know, are sons of Commodore Perry and one, of course, is the son of the Secretary of War. That's three."

"Yes." Alexander smiled. "The fourth is strictly a family matter. A lad from Louisiana named Adrien Deslonde. My brother John is married to his sister Mathilde. I suppose the boy is sort of a brother-in-law of mine. I have never seen him."

Wales made no reply and Alexander wearily decided that there

175

was little point in seeking to warm so chill an association. Unfortunate, for the brig was far too small to comfortably berth any ill will. It could only be hoped that Wales would attend his duties with alacrity.

Alexander concluded his examination of the *Somers* and repaired to his cabin. Captain's Clerk Oliver Hazard Perry, the Second, was waiting for him there.

"Your face is familiar, my boy. Do I know you from another voyage?"

Oliver laughed. "I woke up in a cold sweat last night. I dreamed that I had called you 'Uncle Alec' in front of the entire ship's company." Then, looking about him, "Sir, this cabin! Good thing you are not fat."

"Hush. The vessel was designed by Commodore Matthew Calbraith Perry, of whom you may have heard. The *Somers,* I am in the habit of saying, is a masterpiece."

"Well, I will get in the habit of saying it, too, if that is what you want, but you will have to admit she is small."

Alexander said, "She really is brilliantly thought out, Oliver. Not an inch of wasted space. Have you any dispatches for me?"

Oliver looked worried. "Dispatches? Should I have?"

"Yes. From your mother. Orders that I look after you and Mattie. Threats of what she will do to me if I do not feed you well and keep you dry and safe."

"No. All she said was—" The boy paused and his eyes sparked suddenly. "What she said was very good, now that I remember it. She said, 'Make Uncle Alec hope that everyone finds out you are his nephews.' "

"That is very good, Oliver."

"Thank you, Captain. I will tell my mother you approve, Captain. May I unpack your chart case, Captain?"

"No. Just get out. You are very impudent."

"I was only trying to get used to calling you Captain."

Alexander raised his head and gazed at Oliver coolly. "My boy," he said, "when this vessel is once under sail, it will not occur to you that I could possibly be called anything else."

Oliver whistled. "That's a good line, too. You have a knack for phrasemaking almost as good as Mother's. You ought to try

176

to write a book sometime." He ducked out of the cabin then, leaving Alexander with a glow of satisfaction. No matter what vexations the voyage offered, they would be lessened by the presence of Oliver and Mattie Perry.

There was a knock upon the door and the sailor ridiculously termed Captain's Hammock Boy entered. "Sir," he said, "your trunk just came aboard." He looked at the cabin doubtfully. "May I bring it in?"

"You may. Here is the key. Unpack it at once, then take it out again."

"And put it where, sir?"

"Oh, you will find a place. Handle things carefully."

"Yes, sir." The man was chubby but sprightly. It struck Alexander that he probably took great pride in being a sailor and would lambaste for a dirty liar the dolt who called him a valet.

"What is your name?"

"Nicholas, sir."

"Very well, Nicholas. We will get on fine together if you never throw away a piece of paper that has writing on it. I will be in the wardroom for the next hour. See if you can get me settled by then."

The purser, whose name was Heiser, was having coffee with the doctor. Alexander had known Heiser for years. He was a man who was always quite certain that fair weather could not last and that the drinking water had in some manner become contaminated.

Waltham, the Negro wardroom steward, brought coffee to Alexander and offered a welcoming smile.

"Where do I know you from?" Alexander asked the man.

"The *Independence,* Captain. Voyage to Russia."

"Oh, yes indeed. I remember you as a good lad." Then turning to Leecock, the doctor, "I trust you will have a lazy time aboard the *Somers.*"

"Not likely. I expect to be nursing colic and prickly heat from here to Africa and back. You know we have seventy-two babies aboard? Seventy-two between the ages of twelve and eighteen."

Alexander said, "We have a few men also."

"Very few. I do not call the midshipmen men. They are young-

177

sters themselves. We have you, Captain, myself, Heiser here, Mr. Gansevoort and three warrant officers."

"And fourteen seamen, doctor."

"Yes, and six or seven of those are still infants. Had I seen the ship's company earlier, I would have requisitioned a hundred gallons of paregoric and several nursing bottles."

"Had you not heard it was a training cruise?"

"No. I understood we were delivering dispatches to the African squadron."

"We are, but the time may as well be employed usefully. Our lads must get their training somewhere. We can impart a great deal of naval knowledge during ninety days. Since all signs point to an uneventful passage, it would be a pity to have the vessel filled with experienced men who would derive nothing but tedium from the voyage."

Heiser said, "Ninety days is a very rough estimate, is it not, Captain? Don't you think we might be away closer to four months?"

"If I thought so, Mr. Heiser, then that is what I would have said."

The doctor yawned. "I hope the children do not break out in chicken pox or anything contagious," he said and strolled away.

Heiser said, "Will you excuse me, Captain?" And followed the doctor.

Alexander sent for his clerk, young Oliver. "Tell Midshipman Deslonde I want to see him. Give me a few minutes with him, then bring Midshipman Spencer here."

"Yes, sir."

Alexander intended to have a private word with each of his midshipmen. Pleasant to begin with this brother of Mathilde's, who would in all probability be a fine boy. And pleasant to have behind him the meeting with Philip Spencer, son of the Secretary of War. He had been inclined to reject young Spencer but Cal had said, "Alec, you cannot do that. The boy is full of hell but, my God, you can cope with a midshipman, can't you? And his father *is* Secretary of War, you know."

Alexander raised his eyes from his coffee cup and Adrien Deslonde was standing before him.

178

"Welcome aboard, Deslonde."

"Thank you, sir."

A tall, slim youth with Mathilde's eyes and a strong chin. Mouth firm, manner easy but respectful. What on earth had he done to his uniform that gave it such dash? Alexander exercised his prerogative of maintaining silence while he studied the lines of the boy's trousers and jacket. He was at length forced to the conclusion that Adrien Deslonde had improved the uniform only by putting it on.

"First time we have had the opportunity to sail together, Deslonde. Have you met Mattie and Oliver Perry as yet?"

"Yes, sir."

"I expect you three will hit it off fine together. They are good lads, too, with records similar to yours. How did it happen that you chose the sea?"

"Perhaps you know that I am one of several sons, sir. We cannot all be planters and in my father's family there were, years ago, men of the sea, officers in the French navy."

Adrien spoke with an accent that was certain to bewilder the seamen. It would be difficult for them to believe that he had been born an American on American soil.

"Is that so? I had not known."

Adrien made no comment. He stood quietly, ready to accept conversation without presuming or dismissal without resentment. Like the Perrys, he expected no special handling for being part of the family.

Alexander said, "I regret we never met before. We have a few minutes now in which to establish an acquaintance. Is there anything you would like to say to me? Any observation you care to make?"

Adrien smiled and lowered his eyes. "I have read all your books, sir. *A Year in Spain* I have translated into French. Would you care to see the translation?"

"Why, yes. I am greatly flattered. Do you have the translation with you aboard?"

"Yes, sir."

"Do see that I get it."

"Yes, sir."

Alexander waited. Evidently there was nothing else the boy wished to say. And as impressed as he had been with the appearance and manner of Mathilde's brother, Alexander was now ready for him to depart. So difficult to make small talk. So difficult. He realized that Cal would have found it quite simple to speak of Mathilde and John and to range lightly over a dozen subjects of interest to the boy. Cal would have laughed and jested and endeared himself with the marvelous quality that in his relaxed moments made of him a jovial god.

Alexander said, "Well, Deslonde, send me the translation and if at any time you wish to speak to me, tell Oliver and he will arrange for you to do so."

"Thank you, sir," Adrien said and withdrew.

Alexander thought over the words he had just spoken. Pompous. Graceless. The boy had been to sea. He did not need to be told that a midshipman did not just dash into the captain's cabin at will. Cal would have said, "Come see me when you feel like it" and relied on Deslonde's intelligence to arrange an appointment.

Oliver was at his side now. "Are you ready, sir, to see Midshipman Spencer?"

"Yes. Send him in."

Philip Spencer entered the wardroom with the air of a man who has been called away in the midst of serious occupation. There was a small frown between his brows, a question in the hazel eyes. He was a medium-sized youth, underweight and depressingly unattractive. Large nose, bad skin and an almost ostentatious untidiness. Good God, had he ever had his hair cut? Alexander regarded him without pleasure and he was aware that Spencer was also making certain judgments.

At last Alexander spoke. He said, "What were you doing just now when I summoned you, Spencer?"

"I was assisting Mr. Wales, sir."

"What were you doing by way of assistance?"

"I was making a chart of duties and assignments."

Alexander nodded. Nothing that would account for the dirty hands and disarranged uniform. "We have never met before, Spencer." In order to consider his next words, he paused, so perhaps he could not accuse the boy of interrupting him.

180

"We have met, sir. I was at both weddings when Commodore Perry's daughters were married. I knew John Hone before Jane married him but I had never known Colonel Rogers till Sarah and he—"

Alexander said, "Your record, Spencer, is not all that either of us could desire."

Philip Spencer's face grew sulky. "May I say something, sir?"

"Of course."

"My father is Secretary of War. That is a very high position, is it not, sir?"

"It is, indeed."

"It is a terrible cross for me to bear. Too much is expected of me. I am supposed to be as mature, as brilliant and as responsible as my father. If I behave like an average midshipman, everybody is appalled. I am supposed to be a model of deportment. Other fellows are excused when I am punished. Other fellows are—"

"The sorry report begins in college, Spencer."

"Yes, sir. I was wild in college. I admit that."

"Then aboard the *North Carolina* you were guilty of malicious mischief."

"Lieutenant Craney *said* I was guilty of malicious mischief, sir."

And for saying so, this boy's father had cruelly persecuted Lieutenant Craney. Only by resigning his commission had Craney saved his sanity. There was not an officer in the Navy who did not know that story.

"On the *John Adams* you were accused of disgraceful and scandalous conduct. Would you like to give me your explanation?"

"I was singled out as an example because I was the son of a famous man."

"I see. You behaved yourself but your former officers lied about you."

The midshipman did not reply.

"Answer me, Spencer."

Spencer smiled crookedly. "Sir, you have placed me in peril. Am I to say to you that officers of the United States Navy are liars?"

"Do you suppose these officers met and agreed in collusion to

181

represent you as a bad lot? Or do you think the fiendish notion to discredit you just occurred to each of them separately?"

Spencer gazed down at the floor and spoke in a quiet voice. "In all honesty, let me say that I have been misunderstood by my officers. I do not call them liars. Forgive me if I implied they were. To the best of their knowledge, I was a bad lot. They could not see that they had driven me close to frenzy with the demands they placed upon me."

"Demands? What do you mean?"

"I mean the thing to which I referred a moment ago, sir. These officers expected me to be the man my father is. Someday I might be, but at present I am young and impulsive." The hazel eyes shot a sudden swift plea straight at Alexander. "Sir, I have not been fairly dealt with."

"Have you not?" Alexander wished the cold coffee in the thick mug had been taken away. It was disgusting. He said, "I have been on many voyages with young, impulsive men. I never thought these adjectives were synonyms for malicious mischief and disgraceful conduct."

Spencer said, "Sir, perhaps you are more understanding."

"No. On the question of behavior that ill becomes a midshipman, you will find me the least sympathetic officer you ever encountered. On this vessel, on this voyage I expect you to go far toward straightening your miserable record."

Spencer sighed. "I will try, sir, but—" He permitted his voice to trail off into sad silence.

"But what?" Alexander prompted.

"May I say?"

"Yes."

"But already I have impressed you unfavorably."

Alexander said, "That is God's truth. You have pleaded that you would be better, happier, more useful if your father were not a celebrated personage. And yet, Spencer, you have taken outrageous advantage of your father's position. There is not another midshipman in the Navy who would talk as you have talked. Any other lad with a record such as yours would have entered here in humility. I saw no sign of humility or of anxiety to prove that you can mend your ways."

"Sir, I can be a model midshipman if I am not hounded and criticized and—"

"Midshipmen do not strike bargains with commanding officers. They adapt themselves to circumstances. You will find my standards for the behavior of midshipmen inflexible. You may go now."

Spencer turned and walked out of the wardroom. Alexander sat unhappily reviewing the conversation. Cal had said that he could cope with a midshipman. Could he really? Would it have paid to have greeted the boy with a cheery promise that on this voyage, by praying, working and trusting, they together were going to wipe out the ugly blemishes on the Spencer record?

Alexander had a sickening presentiment that in dealing with Midshipman Philip Spencer, there was no method devised by man that could possibly pay.

George Peter Alexander Healy, who had just finished a portrait of President Tyler, was now painting Mathilde. For the sittings she wore a black velvet ball gown trimmed with marabou feathers and scarlet geraniums. The portrait would hang in the drawing room at Belle-Point and when Mathilde thought of Belle-Point, there was an expression in her eyes that Healy yearned to capture.

Mathilde did not care for Washington but there was no one to whom she had ever breathed her secret. No one to whom she could breathe it, for John's conversation was studded with references to the time "when we take a house here." Mathilde knew, for she had been taught by her mother, that a woman must be happy where her husband found happiness and that it was a poor wife indeed who made excuses instead of a home. So Mathilde had created in the suite at Willard's a Louisiana outpost. She had banished the hotel waiters and despite lamentations and tears, she had pressed the baby's nurse, her personal maid and John's valet into serving the table when John wanted a few gentlemen to a quiet dinner unobserved by newspapermen. Over protestations that almost equaled those of her servants, she had convinced the hotel chef that *daube glacée* and *gombo z'herbes* and many another delicacy could be prepared with no trouble at all if only her recipes were carefully followed.

John expressed his appreciation in a way she thought adorable.

He would pluck the baby from her crib and holding her high over his head, he would look up into the sleepy little face and say, "Do you know you have the most wonderful mother in the world? Do you know what she did?" He would then proceed to tell the baby that her mother had been clever enough to ship the *brûlot* bowl and forty pounds of Creole coffee to Washington. "I can tell you, young lady, that my guests had a breakfast Sunday morning they will not forget. *Calas tout chaud,* preserves of Tangipahoa strawberries, *la cuite* with pecans to spread upon their toast. To look at her, would you not swear that she'd pack only worthless things such as jewels and clothes?" Then pausing to glance at Mathilde with mock annoyance, "You must not listen to the private conversations I conduct with Rosina."

She had named the baby for her favorite aunt. John had named the first child and he had insisted that she must be another Mathilde.

"But, John, they will call us big Mathilde and little Mathilde. How dreadful for me if ever I should really become big Mathilde."

He had laughed. "Your waist will measure eighteen inches for a hundred years, my love. After that, we will change our daughter's name."

Little Mathilde was three now, yellow-haired, bronze-eyed, a conversation piece in Washington with her precise manners and French accent. Rosina would be much like her. Enchanting children, to be sure, but, oh, their mother wondered, where was the son for her to place proudly in John's arms?

Not that he had complained, but Mathilde knew that for Creole men, no marriage was complete without a son, and her New York-born husband was very much a Creole. Like her father and the other gentlemen she had known throughout her life, John saved his compliments and expressions of sentiment for moments when they were alone. It amused and somewhat embarrassed her to hear Northern men remark on their wives' beauty or to see loving glances exchanged between a couple. And to her amazement, Mathilde had discovered that with their husbands' approval, ladies of Washington and New York often sat at a dinner table where politics or business was being discussed. She was happy that John expected no such thing of her. It was her responsibility to make

184

certain that the food and service were all that could be desired. After that, a wife correctly retired, leaving the gentlemen to their conversation.

Her favorites among John's guests were Senator Buchanan of Pennsylvania and Mr. Polk, the ex-governor of Tennessee. Though they often kept John talking into the morning hours, she thought them both very gentlemanly and was not surprised at John's conviction that Mr. Polk would be the next President of the United States.

John knew everything. She would hear him sometimes as she sat in the small room off the parlor with her fancywork. He would be informing his guests of such astonishing things as what Massachusetts would do at the convention, what Ohio would do. She heard, too, doubts expressed concerning Louisiana and she would hear John say such things as, "Let me worry about Louisiana, Jim. Good Jesus, if I cannot deliver Louisiana, I might as well drop dead. As a matter of fact, if I do not deliver Louisiana, that is exactly what I shall do."

She would sit in the small room, listening to the clink of glasses, picturing how Mr. Buchanan's light-blue eyes must be flashing as he spoke of "that cypher Tyler" and how Mr. Polk's penetrating gray glance must be caught as John unfolded further plans.

"Actually, I think I will make it my business to be here next year," John said. "I always wanted a Congressional seat and that would be the time to be here, when I can control things somewhat."

"Can you guarantee yourself a Congressional seat, Slidell?" Mr. Polk asked.

"Well now, my friend, if I can guarantee you Louisiana, does it not seem logical that I can manage for myself a small token of New Orleans' esteem?" Mathilde heard John laugh as he recalled something out of the past. "I did get licked once, you know, but that was long ago."

Mr. Buchanan's voice, mild and sweetly modulated, inquired about John's law practice. "Will it not suffer during your absence?"

"I think Judah Benjamin will keep an eye on it for me. He is my dearest friend and, in my opinion, the greatest lawyer alive."

"Oh, yes, Judah Benjamin. Do you not have a brother who is also a lawyer? What has become of him?"

185

Mathilde was amused by the ironic note in John's voice as he answered Polk—Polk, who had wondered if John could win himself a Congressional seat.

"My brother is still around, Jim. He was such a good boy that there was just nothing to do but make him Chief Justice of the Louisiana Supreme Court."

She was even more amused by the respectful silence that followed that announcement.

A split second before the silence became too marked, Mr. Polk spoke. He said, "That must be—er—very gratifying, to have your brother in such a lofty position."

"If you mean it must be very helpful, you are quite wrong. My brother takes himself and Louisiana seriously. He is in the habit of deciding cases on their merit, which is a stuffy and rather unimaginative way of handling things—also extremely lacking in fraternal loyalty. I think he even resents it a little when I call him by his first name."

The gentlemen chuckled and Mr. Buchanan said, "Yet you must have been somewhat instrumental in helping your brother to—"

"Oh, he admits I helped a little. He feels that his superb qualifications and abilities would have gone unnoticed without my slight assistance but that his gratitude is not owed to brother John but to the State of Louisiana. A peculiar lad, my brother Thomas, and though no genius like Judah Benjamin, he is still one hell of a good lawyer."

"Speaking of your Louisiana lawyers," Mr. Polk said, "one never hears of John Grymes any more."

"No. Poor old Grymes, drink and gambling have done for him. He is finished. He sits in the Boston Club telling all the young men about the old days when he represented Lafitte, the pirate."

"The Boston Club? The Elkin Club is then no more, Slidell?"

"No. It passed in the panic of thirty-seven."

Mr. Polk said, "That must have been an astounding place. I heard that at a party there one evening, the members undertook to drink twelve bottles of wine each, topped off by a quart of anisette. I heard, too, that you and Grymes divided the purse that had been collected for the winner."

"That is true but I was smarter than Grymes. For the sake of my brain, my liver and my stomach, I always made it a point to abstain from alcohol for weeks after a demonstration such as that. Grymes liked to keep in practice. In the end, it made a dull fellow of him."

"And the gambling ate up his money?"

"Yes. He has not a worry in the world now. He need no longer wonder what investments to make or at which card table to squander his income. His old friends see that he is fed and housed. Even his burial place has been purchased, so Grymes is a thoroughly carefree fellow."

There was another silence then while the gentlemen thought about John Grymes and during the silence, Mathilde heard no tinkle of bottle or glasses.

After a time, Mr. Buchanan said, "Personally you have done very well with real estate and railroad stock, have you not?"

"Yes. I have no complaints."

"And you should have none. For many years, you have been in a position to know much about impending improvements in your state, have you not?" Mr. Polk asked.

"Well, yes, but like an old man giving his recipe for longevity, I will say this: there is no substitute for being lucky."

"And daring," Mr. Buchanan added. "Did I not hear that you recently acquired a considerable piece of land in the Houmas tract?"

John said, "Why, I have never heard this transaction of mine described so delicately before. The newspapers refer to it as a conscienceless land grab." The gentlemen's laughter filled the room. "I am having a little trouble getting the title clear."

So the title to those twenty thousand acres was in doubt? Mathilde, bending over her work, thought again how wonderful was a Creole marriage. She was not obligated—indeed it would reveal a shocking coarseness—to make inquiries concerning the Houmas tract or any other of John's financial dealings. A Creole husband valued his wife's happiness so highly that he inflicted none of his worries upon her. A Creole wife was never subjected to the emotional agony of a husband's business failures. In time of trouble, she was simply informed that the utmost thrift must now be exercised. Unlike her Northern sister, she was not asked to endure

187

painful explanations or self-recriminations, nor was her advice solicited on what now should be done. In lean seasons, she was expected only to produce a modest *soupe-en-famille* and with her smile, gentle graces and a few flowers, make of the dinner hour a pleasant and heartwarming occasion. And at night, she was expected to lie in her husband's arms, if such was his wish. The soft, dark shadows had not been created so that a man could answer questions about money, future prospects and the market bill.

Backed by the power of a corrupt machine and surrounded by bullies, Slidell takes upon himself the right of saying who shall fill every public office in the state. Let any man who doubts Slidell's sinister influence visit the groggeries of St. Charles Street.

With horror she had read that item in *The Daily True Delta.* For a moment, she had stood trembling, half sick, but the moment had passed. The newspaper spoke of a man she did not know. And did she want to know him? Of course not. Then why admit he existed? Why say to her husband, "Was that not a terrible thing the paper said of you?" Only a woman intent on driving happiness from her life would recognize the news item as a reality. Reality was a man who brought her jeweled trinkets, a man who stole into the nursery and awakened his children for the joy of holding them in his arms.

"Good night, Senator. See you in the morning. Yes. Ten sharp."

Mr. Buchanan was leaving. Mr. Polk? No. She heard the clink of glasses again. She sensed the settling down for a long talk, visioned the eyes of the two men cleared of laughter, gazing soberly into the future.

"Jim, you know you will have to do something for Buchanan."

"Cabinet?"

"Probably."

"What about you, Slidell? What can we do for you?"

"I will tell you when the time comes."

"That sounds frightening. You had better tell me now."

Mathilde heard her husband sigh heavily. "Truly, Jim, I do not yet know what I want. 'Lawyer and politician' are vague terms. Christ, they could apply to a pipsqueak just out of law school who

188

wants to be an alderman. I am dreaming of a position unique and honored."

"Well, Congress will be——"

"It will do for a time, but there are many Congressmen. It is not a great mark of distinction. Moreover, my friend, that will be a gift from my city, not from you. I will still be looking forward to some evidence of your appreciation."

"Of course, Slidell. When the time comes . . ."

Beneath the skylight in his small cabin, Alexander made his dull, colorless entries in the log of the brig *Somers*. The entries were dull because nothing of interest had occurred on the voyage. The language was colorless because Alexander was self-conscious regarding his avocation. He wanted none who read the log to curl a scornful lip and mutter "the novelist's touch."

In a desk drawer there were other writings of Alexander's. Notes on a projected biography of Commodore Stephen Decatur and, at last, a completed manuscript of the life of John Paul Jones. He hoped that he had not done an injustice to Pierre de Landais. God knew he had dug deeply in his effort to give the Frenchman his day in court. All evidence available had been in favor of Jones and the book would go to the printers some time in January with De Landais once more convicted without a trial. Alexander believed he had been fair. He could only hope so.

His eyes and mind turned again to the log. Contact made with the sloop *Vandalia* and dispatches delivered. A brief tarrying at Madeira and preparations made for the voyage home. What else had happened? Oh, the usual. A few floggings for disobedience or thievery. Some illness. Everything routine. The apprentices studying with good will their courses in navigation, mathematics and astronomy, finding the standard excuses for not delivering their written exercises, receiving the customary punishments. A numskull or two in the classes, which was to be expected. Lectures on morals and hygiene, religious services all conducted by the captain, listened to respectfully. If he were forced to find something extraordinary to enter in the log, he would have to record Wales's continued cool dislike for his captain or Midshipman Philip

189

Spencer's penchant for the company of his social inferiors. Alexander could have understood a nature that sought retreat on the crowded *Somers,* but Spencer obviously had no passion for solitude. He was gregarious enough but one never heard his laughter blended with that of other midshipmen. His companions were selected from among the seamen and ashore at Funchal, he had stood treat so lavishly for the giant boatswain Cromwell that it had taken the man two days to recover. Mr. Secretary of War Spencer had provided spending money with a careless hand.

Alexander made a conscious effort to divert his thoughts to a brighter subject. How fine a sailing master Mattie was! It was always heartening when the young son of a distinguished father— Such cheerful musing was not to be. It was interrupted by the sound of swiftly running feet. He hurried to open his door before the knock came. It was Oliver.

"Captain, there is a strange vessel pursuing us. For a time we thought— But now—"

Briskly but with full composure, Alexander moved to the deck. When the moment of excitement had passed, he must reprimand Oliver for the manner in which he had delivered his message. Like a flustered schoolboy. Broken sentences. Confusion of thought. Had he closed his mouth after his one completed statement, praise might have been in order.

Alexander swept the seascape with his glass. There was no mistake. The following sail was making every effort to overhaul the *Somers.* He summoned Lieutenant Gansevoort and gave his orders sharply and concisely. Small arms were loaded and served out and the men posted and ready. The *Somers* could outrun anything under canvas but Alexander knew the demoralizing effect a mysterious pursuer could have upon a youthful crew. Boys of less than fifteen years Alexander sent below and in crisp, businesslike tones, passed the word among the others that probability of action was slight but that if necessary, they would stand and fight. He had, he told them, every confidence that each man would perform in a manner creditable to the United States Navy.

Orders were then given to permit the stranger to draw within hailing distance. By that time the sky had darkened, making the hoisting of signal flags impracticable.

190

"What ship is that?" Alexander trumpeted.

For reply, the same question boomed back to him across the blackening water. "What ship is *that?*"

Alexander stiffened and Gansevoort glanced swiftly about as though to evaluate the readiness of the men.

"I hail you again," Alexander called. "I expect a proper answer. What ship is that?"

There was a silence and the apprentices peered intently into the darkness. Then, riding on a light wind, came the welcome word. "This is Her Britannic Majesty's frigate *MacBride,* thirty-eight guns."

"This then is the United States brig *Somers,* ten guns," Alexander trumpeted.

Conversation was now at an end, tension relaxed, but surprisingly, the steady pull of oars could be clearly heard coming toward them. The *MacBride* was sending a boat and shortly a young British lieutenant stepped aboard the *Somers* to apologize for the rudeness which had been displayed.

"We watched you for some time without liking you very much," he said. "You do not look very tasty. Obviously built for speed, you have rather sinister lines. You might have been a slaver or some other sea scourge."

The lieutenant had a drink with Alexander and Gansevoort and that was all there was to the encounter except for one small detail. When the British explanation for such peculiar behavior had been passed on to the men, Philip Spencer laughed pleasurably and his eyes sought the eyes of Cromwell, the boatswain. Apparently, Spencer had voiced some thoughts of his own on the build of the *Somers* which were similar enough to those of the British to delight the lad. His glance at Cromwell had plainly said, "What did I tell you?"

Alexander thought, "I do not like Spencer so what he does is annoying to me." And later, when a drawing of the *Somers* with a skull-and-crossbone flag at her mast was circulated throughout the brig, he found it not at all amusing. "Suppose Oliver had drawn that? Would it be amusing, then? I know it is Spencer's work and therefore I find it offensive. Yet why should it be? I smiled at the British lieutenant's words. Mistaking us for an evil vessel is funny, is it not? I am not fair to Spencer."

And yet the boy had given no trouble of importance. Waltham, the wardroom steward, had mentioned—saying that he thought it his duty to do so—that Spencer quite regularly bought rum. Too regularly, Waltham thought.

"I have not seen him intoxicated, Waltham."

"No, Captain. He don't buy much for himself. He gives it away. Any man aboard can get all he wants by just telling Mr. Spencer he wants some."

"Do you mean that he permits the younger boys to—"

"No, Captain. He ain't even polite to the younger boys, let alone give 'em a drink."

Odd. Everything about Philip Spencer was odd, still perhaps his case was a sad one. Alexander knew for a fact that Adrien and the Perry brothers disliked Spencer. Undoubtedly, the boy hungered for friendship and knew no means of gaining it save by shopping for it. It would be a good time, he thought, to meet privately with Spencer again.

Concealing the odious drawing of the *Somers* beneath a pile of papers, Alexander directed Oliver to fetch Midshipman Spencer. When the lad stood before him, Alexander was struck immediately by the change his personality had undergone since the first private talk. He was not frowning now and the hazel eyes glowed glee-fully. True, he looked no tidier for his weeks at sea and had not yet had his hair cut, but Alexander thought he had here a happier Spencer than the one who had sailed out of New York.

"Well, Spencer, how do things go for you?"

"Fine, Captain."

"I am glad to hear that."

Spencer laughed. Why? Sometimes young men laughed as a result of nervousness but Philip Spencer was not noted for his awe of superior officers. Had he been drinking? Alexander decided that such was not the case. Was it possible that Spencer bubbled with a new-found joy in living because he had discovered, meretricious though it was, a way to make friends?

"Has the voyage thus far been a satisfaction to you, Spencer? Do you feel you are doing your job well, that you are being accorded fair treatment?"

"Oh, yes, Captain." The curious laughter again. "The voyage has been a great satisfaction."

"There has been harmony between you and others in the steerage?"

"I think them fine fellows, sir."

"Yet your closest friends are on the berth deck. Is that not so?"

"Yes, that is so, Captain. I trust you do not object."

"I would not say that I object but I am disappointed that your companions have not been chosen from among your own mates."

Spencer did not reply but his silence, Alexander thought, was without sullenness. And certainly Spencer had as much right to avoid the Perry brothers and Adrien as they had to avoid him.

"I know from my own youth that many of the ordinary seamen are very interesting."

"Oh, yes, sir." The laughter again.

Alexander said, "Why do you laugh, Spencer?"

"Your pardon, please, Captain."

"It is not a question of manners. I would just like to know what is amusing you."

Spencer gazed up at the skylight and as he did so, a soft, frosty gleam played upon his unattractive face, giving it for the first time in Alexander's experience a childlike innocence. Even the overgrown, unruly hair seemed suddenly pathetic, symbolic of the neglect Spencer had suffered all his life. For what had John Canfield Spencer done for his son beyond giving him too much spending money and using his influence to keep the boy in the Navy?

"I was laughing, sir, because someone had told me a humorous story just before I was summoned here."

Alexander accepted that. "I see," he said. "Well, Spencer, if there is anything you wish to say to me at any time, I am available."

"Thank you, sir." Now the laughter was soundless but visible in the hazel eyes.

It was three days later that Lieutenant Gansevoort entered the cabin, looking troubled.

"Everybody is getting tired of the voyage, of the *Somers* and of everybody else," he said.

Alexander raised his eyebrows. "This has not been a long voyage, Mr. Gansevoort."

"I know it. I guess I am seeking an easy explanation for a certain disquiet, a certain—"

Alexander sat up straighter in his chair. Only today he had sensed the same restlessness of which Gansevoort spoke and in reviewing the past forty-eight hours, had had to list several dissatisfactions. There had been a dilatory response to orders, an inordinate number of punishments for fist-fighting and then that matter of the jib. Alexander had ignored the incident, for he had felt any emphasis placed on it would but serve to make him ridiculous; Cromwell, pitting his giant strength mightily against a high wind, had suddenly shouted, "God damn this jib and its lacing and the God-damned fool that invented it."

There was not a man aboard in ignorance that Alexander himself had designed that particular jib-lacing. Still, in his frustration and rage, Cromwell could have forgotten. Alexander had chosen to let the matter pass.

"They are getting good rations, Captain, and none of them have complained about close quarters. Point is, there is nothing for them to be disgruntled about but many of them act like men with something on their minds. They gather in clusters and carry on like a convention of crows. When I approach, they fall silent and scatter. Do you want me to tell you something odd and disturbing sir?"

Alexander smiled coldly. "Of course not, but if it is happening, I must hear about it."

"Well, in his seamanship classes, Cromwell has been an absolute tyrant with apprentices, sneering at them, punishing them, purposely misunderstanding them in order to vent his bad temper. Suddenly, overnight this has changed. He is a docile Saint Bernard, a loving companion to the children. What does it mean, Captain?"

Alexander shook his head. "I do not know, Mr. Gansevoort."

"Do you place a seaman named Small, Captain?"

"No."

"He is appropriately named. Short, slim, quiet. He has become an intimate of Cromwell's and of Spencer's. The three of them

194

spend every possible moment together. They whisper and they write what are apparently notes to each other. There is a constant passing back and forth of notes."

"Schoolboy antics," Alexander said.

"Yes, but Cromwell is a man, one of the biggest men I ever saw."

"This is no index to his mental development, Mr. Gansevoort." Alexander rose from behind his desk. He realized that it had been his impulse to pace. He sat down again. The cabin had not been designed for a perplexed captain.

"I think the men need a good firm talk, sir."

Alexander eyed Lieutenant Gansevoort with disappointment. He had expected something better than that from him.

"What would you suggest? That I forbid them to write notes? That I reprove Cromwell for having taken a milder tone with the lads? That I announce that henceforth no one is to call the captain a God-damned fool?"

Lieutenant Gansevoort reddened. "I know you can make it sound silly, sir—"

"My problem is to make it sound intelligent. Until we know what the matter is, until there is something we can safely issue orders for or against, I will tell you candidly I do not know how to give them that 'good firm talk' they need."

"Well, they could obey more quickly."

"Yes, that they could, but punishments are already in force for dawdling. I could have the number of lashes increased but you know as well as I that disobedience is only a symptom. I would like to know the name of the disease."

When Gansevoort had taken his troubled eyes away, Alexander went above and walked the deck with lively step, feeling the spray like powdered glass striking his face. The ocean had a curiously oiled look and seemed darker in color than was usual. The sunset, too, was notable, with chains of gold-tipped clouds resembling jagged mountain rocks. By moonlight, Alexander had often seen the sails take on the appearance of having been made of satin. Never before at this hour had he seen them look so smooth and beautiful. A good omen, no doubt, to the superstitious.

He walked, stopping here and there for a word. How much was imagination? Did he see in some eyes the same mocking laughter

195

he had caught in Spencer's? Why was the loquacious Waltham suddenly a silent man with a withdrawn expression?

"Are you feeling quite well, Waltham?"

"Yes, Captain." Only that from Waltham, who regarded himself as an old friend of Captain MacKenzie's.

Alexander lingered in the wardroom, requesting a cup of coffee be brought to him. There was a good chance that Waltham yet might become talkative. But Waltham said no further word and Alexander thought there was a mournfulness in the dark eyes.

He took but a few swallows of the coffee and proceeded on his tour of reconnaissance. Certainly the vessel herself was in perfect order. Every rope, every implement was in its place, decks as clean as though still unused, brass mountings shining like mirrors. He took comfort from the fact that with industry and skill, the men of the *Somers* had produced this pleasing effect, but the comfort was dissipated by a sudden burst of laughter that followed him as he passed the pumping station. In annoyance, he told himself to forget the laughter, that there was nothing in it to rouse either distress or anger. These were young men and a lighthearted crew was a good crew. What in God's name had given him the ugly idea that they had laughed at him? There was no reason why they should, but he could give them a reason. He could retrace his steps and standing before them, make a painstaking inquiry into the cause of their high spirits. No, no, the whole thing was fanciful and yet Gansevoort, too, had felt mischief abroad.

Worried, he descended the ladder. Nicholas was in his cabin, tidying the overburdened desk. It seemed to Alexander that the chubby Nicholas looked as mournful as Waltham.

"Anything wrong, Nicholas?"

Nicholas shot him a startled glance. "Wrong, sir? Oh, no, sir. I was just cleaning up a bit. I will get out of your way now."

Alexander let him go. Questioning Nicholas would be a fool's pastime. Oliver came to the door.

"Captain, Midshipman Deslonde has requested a minute with you."

"Very well." And as Oliver turned, "Wait. I myself would first like a minute with you."

"Yes, sir." The boy stood attentively, his eyes fixed upon his

196

captain. Alexander, looking carefully at Oliver, thought him rather pale and tense. It was the moment, Alexander thought, for them to relax the sustained effort of being no more than captain and clerk.

"Oliver," he said, "what is the matter?"

"With me, sir?"

Alexander rubbed his hand wearily across his face. "With you, Oliver, and with the *Somers.*"

Oliver moved closer and dropped his voice. "Uncle Alec, talk to Adrien."

"Does he have the answer to the question that I asked you?"

Oliver's eyes became expressionless. "Uncle Alec, talk to him."

Alexander sighed. "Send him in."

Midshipman Deslonde entered, wearing a pallor and tenseness equal to Oliver's.

"Captain, Midshipman Spencer and I had words within the hour. Though harsh and angry, they were the result of nothing important, so if you do not mind, I will omit the cause of our disagreement. What followed is, however, a matter for your attention, I do believe. It was, I will confess, my impulse to strike Spencer but I controlled myself and left the steerage apartment. Outside, I encountered Seaman Small, who had evidently heard the entire exchange. He addressed me most disrespectfully, saying that I was a fool to antagonize Spencer." Adrien paused and swallowed hard. "It is not easy to repeat the rest of this seaman's words, sir. You may be inclined to doubt me."

"I will not doubt you, Deslonde."

"Then, sir, I will say he looked at me contemptuously and said, 'You are slated to walk the plank, anyhow, but now you may first be tortured.' " Adrien fell silent and regarded Alexander questioningly.

Alexander said, "Oh, yes, that's of a piece with Spencer's childish drawing of the *Somers* flying the pirate flag. Little things amuse little minds. What happened next, Adrien?"

"Next?" Adrien stared incredulously at Alexander. "Next, sir? Why, next I informed the clerk that I desired to see you."

Alexander nodded. "Small must be punished for addressing you disrespectfully and I think Spencer's fevered brain needs to be cooled off. He has read too many adventure stories and is entertaining his friends by recounting them. I do not like it a bit. Thank you, Deslonde, for coming to me."

Midshipman Deslonde, precise officer and lad of exquisite manners, surprisingly enough seemed not to realize that he had been dismissed. He remained standing beside the desk, staring in wonderment at his captain.

"Was there something else, Deslonde?"

The lad was slow to reply. At length he spoke. He said, "No, Captain," and withdrew from the cabin.

After he had gone, Alexander regretted that he had not said a word concerning the translation of *A Year in Spain*. He must remember to congratulate Deslonde sometime on having done a very acceptable piece of work. Just now he had other things on his mind. Damn Spencer, anyway, for complicating matters by overheating the weak minds of seamen with all that buccaneering rot that passed for literature in some circles. There should be a law that no one under thirty be permitted to read books in which criminals of land or sea were pictured as romantic fellows who led exciting lives. This game of Spencer's had made Small bold enough to forget that Adrien was his superior. A few lashes now would go far toward sharpening his memory in the future.

Why had this report of Adrien's seemed so significant both to him and to Oliver? When something really troublesome was disrupting life aboard, how could they possibly inflate a seaman's impudence to the point where— Alexander's jaw dropped in sudden amazement. Why, of course. These youngsters, Oliver and Adrien, were making no issue of Small's disrespect. It was his actual words that had shaken them. They had taken quite seriously that foolish threat of Small's. Alexander shook his head unbelievingly. Such bright lads they seemed, too. Still, they were of an age with Spencer. Their minds were as subject as his to being inflamed by wild adventure stories.

He called Oliver to him. "My boy, I have listened to Adrien's complaint against Seaman Small and I order a half dozen lashes for that stupid fellow."

"Yes, sir," Oliver said, his eyes still expressionless.

Alexander saw that he had been quite correct in guessing that

198

Oliver and Adrien had read menace rather than impudence into Seaman Small's words.

He smiled at Oliver. "Can you not see that if ten years ago all you lads had been herded together in a boarding-school dormitory, Spencer would have terrorized you with ghost stories? His friends would have been warning you that particular rooms and hallways were haunted."

Oliver said nothing.

"It is his way. I presume it gives him a feeling of importance. I will not say it is harmless, for I do believe that anything which stirs the imagination too turbulently has a grave effect upon the nerves. However, this being a vessel of the United States Navy, I doubt that we need worry about either ghosts or pirates. Let us put Spencer from our minds and return to the matter I raised several minutes ago. What is going on aboard this ship which has caused a strange restlessness?"

Oliver said, "Naturally, the men do not confide in me."

"No, of course they would not. How about Thompson or Hays or—"

"Sir, Spencer is the only midshipman who has wooed the berth deck."

"Do you suppose the master-at-arms—"

"He is disliked by Spencer and—"

"Spencer is rather an obsession with you, is he not, Oliver? I say again, let us put him from our minds and try to solve the puzzle of what worm has eaten into the firm apple of shipboard harmony."

The following day was a busy one for captain and crew. The sea rose in short, convulsive heaves and frowning ramparts of dark clouds threatened ahead. Wind and rain descended upon the *Somers,* screaming and beating at the brig demonically. Every man aboard was drenched and weary by nightfall, when suddenly the moon, looking bleared and sickly, peered through a thin gray squall. The wind settled and though the moon was driven back, the rain when it returned was only a light drizzle and the work burden of the brig reverted to normal.

Alexander ate his evening meal and went to his cabin. Waltham had served very badly. Absent-mindedly, one might say. He had forgotten to offer the potatoes till they were quite cold. There had been no vinegar on the table and the man had completely neglected to brew the Captain's tea. Had the afternoon's rough going disorganized Waltham so thoroughly? Or was his lapse related to the matter on which today Alexander had had no time to ponder?

Lighting his desk lamp, Alexander seated himself and made ready to bring the log up to date. Latitude, longitude, the less than dramatic encounter with wind and rain. He had not entered Adrien's complaint against Seaman Small, for it had seemed a matter beneath attention. Moreover, it had not been submitted as a complaint. And yet— Though Adrien's recital had struck him as pointless and overrated in importance by both Oliver and Adrien, he now had a strong impulse to mention the incident.

There was a knock on the door and at his command, Warrant Officer Wales entered the cabin.

"Good evening, Mr. Wales."

"Good evening, Captain." Wales's wide mouth grimaced. "That is only a formality. It is not a good evening at all."

"The rain does not disturb me. There is no evidence that a storm of any magnitude approaches."

"You will change your mind in a minute, Captain."

Alexander bridled and said coldly, "You obviously have information not available to me."

"I am about to make it available to you." Wales glanced around the cabin as though searching for a chair. There was none except the Captain's and Alexander was relieved of the unpleasant necessity of informing Wales that he had not been invited to sit down. "Captain, I am not two-faced like some men and I must say that neither are you. Apparently it has been very plain that there is no love lost between us. Maybe I have been careless at times with remarks. I do not remember. In any case, I have been listed as an enemy of yours."

"Mr. Wales, have you been drinking?"

"No, Captain, I have not been drinking," Wales said in annoyance. "I have come to tell you that this impression some people got that you and I are enemies is going to save our lives."

Alexander was not at all sure that Wales was sober. He kept his gaze fixed upon the man, studying the way his body accommodated

200

itself to the rise and fall of the choppy sea. The eyes seemed clear enough, speech the same.

"Now, you tell me, Mr. Wales, how our lives are going to be saved simply because you and I are so honestly critical of each other."

Wales leaned across the desk and spoke dramatically. "Because I obviously am not partial to you, sir, I have been invited to join a mutiny!"

"What?" Alexander sprang to his feet. "Mr. Wales, that word is not lightly spoken."

"Indeed it is not, Captain. I speak it knowing full well that I run the chance of being judged a madman by you or being murdered by the conspirators. Sir, in God's holy name, I beg of you to listen to me well. Aboard this ship there is nothing short of mutiny being planned."

Alexander gasped his bewilderment. "I cannot credit this. I am not a harsh captain. I have never—"

"It has nothing to do with your treatment of the men. It is the *Somers* herself that has inspired the plot." Once again, Wales glanced about the cabin.

"Come," Alexander said. "Let us sit here." He walked toward his narrow bed, where Wales and he seated themselves. "Now talk, Mr. Wales."

"Yes, sir. Last night Philip Spencer communicated to me the entire scheme. I would have come to you today but for the squall. He told me that he is leagued with about twenty of the crew, that they plan to murder you and the other officers and commence the business of piracy. They swore me to secrecy—"

"They?"

"Yes. Seaman Small was present for a time. He congratulated me on having joined them."

Alexander's eyes narrowed as he sought to prove it all a nightmare. "Mr. Wales, are you sure that you are not the butt of a bad joke? Can you be certain this is not a frolic of boyish fancy—uproarious to a lad and something quite different to a man?"

"Captain, Spencer's manner was earnest and grave. You can take my word that nothing facetious was said. This young villain knows the capabilities of the *Somers* as well as you do, sir, and knows exactly how she can be put to a despicable use. He mentioned that she was of sufficient strength to overcome merchantmen but that if pressed by a superior force, she was small and light enough to retire and hide herself in shoal water. He said that he would have the booms cut away and the launch thrown overboard. He said that she was capable of supplying herself from her conquests. That never would she want for men, naval stores, provisions or water, that she could make her home on the seas without ever entering a port. Before God, Captain, does that sound like a boy having a joke?"

"No, Mr. Wales. It does not." Alexander turned his face away and closed his eyes. A deathly sickness had swept over him as Wales spoke.

"He asked me if I could be put on the list as a certainty and I told him that I could. He then said that if I was lying, my throat would be cut. He told me that all the youngest boys and the 'goody-goodies'—his word, Captain—would be forced to walk the plank. He repeated that he had twenty strong followers. I have no doubt that Cromwell is one."

"Very likely." Alexander now wanted nothing so much as to be alone with the dreadful information Wales had brought.

"What shall we do, Captain?"

"Nothing tonight, Mr. Wales."

Wales's face plainly expressed his astonishment and disapproval. Alexander knew what the man was thinking. Possessed of knowledge of the danger, one could think only of the narrow steps and small companion scuttles of the *Somers*. Two or three desperate mutineers standing on deck could cut down any number of faithful officers or men attempting the ascent from below.

"You have spoken to no one else, Mr. Wales?"

"Sir, I am not trying to have my throat cut."

"These men have done much writing and you spoke of a list. Tomorrow we will make a search."

Wales stood up. "Captain, if you find no written directions on how to conduct a mutiny, will you doubt all that I have told you?"

"No," Alexander said. "I am convinced you have spoken the truth as you believe it to be. However, mutiny is so monstrous a crime that it is difficult to accept that a boy could conceive such an

202

idea. There has never been mutiny on a vessel of the United States Navy. It is an atrocious thing. Think of it, Mr. Wales!"

"I have thought of it for many hours now. Sir, because you have not heard the crisp, matter-of-fact manner in which this boy outlines his plot, because you have not seen the determination in his eyes, I must beg you to take on faith what I have told you. The danger is great. You must make haste to settle this matter."

After Wales had gone, Alexander remained seated on the bed. His sick stomach and his racing heart had grasped the horror of the situation long before his mind readied itself to do so. Mutiny. The word was so vile, one hesitated to speak or even think it. Yet aboard this brig, it had been spoken, thought and plotted—and by an eighteen-year-old boy. Viciously this boy had schemed to subvert an American vessel of war to piracy. A vessel born into a great naval family and consecrated as a defender of her country's glory.

In agony and grief, Alexander brought to mind faces of the men aboard. Who were the faithful? Who were the mutineers? Never would his ship be taken from him. Not through a fault of his would the United States Navy seek upon the seven seas a scourge that had once been an honorable vessel. The talents of the *Somers* would not be turned to the depravity of piracy. Not while he lived. And he must live long enough to save the *Somers*.

For hours, as he sat rigidly where Wales had left him, his thoughts ran over and over the terrible possibilities confronting every man aboard. Time and again recollections came to him of the uneventful voyage to the African coast, how sure he had been that all was well. The sky was lightening when his weary, suffering brain, anxious to rest, suggested to him that somehow Wales had made a shockingly grave error. Wales had been intoxicated. Wales had not recognized that Spencer was making a joke. Wales was inclined to hysterical exaggeration. Wales disliked his captain and would go to any lengths to— Alexander collapsed despairingly upon his pillow and knew an hour's fevered sleep.

When he awakened, he sent for Lieutenant Gansevoort and told him all that Wales had said, even adding what had seemed so short a time ago a childish inanity—Seaman Small's words to Adrien Deslonde. Gansevoort listened quietly, wasting no time in expressing horror or doubt. Only a twitching nerve in his temple revealed his emotion.

"I would like to keep the matter quiet until we are ready to take a definite step," Alexander said. "Therefore, I am going to ask you to personally search Spencer's effects."

In Spencer's razor case, Gansevoort discovered a page torn from a book on geometry. It was the last page and one side of it had been left blank by the printers. Now it was covered with markings in Spencer's hand. Gansevoort brought it to Alexander.

"It is probably a code, sir. I do not understand it."

Alexander glanced at it. "It is Greek," he said. "And I know no more Greek than you. If—"

"Greek, sir? Midshipman Rogers is familiar with it. At least, so he once claimed."

Henry Rogers, an overgrown puppy with an ingratiating manner, was summoned and the torn page set before him.

"Can you read that?" Alexander demanded.

Rogers scanned the paper. "Why, yes, sir. It is mostly just names." He smiled. "Lots of the apprentice boys and seamen. Do you want it all written out, Captain? Name for name, word for word?"

"I do, indeed, Rogers."

"Yes, sir." It was clear that Rogers thought it a rather idiotic assignment. "I will bring it back to you within—"

"No. You stay right here and translate it for me."

"Yes, sir."

It took a surprisingly short time, but Midshipman Henry Rogers' face was white when he handed his finished paper to Alexander. There were three columns of names. The headings read "Certain," "Doubtful" and "To be kept willing or unwilling." Underneath there was the statement: "If any not marked down wish to join after it is done, we will pick out the best and dispose of the rest." Following that was a neatly detailed plan of the chief conspirators' stations for the moment of the massacre.

Alexander read the paper through, noting that Wales had been listed as certain, that Doctor Leecock and Waltham were among those to be retained even unwillingly, that E. Andrews was marked in the certain column, though no man aboard bore that name. After a moment, he passed the paper to Gansevoort.

"Rogers, thank you for your assistance. You are ordered to mention nothing that you may have learned here."

"Yes, sir."

Rogers left the cabin and Alexander turned to Gansevoort. "Any doubts in your mind, Lieutenant?"

"No, sir."

"Have Philip Spencer placed under arrest immediately."

"Yes, sir." Gansevoort moved swiftly toward the door and paused there with an odd expression upon his face. "Captain, an awkward thought. When we have the irons on Spencer, where are we going to put him?"

"Why, in the hold, I suppose, Lieutenant."

"Sir, there is not an inch of room. He will have to be handcuffed and ankle-ironed and left in the after part of the open deck."

"But the deck is flush fore and aft. He will be in full view of the crew."

"There is no help for it, sir, and it is possible that the sight of Spencer in irons might have a salutary effect upon the men."

"It is possible, Lieutenant." Weakly Alexander sank into his chair, covering his face with his hands. Handcuffs and ankle irons on an eighteen-year-old boy. Where was the world heading when evil seethed in a brain so young?

After a time, he rose and moved on to the miserable business of confronting Spencer. The midshipman, shackled, sat against the bulkhead, sullenly watching him approach.

"Spencer, this is a terrible situation for us all. You have wickedly, criminally planned—"

"I know. I was born wicked. I am always in trouble. I am used to it." The hazel eyes dreamed out at the open sea. "I am not answering any questions."

"I have not asked any. There is nothing in doubt. Your Greek paper makes everything extremely clear."

"Does it?" Spencer's gaze was contemptuous.

"I must remind you, Spencer, that your arrest has not given you license to address me insultingly."

205

Spencer said nothing.

"Is there any word you would like to offer in your own defense?"

Spencer shook his head.

Alexander said, "Answer me properly, Spencer."

Spencer was quiet for a moment longer, then he said, "There is nothing I want to say, Captain."

"Very well." Alexander walked away. Naval procedure, he thought, had its moments of grim humor. Philip Spencer had cold-bloodedly planned the murder of his captain, yet it seemed in order to chide him for a lapse of proper address.

During the morning hours, it became clear that the arrest of Spencer was having no sobering effect upon the men of the *Somers*. Those named in the Greek paper were manufacturing reasons to steal aft under pretence of some call of duty, so as to be near Spencer, watching an opportunity to communicate with him. Hostile glances were flashed at both Alexander and Gansevoort. The two met in the Captain's cabin.

"What is the next step, Captain?"

"More arrests, I fear."

"In your opinion, who is this E. Andrews on the 'certain' list?"

"Cromwell, of course. He is the oldest and most experienced of the lot. He saw the dangers, not the glories of being identified as a mutineer. Somehow he talked Spencer into letting him use another name."

There was a tap at the door and Oliver entered with the word that Heiser wished to see the Captain.

"Have him come in."

Heiser, breathless and wild-eyed, brought the chilling news that the handspikes, heavers and holystones had been mysteriously removed from their customary places.

"And also, sir, two articles which were considered souvenirs now must be regarded in another light entirely. An African knife and battle-ax are at this moment being sharpened by McKinley and Green. McKinley was overheard to say that he would like to get the knife into Spencer's possession and that—"

"Where did you gather all this information, Heiser? Who reported to you the disappearance of handspikes and heavers and who—"

206

He was interrupted by a crash from the deck and sprang toward the ladder, with Gansevoort and Heiser behind him. A glance revealed that the main topgallant mast had been carried away. The aimless milling about of what had been a well-trained, well-organized crew struck Alexander with horror. He bellowed orders and watched the alert response of some of his men and watched, too, the way a dozen or more turned their heads questioningly toward the shackled figure as though for further instruction.

Adrien Deslonde hastened to Alexander's side. "Small violently jerked the weather-royal brace with full intention to carry away the mast. I saw him myself and it was done after consultation with Cromwell. I swear it, sir."

And it was clear that Adrien was not mistaken, for both Small and Cromwell took no step toward aiding in the sending up of the new topgallant mast till Philip Spencer had given the signal to obey. Then, with disappointment evident upon their faces, they moved to the work. Alexander guessed that they had planned confusion and turmoil, thinking it the ideal climate in which to begin battle and bloodshed. Their strategy was sound enough and, he reasoned, had been defeated only by Philip Spencer's unwillingness to sanction an idea he had not originated.

When the mast was raised, Alexander gave the order for Small and Cromwell to be placed under arrest, and now three figures in irons sprawled upon the open deck and terror stalked the *Somers*.

Spencer's potential followers were openly sullen and morose, missing muster without excuse, expressing in ominous tones their displeasure at the prisoners being kept in irons, communicating with the three by glance and signal. One of the missing handspikes came out of its hiding place after Midshipman Tillotson had been insolently disobeyed by Seaman Wilson. Tillotson had reported the man to Gansevoort and an hour later, with back turned, had been attacked by Wilson, brandishing the weapon. Wilson, shackled and snarling, was thrown with the other prisoners and was soon joined by Green, McKee and McKinley. Not a man on the brig, loyal or villainous, could be unaffected by the sight of seven men involved in the crime of mutiny.

In the tiny cabin, Alexander met with Gansevoort, Heiser and Wales to speak and to listen. Three days had passed since Spencer's arrest and each day had brought new dangers, new fears.

Gansevoort said, "It requires an omniscient eye to select those if any on whom we can now rely. To have the Greek paper is not the great help that at first flush it seemed. From actions aboard, it is easy to guess that Spencer's boast of twenty staunch followers was a modest estimate."

"Well," Heiser ventured, "why don't we hold an investigation with questioning and—"

"That would be worse than useless," Alexander broke in. "There is not space to hold or force to guard any increased number of prisoners. Besides, suppose we hold a court of inquiry, then what? Then we have informed a large number of our crew that when they reach the United States, they will be punished but that in the meanwhile, they may run loose and are expected to perform their jobs in good order. Mr. Heiser, does this sound like a truly workable plan to you? Do you not think these men might choose the black flag here and now?"

Wales said, "Of course they would. They are about to do so at any moment as it is. All that is needed is for one man to feel self-confident enough to take the lead. As soon as that one man is appointed by himself or the others or by a signal from Spencer, we are going to be rushed. We are going to be rushed and murdered."

"That is extravagant language, Mr. Wales. We are not going to be rushed and murdered," Alexander said. "We are going to bring the *Somers* into New York harbor safe and sound."

"Of course, I agree with the Captain," Gansevoort said thoughtfully, "but the conspiracy is ferocious and desperate. The instinct of discipline has been lost. Anything is possible when anarchy has the upper hand." He paused, then added, "Everything on a ship is a weapon. Implements of wood and iron are available for close and hasty combat no matter where a man stands. And we are positive of so few and suspicious of so many."

"We ourselves must stand sentinel," Alexander said. "Under arms day and night, watch and watch about. Those of us present, the Perry brothers, Deslonde and the other midshipmen now have the responsibility of the *Somers*. A great deal of labor we have as well, for we are too uncertain of where trust may be placed."

And when he was alone again in the cabin, Alexander lowered

his head into his arms and wept, for he knew full well what must be done, what in the end would be done. With all his heart he had loved the Navy and now he must act in accordance with the Navy's implacable laws. And when he did, when he gave to his ship that protection necessary to preserve her honor, he knew he would lose forever the Navy to which he had dedicated his soul.

Where had he failed? How had he failed? He who had tried so hard, who had yearned so passionately to be a great officer. It came to him as he wept there aboard the *Somers* that it was as foolish to strive for greatness as to seek to storm the gates of heaven. It was given or it was not given. One did one's best and if fortune smiled, there was a reward. One did one's best and if fortune frowned, an eighteen-year-old boy with murder in his heart sailed aboard one's ship. And Alexander sobbed like a girl for the dreams he had had, and he felt no shame. God knew his tears were his to shed if he so desired, for it had not been with an egotist's rage for fame that he had held precious his naval career. Another field had given him fame enough to satisfy any egotist. It was for love that he had served the Navy. To have someday that love returned was what he had lived for. Now the hope was gone. Yes, he would bring the *Somers* safely into New York harbor but at a price. Dear God, at what a price.

And after a while, he dried his tears and walked the deck as a captain should with assurance and dignity. Stern-faced, he inspected the prisoners, satisfying himself that they were clean, well fed and comfortable within reason. The prisoners averted their eyes but not before he had glimpsed hatred and anger. Only Cromwell, the giant boatswain, was mild-mannered and respectful.

He said, "Captain, may I speak, please? Captain, I am innocent of any plot against you or the ship."

"Are you, Cromwell?"

"Yes, sir. Before God I swear I am innocent. I know nothing of any plot, if there is such a thing."

"You are the only man aboard who can be in doubt."

"I cannot speak for others, sir, but I am innocent." He leaned closer to Alexander, squinting up at him from the deck. "Surely, Captain, you did not find my name on any suspicious paper or anything."

209

"No, Cromwell, I did not find your name. You were careful about that."

Now Spencer, seeming with effort to shake himself from lethargy, spoke. He said, "Cromwell is telling you the truth. He is innocent."

Alexander shifted his gaze to Spencer. The calmness and detachment of his tone suggested unawareness of how implicit was his own guilt in the words he had used to defend Cromwell. Alexander knew Spencer too well to think him naïve or thick-skulled. And in a sudden wave of painful clarity, Alexander recognized a kinship with Spencer. Here was another human who understood the stupidity of quarreling with the inevitable. There was good fortune and there was bad and Philip Spencer, in handcuffs and ankle irons, knew it to be a truth. He expected nothing for himself but that which naturally follows those marked for misfortune. The red-haired captain, towering above the prisoner as a symbol of decency and authority, was shocked to find himself looking with sympathy upon Philip Spencer. This tragic lad had forged his own shackles. But he could not have done so, could not have found the way, had fortune favored him. And because fortune had favored neither the prisoner nor the red-haired captain, they would be each other's undoing.

"Spencer, if there is guilt, if you do not deny your own, how is it possible for Cromwell to be innocent? He was your constant companion."

The hazel eyes met Alexander's. "I tell you he is innocent."

"And do you think there is a reason why I should accept your word?"

"Yes. I have nothing to gain by defending Cromwell."

"Nothing to lose, either, Spencer."

"That's true," Spencer agreed and withdrew himself from the conversation. His eyes went back to contemplation of the sea.

"I am innocent, Captain," Cromwell said again. "Before God, Captain, I am innocent."

And though it was logical that a man who could plot mass murder would not hesitate to speak an untruth, still it was difficult to understand why Spencer spoke only for Cromwell. The boatswain was as guilty as any. No action of his could be interpreted in his favor and four midshipmen, prior to their knowing the significance

210

of the Greek paper, had seen it in Cromwell's hands while Spencer whispered explanations.

"I thought," Midshipman Rogers had told Alexander, "that Spencer was teaching him geometry."

It was fantastic to turn from the seven men in shackles to the wardroom, where a class of apprentices awaited him. This was a training ship and the training would continue, but there was an element of frightful absurdity here which Alexander recognized. Some of these apprentices were, in physical strength, already men and doubtless a percentage of them were Spencer's followers. Others, with slim, childlike bodies inadequate for the rugged demands of piracy, would be drowned like unwanted kittens in the event of a triumph by the mutineers. And so he, the captain, sat among those who could possibly become murderers and those who could possibly become their victims and ridiculously gave the arbitrary rule for measuring tonnage.

"Measure from the fore part of the main stem to the after part of the stern post above the upper deck; take the breadth thereof at the broadest part above the main wales, one-half of which breadth shall be counted the depth; deduct from the length three-fifths of such breadth; multiplying the remainder by the breadth and the product by the depth; divide by ninety-five; the quotient is the tonnage."

He watched them take notes, some faces wrinkled in pained perplexity, others bright with interest and faith that soon the rule would be as clear to them as to their captain.

Reminding himself of a schoolma'am stubbornly ignoring the fact that the classroom was on fire, Alexander continued, "This will give you the basis for figuring your space for handling guns, berthing the crew and storing provisions, ammunition and water."

"Sir, could you repeat the rule?"

"Of course. Measure from the fore part of the main stem—"

Remarkable that any of them could tear their thoughts away from the seven men in shackles.

Oliver had admitted Lieutenant Gansevoort to the captain's cabin and he left them together as Alexander entered. The cabin was in disorderly condition. Nicholas had declared himself ill and the doctor had informed Alexander that the dizziness of which

Nicholas had complained was caused by an alarmingly rapid heart-beat.

"Captain, I must tell you that a crisis may suddenly be forced upon us," Gansevoort said as the door closed behind Oliver. "It is common knowledge that within a week or so we will be not far from the Island of St. Thomas. A rumor is sweeping the ship that we plan to put in there and leave the seven prisoners and all men under suspicion in the care of the British government till a larger American vessel can pick them up and bring them home for trial."

Alexander nodded. "It is a thought that would come naturally to any man aboard."

"Yes, a fearsome thought. The unconfined culprits, sir, will not wait patiently to be thrown in irons and sent home to positive doom. I detest Wales's dramatic language, Captain, but there is reason to fear we will be rushed and murdered."

"Yes," Alexander said. He sat down and bent his head, fixing his eyes upon the log of the brig *Somers*. For a hundred hours now, he had known that there was no hope, that inexorably the moment of decision was drawing near. There was only one thing to do and only one prayer to offer—that Gansevoort's mind remain strong and clear enough to be uninfluenced by what his captain thought. "For I may be wrong. And if I am wrong, I want no agreement from Gansevoort. Let him fight me, dear Lord, if there is another conclusion than the one I have reached."

"As I see the matter now, Captain, piracy is no longer the dream of these men. It is but the second crime into which they will be forced in order to protect themselves for having committed the first. They are thinking of those seven prisoners, any one of whom, by turning State's witness, might insure their own conviction."

"I know," Alexander said.

"The black flag is now their surest protection. Captain, they will attack us and release Spencer and the others." Gansevoort drew closer and said, "They have to do it, Captain. It is only over our bloody bodies that they can free Spencer and they must have Spencer or Cromwell or Small. No other man among them can navigate a vessel!"

So Gansevoort had realized that, too. Closer and closer to the inevitable. Dear God, is there another way?

212

"Captain." Gansevoort dropped his eyes and his voice shook. "Please do not take offense. I only want to help you. Someday I hope to command a ship and I will be grateful then if help is offered me. Sir, would you permit a discussion of this matter among the officers and warrants?"

"I have not discouraged discussion, Lieutenant. We have had—"

He paused as Gansevoort's face flamed red.

"I meant without your presence, Captain."

"I see."

"It is this way, sir, and you must know it. Some will venture no word unless certain that it is one they have heard you speak. Let us talk in private and then we will tell you what opinion we reached. You need not accept it. It may be of some help but in the end, the responsibility is yours, the decision is yours, and I know that well."

Alexander looked away from Gansevoort. He said, "The high seas offer no learned jurists with whom I may consult. I will appeal to the best and only counsel within my reach. I shall send a written request to certain men. Thank you, Mr. Gansevoort."

Within the hour, they gathered in the wardroom. Gansevoort, Heiser, Mattie Perry, Wales, Leecock and Midshipmen Rogers, Thompson and Hays.

Alexander ran the vessel while Tillotson, Adrien Deslonde and Oliver Perry, armed and alert, patrolled the decks. With melancholy certainty, Alexander knew what opinion would issue from the council below. There was no other. He was aware even now of the boiling hostility that surrounded him. It was reported that Adrien had stopped only at gun point a man intent upon communicating with Spencer. And Alexander thought of the quotation that "Nothing emboldens sin so much as mercy." And on this day, he thought it true.

And on this day, too, the sea had never been bluer nor its siren song more sweetly pitched to enter the heart of the red-haired captain who had loved it well. He scowled to keep the tears from his eyes and swallowed hard the lump of misery that rose to his throat.

Solemnly aware of the true question confronting them, the men in the wardroom made no hurried business of their deliberations. The hours passed and a night of star shine came down upon the

Somers. Only the evil and those suspected of evil were allowed to sleep. There was a need for armed men, and few who could be trusted. The gathering in the wardroom could be a fatal provocation, so there was no rest for the trustworthy. The night dragged by and at dawn the court had not adjourned. Alexander and his men took no ease and substituted coffee for sleep. And it was hours and more hours till twilight colored the sea with rose-and-purple light and suddenly the deliberations were ended.

To Alexander came a note from each of the men who had sat in judgment and there was no disagreement. The ringleaders of the mutiny were Spencer, Cromwell and Small. In the opinion of those who had weighed the matter carefully, these men must die.

Gansevoort, the spokesman, summed up the situation as it had been seen in the wardroom.

"We do not believe there is a chance of bringing the *Somers* into New York harbor with these three men alive. A single concerted rush can overpower the officers and free the prisoners. There is no intention of permitting us to deliver Spencer and the others to duly authorized court-martial ashore. The closer we come to New York, the greater our danger. We believe fast action is necessary but our hearts and abilities are with you, Captain, no matter how you decide."

Alexander dropped into a chair and asked for a drink of whisky. He downed it quickly. There was no time to rest. And in thinking of what must now be done, he was not certain that he would ever rest again.

In the dim, shuttered house at the Brooklyn Navy Yard, John Slidell faced his brother across a luncheon that had been brought to them on trays. John had not seen Catherine. She was, he had been told, lying in her room in a state of collapse. The two men sat in Alec's office, which had a cathedral-like atmosphere. Far too grand, John thought, for a room dedicated to Alec's writing. The chairs and tables were exquisite Spanish antiques purchased on that profitable leave of Alec's when he had written his most successful book. Idly John wondered if his brother could be induced to sell the contents of this room. There were corners of Belle-Point crying for such furnishings. So like Alec to use them at the Navy Yard house instead of at Tarrytown.

"Listen," he said, "I have come all the way from New Orleans to see if I can be of help to you, so do not ask questions that will result in time-wasting, disagreeable discussion. I am not without influence so let us see how I can serve you."

Alec shook his head. "Influence is a meaningless word in this—"

"Oh, for Christ's sake, Alec, influence has never been a meaningless word. During the first winter, cave men found out that having the right relatives got them a seat closer to the fire. Now, look here, my boy. It is not wise for me to do anything about the court-martial unless, of course, they decide to shoot you. But I understand that if the Navy finds you not guilty, Mr. Secretary of War Spencer is planning to have the civilian courts try you for murder."

"But surely even civilians would see that the executions were necessary."

"Wait a minute. Even the Navy is not yet convinced that they were. You have not been court-martialed, you know, to receive a medal. There are about a million people on both sides of the Atlantic who think you were a little hasty with the yardarm." John chewed thoughtfully. "I know nothing about how verdicts are arrived at in the Navy, but I can tell you something about civilian juries. People are sentimental about people. This is the tack you would have to take: you would have to convince twelve good men that Spencer, Small and Cromwell were potential murderers of boys you loved. Your own nephews and Mathilde's brother. You would have to convince them that the safety of these fine, adored youngsters meant everything to you."

Alexander paled. "My God, John, that is contemptible. As commander of the *Somers,* I had my duty to the United States Navy, not to my family."

"Civilian courts understand self-defense, too. These bloody little bastards would have murdered you without blinking an eye."

"Yes," Alexander said, "but I implore you to try to understand the situation. The lives of military men whether on land or sea are plighted to their country and compared to the honor of that country, individual life is as a drop of the ocean. The nation's honor was at stake, John. An American vessel of war was about to be-

215

come a piratical cruiser. I did not hang those men to save my life or the lives of Cal's sons or Mathilde's brother. I hanged them to save the *Somers*. It was my duty."

John said, "To hang three men for a chilly little thing like duty —well, I think a jury might look upon you as a hardhearted customer. Alec, couldn't you have possibly brought these men home alive?"

"I expect to prove at my court-martial that I could not. There will be those to say I could have done so. Before God, John, I had not the force to guard them. In a cell with locks and bars, the problem is simplified but—"

"Could you not have locked them in your own cabin, for instance, with an armed man or two patrolling outside? Surely it would have been better for you to have slept on the deck than to have invited all this—"

"You have not the slightest idea what my problems were, have you, John? The *Somers* has only thin and frail partitions below, through which a man could force his way from the brig's stem to her stern by the shove of a shoulder or the push of a foot."

"Oh?" John raised his head and looked down his nose at Alexander. "So the brainy Commodore designed a pretty piece of floating bric-a-brac, did he?"

"He designed a magnificent vessel." Alexander poured himself a cup of tea and gazed into the faraway. He said, "I have not yet seen Mother. Will you tell her that I apologize for having taken her name?"

John choked on a swallow of water and coughed violently. His face was purple as he spoke. "Shall I have the choir from Grace Church accompany me as I tell her? Apologize to Mother!"

Alexander did not reply. He sat back in his chair and stared unhappily at his brother. He had not expected much from John but life was so bizarre. Why should it not have turned out that John was the one comfort in his hour of despair?

Catherine had said, "You must have been mad. You have ruined us."

And Cal—Cal had looked at him with a freezing glance. "There must have been another way, Alexander," he had said.

"No, there was no other way, Cal."

216

"God damn it, I would have found another way."

And perhaps Cal would have. Oh, certainly, he would have. He would have known how to tame Philip Spencer. He would have brought young Philip home alive and not even in irons. He would have laughingly delivered him to the Secretary of War, saying, "Here is your cub, Mr. Secretary, wild but not so wild today as when we first met." Yes, Cal would have known how to do that. And suddenly Alexander felt tears upon his cheeks and turned his face away from John.

John said, "It is a bad toss, Alec. I am sorry."

Alexander fumbled for his handkerchief. "Merciful God, John, *was* there something else I could have done?"

John nodded. "Yes, Alec, you could have hanged Small and Cromwell."

"I did!"

"But you also hanged the son of the Secretary of War. That does not make sense. You just do not hang the sons of important men unless you are looking for trouble."

"I was well aware of John Canfield Spencer's importance and that he would use the power of his position vengefully, but I could not have hanged Small and Cromwell and permitted his son to live. That would not have been justice."

"It would have been damn good thinking, though. Two dangling bodies would have quieted your insurgents just as well as three. The sight might even have sobered young Spencer. If not—well, one little son of a bitch cannot be all that difficult to guard."

Alexander stared in wonderment. "Is it possible that you do not know how unconscionable your thinking is? Can it be that you go through life giving no thought to honor or decency? Do you truly act only in the interest of expediency?"

John said, "Let us put it this way—I would not have gone to the Crusades."

Alexander rose and carried his tray into the corridor. Even the sight of food was an abomination. When he returned, he poured himself a drink from the decanter upon his desk. "John," he said, "I find myself in need of one of two things—a kind word or solitude. Which do you feel disposed to offer me?"

John lighted a cigar and sat back in his chair. "Because you are

217

a writer, I guess it is only natural that you place such a ridiculously high value upon words. If I said to you, 'Alexander, my brother, I love you more than anything on earth,' you would treasure that statement. And if I added, 'What you did aboard the *Somers* is what any great captain would have done,' you would probably faint with delight. All right, I can say those things if you want to hear them. Utter hogwash, but I have nothing against hogwash when there's a market for it." John paused and examined his cigar with interest. "You would thank me for empty words, Alec, but I have not had so much as a warm handclasp for having dropped every God-damned thing in New Orleans to come running to your side." John stood up and walked toward the door. "I will give you your solitude, Alec. We were never soothing to each other."

Alexander raised his glass, drank slowly and looked away from his brother. "I regret that I have shown no appreciation. Forgive me. I am not myself."

"That is an excuse that always irks me. No man ever evokes it when he has behaved with admirable courage or kindness. Only when he has conducted himself unacceptably is this sickening disclaimer called into play. Do you wish to imply that ordinarily you are a hell of a greathearted fellow? No? Then do not use the phrase. Say instead, 'Forgive me. I am myself.' "

Alexander said, "I never know how to answer you."

"Of course not. In debate, lawyers always slaughter writers. A writer can express himself only with a pen."

The brandy glass crashed suddenly upon the hearth and Alexander turned hot, angry eyes upon John. "Will you stop saying that I am a writer? I am a Navy man. Are you a gardener because camellias grow at Belle-Point? No, you are a lawyer. And, by God, I am a Navy man. Do you understand that? I am a Navy man."

As Alexander's voice rose shrilly, John walked toward him and laid a hand upon his shoulder. "Yes, you are. That is why you have self-control enough to limit your outbursts to the breaking of a glass. Tom or I, in your situation, would go to pieces, but because you are a Navy man, you are disciplined. You know how to steady your nerves, how to combat hysteria."

It was not the time to give Alexander solitude.

218

I had better go to Washington. I had better see the Secretary of the Navy. How thick is he with Spencer? I will have Buchanan find out. Maybe Tyler could help. Do I know anybody Tyler likes?

How pure was a naval court-martial? Were the damn things composed of shining-eyed demigods like Cal Perry? Or could the prosecution ever be induced to take things easy? Cal, for God's sake! Cal would heroically march Alexander out and personally hang him if the Navy said that was the thing to do.

I think I will go to Cal. I will say to him, "If you can give me a hand here, Cal, I would appreciate it. After all, by taking stern action, my brother probably saved the lives of your two sons."

No. When you were in trouble, you could never go to people of Commodore Matthew Calbraith Perry's sort. Such people were for the happy times when you needed no favors. For favors, you turned to a man who had sinned a little, a man with a sad knowledge of what the world was really like. Twelve hours to Washington. Twelve hours back. At least twenty-four hours there. If only Catherine had been strong enough for Alec to lean upon through this dismal ordeal. John glanced at Alexander. His eyes looked heavy and ready to sleep.

"I will see you in a few days, boy. Try to get some rest. Eat a little, too, will you?"

Alexander nodded absently. "John."

"Yes?"

"John, I did what I thought was right."

"Of course you did."

"But if nobody else thinks I did right— Do you see what that means? It means my judgment is completely erratic, that I do not reach sane, sensible conclusions."

"Well, Gansevoort and the other fellows saw things just as you did."

Alexander shuddered. "I know. That is why I cannot sleep. John, I keep thinking they saw things just as I did because they were looking through my eyes."

John reached for the decanter. God, what an imagination! "Alec," he said, "if I didn't know you were a Navy man, I would swear you were a writer."

. . .

219

"Moorings" was especially beautiful that year. The winter had been mild and March, when it came to Tarrytown, breathed as warmly and softly as May. Then April had accepted the joke and pretended to be June.

Janie Slidell Perry had been grateful for the good weather, for Cal had decided back in December that they could not be a part of New York's social season that winter. There had been nothing to do but walk the countryside, take an interest in repairs on the outbuildings and play the part of a country wife. Janie had found the whole thing tiresome.

"Yes, 'Moorings' for the winter will be charming," she had said to Cal. "So gay and stimulating. How sad that you will miss it all."

"Now, do not be sarcastic, Janie. You have no choice and I should think to retire from questions and comments would be your natural wish."

"Well, it is not. Would it be yours?"

"What a silly question! I am Commandant of the Brooklyn Navy Yard. Can I spend the entire winter at 'Moorings'?"

"No, you cannot, and I envy you your luck."

He had shaken his head in mystification. "I do not understand you. Your brother has been court-martialed. Your sons are witnesses in one of the most sensational cases that ever shook the country. Do you mean that you would actually like to expose yourself to the stares and remarks and—"

"Oh, for heaven's sake, Cal, I would be in the parlors and ballrooms of my friends. They would not—"

"I prefer you to stay at 'Moorings.' It will not be very long, dear—"

"Unless the Navy decides to execute Alec. Then you will think it only proper for me to mourn him forever."

"You are very callous. Do you have no pity for your brother?"

"Of course I have, but he has exposed us all to a terrible ordeal. The London newspapers are calling him a murderer, a coward and a fool. It is almost more than—"

"The London newspapers have been damned insulting to an officer of the United States Navy."

She had broken down then and laughed. Somehow, and she was never quite sure why, Cal was wonderfully funny when speaking

220

what to him were the most awesome words that could be enunciated —The United States Navy. Was it because he was never more endearingly boyish than in his most solemn moments? Was it because to her the United States Navy was only the firm for which he worked? After all, an excess of loyalty to the New York City Shoe and Gaiter Company could be a pretty ridiculous thing.

Now, leaning against a trim fence, gazing across the meadow, she thought how long and dull the stay at "Moorings" had been but how correct Cal's decision. Time had revealed that the parlors and ballrooms of her friends had not, by any means, been crowded with Commander Alexander Slidell MacKenzie's well-wishers.

Caroline, her youngest, riding the black colt Monsoon, came into view and outlined against the spring sky, horse and rider seemed to Janie beautiful beyond imagining. Caroline, her yellow hair free in the sunlight, directed Monsoon to pause and beneath the budding trees, the two young things held themselves motionless and magnificent. Janie wondered if either the black colt or the yellow-haired girl sensed a relationship with spring and she thought of her own springtime when she had dreamed of marrying the quiet lad in midshipman's uniform. Of what did Caroline dream?

Janie called to her, and Monsoon moved slowly across the sunlit turf. A boy came from the stable, assisted Caroline to dismount and led the colt away.

"Did you have a nice ride, dear?" Janie asked.

"Lovely." Caroline's eyes were very gray. Those who knew her well looked to them to tell whether or not she was pleased. Caroline was an unsmiling girl, to her father an eternal oddity.

"Young girls are supposed to giggle and laugh and whisper together, Janie."

The girl pleased Janie. She liked Caroline's haughtiness, her aloofness from the pink-cheeked gigglers, her talent for choosing clothes that were right for her. She liked the thought that Caroline was as she had been. She liked the thought. She knew that at sixteen, she had not been as interesting as Caroline. This girl had the fine, clear mind of Matthew Calbraith Perry, spiced with just enough Slidell flavoring to give it style.

They walked toward the house, Caroline's stride graceful and swift. Too swift.

"I refuse to run along at your side, panting, my dear," Janie said. "Meet me for tea in my sitting room."

Caroline slowed down. "Was there something you wanted to tell me?"

Janie experienced a small resentment. If there was no message for her, Caroline would just hurry along. Was that it? Rather damned unfriendly. And yet Janie had had daughters who had clung to her arm and not a one of them had meant as much to her as Caroline.

"Yes. There were two letters today. One from Father and one from Aunt Mathilde."

Caroline stopped dead on the path. "The one from Father— what did he say of Uncle Alec? Has the Navy Department announced the court-martial verdict?"

Janie nodded. "The court-martial has found Uncle Alec not guilty."

Caroline closed her eyes and breathed deeply. "Thank God," she murmured. "Oh, thank God."

Really! All this emotion over Uncle Alec? Why, the child had yet to knit him a scarf for Christmas or embroider his initials on a handkerchief. And yet perhaps she was being unfair to Caroline. It could be that Caroline had suffered for her mother's anxieties. Or it could be that for her Aunt Catherine's sake, Caroline was grateful. It could be—

"Think of the shame that would have fallen upon us if he had been executed," Caroline said.

"Oh, yes, indeed, Uncle Alec would never have got over it," Janie replied grimly. But she was content with Caroline's remark, for it assured her that she still understood the child. She did not even mind now that Caroline was floating fifteen feet ahead of her. Suddenly the girl stopped once more as a new thought struck her.

"What about the civilian court?" she asked. "Will he be tried there?"

"No, darling. God is very good. He heard your prayers and will preserve our social position."

As Janie watched her daughter flash through the orchard, past

222

the rose garden and beyond her range of vision, she thought about the other piece of news. Caroline would like that, too.

They met for tea a few minutes later in Janie's pearwood sitting room. Caroline had piled her hair atop her head and had changed from her riding habit into a flowered cotton wrapper. Her pale golden skin glowed with memories of a day spent outdoors. These were lovely moments, Janie thought, listening to the sedate tinkle of china cups. Teatime with Caroline. Secretly Janie thought this child the most wonderful Perry of them all. She hoped that somehow here in this room during the long winter of withdrawal, she had established an intimacy that would last her lifetime. When this child was married to some dull and weedy young naval officer, would they still have an occasional friendly cup of tea together?

Lord, how middle-aged her thinking had become. How muddled and illogical. First of all, it was not a positive fact that Caroline would marry into the Navy. Then, most young naval officers were neither dull nor weedy. They inclined to be good-looking and/or pleasantly amusing. The only dull and weedy one she could remember was Raymond Rogers, whom her baby sister, Julia, had married, and he was now a sort of naval celebrity, the youngest captain on record. If she had any sense, she would pray for Caroline to do as well as Julia had.

As the tea was served, as the dainty sandwiches and jewel-like pastries were set before them, Caroline gazed through the large window out at the gardens, contentment in her eyes.

"I am so pleased about Uncle Alec," she said when the maid had gone. "So pleased and rather surprised."

Janie looked up quickly from her tea-pouring. "Surprised, dear?"

"Of course. Aren't you?"

"Not at all. It was necessary for Uncle Alec to hang three mutineers. The court-martial, not being a stupid body of men, saw that it was necessary."

"Yes, I suppose so," Caroline said, accepting the cup from her mother. "Did you read all the testimony, all of Uncle Alec's beautifully written defense?"

"Not every word."

"I did," Caroline said. "I read every word." She reached for a small mocha tart. "I would not have acquitted Uncle Alec."

Janie gasped. "Caroline!"

"Why are you so horror-stricken? By your own admission you did not read everything available. In my opinion, Uncle Alec— But you would not be happier for knowing my opinion. What about the letter from Aunt Mathilde?"

"Oh, yes. She has asked us to entertain a young couple from Louisiana. Lieutenant and Mrs. Beauregard."

"Navy?"

"No. Army. They have been married about a year and a half. She was a Villère, which your Aunt Mathilde assures me is something very fine to be. Seems that young Mrs. Beauregard's grandfather was the first Creole governor of Louisiana. She will be very elegant, I am sure."

"We will entertain them in the city?"

"With several days here as well. They are bringing young Caroline Deslonde with them. Queer the Deslonde family also has a Caroline. I do not think I ever noticed it before."

"I did. Is she visiting us, too?"

"No. She is being enrolled in a school in the city. The Beauregards are simply looking after her on the journey north. More tea, dear?"

"Yes, thank you." Caroline helped herself to two small sandwiches. At teatime, she always began with the pastries and Janie pretended not to notice. It was almost the only childishness left in Caroline—the fear that sandwiches first would leave no room for sweets. "I shall be very glad to see the Beauregards, Mother. We have been fearfully isolated and for such a long time."

A very long time. Since that day in December when the brig *Somers* had arrived in the bay and for twenty-four hours had lain mysteriously apart from the other shipping, permitting nobody to come on board till Lieutenant Gansevoort had carried his message to the city of Washington and the Secretary of the Navy. And now they were both thinking of the court-martial again.

"Did Uncle Alec receive an honorable acquittal?" Caroline asked.

Janie was startled. "Now, how did such a question come to your mind?"

"I told you I read every word that was printed. Did he?"

224

"As a matter of fact, he did not. It was just an acquittal."

"Still—" Caroline began and then fell silent.

Janie leaned toward her across the small, wheeled table. "You were going to say, 'Still, he was lucky to get that.' Isn't that what was on the tip of your tongue?"

"Exactly. Mother, for the love of heaven, do not tell Father I said so, but the Navy was terribly tender with its favorite author. If I were Secretary of War Spencer, I would personally kill Uncle Alec and I would kill the Secretary of the Navy, too. Somehow, somewhere, somebody pulled everything into a shape that was awfully comfortable for Uncle Alec."

"Why, such a thing cannot be done, child."

"Now, stop sounding like Father. You are not in the Navy."

"But right is right, Caroline. This Spencer boy was an evil, vicious, loathsome—"

"Absolute devil, whom you invited to two weddings."

"I did not invite him. I invited his father and mother and they brought him."

"And at both weddings you noticed that he was evil, vicious and so forth?"

"Well, of course you know that I never noticed him at all. He was, however, as has been proved, a young man of villainous intent. Mutiny, Caroline, is a crime so dreadful that—"

"Yes. Father told me." Her eyes turned again to the garden. "Mother, be very smart when you go back to the city. Do not discuss the matter of the court-martial with anyone."

"I know this is going to be hard for you to believe, Caroline, but I am generally considered an intelligent woman."

Caroline pushed her chair back from the table and studied her mother thoughtfully before she spoke. Then, "Yes, you are an intelligent woman but you might still quiver with righteousness on the subject of Commander Alexander Slidell MacKenzie. Just now you were very quick to establish Philip Spencer as the most fiendish character who ever sailed the seas. Do not do it in public, Mother. You may run into somebody who has read more of the case than you have."

Janie sighed. "Very well. I guess I had better know. Where is the pitfall?"

"It's in dear Uncle Alec's elaborately written defense. A person reading it has to wonder a little. By his own words, at the peak of danger, just when mutiny was about to explode at any second, he ran the brig with only Oliver, Adrien Deslonde and another midshipman. Does it not seem to you that this was the ideal moment for the mutineers to charge, if mutineers there were?"

"Why, Caroline Perry, what a thing to say!" Janie stared at her daughter in bewilderment. "Do you think Uncle Alec regarded the hanging of three men as good sport?"

"No. I just think Uncle Alec overestimated the danger."

Janie shook her head. "You are without a doubt the most arrogant young woman I ever saw. You think that at sixteen years of age, sitting in a farmhouse in Tarrytown, New York, you can see the whole thing more clearly than an experienced Navy commander right on the scene saw it?"

"Oh, very definitely," Caroline said. "I can weigh the matter without getting nervous. Uncle Alec could not."

"You are impossible." Janie, a little nervous herself, reviewed swiftly all she had read and heard of the horrible affair. "Oh," she said suddenly, happy to be able to argue a point. "While Uncle Alec was running the brig with just the three boys, the mutineers did not dare strike because Gansevoort and all other officers were gathered in council in the wardroom. They were awake and ready in case—" She allowed her voice to trail off as she saw Caroline's eyes fixed sadly upon her.

"Mother, in another part of his defense, Uncle Alec spoke of the impossibility of ascent from below by officers and other faithful men. He said the companion scuttle was so narrow that one by one they could be murdered as they appeared. It seems to me that he set up the ideal conditions for mutiny and then nothing at all happened. How does it seem to you?"

"It seems to me," said Janie stiffly, "that your Uncle Alec did what he thought right."

"Yes, of course he did, but more than that is expected of a naval officer. He is supposed to do what *is* right." Caroline moved back to the table and chose another sandwich. "A pity, was it not, about Leecock, the doctor, committing suicide before the court-martial had endorsed the hangings?"

226

"A great pity, but he was in poor health."

"Yes, but I keep wondering . . ."

With but one bite taken from it, Caroline dropped the sandwich, now unwanted, upon her plate. "All this has only been my thinking on the subject and I may be wrong. Forget everything I have said."

"With pleasure, young lady. You have said some dreadful things."

"They are dreadful only if they are true. Actually, I was just expressing ideas which the Judge Advocate might have offered had he ever found the courage to speak up. I am perfectly certain Uncle Alec did what he thought was right and I am delighted with his acquittal. Now let us talk about the clothes you will want to buy me for the Beauregards' visit."

John Quincy Adams, an ex-President who wished to continue service to his country, did not regard a Congressional seat as an insult to his past achievements. However, he looked sourly upon some of his colleagues.

"The day was consumed by the dullest of speeches," he wrote to a friend. "James E. Belser of Montgomery, Alabama, against the tariff, Richard Brodhead of Easton, Pennsylvania, for it and John Slidell of New Orleans on both sides."

Mr. Adams would have been cheered to know that the voice of John Slidell of New Orleans would not be heard very often in Congressional debate. It was a busy year for John Slidell. Louisiana, he had promised, would go for James K. Polk but Polk's opponent had turned out to be Henry Clay and Clay was alarmingly popular in New Orleans.

"How is it down your way?" Buchanan asked anxiously.

"Splendid. Best weather in twenty years."

"You know what I am talking about, Slidell. How is your state going to vote?"

"Democratic, that is how. Next question."

"My next question is this: are you sure?"

"Now, listen. You worried like this in Baltimore at the convention. When some of the boys wanted Van Buren again, you were ready to believe that we were licked. I kept telling you that Polk would be nominated but you fretted just as you are fretting now. Take my word, Louisiana will go for Polk."

"I hope you know your state. We have to have Louisiana."

John laughed. "Why is it that everybody always has to have Louisiana? I am constantly told that if I fail to deliver Louisiana, I have mortally wounded the party. I live for the day when somebody will tell me that this time the party does not need Louisiana."

"When somebody tells you that, Slidell, go home weeping, for it will be a polite way of saying that the party does not need John Slidell. The party will always need Louisiana. Tell me honestly, do you think you can deliver it for Polk?"

"Oh, for God's sake, have I not just told you—"

"Yes, you have just told me but I cannot help being concerned."

Neither could John. It was not easy to forget the way New Orleans felt about Henry Clay and his two daughters, who had married prominent Orleanians and settled in the Garden District. It was not easy to forget that Clay's visits to the city had always been celebrated with parades and entertainments and a ball at either the St. Charles or St. Louis Hotel. Of course, Clay also had enemies in New Orleans. Enough? No, not enough. It was easy to like Clay.

"I am very fond of him myself," John thought. "What can I do to ruin him in Louisiana?"

Sometimes, in the middle of the night, he would leave his bed and go quietly to sit alone with a drink and a square look at his problems. James Knox Polk. A spare man of unpretending appearance and middle stature, a small head, a full, angular brow. What was heroic about him? So far only battle cries. "The Whole of Oregon or None." "Fifty-four Forty or Fight." And John Slidell knew all this was meaningless to Southerners. Was there a Louisianan whose heart beat faster at the thought of possessing Oregon? Of course, Polk also wanted to possess part of Mexico and extend the realm of slavery into the new states which would be carved from the annexation. This was interesting to Louisiana. But interesting enough to outweigh the fact that Polk was a Mason?

"I must like trouble," John thought bitterly. "I knew Polk was a Mason when I let myself in for all this. I knew his wife was a strict Presbyterian who shuns 'the vanities of the world.' They are certainly an untasty dish to serve up for Louisiana's consideration. I must have been mad."

He thought of his friends in New Orleans. Or did he have any when it came to electing James K. Polk? The whole damned Bar Association would go for Henry Clay. Mazureau, Soulé, Roselius, Judah Benjamin—all of them were Clay men. Even Chief Justice Thomas Slidell.

Sitting with his drink and a cigar in the predawn hours, John thought of Edward Livingston. He thought how Edward, too, had once sat in this city, tormented with the fear that he would not win Louisiana for his candidate. Edward had picked up a pen and asked a young friend in New Orleans to help him elect Andrew Jackson and the young friend had helped.

"But today there are no youngsters like that," John thought mournfully. "What has become of the ambitious, imaginative ones? I would give much to have a fine young fellow to whom I could call for assistance as Edward called to me. But the world has changed. Where is the boy now who could think of anything as effective as my labeling old John Quincy Adams an anti-Catholic?"

And there was a night when he had dwelt so long and dismally on James K. Polk's affiliation with the Masons that he went to the bedroom and awakened Mathilde.

"In a few hours, you must begin packing and arranging to return home," he told her.

She sat up and stared at him with heavy, sleep-filled eyes. "What has happened?" she asked.

"Mr. Polk joined the Masons and his wife is a Presbyterian, so you will have to get up."

"What, dear?" In the moonlight, she looked as bewildered and helpless as a little girl. He regretted that he had not let her sleep at least till sunup. "John, I do not know what you are talking about."

"No wonder. I was being silly. Try to go back to sleep."

"You said we were going home."

"We are as soon as we possibly can."

"But you have your Congressional seat."

"We will pack it and take it with us. Go back to sleep."

She threw the blankets off and sprang from the bed. "If we are going home, I have a thousand things to do," she said. "I have dinners out and dinners here to cancel. I have four dresses at the seamstress to pick up and I personally want to pack the china. Now, about the ball at the British Embassy—"

"Wait a minute. Have you thought this over? Are you quite certain we have to go?" John asked her.

She ignored his nonsense. "Do go wake the servants. I will want breakfast at once so I can be at my desk by six. You cannot think how many apologetic notes I will have to write. Oh, by the way, will we be returning to Washington?"

"Yes. After election."

"Very well. Then of course I shall not take the china home. Now, let me see—" She had flung open her wardrobe door and was reaching for a dressing gown. "People will ask why we are leaving. What would you like me to tell them?"

"Something very Creole."

Buchanan had gone to Pennsylvania and John wrote: "I shall leave here tomorrow for New Orleans. I have not the slightest apprehension respecting the vote of Louisiana but I should not feel satisfied with myself were I absent from my post on the day of battle."

He knew Buchanan would not be fooled. Buchanan would know that he was sick with apprehension. Buchanan would be sick, too.

"I do not know," John thought, "what I can do in New Orleans when I get there except talk. And what do you say against a man like Clay?"

During the ten-day journey, he must think of something to do, something to say.

"How will your state vote, sir?" he was asked many times along the way.

"Democratic, my friend. My state will vote for the greatest candidate since Jackson."

Sometimes people smiled and murmured that the most populous city was not a Democratic stronghold and John smiled back at them, thinking that a lot of these fellows were going to lose money when Louisiana's votes were tallied. He knew now how to beat Henry Clay. It would be an expensive undertaking but, he reasoned, what were donations for but to be used in behalf of the donor's favored candidate? And it gave him a warm, pleasant feeling to

230

know that he could defeat Clay without saying a word that would damn so honorable and admirable a man.

Election day dawned clear and bright in New Orleans and Clay's supporters rushed enthusiastically to cast their votes. Those who rose early enough and who caught a glimpse of the wharves were amazed to see so many steamboats taking on so many rough-looking, hard-faced men. Well, they concluded tolerantly, even these low creatures had a right to celebrate Clay's victory and were evidently arranging some sort of riotous drinking bout on the river.

John Slidell had risen early himself that morning and as the steamboats were filling, he, in a black silk dressing robe, was having coffee in his Royal Street house. Plenty of time to cast his vote for James K. Polk later in the day. At the moment, he had business which needed his attention. He was not breakfasting alone. A half dozen men had joined him at this tedious hour of the morning and though they had dressed for the occasion, he thought them all rather lacking in style. However, being a gentleman himself, he treated them as honored guests. He saw that his serving boys fed them well and he disregarded the table manners of these horribly jolly fellows.

"Now, you are quite sure you understand?"

"Yes, sir, Mr. Slidell. Don't have a worry. Don't have a care. We understand."

"Good. Just what is it you understand?"

"Well, we steam up and down the river and drop the boys at the different polling places and see that they vote for Mr. Polk—over and over."

Inelegantly phrased, John thought, but the spirit of the outing had been properly captured.

"Now, you must remember," he said, "there is a great deal of refreshment aboard the boats. It would be pleasant to serve it liberally and with the feeling of good fellowship but watch your men carefully. Make quite certain they know where they are each time they disembark. When they hold up their right hands and swear they are residents, it would be a pity if they did not know the name of the place."

"Yes, sir, Mr. Slidell. Anybody who don't know where he is gets no more to drink and no dollar at the end of the day."

231

"I have an additional suggestion," John said. "Why do you not mention that anybody who—er—don't know where he is gets no more to drink, no dollar at the end of the day and some form of corporal punishment administered by his comrades for having embarrassed them. Now, is there a competent leader for each boat?"

"Oh, yes, Mr. Slidell."

"Splendid," John said. "I think you had better get started. Such a nice day. It will be lovely on the river."

When they had gone, he had the room aired and he lay a long while in his bath. Practical politics was such a disagreeable business. Later, he dressed carefully and went to cast his vote, after which he drove out to Belle-Point, where Mathilde and the children were staying. He was looking forward to the day. The children adored having him read stories to them.

No sense in returning to the city before Thursday. There would be no definite vote count at least till then. On Monday, they ought to start back to Washington. It really seemed too bad they could not remain here, but there was much that had to be done in Washington and it would be rather wonderful to see so many surprised faces—Buchanan's among them. Perhaps he should be cross with Buchanan for having had so little faith in him.

But he found it difficult to be cross with Buchanan. Such a decent fellow, so willing to admit his own errors. In his parlor at Willard's Hotel, he embraced John and promised never to doubt him again.

"I thought sure Louisiana would go for Clay. You are a magician, Slidell."

John nodded. "Of course I am and like all magicians, I am suffering from the vulgar destructiveness of the public. Everyone wants to know how the trick was done."

Buchanan said, "Here is one man, my friend, who does not want to know."

"Well, avoid the newspapers, for I understand Clay's admirers are rather put out at having been bested. They are crying dramatic words like 'fraud.' "

Buchanan daintily dusted some lint from the sleeve of his well-tailored black coat. "They will grow accustomed to Polk and even become fond of him. He will be a great President."

"Yes, of course," John said. "Has he been in touch with you yet?"

"Only socially. He is, I would say in the vernacular, sizing me up."

"What in hell for? I have told him you are just the right size for the State Department."

Buchanan smiled gently. "He is a man who enjoys thinking that he makes his own decisions. A harmless delusion, Slidell. And he will like me better for having selected me himself. When he is quite certain that I am sufficiently expansionist minded, he will—"

"I hate all this waltzing around. My God, he could not get a better Secretary of State than you, with your experience as Minister to Russia. He knows it, too."

"I am sure he does, Slidell. However, what would be your advice if he offered me something slightly less magnificent?"

"You must refuse. Do not forget that you and I have plans for the future. We cannot afford to have you accept any position unless it brings you the greatest prestige and honor. Besides, this bloody Presbyterian Mason owes me a hell of a favor."

Buchanan smiled thinly. "I liked," he said, "the part about my experience as Minister to Russia qualifying me so splendidly for the appointment."

"Well, you will get it."

And of course he did.

By the following summer, John knew what he wanted for himself from Mr. Polk. Mexico loomed largely in the thoughts of every man in Washington. Nothing since 1812 had been as momentous a challenge.

"Send me down there," John said. "Perhaps I can avert war."

"Oh, we can avert war," Polk said. "That is not the problem. If we simply leave the boundaries as they are—"

"Now, really, Mr. President." John looked at Polk in some annoyance. "You did not think my intention was to use my persuasive Spanish only in the interests of *status quo,* did you?"

"And you do not think you are going to *talk* Mexico out of a large piece of territory, do you?" Polk demanded.

"It would interest me to try."

"Let me think of something better for you to do, Slidell."

John shook his head. "It is this I want, Mr. President. I would like to be appointed Minister to Mexico, with, of course, a reasonable amount of authority to negotiate."

Polk said, "You would be given all ordinary powers and some perhaps a little extraordinary, but permit me to offer a word of advice, Slidell. Never undertake the impossible."

"Good advice, sir. Thank you."

Never undertake the impossible! Delivering Louisiana to a Mason, then, was an everyday occurrence, was it? Presidents! No matter what you did for them, the bastards always thought they had reached the top by their own personal charm and unassailable integrity. One day, a man was a worried, nervous candidate, looking anxiously to you for a reassuring word. The next day, he was dignified and imperturbable, wrapped in the comforting illusion that he had been that very sacred object—the people's choice.

In September, John, Mathilde, the children, two secretaries and a railroad car filled with luggage and house servants departed for Mexico. At Jalapa, they were detained by courteous but somewhat chill officials of the Mexican government. John's credentials would, of course, be presented in Mexico City—but not just now. He would be informed when his journey could be continued. For the present, he was requested to wait in Jalapa.

"Wait? Wait where?"

The officials shrugged. Unfortunate that Señor Slidell had thought it wise to bring his family, his secretaries and so many servants. There were, as he could see, no conveniences in Jalapa for such a household. Perhaps the señor would like to return this evening to the United States. The señor was damned if he would like to do that. He was the accredited minister to Mexico and wished to present his credentials in Mexico City. Surely someone of sufficient importance could be reached who would authorize his continuing. More shrugs. Could a letter be delivered to the American ambassador? Perhaps. One was never certain of anything, was one?

Two cars were detached and left on the siding. In fury, John watched the train chug its way toward Mexico City.

He said, "They hope to make us so uncomfortable that we will gladly go home."

"Perhaps we are not liked," Mathilde commented.

234

The older secretary, a man who had been in John's employ for several years, said, "Any orders, sir?"

John glared at him. "Of course. Fill the inkwells and empty the waste baskets and see that I have a small baked chicken and a cold bottle of sauterne on my desk at noon."

"Sir?"

"Oh, go lie down. Any orders!"

Mathilde, leaning back in the dusty red-plush seat, stared up at the lamp in the car ceiling. "We will have to find a way to feed the servants."

"Is that your only worry?"

"Have you any ideas, John?"

"Not yet. For God's sake, we just got in this predicament. Give me a chance to think."

She sat quietly, gazing out the window. Under the watchful eye of their nurse, her children played in the fresh morning air. They had had breakfast and there was an ample supply of fruit in the hamper. For many hours, the children could be satisfied and cajoled, but a woman who did not feed her servants at least one hearty meal a day was a disgrace to an entire social system.

John stood up. "The town has to have a mayor," he said. "I will go see him. I will take Dupré with me. La Sage can stay here. I will leave a pistol with him."

She said, "I believe the hostility is between governments, dearest. I do not think the people are angry at us or, for that matter, aware of us."

"Even so," he said.

She followed him with her eyes as he stalked toward the town, little Dupré at his side. This husband of hers, so tall, so good-looking, so utterly splendid. True, his hair was turning white but she was no longer young, either. Well past thirty now.

When he was out of sight, she put on her bonnet and patted hopefully at the wrinkles in her blue linen skirt. "Come," she called to Mr. La Sage. "We, too, shall take a walk." And when he looked concerned, "Bring the pistol if you must, but for pity's sake, do not let anyone see it or they will think we are what they think we are."

John was already back from his call upon the mayor when she returned.

"Where the hell did you go?" he demanded. "You had me worried."

"I am sorry, dearest," she said meekly. "Did you see the mayor?"

"Yes, I saw him."

"And?"

"And the son of a bitch shrugged. He was as helpful as the other officials. He suggested we go back to the United States." He bit into an orange and said, "I think we can pay one of these poor families around here to feed us and La Sage and Dupré, but the blacks are really a problem. Have you any really good Creole ideas on how to take care of your servants, madame?"

She nodded. "Oh, yes. It is attended to. I went to the priest and explained our plight. His housekeeper, who happens to be his sister, is now preparing a *guisado* of vegetables and goat meat, which she will give the servants in the patio. We will of course eat indoors—eggs, I believe. Tonight, the children and I will sleep in the parish house. By tomorrow, the good woman will be organized to feed the servants regularly and if we are here—"

"We will be here till this nonsense is cleared up. I must say that I think you are rather wonderful, Mathilde."

"Only practical. In trouble, one turns to a priest. My mother taught me that." She opened her purse and holding it upside down, shook it violently. Not as much as a picayune dropped into her lap. "And a priest always has a poor box and plans for a new church," she said. "My father taught me that."

John laughed. "If they take care of us in this foolish mess we are in, I will make the poor box bulge."

"They will take care of us. There is much food here. It is only a matter of paying for it and its preparation."

"We will probably be out of here by tomorrow evening."

On the third day, the Mexican officials returned with the news that it would be perhaps another week before the cars of the United States Minister could be attached to a Mexico City train. Very unfortunate. Why did not the Minister go home? It could be arranged very neatly to carry him back to the United States. There would be no dilemma at all if the Minister would recognize that for the present, Mexico City was quite unprepared for his arrival.

John knew the futility of rage but he was not yet ready to admit

236

defeat. For three weeks, he accepted excuses and explanations, all delivered in bland voices accompanied by fatalistic shrugs. Did not the United States Minister to Mexico think it would be very sensible at this time to remove himself to the comforts and conveniences of his own country?

During the fourth week, the Slidells moved into a house which a widow had donated, fully furnished, to the church.

"It is for sale," the priest told them. "But I see no reason why the church cannot rent it to you. The poor can use the money."

"And," John remarked to Mathilde, "it costs no more than if we wanted to rent two or three floors and the main ballroom of Willard's Hotel."

During the fifth week, a letter was actually delivered from the United States Ambassador in Mexico City. Mexico, he wrote, declined the honor of accepting Mr. Slidell and his credentials. Mexico, as a matter of fact, was in a mood to ask the Ambassador to leave.

"I'll be God-damned if I will stand for that," John fumed.

Mathilde said nothing. She shook a large, hairy spider out of a lace gown she had intended to wear to the Mexican president's palace and observed with interest that her stomach was sick. How ridiculous! Surely the sight of an ugly insect could not nauseate a sensible woman.

John wrote hot letters to Washington. Washington wrote cold letters to Mexico City. For three months, the letters went back and forth but at last the letters were at an end and John Slidell returned to the United States just as had been suggested by the Mexicans in the beginning.

Not until they were safely back in the United States did Mathilde tell him that she was pregnant.

He drew her into his arms and said, "What a nuisance you are. Any normal, self-respecting woman would have told her husband a thing like that in Jalapa, hundreds of miles away from a good doctor. What's the matter with you? Have you no consideration?"

She laughed and hid her face against his shoulder. "It will be a boy this time," she whispered. "I have prayed and lighted candles and—"

"We could have used such activities as that on behalf of the

Mexican mission, madame. I have no objections to a third daughter and I would have dearly loved being received in Mexico City."

"The saints and I hold ourselves aloof from politics," Mathilde said primly.

"Very wise of the whole bunch of you."

He felt like the man in the old story who had been permitted one wish and one wish only. Polk was not to blame that he had chosen to be Minister to Mexico.

And there was war. It was strictly the affair of military men and lacked the spark to fire an average American's imagination. It had nothing in common with the glorious goal of the Revolution or the honest flame of resentment that 1812 had ignited. The Army was at war with Mexico. The people, though they felt themselves uninvolved, wished the Army well. It was their Army, even if it had marched away on some bloody errand not very clearly understood. When victory was theirs, the Rio Grande was the new border and a great many Spanish-speaking people were Americans. Very odd but a reason for parades.

Mathilde said, "War is a terrible thing but it is over now and we can be proud indeed of the support Cal's fleet gave General Scott in taking Vera Cruz. Julia's Captain Rogers and Sarah's Colonel Rodgers, too, were heroes. Even among our friends there were remarkable accomplishments. Pierre Beauregard distinguished himself so extraordinarily that he received a golden sword."

"Splendid," said John heavily.

"Are you not happy for them?"

"I am divinely happy for them."

"You do not sound so."

"Mathilde, if they had let me into Mexico City, I guarantee you there would have been no war. Medals, brevets, gold swords! Of course, the God-damned Army and Navy would not have been at all grateful to me, but if I had had the chance to present my credentials, you would have had the most famous husband in the country—the man who averted war with Mexico."

She stared down into the crib where slept her small son, Alfred Deslonde Slidell. "Dearest, if you are hating the Mexicans because they robbed me of having the most famous husband in the country,

238

you can cease. If you had attained that position, what would we have that we have not?"

"You know that is a foolish question, Mathilde. You understand life and me too well to have asked it."

She gave him a pretty, doll-like smile. "It is delightful that you think so highly of my intelligence," she said in a cool, faraway voice, "but I am still a simple plantation mouse. There is much I do not understand."

He knew what she was trying to say. She was begging him to keep it a Creole marriage. More and more often he realized that she was in figurative retreat from him. He had married her with no thought or even desire to find behind those light-brown eyes a good sharp mind. That mind had been no part of the bargain. It was not her wish to be an intellectual companion, a confidant or a sounding board for ideas. She was wife, mother and hostess, a simple plantation mouse. A Creole woman.

"She could be everything to me." And even as the thought came, he disliked its whining note, its weakness and falseness. Could she discuss with him the shoddy manipulations that had beaten Henry Clay in Louisiana and still, in his eyes, remain the most elegant woman in Washington? Could they laugh together over a drink while he told her the story he had spread years ago about John Quincy Adams? Could they do that and continue to treat each other with the utmost respect? They could not and she was warning him that they could not.

He placed his arm about her waist and drew her from the nursery. "Sweetheart," he said, "forgive me for not being sufficiently grateful for all the beautiful things I have." She raised her lips to him. He kissed her, then added, "I will not mention the mission to Mexico again."

"Oh, I think you could mention it among your friends," she said playfully.

"I will remember to do that, Mathilde," he promised.

Joseph Gungl's well-known Berlin orchestra was playing at Burton's Theatre and Jane MacKenzie Slidell, having always had a weakness for the lighter German music, decided to attend one of

Gungl's concerts. She had expected to go alone, with only her coachman's arm to lean upon. It was delightful to be offered the companionship of her granddaughter Caroline Perry.

"But, dear, you will not care for the music. It is all treacle and tinsel and sentiment."

"Why should I not like treacle and tinsel and sentiment?"

"Because you are so young."

"Are you going to turn out to be a conventional grandmother? Are we going to seem like children to you forever? After all, you know I am twenty-one."

And the prettiest girl the family had ever had, even taking into account her pretty sisters and her mother, Janie, as a young girl and the sad, shadowy ghost of long-ago Ellen. Yet pretty was not the word for Caroline. Perhaps the girl was beautiful, but a grandmother could not be sure. Jane knew only that Caroline's was the most arresting face she had ever seen. Those huge gray eyes that found very little worthy of interest. The golden skin so clear and warm. Strange how Caroline had always chosen to pile her hair in the coiffure of an older woman and to wear high-necked frocks in a season when a bosom view was again in fashion. Obviously she liked the appearance of severity. It certainly suited her. She had, her grandmother thought, the look of a medieval princess in a touchy humor.

Burton's Theatre was only the old Palmo Opera House with a new owner and new decorations. The seats had been recovered in a rich shade of crimson and there was more gilt on the ceiling and walls than Jane remembered from the past. Her sharp eyes examined the carpeting in the aisle and decided that it was the old carpet, which had been subjected to a vigorous cleaning. She grunted in annoyance. Mr. Burton might have spared the additional gilt. She disliked the implication that patrons would be so dazzled by a generous display of gold paint that they would never notice the carpet. Vindictively she took satisfaction in observing that the concert had not drawn a large audience. She and Caroline were alone in their row and the back of the theatre was almost empty. Served Mr. Burton right.

But when the music began, Jane melted and forgot about the carpet. She closed her eyes and permitted pictures to form in her mind. Bright winter stars shining on the frosted roofs of a Bavarian village. Sleigh bells sounding silver tones in the depth of the Black Forest. A picnic on the banks of the Danube. The cottage where a wood-chopper's plump wife baked small cakes for red-cheeked children. The splendor of a palace ball.

She opened her eyes once and saw that Caroline was listening attentively, trying, in the way of an intelligent person, to grasp what made others respond to this music. Jane patted Caroline's hand approvingly and returned to enchantment. Later, during a passage composed for violins, she glanced at Caroline again to see if the girl could possibly be immune to this sweet magic. In that instant, before giving herself back once more to the music, Jane caught sight of someone she knew. He was sitting four rows in front of her and to the left. His head was bowed and she knew his eyes were closed, his heart in surrender to melody and memory. Even without seeing his face, she knew she was not mistaken. The young man was August Belmont.

And now she no longer heard the music. Her imagination was occupied with quite another matter. He appeared to be alone. Surely if he had married, he would have brought his wife to hear Gungl's concert. She glanced at Caroline again, this time so appraisingly that the girl thought it very odd indeed.

"Is everything all right, Grandmother?"

"I hope so," Jane whispered. "It could be. It actually could be," she added cryptically.

At intermission, she called an usher and gave him a coin and an order. "The dark-haired young man sitting alone over there. Tell him that a lady wishes to give him her glovemaker's address." And as the usher and Caroline stared at her, she continued, "Then indicate to him where I am sitting."

Doubtfully the usher turned to obey. Caroline said, "Nice girls do not do such things, Grandmother."

Jane laughed. "I met him once and that was seven years ago. It will be interesting to see if he remembers me as pleasantly as I remember him."

Seven years ago. Caroline had been a child. What an amazing thing if he were still unmarried. One would not have wagered a penny on his being single for another six months.

"Who is he, Grandmother?"

"August Belmont."

"And is August Belmont anybody important?"

"Child, by any standards."

Jane watched intently as the usher bent above him, delivering her message. She saw his brows draw together in puzzlement. A second later, he was smiling and looking about the theatre. She waved her small gloved hand and immediately he rose and started to walk toward her. She was startled to see that he limped as he walked but this young man would not have been August Belmont if the limp had not somehow added to his fascination.

"Mrs. Slidell, Senior. What a delight!"

She offered her hand and he took it affectionately in both of his. She performed the introduction and asked him to seat himself.

"The parents of this particular granddaughter," she said, "are Commodore and Mrs. Matthew Calbraith Perry, whom you met at the Robinsons' that evening."

"Oh, yes," he said. "Such charming parents to have." But he scarcely glanced at Caroline. "We have so much to say to each other, Mrs. Slidell, Senior. To begin with, I must warn you that you are in for a disappointment. Never again can we dance together."

"That is a disappointment," she said. "And since at a scant seventy-two I cannot be expected to sit on the sidelines, you must forgive me for seeking other partners. What happened to you, Mr. Belmont?"

"I was an idiot. I fought a duel."

"You have my sympathy and I am in complete agreement with you. You are an idiot."

"Do not tell the Rothschilds. They still think me very bright."

"They were always partial to you, as I remember."

"Yes. They permitted me to spend a few years in Austria so that I could be consul general there. It was very romantic."

"I know. Waltzes and castles and duels."

"Correction, madame. The duel was fought against the quaint background of Elkton, Indiana."

"I never heard of the place."

"We were very quiet." He surveyed her in silence for a moment. "You are as tiny as I remembered you."

242

"But my hair is whiter and now when I run upstairs, I become breathless. Oh, already the musicians are returning."

"A plague upon them for gulping their beer," August Belmont said. "May I remain seated here with you ladies? And will you have supper with me afterward?"

"Do come to my house," Jane said. "Supper is in preparation there. Do you have a Mrs. Belmont?"

"No, I do not."

It was difficult for Jane to give her full attention to the second half of the concert. There was no Mrs. August Belmont but he and Caroline had not been impressed with each other. She realized that under the influence of the honey-sweet music, she had actually expected them to exchange glances and perhaps to pale slightly in sudden wonderful recognition that here at last was love. But why did they not see what she saw? How could he look at Caroline and be blind to the loveliness of that cold, proud face? How could Caroline ignore the fact that August Belmont was the most attractive man she had ever met?

When the concert was over, they drove in Jane's carriage to the house on Thirty-second Street. August Belmont wandered about, admiring all Jane's favorite possessions, asking the history of the bishop's clock, commenting on the workmanship of the fire screen, examining with interest a curious little eleven-sided, porcelain-topped table that had come to her from New Orleans.

Caroline had vanished, reminding Jane hopefully of a bygone day when this girl's mother, at the sight of a young midshipman, had scampered upstairs to change to a more becoming frock. Caroline would do nothing so obvious—but could it be that she was re-combing her hair or biting her lips to make them very red?

During her absence, August Belmont seated himself beside Jane and said, "One never knows whether a word of sympathy is acceptable or not, dear lady, but I cannot let you think me unaware of your sorrows. Throughout the court-martial I was greatly concerned and at the acquittal my heart sang for you. Then when I heard of Commander MacKenzie's death, I was shocked and grieved. A terrible thing."

"Mr. Belmont, he did not care to live any longer."

243

His dark eyes were sad. "Many newspapers were unkind to him but there were some—"

She said, "I do not think the newspapers broke his heart. No. I believe he wanted death because he felt that the trouble aboard the *Somers* would have been handled in another manner by another commanding officer. And he did want death, Mr. Belmont. If you could have seen the way he rode the horses at Tarrytown when he came home. He was pursued by devils. Incidentally, the horse from which he was thrown belonged to Caroline. I do not think any of it matters. Not the horse, not the court-martial, not the newspapers. Alec was dead the day Philip Spencer and the others were hanged. I count his death from then. Philip Spencer and he killed each other."

August Belmont said almost fiercely, "But why? Good God, why do such things have to happen?"

"If I were a proper old lady with a heart filled with love for the whole world and a mind filled with sugary notions, I would say that everything has its purpose, that nothing is tragedy or waste. I would point with pride to the new naval academy at Annapolis and say, 'My son was the instrument chosen by Fate to dramatically illustrate that this wonderful school was needed.' "

"And it is not a farfetched idea. If such an academy had operated in the past, Philip Spencer would have been weeded out in a classroom and never sent to sea at all."

"Yes. Mr. Polk's Secretary of the Navy, Mr. Bancroft, tells me that Alec's ordeal was his inspiration for the establishment of the school. He assures me that no commanding officer will ever again be forced to contend with a boy like Philip Spencer."

"That," he said with solemnity, "is something rather wonderful, is it not? Commander MacKenzie will be remembered always by his brother officers for—"

She smiled wryly. "Pardon, Mr. Belmont, but Commander MacKenzie will be remembered not at all. To utter his name has been forbidden by naval etiquette. It seems that he is a controversial matter, which means that even gentlemen take to breaking each other's noses when he is mentioned. By common agreement, he is to be forgotten." She patted the shining silver curls at the back of her neck, rearranged the cloud of tulle upon her shoulders and asked, "Now would you like to tell me about the duel?"

"No," he said. "I would like to tell you that your house looks just like you."

"You mean that it is—"

"No, I do not mean that it is popeyed."

She laughed. "Fancy you remembering."

For supper there was capon and salads and a variety of small, enticing dishes and there was both conversation and prattle.

"Tell me of the John Slidells, Junior. Not the things one can read anywhere but how they are, really."

"They are bursting with good health and they are in Havana."

"Why are they in Havana?"

"They are probably thinking of buying it."

"That is a possibility," August Belmont said seriously. "There is much talk of how Cuba can be taken from Spain." He turned to Caroline. "Your parents are well, I trust."

"Yes, thank you. Very well."

"Do you live here, Miss Perry, with your grandmother?"

"I am just staying tonight. I live with my parents."

"And where are they living?"

"At present, in the house at the Brooklyn Navy Yard."

He watched the sparkle of golden wine as the butler refilled his glass. "May I call?" he asked.

"Would you really want to? It is a dreadful trip. Ferry and all, you know."

"I am accustomed to the discomforts of travel."

"Then come to dinner on Sunday the twenty-seventh."

"Thank you. I will be there."

So they had not been unaware of each other, not for a moment. A strain of romantic German music was running through Jane's mind.

"When it leaves me," she thought, "I will be realistic again. I will remember that a gentleman's dining at the home of a young lady does not guarantee love, marriage or even another meeting."

But the romantic melody repeated itself again and again.

"Is he not charming, Caroline?" Jane asked when August Belmont had taken leave.

245

"Yes, he is. He is too charming."

"What do you mean?"

"Does not common sense tell you, Grandmother, that he has misrepresented himself to you? He is actually an adventurer who is wanted by the police of Europe for the murders of helpless women and orphan children."

"Caroline, what are you talking about?"

"I am talking about August Belmont. Nobody could be all that he is and still have substance and importance and a good family and—"

"Why, he has bewitched you."

Caroline said, "If that were so, then I would have to find a way to bewitch him in return, would I not?"

Jane said, "I think sorcery has already come quite naturally to you, my dear. Does he look like a man who often journeys to Brooklyn?"

Cal had shut himself away in the library at "Moorings" to explore with the help of books and charts a strange, faraway land of which Janie had barely heard. After a week of loneliness and resentful glances at the closed door, she had delivered an ultimatum.

"If you will not come outside for the noonday meal, then I shall join you inside."

"Janie, I have no time to come out. There is so much—"

"Very well. While you are eating from your tray, I shall eat from mine. At least for a few minutes, we can talk and be together."

He had had to be gracious and admit her to the library, though she knew she made him nervous.

"Janie, for the love of God, do not set your teacup there. Those charts cost the government thirty thousand dollars. And not on the books, sweetheart, please not on the books. They were loaned by a London collector and are very rare."

"Do not get upset. I will be careful." She sat down and beamed at him, her tray upon her lap. "There now, isn't this cozy?"

"Well, yes."

"We do not have so long to be together, Cal." She cast a sullen

246

eye toward the charts. "I feel as though you were going to the moon."

"So do I," he said soberly.

"Do you know the exact date of sailing yet?"

"No, not yet. I have been assured twelve ships. I suppose we will set the date when the ships are close to readiness."

She sighed. "Oh, it all seems so dangerous and so foolish. Why can't Japan be a hermit if that is what the Japanese want? Must we act like a boy poking a stick into a nest of hornets?"

"Yes, Janie, we must."

"Why?"

"Because a hermit is a bad neighbor."

"Nonsense. He never knocks on your door while you are washing your hair, nor does he come seeking to borrow an egg or to snoop into your family secrets."

"That is perfectly correct and neither will he help if your house catches fire or you have sickness or need someone to watch the children for a moment."

"But what can the United States possibly want of Japan?"

He was silent and slightly irritated. With high enthusiasm and what he had considered to be extremely colorful broad strokes, he had already sketched for her the picture of what he saw himself accomplishing. Supplies and refuge in Japan for American ships in distress. Shelter for shipwrecked seamen. A trade agreement—

"Stop sulking, Cal. Tell me what we need with Japan?"

"I told you."

"No, you did not."

"You mean to say that you do not remember my telling you that the Japanese are throwing our shipwrecked sailors in prison and forgetting all about them?"

"Oh, yes," she said penitently, "I do remember now. You told me and I said the Japanese were beasts. I still think so."

"Well, they are not beasts. They have a culture and—"

"I do not care about their culture. If they have no wish to help men whose lives are in danger, then they are beasts."

"I see I am not going to change your mind about that."

"No, you are not, but tell me again, Cal, about the expedition. Educate me."

"What? At this late date?"

"Please."

He decided to be mollified, for there was nothing in the world he wanted more than the opportunity to talk of the United States' mission to Japan.

"Well," he said, his eyes resting dreamily on the charts, "there is the matter of trade relations. England, France, Portugal and Russia have all failed to establish agreements with Japan. It would be a very notable triumph, Janie, if the Navy was able—"

"The Navy? You mean if Matthew Calbraith Perry—"

"No. I mean the Navy."

"Oh, you and your Navy!"

He nodded. "Me and my Navy. The Japanese tried to kill Commander Whiting. They told Commodore Biddle to 'Go away and do not come back any more.' The Navy has enormous courage, let me tell you, to once again attempt contact."

"Did I hear you correctly? Did you say *the Navy* has enormous courage?"

He smiled at her. "It really has, you know." He selected one of the beautifully bound books and turned the pages with great care. "I am going about all this differently from anyone else. It is not enough to know the waters or the resources or the fortifications of Japan. I am learning their history, customs and manners. I am trying to figure what my reactions would be if I had a Japanese background. Understanding them could make all the difference, you know."

"I suppose so, Cal."

"The other men who have tried to penetrate the country have behaved exactly as though they were dealing with Europeans. You cannot communicate with Japan on that basis. An entirely new precept is needed. You see, Janie— Oh, darling, what are you crying about?" He went to her and took her in his arms. "Please, Janie, I can stand anything but your tears."

"I get so miserable when I think about it all. You will be gone for years."

"No, dearest. I would think not more than eighteen months or so."

"That is long enough, Cal."

248

"But you will be with Caroline and August and they have promised to take such good care of you."

"And who has promised to take good care of *you?*"

"Janie, Janie dearest, you know I will be safe. I have a lucky star, a rabbit's foot and a blue Bible. Try to smile. Just a little. I have gone away before and you have not cried."

She dabbed at her eyes with his large handkerchief. "I know I am not being helpful but I feel very sad today and depressed about everything. I was going to make this tray meal so jolly and tell you nothing of a dispiriting nature but I am not very good at such performances. There was a letter from Mathilde that just crushed me. Young Mrs. Beauregard died."

"Oh, my God. That sweet little woman."

They were silent, thinking of the time that Laure Villère Beauregard had been their house guest. Such a gentle, quiet little thing. They thought of her bright face at the theatre and her graceful horsemanship and how keenly she and her young husband had enjoyed everything in life.

"She died in childbirth. The baby lived. Pierre at least has the baby for which to be thankful."

"Piously spoken, Janie, but I will tell you that to have exchanged you for a child would have given me scant reason for thanks."

"I guess I was only trying to cheer myself with the thought that Pierre is not completely desolated." Her tears gathered again. "Cal, it is really a horrible world, don't you think?"

He shook his head. "It has sorrowful moments but I have had much happiness."

"So have I but, oh, it is a melancholy day and I will be melancholy with it and say that we are separated too often."

"Yes, but that is the way of a Navy marriage, Janie."

He spoke very complacently, she thought, and her eyes, still blurry with tears, returned to the charts. It seemed to her that she had spent all her life watching Cal prepare for a voyage or waiting for him to come home from one. In other years, she had detested Cal's Navy, for it had led to a very dull existence. She had passed the time by filling her closets with the latest fashions and bemoaning that she had no place to wear them. Now, ironically, when the whole exciting world of Caroline and August Belmont had opened to her, she detested Cal's Navy only because it took Cal away from her. Clothes and social glitter meant little now. Only the big man with the bright-blue eyes and the wonderful laughter had any meaning for her. Did she love him more today than when they were young? Or was it only that she was ready now to sink into a comfortable, quiet limbo of elderliness with a comfortable, quiet retired husband at her side?

"Would you ever consider retiring, Cal?"

"Naturally, when the time comes. There is lots to be done before that, though."

"Still, if we are to have any life together—"

"What a goose you are, darling. We have had a beautiful life together. And when this Japanese business is settled, we will rest and play till we are tired of resting and playing. We will take a holiday someplace where you can wear all your prettiest clothes and dance after dinner every evening."

She smiled bleakly. He had not observed that she was no longer the girl for whom he had planned the holiday. It should be flattering that in his eyes she remained the same but there was the unpleasant probability that for some time Cal simply had not noticed much about her. Cal, who overlooked nothing that occurred on a naval base or aboard a ship.

"Cal, I wonder if you still love me."

"Love you? Why, you are all the world to me."

"No, that is not so. You have the Navy."

"But the Navy is not something I can kiss or hold in my arms— like this."

That was true enough but still he had not said that the Navy meant nothing at all compared to her. And the girl who had wanted to marry a dedicated Navy man, the brother of Oliver Hazard Perry, had not asked him to say it. Only an aging woman who had lost her taste for dancing could be pathetically foolish enough to dream now of having his whole heart for herself alone.

She said, "I suppose you have to get back to your studies."

"Yes, I really do. It was fine having you with me, dear."

She could tell that he had already left her. His mind was across the Pacific in a strange land which she could not imagine and would never see.

"I will leave you to your work. Until dinner then, Cal."

"What? Oh, yes, certainly. Dinner."

Senator Pierre Soulé of Louisiana was appointed Minister to Spain and the Governor of his state surprised no one with his choice of a successor. Bitterly the New Orleans newspapers commented that it was only fair for the Governor to appoint John Slidell Senator since John Slidell had appointed him Governor.

John, Mathilde, their daughters, their son and fifteen servants arrived in Washington. John took over the largest, most luxurious house available and Mathilde took over the position of leading Senate hostess. The senior Senator was Judah Benjamin, who, although not of Slidell's political faith, was a valued friend and agreeable companion.

"I have acquired another relative since I saw you last," John told Benjamin. "A new brother-in-law. Mathilde's sister Caroline Fernier Deslonde has married the widower Captain Beauregard."

The widower Captain Beauregard. Where did the years go? He had been in Maspero's with André Deslonde when the sugar planter Jacques Toutant-Beauregard had entered and spoken of his eleven-month-old son. The widower Captain Beauregard. By God, there was something dishonest about time when it could so confuse a man. It seemed impossible that almost thirty-five years had passed since that day. And he remembered that André had offered Mathilde to Jacques for his young son. Jacques already had a Villère arrangement and André had been slightly vexed. How strange, the patterns of life. One of André's daughters would still marry this young Beauregard and Mathilde would be the bride of her father's friend, the New Yorker who sat in Maspero's that day.

John sighed. So long ago. He could almost count himself an old man were it not for his extraordinary good health and the cultivation of young companions. As, for instance, that amazing dynamic figure of international importance who had married his niece Caroline Perry. Belmont, the American representative of the Rothschilds. Belmont, with his brilliance and courtliness. Belmont, who had drawn from John Slidell the awed admission, "I never saw such luxury."

John and Mathilde went frequently to New York to visit the

Belmonts. Their home on Fifth Avenue at Eighteenth Street was a marble palace housing an art gallery and ballroom. It also housed, at a fantastic salary, the best chef in New York and it was August Belmont who had taught the city the artistry of a perfect dinner. It was August Belmont, too, who startled New Yorkers by building stables as magnificent as the house and dazzled society by the costliness of his blooded horses and the originality of his carriages. His wife, the gorgeous Caroline, proclaimed uncontested queen of the beau monde, saw Fifth Avenue on fine afternoons from a shimmering jewel box drawn by two snowy mares.

"I never thought," John said, "that I would live to see the day when I would be a poor relative."

"It is good for our souls." Mathilde laughed. "I always return to Washington feeling very humble. Caroline buys fifty ball gowns a year."

"I hope you asked her what she does with the discarded ones."

"As a matter of fact, I did and was very disappointed. She divides them among her sisters. Her poor old Aunt Mathilde gets nothing but her castoff jewels. Look, John." She snapped open a small velvet box and he stared down at a bracelet of flaming rubies. "I can never wear it in New York. It was August's St. Valentine's Day present and it might hurt him to know that she hates it. She does not think rubies are becoming to her."

"Poor child. Her life is very difficult. We must give her something very nice for Christmas," John said. "Why do you not knit her a good warm scarf?"

"Oh, John, with wool at its present price! Could we afford it?"

"I'll be God-damned if staying with the Belmonts does not cause me to ask myself things like that."

Jane MacKenzie Slidell had declined to live with the Belmonts though they had begged her sweetly to come to them.

August said, "We thought if we named the baby Jane, you would surely—"

"You named her for Caroline's mother. Not for me."

"Not so. Did we name her Janie? We named her Jane, with no silly tag ends on it. Do come to us. You can sit on a pillow and sew a fine seam and dine upon anything that delights your small stomach."

Jane looked at him lovingly. "August," she said, "would you believe that when I was praying for you and Caroline to marry, I did not know you were so hideously wealthy?"

"Not for a minute will I believe such a thing. I think you nipped over to Europe, investigated my inheritance and questioned the Rothschilds concerning my potential. *Then* I think you started praying."

Most times she laughed in silence, for things happened at the Belmont home that she could share only with the memory of John, Senior. With him she laughed because in the marble palace jewelers bowed obsequiously to Caroline and hopefully laid their wares before her. Materials were designed and woven with Caroline in mind and carried to her for consideration. Furs and feathers from all over the world came first to the house at Eighteenth Street. Here, too, visiting royalty was entertained by the haughty Mrs. August Belmont, who was the granddaughter of a soap-boiler.

August embraced his wife's entire family with enthusiasm and affection, deluging them with gifts and invitations.

"But I still do not know my illustrious relative Chief Justice Thomas Slidell of the Louisiana Supreme Court," he complained to John. "Why do we not suggest that he take a few months of rest in Washington and New York?"

"He bores me," John said. "He would bore you."

"Really? I understand he is an intellectual giant."

"He is intellectually gigantic on the subject of law, August. I am not excited by the company of people who are at home only with scholarly concerns. That does not command my respect any more than concentrated money-grubbing does. Single-sidedness is always a bore. I have never understood why the man who has nothing but learning is to be more respected than the man who has nothing but money. They both lack the ability to live gracefully. They both have damned limited horizons. They both have failed in a rather important test. Yet each regards the other with pity and contempt."

August said, "That is a very interesting point of view but not to me. I still want to know your brother."

"Why? He is not even a Democrat."

August, that many-sided individual, somehow found time for music, art, horses, entertaining, traveling, the banking business and

253

the welfare of the Democratic party. "That settles it," he said. "If he is not a Democrat, he is not my uncle-in-law. I cast him off."

"I could tell you even worse about him. He saves money."

"No!"

"Not much, of course. Louisiana does not pamper her chief justice, still he manages to put by a picayune here and there. I am willing to bet that after ten years of thrift, he has a cozy two hundred dollars laid away."

"Ah, but what a luncheon a man could have for that, John. Does Thomas have a romantic attachment?"

"I should not think so. Thomas is very respectable."

"Actually, you Slidells are all very respectable."

"I resent that, August. It suggests we have no imagination."

"You have imagination. Every one of you. Still, does it not strike you as odd that with such a large and handsome family, no one has ever become embroiled in a scandal?"

"You do not read the newspapers, August."

"I am speaking of romance. When members of your family marry, searching ceases and you are apparently faithful world without end. Why is that, John?"

"I think it is because we are very mature people, August."

"Mature? Or frightened of public opinion?"

"August, my dear friend, you tell me what maturity is if it is not a weary knowledge that no ecstasy that lasts but a moment can be an intelligent swap for dining *en famille* at the White House."

August laughed. "Such bitter wisdom and so characteristically Slidellian. I do not know whether I love you, your mother or Caroline best."

"My mother and Caroline are not Slidells."

"A technicality, John. Will you come driving with Leonard Jerome and me this afternoon? We want to look at some property. We are thinking of building a race track one day."

"Spendid. I could tell my grandchildren I was present when the site of Jerome was decided upon."

August looked injured. "Jerome! It never crossed my mind that the track would be called Jerome. I was thinking of Belmont."

Leonard Jerome, the man John thought of as August's playmate, was a dark six-footer with an enormous mustache. He was not famous for a conservative way of life or for his unwillingness to meet a challenge. August's stables had challenged him mightily. Leonard had found it necessary to do his own over. They were now paneled in black walnut with floors smartly carpeted in crimson. John had not seen all of Leonard's house, only the ballroom, and on the particular evening he had seen it, he had been fascinated by two fountains—one sending forth champagne, the other French perfume.

John hoped Leonard would not arrive today in his coach with its tetrad of wild horses. Leonard had recently perfected the art of driving four-in-hand and the horses had perfected the art of capering and rearing.

"It is only a trick," August said to John. "The horses are not really dangerous. They are only trained to appear so."

"Very comforting," John said, observing that the magnificently uniformed lackeys sitting behind on the coupé were white-lipped.

Leonard, on the box, the reins in his hands, welcomed John happily. "Greetings, Senator Slidell. Ah, you are in for a glorious day."

John, looking at the lunatic horses and listening to Leonard joyously cracking the whip, said, "I hope so, for it could be my last."

"You are a droll one, Senator. Here we go!"

And the four horses rushed up Fifth Avenue with Leonard Jerome shouting and the lackeys praying.

"I must have one of these coaches built for myself," August said, his eyes bright with excitement. "Is it not an experience?"

"I cannot argue that point," John said.

He was thinking of the day that he and John Grymes had driven out the shell road to find a property on which to build a private club. What simple bumpkins they had been and they had thought themselves so elegant, so worldly. Leonard and August would find a description of that day very quaint, no doubt. The carriage built in Philadelphia of which John had been so proud. Two horses, only two. A few acres of land on which to establish a club. Grymes and he had been the country cousins of these fellows and they had not dreamed of money as it was possessed by Leonard and August.

Leonard's demon horses plunged on to the sound of his shouts and cracking whip. After a time, even danger loses its urgency.

255

John began to notice that the coach was uncomfortable, that the roads beyond the city were not constructed for such madness. His thoughts continued their backward sweep and after a time, he spoke to August in tones of sorrow.

"August," he said, "I am an old man."

"Not so, John. I can see you are beginning to enjoy this."

"No. If you observe a peaceful, musing look upon my face, it is because I am thinking of the past. There was a beautiful girl in a black velvet riding habit mounted upon a very spirited horse. I sat in my father's carriage and regarded her with longing."

August smiled. "Even though this was many years ago, I would deny that you are an old man, for you look too enraptured, remembering that beautiful girl."

John sighed. "August, you misunderstand. I am remembering the comfort of my father's carriage."

Cal Perry, on the deck of the *Mississippi,* peered through his glass at the shore of the mysterious little empire whose insular solitude had challenged the Western world. He knew that his ships were the first steamers the Japanese had ever seen and he guessed at the astonishment that must have shaken them at sight of these monsters approaching directly against the wind. Ruefully he admitted to himself his disappointment in not having been able to enter the bay with a spectacularly impressive fleet. Had he insisted upon the twelve ships that had been promised, he thought he might have died of old age, still insisting.

He had come away with four ships. The frigates *Mississippi* and *Susquehanna.* The sloops of war *Saratoga* and *Plymouth.* To compensate for this relatively meager showing, he had demanded with emphasis and persistence that he be given officers of imaginative turn of mind. For the somewhat theatrical tactics he intended to employ, he needed more than men with sparkling little Mexican victories and years of devotion to the Navy behind them. Noble, conscientious officers noted for courage and integrity were plentiful but they did not all possess the additional gifts for which Cal searched. Originality, inventiveness and a flair for being ridiculous in a thoroughly dignified manner were essential to the assignment.

"The Japanese are a very ritualistic people. Casual manners, good fellowship and all cheery, brotherly attitudes toward them are completely ineffective," Cal told the officers he interviewed. "They do not admire humbleness and have only scorn for the offer of a friendly hand. To them, if a man is humble, it is because he knows himself to be contemptibly inconsequential. If he is friendly, it is because he is weak and frightened. It is difficult to describe what I am looking for. I want men who can be cold and distant and at the same time— Well, in order to be any good at this game, you are going to have to know how to play without instruction and how to make up rules as you go along."

Captain Franklin Buchanan—no relative of the more famous James—had smiled at Cal's words. He had been the first superintendent of the Naval Academy at Annapolis. He said, "Sir, you have described almost exactly midshipmen and the qualities needed to deal with them."

Captain Buchanan was now Cal's right hand and commander of the *Susquehanna*. Captain Adams, a distant relative of the great New England family, had been chosen for his scholarly comprehension of all Cal had to say of the Japanese. Cal favored, too, the chill lordliness of Adams' manner, which was a façade for a warm heart and a humorous view of life. Lieutenant Contee, a young man of quick wit and rare intelligence, had struck Cal as the sort he would like beside him in any contest. These three and a Japanese-speaking Dutchman, in the uniform of an American seaman, completed Cal's staff for all personal contacts with representatives of Japan.

Now, lying off the coast of Uraga, a city twenty miles from the capital, Cal and his officers watched a cordon of small boats putting out from the shore.

"Foreign ships in the past have permitted the natives to catch at chains and clamber aboard to satisfy their curiosity," the Dutchman told them.

"See that a hard watch is kept to prevent such familiarities as that," Cal said to Lieutenant Contee. "We are a very haughty, very exclusive people."

He went below then and as had been rehearsed, left the encounter to the others. The *Mississippi* was soon surrounded by Japanese. Sharp, staccato speech filled the air as dozens of lively, athletically built young men attempted to swing aboard the ship. Contee shouted his orders and the trespassers were shaken off the chains and popped into the bay, where they swam about like frenzied goldfish.

"What swimmers they are!" Adams remarked. "I hope they will not test our supremacy by pushing us overboard."

A cushioned and canopied boat came into view. It was larger than the others and its passengers were an elderly man and a younger, both dressed in elaborate and colorful clothes. The younger man called to the officers.

"I am interpreter."

Captain Buchanan murmured to the Dutchman, "We will use their man and keep you a secret as long as we can. Make yourself look busy and keep listening." He gazed down at the luxurious little boat and its occupants. "Here we go, boys. First chapter in our own little adventure story. Take over, Lieutenant."

Lieutenant Contee nodded and called out, "For whom do you interpret?"

"For him," shouted the young Japanese, gesturing. "Yezaiman, Vice-Governor of Uraga."

"And why did the Governor himself not come?" Contee demanded.

The question was presented to the elderly man, who shot a startled glance at Contee, then spoke at some length to the interpreter.

"Vice-Governor willing to come aboard for conversation."

"Is he?" Contee said. "Tell him we will have to think it over, for his rank may not entitle him to board this ship."

Buchanan said, "Poor bastard looked quite stricken at that snub, didn't he? We will have to watch carefully now and give consent just before he grows peevish and departs."

The officers assumed judicious expressions, stared thoughtfully at the Vice-Governor and began to speak of the weather, which was rather humid. Some fifteen minutes later, when they had run out of small talk, they permitted Yezaiman to come aboard. He was a brownish, oily little man with a heavily pomatumed topknot. In the capacious sleeve of his silken robe, he carried innumerable paper handkerchiefs, with which, in the course of the interview, he

258

mopped his perspiring forehead, discarding them on the deck after a single use. Wonderful idea, the Americans thought, filmy squares of paper that could be tossed away. An Oriental novelty to remark upon in future discourse on odd native customs.

"Vice-Governor wishes to speak with leader of squadron, please."

Contee gasped dramatically and stared in horror and wonderment. "Why," he said, "such a request is without precedent. You must tell the Vice-Governor that the Lord of the Forbidden Interior who is master of these great ships is not permitted conversation with any man below the rank of Cabinet Minister. To others he may speak only when issuing an order."

Yezaiman digested this information and studied with interest Buchanan and Adams, who stood a few feet away, seemingly absorbed in the movements of the miniature flotilla. They were older and would certainly be more sensible than this annoying boy.

"Vice-Governor wishes speech with other gentlemen," the interpreter said, indicating the captains.

"Quite impossible," Contee replied. "Those gentlemen may not speak to any personage below the rank of Governor. I am the only one permitted to converse with you and I am authorized to say that our mission is amiably disposed toward you."

Swiftly came the response through the interpreter. "According to the laws of Japan, Nagasaki is the only place where foreigners may be received. It will be necessary for you to go there."

Contee said, "The Lord of the Forbidden Interior has come purposely to Uraga because it is near the capital, where reside men of sufficient magnificence to receive him. He will not go to Nagasaki and will allow of no indignities. Moreover—" Contee interrupted himself at a signal from Captain Buchanan. "How unfortunate that this conversation must now be terminated. It is the hour for drilling our crews. We make it a practice to keep our men at wartime readiness."

From the small boats in the bay, the Japanese watched the military maneuvers of sailors and marines. They saw the flash of unfamiliar weapons and heard harsh voices bark orders they did not understand.

"Nagasaki, eh?" Cal said when a report of the encounter was

259

presented to him. "Nagasaki, and President Fillmore's letter dropped into a Japanese waste basket along with those from France, England, Portugal and Russia." Cal shook his head. "No, as you told him, we are not going to Nagasaki."

"By the way," Lieutenant Contee said, "it occurred to me today, while speaking with our visitor, that by the time we finish this business, Mr. Fillmore might not still be President."

"I know," Cal said, "and the first person who makes this confusing observation to any Japanese gentleman is going to be sent home in a rowboat."

All night long, beacon fires blazed on the hilltops surrounding Uraga and an alarm bell tolled portentously. Evidently it was not Japanese reasoning that in the face of uncertainty, a good night's rest would be a fine thing for the people of the city. Cal, lying wakeful in his comfortable cabin, listened to the bell and hoped there would be no conflict. What a triumph it would be to bring this thing to a successful conclusion by force of careful planning and constructive thinking. He thought of his brother Oliver, dead all these many years. Would Oliver recognize a trade treaty with the Japanese as a great accomplishment? Or would Oliver ask sneeringly, "What the hell are you? A sailor or a diplomat?" Would he respect a naval action in which it was the hope of the commander that no blood would be spilled?

At seven o'clock the next morning, two large boats brought the Governor of Uraga and his attendants. It was explained to the Americans that he had been ill on the previous day and that he now wished to board the *Mississippi* to confer with the foreigners.

The Governor was a brisk and arrogant man named Kayama. He, too, had his pomaded topknot, his marvelously embroidered robe and his supply of gauzy paper handkerchiefs. In addition to all this, he carried a bright fan, which he handled with the dexterity of a magician. He understood thoroughly why the Lord of the Forbidden Interior had not bothered to present himself to a mere Vice-Governor. Today, of course, he would step right up and have an exchange of opinions with the august personage who awaited him. The fan, at this point, disappeared into some mysterious silken fold at the back of Kayama's neck.

"I am sorry," Captain Buchanan said. "Your rank, though it

may be dazzling to many, is not of a grandeur to allow for a meeting with the Lord of the Forbidden Interior."

The Governor apparently did not believe that the interpreter had got that quite right. There was a minute or two of argument and anger, then a sulky silence while Kayama reached once more for his fan, which had a language all its own. Its swift little beats upon the air now expressed that it was perfectly furious.

While the stillness lasted, Buchanan continued, "The Vice-Governor, because of his lowliness, could not address me or my distinguished brother captain. You are fortunate that your position permits of conversation with us, for we can answer questions if you happen to have any."

"What is the purpose of the mission?"

Ah, that must be answered by Captain Adams, as it concerned Noble Activities and Praiseworthy Intentions, which came under his jurisdiction.

Captain Adams moved a step forward and spoke. "The purpose of the mission is to establish golden harmony, and therefore we come peaceably, as I am sure you have been informed. I repeat this only so that it may take firm root in the minds of us all. The Lord of the Forbidden Interior brings a letter to the Emperor from the great American President. He will deliver this letter with appropriate formalities."

Kayama and the interpreter needed only to exchange a word or two to arrive at a reply. "You must go to Nagasaki. You have been told to go there. Why do you not go?"

"Captain Buchanan," Captain Adams said. "I believe that it is not given to me to answer inquiries already spoken. If I am not mistaken, you are the Guardian of the Related Question, the Contiguous Information and the Repeated Declaration."

"Yes, yes, of course. We do not go to Nagasaki because the Lord of the Forbidden Interior is going to deliver his letter to more resplendent beings than any who dwell in Nagasaki."

There was a sudden flutter of conversation among the Japanese. It quieted as Kayama directed a sharp order to the interpreter. Just as sharply, it was passed to the American captains.

"You are to go to Nagasaki and at once."

Both captains shook their heads. "Oh, no," Captain Adams said.

261

"Tell him he simply does not understand. The Lord of the Forbidden Interior will deliver the letter addressed to the Emperor only to a suitably high-ranking person. If no proper arrangement is made for this, then he will go ashore with a well-trained force and find such a person for himself."

The fan snapped closed in horror and perspiration appeared on the forehead of the Governor. A half dozen of the paper squares were whipped from the embroidered sleeve. When he opened his mouth to speak, he choked and swayed weakly against a member of his staff. The interpreter knew what his master had wished to say.

"If foreigners land, they may step on ground which will then be defiled."

"That would be a pity," Captain Buchanan said. "But if the master of these wondrous ships must search unguided for a man who equals himself in greatness, then such a thing could certainly happen."

The fan spread in hysterical, breathless protest. The Governor and his entire staff broke into rapid, nervous discussion. When it was at an end, Kayama said that he would send to the capital for instructions and that four days would be required for the operation.

Buchanan made a helpless gesture with his hands. "How heartbreaking! The Lord of the Forbidden Interior is not permitted to wait more than three days for anything on earth. Now you must pardon us. We have matters of unusual significance to ponder upon."

The fan fainted and allowed itself to be carried to its silken resting place. The Governor and his party returned unhappily to their boats. The Americans looked questioningly to the Dutchman, who unobtrusively had been polishing some brasswork.

"Is there anything we do not know?"

"Nothing important. Their interpreter does excellently, even transmitting the spirit of your words. They think it in order to send you tomorrow some businessmen of Uraga. Persuasive gentlemen."

"Of course," Cal said upon receiving this information, "we would not allow their shopkeepers to board under any circumstances and tomorrow happens to be Sunday. The visitors must be told that it is our day of ceremony and worship and that we expect them to depart quietly."

And on Sunday morning, wealthy Uragans who had been denied permission to board the foreign ships sat disconsolately in their dainty boats in the bay listening to the voices of the Americans raised in song. It was perplexing. It became disturbing when the interpreter, catching some words, informed them that the song concerned "nations bowing with solemn joy before the awful throne of somebody named Jehovah."

Doctor Morrow, the horticulturist of the mission, stared wistfully through a porthole at them. "I am lowly and insignificant myself. I even have a few shopkeepers in my own family. Could I not speak to those fellows?"

"What about?" Cal asked.

"Rice," said Morrow, becoming serious. "I dream of getting just a few grains of their local variety in my hand."

"Not just yet, Doctor."

Morrow's eyes expressed his disappointment. He said, "There are things you perhaps do not realize, sir. You may, as a gift, receive from the Japanese a hundred pounds of rice. You may, by force, take from them a ton, but for scientific reasons this might be useless to me. The handful I could wheedle in friendly interchange could possibly be of intrinsic value."

"Do not be mysterious about your specialty, Morrow," Cal said. "You want kernels in which the germinal vesicle is intact. Isn't that what you are talking about?"

"Yes, sir," Doctor Morrow said, somewhat deflated.

A great part of the day Cal spent reading his small blue Bible. It vexed him to find his mind wandering often from the holy word.

Just before Cal's departure, August Belmont had been appointed Chargé d'Affaires at The Hague. Cal had urged Janie to accompany the Belmonts to Europe. She had been undecided. Had she in the end gone with them? Had they arrived safely? There were always the storms at sea, the shipwrecks, the transatlantic liners that sailed away in happy excitement and were never again seen by human eye. No point in giving room to such thoughts. It would be months before he had word of Janie.

With the blue Bible in his hands and Janie in his mind, he could not but remember the evening when they had both entered his life. Who was still alive to remember that evening with him? John Slidell, Senior, was gone and the daughter Ellen, whom Cal scarcely could call to mind. Oliver, of course, and Alec. And Edward Livingston. Yes, and now that he thought of it, the friend of Oliver's, Richard, who had been Ellen's husband. Six members of that dinner party, half of the total present, were now dead. Well, was that strange? In a few more years, it would seem odd to no one that all twelve had departed this life. Even Kayama and Yezaiman would have gone to some silky, papery hall of judgment.

Cal gripped the blue Bible more firmly in his hands. Were Kayama and Yezaiman the true reasons for his inability to concentrate on the scripture? Had he only substituted Janie in a futile attempt to drive Navy business from his mind? Navy business must wait. This was Sunday, a day for meditation and prayer. But he was an American and was it Sunday in the United States?

Irresistibly he felt himself drawn to the cabinet in which, under lock and key, rested his credentials and the President's letter to the Emperor. For the hundredth time, he gazed upon the documents, assuring himself that his designs had been properly carried out, torturing himself with the question of whether or not his designs had been worthy of such faithful execution. Each document was of folio size and beautifully written on vellum, not folded but bound in blue velvet. The seals, attached by cord of interwoven gold and silk to pendent gold tassels, lay in a small circular box of pure gold. He was haunted by the fear that all his careful preparations might fail, that in the end it might be proved to him that he had been a dreaming fool, that thought and patience could never take the place of blood and death. He supposed he could beat these people into submission but as they knelt in defeat, agreeing to all that he had demanded of them, would he feel any satisfaction? But, oh, God, if thinking and planning could result in Japanese-American rapport, then perhaps he would have lighted a torch to guide the way forever more.

Two full days passed and there was no contact with the Governor of Uraga or any other Japanese official. The small boats and

264

the swimmers played about in the bay but the chains were no longer touched, no effort was made to board the foreign ships.

Cal and his captains with Lieutenant Contee sat in frequent sessions, arranging the formalities that would accompany a peaceful delivery of the President's letter—touching grimly, too, upon what must follow Japanese insistence that they proceed to Nagasaki. The suspense was maddening to every officer and man upon all four ships but to Cal Perry, who had entertained the outrageous notion that he could think like a Japanese, the silence from Uraga was agonizing.

On the third day, the Governor's boat appeared alongside the *Susquehanna*. Kayama, his party and interpreter were received aboard by Buchanan and Adams. Greetings were crisp and cool but the message was favorable.

"Your President's letter," said the interpreter, "will be accepted with fitting ceremonies by men of superior rank."

"Very well," Captain Buchanan said indifferently. "It remains now to determine how superior the rank of the men and what you mean by fitting ceremonies."

"The men," the interpreter said, "will be selected from constant and welcomed visitors to the Imperial Palace."

Captain Buchanan did not need a course in Kayama's language to understand what followed this announcement. Every man of the Governor's party was holding his breath and watching anxiously for American reaction. The fan paused in midair and leaned forward to listen intently.

"Constant and welcomed visitors to the Imperial Palace?" Buchanan asked. "This is regrettable, for the Lord of the Forbidden Interior is permitted to treat only with men who have no need to visit the Imperial Palace. Only men who reside there would be acceptable recipients of the President's letter."

The fan sighed audibly. Dispiritedly Kayama conversed for a time with members of his party, then passed to Buchanan the word that those who received the President's letter would indeed be residents of the Imperial Palace. As a matter of fact, they would be princes. Inwardly Buchanan smiled. Kayama had so hoped to report to the capital that by shrewd manipulation, he had suc-

265

ceeded in spending less prestige than had been authorized. Well, he had done his best.

"Now," Captain Adams asked, "exactly what in the Governor's estimation are fitting ceremonies?"

Naturally, the proposed formalities did not meet with the Americans' satisfaction. No, no, there must be a pavilion especially erected for the occasion. Surely the Japanese, who built so swiftly of such agreeably airy materials, could produce an exquisite meeting place within a few days. The Lord of the Forbidden Interior could not be expected to enter through the curtains of any enclosure that had suffered the presence of lesser men. The President's letter could not be exposed to atmosphere contaminated by the breath of those who had conversed of ordinary matters. Incidentally, the pavilion hangings would be of a gossamery silk, would they not? The Lord of the Forbidden Interior was pledged to regard as an insult the use of inferior materials, for it was conceivable that a breeze might cause a drapery to touch his person. And, oh, yes, there must be a magnificent scarlet box prepared by the Japanese in which to deposit the honored documents when they were delivered.

"We are going to have to give them quite a show, sir," Captain Buchanan said.

Cal nodded. "It will be exactly as planned. Every man understands that pomp and parade were never more important."

It was three days later, on a misty blue morning in mid-July, that the *Susquehanna* and the *Mississippi* moved down the bay and inshore to their historical rendezvous. All Uraga stood on hilltops to witness the landing of the foreigners. At a signal from the *Susquehanna,* three hundred officers, sailors and marines filled fifteen launches and cutters and in stately procession approached the beach. When they had gone halfway, a salute of thirteen guns from the flagship boomed the awesome tidings that the Lord of the Forbidden Interior, upon whom no Japanese had yet been privileged to gaze, was embarking in his barge.

The Uragans knew not where to look. The barge was a compelling mystery, yet upon the shore, huge men were forming themselves into inhumanly straight and motionless lines. The watchers stared in fascination and some fear. Those closest observed that

266

many of the strangers had eyes so light in color that doubtless they were blind.

A wave of nervous excitement possessed the hilltops and the paths leading to the landing place as the Lord of the Forbidden Interior himself stepped ashore. A man as huge as the others, eyes the color of the summer bay, gorgeous clothes that glittered with round gold pieces of ornamentation above his heart and gold upon his sleeves and headpiece. How odd he was, how frightening. There was a sudden gasp from the Uragans, for now, on either side of the mighty foreign lord, had appeared a man as tall as a tree, as black as night, as wide in the shoulders as two earthly beings. A hundred of the light men arrayed themselves before the great visitor as he walked forward. Many more followed, still in unbelievably precise order. Now came two men gigantic beyond description. They carried on thick, polished poles immense rectangles of silk in red, white and blue that fluttered in the morning wind. Then there were more men, straight and tall, and it could be seen that some had hair like the gold fringe that decorated the large pieces of silk. But that became as nothing, for behind them marched two very young boys, identical in appearance, with hair that struck wonderment to the hearts of the beholders. It was hair such as never had been imagined, for it was the color of fire. Between them these youths carried a rosewood box with lock, hinges and mountings wrought of gold. It was known to all that the box contained the messages to the Emperor. And it was known, too, that these twin amazements had been sent into the world for the sole purpose of performing today the task of bearing the rosewood box.

Kayama and his interpreter walked near the head of the procession but to the side. It was understood that no man other than his own warriors could precede the Lord of the Forbidden Interior. Understood, too, by that great personage was the need for Kayama to indicate a route to the reception pavilion that crossed no worshiped ground.

"As you know, we have not come with any desire to harm you," Captain Buchanan had said. "It is not our wish to violate your sacred conventions. However, it is without precedent for the Lord of the Forbidden Interior to have walking before him a man of

267

inferior position who is still a man he cannot order into battle."

The matter had been settled in a way reasonably satisfactory to both parties but Captain Buchanan had had the last word, using the Dutchman to speak it so as to insure Kayama's receiving the full message. "Make quite certain that as the interpreter points out the road, he does not appear to be giving commands to the Lord of the Forbidden Interior. Insist that he keep his eye upon the vanguard or much displeasure will be generated."

The reception pavilion was magnificently draped in soft silk the shade of violets. Three chairs, lacquered a bright black, were the only furnishings save for vases of flowers and the scarlet repository for the documents. As the Americans entered, two men of appalling dignity rose and bowed. Their garments glistened with gold and silver thread and elaborate adornments. Each wore two swords at his side and as a mark of royal birth, their hair was shaved to the skin except at the temples and low upon the neck. Cal returned the bow and was invited to seat himself beside the princes.

A long silence then followed. No American knew the purpose of the silence or observed the signal which broke it.

"If the American documents are ready to be delivered, they are ready to be received," the interpreter suddenly announced.

Cal beckoned and the two huge Negroes marched to the scarlet box, where they stood in imposing splendor as the flame-haired bearers of the documents advanced and transferred their precious burden to them. The Negroes, with deft and quiet motions, opened the rosewood box, displayed the documents in their blue velvet bindings and the seals in the solid-gold container, then, leaving them upon the lid of the scarlet receptacle, retired.

Cal stood then, bowed to the princes and informed them through the interpreter that in three days he would depart, returning again in the spring to receive the answer of the Emperor.

There was but one question asked him.

"Will you return with all four ships?"

"I will return with more."

He bowed again and withdrew from the silk-draped pavilion and the first phase had ended. Now there would be the long and tedious winter at Hong Kong, the terrible season of wondering and doubt.

"We at least commanded their respect," Captain Buchanan said at dinner. "We were accorded honors that no foreigners before ever enjoyed. They will not dismiss us from their minds as other nations have been dismissed."

"That is true," Cal agreed. "Because it was surrounded with ceremony and drama, the President's letter will not be carelessly tossed aside and forgotten."

Captain Adams smiled. "Sir, tell us your guess on the outcome of all this. You have proved you can think like a Japanese."

Cal said, "Tonight I am so weary that I cannot even think like an American. I guess the whole business has been a strain and, boys, we are still so far from finished."

The letters to Jim Buchanan in England were so frequent and so lengthy that John wondered if they were all read in their entirety. He wondered, too, if Jim realized the importance of the many hints, warnings and suggestions the letters contained. If a man wanted to be President, he could overlook nothing. And how Jim wanted to be President! And how smoothly he lied to newspapermen. That incredible little note Jim had written to Benjamin Perley Poore, Washington editor and correspondent!

Actually, Mr. Poore, this mission to London is tolerable to me only because it will enable me gracefully and gradually to retire from an active participation in party politics. Should it please Providence to prolong my days and restore me to my native land, I hope to pass the remnant of my life at Wheatland, my beautiful home, in comparative peace and tranquility.

A copy of the note was on John's desk with a question scribbled upon it by Ben Poore: "Senator, did you know Mr. Buchanan felt this way?"

John had replied that yes, he knew Mr. Buchanan's wish to shrink from the fierce white light that beat upon the city of Washington but he also knew Mr. Buchanan's selfless devotion to his country.

When he realizes how earnestly the people cry for his leadership, I feel sure that he will put aside all personal desire and that he will bravely, generously consent to accept the arduous task for which only he, in today's world, is fitted. With no encouragement from Mr. Buchanan I shall continue to work toward the glorious day when he will assume the highest office in the land. It is my belief that he will sacrifice his private dreams to the public need.

Carefully John now reread the pages he had just written to the Honorable James Buchanan, United States Minister to Great Britain. Had he included all that had come to his mind on sleepless nights? Had he stated emphatically enough that Jim must arrange within the next eighteen months to spend at least six weeks in the United States? A leave from his London post would be of incalculable value. Jim could visit New Orleans and make friends there with the old-line Whigs who might be just about ready to enter the Democratic fold.

Even in London there were things Jim should be doing. How about Cass and Douglas? Had Jim written to them as had been suggested in an earlier letter? Furthermore, quite spontaneously—and disconnected from any specific political action—Jim must remember to drop a perfectly lovely word in praise of Franklin Pierce. If troops were withdrawn from Kansas, Jim was to denounce the President furiously, otherwise Jim was going to lose Northern support. ("You understand, Jim, this has nothing to do with your stupendous admiration for Pierce as a man.") Jim was not to forget to keep a watch on Lancaster, Pennsylvania, newspapers, as any indiscreet remarks of theirs would be attributed to Lancaster's most prominent citizen. And Jim was to cultivate Pierre Soulé, the Minister to Spain, as they met over this miserable Cuba business. Not a damn thing could be gained by Soulé's friendship and yet his hostility could poison a man. There were a great many things to keep under control and it must be remembered above all that Jim's year was coming up and that it would never come again.

And, Jim, you will be interested and pleased to hear that I am thinking of establishing a newspaper. It will be a fine, highclass periodical that just happens to favor James Buchanan for President. August Belmont is warmly interested and will get some of his friends to help finance the undertaking. The man I hope to engage as editor is a talented fellow and would know just how we want the news handled. His integrity is slightly dubious but his brilliance is beyond dispute and I think self-interest would hold him in line. I also think—

Mathilde walked into the room dressed in a garnet-colored traveling costume accentuated by a tiny hat with a garnet-eyed bird perched upon it.

"Dear," she said, "it is time to leave."

"Is it really? I am all ready but for closing this letter."

Jim, I will write you more from New York where I am going this very minute because my mother is desperately ill. For God's sake, Jim, do not make any more secret promises to anybody without us talking it over.

She was desperately ill, as John had told Buchanan. They did not need the doctors or nurses to inform them that Jane MacKenzie Slidell was on her deathbed. She would never have sent for them if within herself she had not known this to be true. Her eagerness to talk and even to laugh created a merciful illusion. There were moments in which it was impossible to believe she would soon be silent forever.

"How lovely that you were in Washington. So close. Only next door. Everyone else is a million miles away. Tom in Louisiana. Julia in California. Janie in Europe. Cal in Japan. Oh, I would love to see August. Caroline, too, of course, but August I adore."

"Everyone adores August," Mathilde said. "He has that indescribable something."

"You mean money?" John asked.

Both women protested. "You know it is not money that makes August wonderful."

"In fact," Jane added, "August makes money wonderful. Caroline will never have a dull marriage."

"No," said Mathilde, "but then your family has no dull marriages."

John, leaning back in a comfortable chair, acting the part of a man who has nothing to do but visit his mother, thought the dedication of his time to her would be wasted if she were not entertained. Mathilde's sweet bromidic utterances were a flat and unappealing diet for a woman who all her life had been more wasp than honeybee. A pity if he was neglecting both the Senate and Jim Buchanan simply to sit in silence while his mother, in her last hours, was overwhelmed by gentle sickroom cant. This was one time when Creole correctness must go.

271

"No dull marriages!" he exclaimed. "Good God, I think Janie and Cal between them have worked out the most devastatingly tedious monotony possible. Not that they don't deserve it."

Mathilde's eyes reproached him. Such talk at such a time. Everyone knew that mothers must die hearing their children's voices raised in admiration and affection for each other.

Jane said, "Well, Janie set the tone of her marriage the first time she ever saw Cal. You remember, John. She gave him a Bible."

Mathilde allowed herself to smile. John knew his mother better than she did.

"The Bible could not have been completely at fault," John argued. "Cal is without a doubt the most predictable, the most tiresome person I ever met in my life. He is a uniform, that is all."

"But a commodore's uniform," Jane reminded him.

"Certainly. That means he was more predictable and more tiresome than most Navy men. And Janie should never have let herself be cured of her mania for clothes. It was what misled people into thinking she possessed some imagination and distinction."

Mathilde said, "But Janie is no longer young. When I am her age, I will not care for clothes, either."

"Of course you will. Look at my mother. She is still mad about them, aren't you, dear?"

Jane smiled at him. God bless him. How dared the newspapers call him a scoundrel?

There was a day upon which John said to Mathilde, "She seems better. I think I will go and spend one afternoon in Washington."

But Mathilde, thinking of the time consumed by the journey, warned him. "You may not be here to say good-by, dearest. She is not better. She has only become more determined to waste no remaining moment."

"What am I to do? I am torn between the demands of my career and the deathbed of my mother."

Mathilde said, "There will come a time when all the important affairs that await your attention in Washington will have been forgotten or recognized as not so terribly important, after all. But never will you think to yourself that it did not matter whether or not you walked away when she had called to you."

And so a secretary of John's came from Washington to Jane's

house in New York and some business was taken care of and some was not, but during her waking hours, Jane MacKenzie Slidell had the company of her son.

For three weeks, she refused the medicine that would have made her insensible to pain. It would also have made her unaware of the bright presence at her bedside. When she consented at last to drink the appropriately dark draft which the nurse brought to her, she drained the glass and said in a small, sad voice, "Oh, God, but it is bitter."

Once more she spoke after that. Only once. "There is," she said distinctly and with considerable annoyance, "a dead horse lying in the street."

Against logic, against will, John moved to the window and gazed into the early-morning grayness. He saw no dead horse lying in the street but he knew one was there just the same. In the back of his mind a memory twitched disturbingly. Had he not been told in childhood some family legend—what had he been told? He could not remember. It was all so long ago. And Mathilde was now whispering to the nurse and leading him from the room.

After that, there was the shuttered house and finally the dreary ride to vault ninety-five at St. Mark's in-the-Bouwerie.

"I have been away from her so long, seen so little of her," John said. "It is absurd that everything should seem different without her."

"It is natural for you to feel so," Mathilde said. "She was your mother."

He was grateful that Creole standards of behavior in the matter of impending death had kept him steadfastly at his mother's side. He admired the Creole way of meeting sorrow with a defiant "You have not startled me for I always knew you were there." He respected the practicality of Mathilde's having packed in Washington an entire wardrobe of mourning clothes for them both and he was pleased with her for not having uttered one fretful word at being separated from the children.

"But," he thought, "I can do without such inspired remarks as 'She was your mother.' Had my mother bored me or earned my dislike through the years, why, then she would have been only a woman who bored me or whom I disliked. I had no contract to love

273

her just because she produced me. Mathilde would not care for such thoughts. She would think of something reproving yet tidily sentimental to say to me. My God, when death comes, Creoles are deathly companions."

It was good to get back to Washington, to the Senate, to the creating of a President. And it was good to behold again, from his position at the head of the long, sumptuously appointed table, the clever, high-spirited wife he remembered. Mathilde, all white lace and diamonds, presiding over a dinner for the new British ambassador and his lady.

Mathilde thought Lord Napier handsome and likable but he had arrived with all the old preconceived notions of the United States.

"I thought Americans were very taciturn, very hidebound people."

"Not Southerners," Mathilde said.

"I thought Southerners had no interest in anything but 'fiddle' music and hound dogs."

"Not Louisianans," Mathilde said.

"I thought Louisianans did nothing but sit in the shade all day counting magnolias."

"Not Deslondes," Mathilde said.

Lord Napier blinked. "Deslondes? I do not know what Deslondes are."

Mathilde smiled sweetly. "Then we have come full circle, sir, for you do not know what Americans are, either."

The ambassador threw a quick glance at his hostess, who looked so soft and girlish. "That was cruel. Do you know the difference between a Cornishman and a Yorkshireman?"

"Let me think a minute," Mathilde said. "I simply adore riddles."

Lord Napier hastened to correct her. "This is not a riddle. I am merely pointing out that you are no better informed on the English than I on the Americans."

"You are perfectly right, sir. Where do I apply for my credentials to the Court of St. James's?"

Lord Napier saw the laughter in her eyes and he laughed with her. "The gentleman to your left is getting off lightly, isn't he?"

"Actually, no. He is suffering because he wants to talk to the guest of honor and I am monopolizing you."

"I have met so many people tonight I have forgotten who he is. Please help me."

"He is Secretary of War Jefferson Davis."

"Oh, yes. And who is the pretty girl in blue seated beside him?"

"That is a Deslonde."

Lord Napier studied the girl in blue for a moment, then said, "I believe I have guessed what a Deslonde is. They all have the same eyes and same shade of hair, do they not?"

"They do, sir."

"And they are very charming. Please show me her husband."

"Captain Beauregard, seated to the right of Mrs. Senator Judah P. Benjamin."

"And Mrs. Jefferson Davis?"

"To my husband's left."

"Is the light-haired lady at the side of Mr. Secretary of the Navy Dobbin the wife of Senator Seward of New York?"

"No. That is Mrs. Senator Clement Clay of Alabama."

"Oh, I met Mrs. Seward casually and I thought—"

Mathilde said, "I doubt that you include social notes in your diplomatic pouches so I will say that we are slightly cliquish. I do not believe you will find Senator and Mrs. Seward at many dinners given by Southerners."

Lord Napier gazed down at his plate. "And I do not believe, dear lady," he said, "that that is exactly a social note."

Christmas in the harbor at Hong Kong was not to Cal Perry an occasion for homesickness. He had spent more Yuletide seasons aboard ship than at his own hearth. His children, his grandchildren, overheated rooms and the confusion of holly, packages and assorted artificial indications of the holiday had always wearied him. On shipboard, the thing was handled sensibly. A quiet Christmas service with a few hymns, a damn good dinner for everybody and an announcement that a merry Christmas was wished to all hands. That was the way to celebrate. All other ways were noisy, tiring, gaudy and only lunatic reasoning could relate them to the birth of Jesus. The Navy alone—well, perhaps the Army, too—understood how to handle Christmas.

There had been a great deal of mail in Hong Kong. Janie was

275

enjoying Europe with the Belmonts. She was missing him but she was in excellent health. At the time of writing, and as far as she knew, everyone else was well, too. Letters from a few of his children who were never very close to him when he was at home moved Cal tenderly. He was touched that they realized his mission to Japan was of infinite importance and that their prayers were with him. He stared at an envelope marked "Mrs. George Tiffany" and admitted sheepishly to himself that had he wanted to write to his daughter Isabella, he would have had to think hard to recall her name. Mrs. George Tiffany. Come to think of it, he could not even recall George.

A letter from his son Bill. How long was it since he had seen Bill? A darling note from daughter Anna. Had she married? Of course. Great heavens, she was a widow already. Cal thought her husband had been named Dick or Dave. He was not sure which. Dreadful. Really dreadful. A man should be in closer touch with his family. The Belmonts he knew all about and Matthew Calbraith Perry, Junior. Oliver Hazard Perry, the Second, had faded somewhat from his mind since the boy had chosen, after that *Somers* trouble, to leave the Navy. Cal thought he might be living in New Orleans. Little Jane had of course married John Hone. Wait a minute. Wasn't there now an even littler little Jane? Whom did she belong to? Oh, yes, the Belmonts. He didn't have to think about her now. She was in the grandchildren department and he did not know exactly how many there were of those.

With Sarah, who had married into the Army, that was the list. He was not out of touch, after all, and it was a comforting thing to know that he was not. A man should always be very close to his family.

But there was so much to think about. The actions of the French and Russian ships, for instance. Right after the new year, their behavior became a matter of great interest to Cal.

"I have a suspicion," he said to Captain Buchanan. "There is entirely too much hustle and bustle going on for this time of the year. Have you noticed?"

"I cannot say that I have. What is your suspicion?"

"That the smart boys of France and Russia plan to cash in our chips. I think they are going to move into Japan, demanding more consideration than they have had in the past, arguing that since we were received, so should they be."

Captain Buchanan said, "Navigation in Japanese waters is so extremely dangerous in winter that they will not leave here now."

"Then they are more fainthearted than we, for we are leaving."

"What?"

"Oh, yes. We cannot take the chance of being beaten out after all our hard work."

Captain Buchanan was silent. There was nothing he knew of the perils of the voyage that were unknown to the Commodore. And it was true that they had not come all this way to assist in satisfying the ambitions of France and Russia.

"How many ships will we have?"

"Seven," Cal said.

"I see the idea did not strike you just now."

"No. I have known we could not wait till spring. Too much activity among those other fellows. Entirely too much activity."

In February they re-entered the bay with three frigates and four sloops of war. This time, they did not anchor off Uraga but steamed fifteen miles beyond to a point only a short distance from the capital. The voyage had been difficult and hazardous. It must be rewarding.

Men with black, glistening topknots again. Embroidered robes. Small squares of paper nestling in silken sleeves.

"Yes, yes, we know who you are. Our government is very aware of you but you must go back to Uraga. Uraga is now the only place where you can be received."

Captain Buchanan shook his head. "You do not understand. The Lord of the Forbidden Interior is not permitted to return to any foreign city where he has already been."

"But he must do so, for only Uraga is possible."

"Uraga is impossible."

"We did not expect you till spring."

"Unfortunate, for we are here now."

"You must go back to Uraga."

"Never," said Captain Buchanan. "Has the President's letter been read by the Emperor?"

"It has been read." Here the interpreter's eyes grew as bland as

277

the eyes of the dignitary. "No one knows more than that the letter has been read."

For many days, Captain Buchanan and Captain Adams met with officials and counselors, but it was always the same. Uraga or nothing.

"I believe," Buchanan said to Cal, "that Uraga, having already been defiled by our presence, is the only possibility."

"And we are positively not going back to Uraga. To do that after all our insisting, would mark us as weaklings, too contemptible to treat with."

"I agree with you. But what shall we do now?"

"There is only one thing to do. We must prove we are not weaklings. We must move the squadron forward toward the capital."

"And enter it by force?"

"No. Not enter it at all. Were I Japanese, I think I would stop the progress of the foreign ships by forgetting all about Uraga and offering discussion in any prominent city short of the sacred capital."

"Do you give the order to move forward?"

"I do. They will despise us if we withdraw and there is no point in further haggling. I have come to do business with the Japanese and to get an agreement that shipwrecked American sailors will be cared for and returned to us. By God, I am not going to fail but I will try everything before violence."

"I know how heartbreaking it would be to come to that."

Cal had a feeling that Buchanan did not know, that no one knew how desperately he yearned to prove that slaughter was not the only answer. How easy it would be to win the support of his countrymen if he blew to pieces half the population of these islands. Those bastards were throwing shipwrecked American sailors into prison. Hurrah for Perry. Certainly hurrah for Perry and oh, by the way, he got us a trade treaty, too, with the little sons of bitches.

And what would it all mean to Perry? Nothing. Any day in the week, anybody at all could obtain mastery if he but possessed the more deadly weapons. To win a victory by the exercise of one's intellect was the only victory worth winning.

The squadron moved closer to the capital, so close that Cal despaired. Had he misjudged the Japanese? Were they so stubborn that they would compel him to march into their holy city? Unless they made some sign, he had no choice, for the fleet would be a laughingstock if he hesitated. Closer to the capital and there was only silence. A terrible thought struck him. Rather than see their city desecrated, they might have chosen their ancient and honorable— Shaking with horror, Cal fell to his knees and prayed. He prayed that by his pride and ambition he had not murdered an entire populace, that he had not played too dangerously with a people whom in his arrogance he had claimed to understand.

When the anchor was dropped, a large and elaborate boat came to them immediately. It was filled with important little men in magnificent robes, who faced Captains Buchanan and Adams and spoke through their interpreter in conciliatory tones.

"The Lord of the Forbidden Interior is not an enemy. This we know. He is not an unreasonable man. This we also know. There are things to which in his greatness he is not permitted to subject himself. The Japanese government has understood that. Now we ask him to understand us. The capital is sacred. If it is touched by foreigners, we do not wish to live. We see that in his view, a return to Uraga is as unthinkable as is, in our view, his entrance into the capital. So we have come to say that representatives of the Emperor wish to discuss certain matters with the Lord of the Forbidden Interior. And we wish to ask if your great one would consider a meeting in the city of Yokohama?"

Captain Buchanan bit his lip thoughtfully. "As you say, the Lord of the Forbidden Interior is not unreasonable. Yokohama might do. Of course, you are planning on building a treaty house slightly more elegant than the reception pavilion at Uraga."

Much more elegant. Silken hangings, of course. Scarlet, perhaps, this time. Gilt and nacre everywhere and flowers never before taken outside the Imperial Palace grounds. Captain Buchanan thought this might be acceptable. He would be prepared to answer in exactly twenty-four hours and thirty minutes.

On a March morning, the Lord of the Forbidden Interior went ashore at Yokohama. Five hundred men and three brass bands accompanied him. The music was loud and martial, the procession

279

more glittering than that presented to the dazzled eyes of the Uragans. The treaty house was as rich and flower-filled as had been promised. The four commissioners of the Emperor were surprisingly cordial, their intelligent faces offering smiles and expressions of warm welcome.

Before the morning had ended, Cal saw that he had a long and tedious task before him. The Japanese were eager to grant their friendship and nothing else. Cheerfully they agreed that it was an interesting idea that countries should exchange goods and opinions.

Well, then, would Japan enter right now, this moment, into a detailed examination of such an exchange as it concerned the two nations here represented? The Japanese gentlemen smiled and said that the subject was too vast to be touched upon so early in the negotiations. Very well. There was, then, the matter of shipwrecked American sailors. Ah, yes, such a pity that their fate was so unpleasant. Cal argued that he saw no reason why they should not be accorded care and protection until a way was found to return them to their countrymen. The Japanese listened politely. The Lord of the Forbidden Interior spoke very commandingly and had so many novel notions. His listeners hoped he would continue to voice his thoughts, which were both fascinating and instructive.

At the end of the day, Cal was weary and slightly dejected.

"What do you think?" he asked of his captains. "Are they laughing? Are they giving me a chance to talk myself out? Are they just waiting till I get so tired of talking that I will go home?"

On the following day, when the greetings were over, the spokesman for the Emperor's commissioners questioned Cal as to the size and population of the United States.

"I am of the opinion," Cal said, "that that is not a suitable subject for the second day. Are any of you gentlemen grandfathers?"

The interpreter asked that the question be repeated. The four commissioners stared first at the interpreter and then at Cal. As it turned out, two of the Japanese gentlemen had grandchildren. For what reason did the Lord of the Forbidden Interior make such an inquiry?

"Because it is a day in spring and very beautiful. On such a day, one thinks gentle thoughts of one's childhood, one's youth and finally of one's happy, honorable position as head of a great family.

Surely, gentlemen, when all time stretches before us, when I plan to remain here for a very long while, we can spend this one day or perhaps this entire spring season in discussing the dutiful sons and daughters that have been given to us and the equally dutiful sons and daughters that have been given to them."

The commissioners exchanged glances and all reached into their sleeves for the little paper handkerchiefs so useful for perspiring brows.

"Let us tell each other the names of our well-loved children and the names of their well-loved children," suggested the Lord of the Forbidden Interior. "I myself have eight children and more than a score of grandchildren, so perhaps I should begin."

He proved his point that day. If time was to be wasted, then he would show them how thoroughly it could be done. If patience was to be tested, the placid Oriental had met his match. The Emperor's commissioners could introduce no subject which the Lord of the Forbidden Interior thought proper for a second meeting, nor would he agree to early adjournment.

"We almost fell asleep," Cal said at dinner. "All of us. That poor interpreter. He was dying to tell me that nobody really cared why this child had been named for so-and-so and the other for such-and-such."

On the third day, the Japanese were ready to talk business. Not ready to agree to anything, but the arguments were stimulating and, Cal thought, revealing. During the last hour, he stated that since the American fleet would be at Yokohama indefinitely, he must have permission for his men to walk in the city and visit public places. Nothing could have been more astonishing than the immediate granting of his request.

That evening, he said to Captain Adams, "The men must be picked carefully and must be made to understand that this is no ordinary shore leave. Anyone who gets drunk, anyone who makes overtures to a Japanese girl, anyone who steals, anyone who behaves unacceptably goes home in irons if he survives the flogging he will receive. Let us cut a small pattern on the first try. Ten of the best boys only."

The conferences continued. Every day, different Japanese of high position were presented to the Lord of the Forbidden Interior.

They lingered to talk with him and to listen to his arguments. It came to Cal as something of a surprise that he had made friends here. There was no longer a contest for contest's sake but a series of conversations in which serious men sought to serve their countries well.

During the second week, the Americans presented an exhibition of their goods for the entertainment of the Yokohamans. Agricultural implements, telegraphy outfits, lifeboats, a miniature railway complete with locomotive and tracks, telescopes, scientific instruments, sewing machines. It was a sensational display and the people beheld it with delighted amazement and deep respect. They were thunderstruck when informed that these marvels were to remain among them as gifts from the great country represented by the Lord of the Forbidden Interior.

In return, they brought to the ships gifts from Japan. Bolts of pongee, lacquered boxes, umbrellas, dolls, brocades, silks, porcelains and four tiny dogs with silky hair and bulging eyes.

Cal and his officers were then invited to witness wrestling matches between enormously fat champions. At the conclusion of this diversion, there were more gifts. Three hundred chickens and two hundred sacks of rice. Cal glanced at Doctor Morrow as the horticulturist found himself a few loose grains to examine. Morrow shook his head sorrowfully as a signal that as far as he was concerned, they were still back in Uraga with nothing accomplished.

In return sociability for the wrestling matches, Cal gave a huge dinner aboard the *Powhatan*. Seventy guests and mountains of food. Lakes of champagne, Madeira and punch. The Japanese thought the champagne very tasty and they approved heartily of American fare. As a climax to the feasting and drinking, Cal showed his visitors the *Powhatan*'s engines in motion and he put to work the daguerreotypist he had brought along for just such a moment.

Captain Adams, watching all the gaiety and good fellowship, asked, "Are the conferences over? Has an agreement been reached?"

"You know it has not," Cal said. "This is only a festive interlude. We will get back to our arguing tomorrow."

Adams shook his head. "You know what I think? I think they

282

are celebrating the treaty without letting us know that they have decided to sign."

"Pleasant to think about, anyway."

"You have shown yourself to be one hell of a diplomat, sir."

"Not yet, I haven't."

"Yes, you have. Do I get one of those tiny dogs if I have called the turn?"

"You could have them all but they are earmarked for girls named Janie, Mathilde and Caroline. If you are right, I will gladly give you Mrs. George Tiffany's."

"Who is Mrs. George Tiffany?"

"Why, she is my daughter Sarah. No. Wait a minute. She is my daughter Isabella. Yes, I am pretty sure she is my daughter Isabella."

Adams grinned. "No man can know everything," he said.

On the last day of March, Cal and the representatives of the Emperor of Japan signed an agreement. It guaranteed aid and protection to shipwrecked Americans; permission for an American ship in distress to enter any Japanese port; the opening of Simoda and Hakodate as stations where Americans could secure water, wood, coal and provisions; the privilege of engaging in trade with residents of Japan.

Topknots glistened, foreheads perspired and everybody bowed to everybody else. The Lord of the Forbidden Interior next extended his hand to each commissioner in turn and squeezed affectionately the short, squat fingers of the Japanese. Then, to everyone's surprise, he wept. With tears upon his cheeks, he walked swiftly from the treaty house before there was time to form the procession.

That night he, his captains and Lieutenant Contee had a private celebration, after which Cal presented the fleet to Captain Buchanan.

"It is yours, my friend. Take it home."

"What do you mean?"

"I have an appointment with my wife. I arranged with the Navy department that at conclusion of Japanese negotiations, I would be free to take a commercial ship from Hong Kong to India and to find my way to Europe the best way I can from there."

"My God, you will hate it," Adams said. "Those commercial ships, I mean. No comfort on the damn things and you can't trust the navigators."

Cal laughed and said dreamily, "I get a year's leave and I am going to wear swallow-tailed coats and striped trousers."

"You will hate that, too."

"Well, while I'm finding out that I do, I will be having a good time. By the way, we must not forget to distribute the daguerreotypes to our little friends here. And remind me to tell our boys tomorrow morning that their behavior ashore helped our cause tremendously."

The Lord of the Forbidden Interior and his staff drank a toast to the stars and stripes and parted solemnly for the night. Their great adventure was over.

The commercial steamers made for deadly dull traveling. Cal had not guessed that the sea could produce such ennui. Worst of all were the long weeks of delay in hot and filthy port cities where he waited for another ship, another packet to take him a few days closer to Europe.

It was, of course, all worth it in the end. It was wonderful to be with Janie and the Belmonts, to see their shining eyes so full of joy at sight of him. He thought it only kind to take Janie out of suspense at the first possible moment.

"I pulled it off," he said. "I made a treaty with the Japanese."

August Belmont threw his arms around him and roared with laughter. "Oh, you are unbelievable, M. C. Perry. Just unbelievable. So you made a treaty with the Japanese, did you?"

"Yes, I did," Cal said stoutly.

August looked at Caroline. "Let us swim in champagne and get very intoxicated and sing sea chanties. Your father made a treaty with the Japanese. Are you not stunned by the news, my dear?"

Caroline patted Cal's cheek. "Darling," she said, "your treaty is rather well known in the Western world. So are you. In fact, you are a famous hero. Where are the little dogs?"

Standing in Jackson Square, New Orleans, looking up at the General on his expensive hobby horse, John silently addressed him. "I helped make you President, sir. If you have any worthwhile

284

contacts where you are, help me to do the same for Jim Buchanan."

For a long while, John stood before the equestrian statue, thinking of the past. The square had been called the Place d'Armes in the days when Jackson had run for the Presidency. Who would have guessed that this revered piece of land, the parade ground of explorer Bienville's soldiers, would someday bear the name of a tough old Carolinian?

Slowly John turned and permitted his admiring gaze to take in the full view of the square. St. Louis Cathedral, the Cabildo, the Presbytere and the splendid twin rows of red-brick and gorgeous iron lacework that were the Pontalba apartment buildings. It occurred to him that nowhere in the United States was there a more beautiful architectural setting.

"I love this city," he thought. "I wonder if it will vote for Jim."

Determinedly he put from his mind recollections of how he had helped the man on the prancing horse to carry Louisiana and how he had not completely trusted to luck in the matter of James K. Polk. He was above such rough-and-tumble today. He was even above his own recollections. The dignity of Senator John Slidell was such that his inventiveness and daring were now limited to the convention hall. Once he had his man nominated, there was little left for him but to exhort his leaders throughout the country to bring their states into the right column. Nobody had told him, in his youth, how to arrive at this lovely result. He had had to think and deliver for himself. Now let the younger men think and deliver and keep quiet about how they had managed. None cared to hear— least of all the distinguished Senator from Louisiana.

But would Louisiana go for Jim? The old Whig party had united with a mad little group called the Know-Nothings and they had placed Millard Fillmore's name on the top of their slate. Some thought Fillmore had been a good President and that the people would send him back to the White House after his three-and-a-half-year rest.

Then there was that new party, the Republicans. They had nominated John Charles Frémont, a national hero. Come to think of it on this Election Eve, who the hell liked Jim? Abolitionists hated him. So did the extremists among the slavery men. Jim was a moderate. Were there enough moderates to place him in office?

The very philosophy of this brand of voter kept him a perpetual question mark, for he usually had no prejudices strong enough to reveal themselves in parade or demonstration. It was not in the cards that unrestrained enthusiasm could be generated for the aloof and soft-spoken gentleman from Lancaster, Pennsylvania. It had only been possible to guide him carefully, to leap forward swiftly when he stumbled and to let Fillmore and Frémont make the mistakes.

"Now watch it, Jim. Religion is a touchy subject. The Know-Nothings are sore at the Catholics and because they back him, Fillmore is certainly going to get tabbed as a pope-hater. Now, on the other hand, it is being whispered that Frémont is a secret Catholic. That is because he and Jessie were married by a priest. Nobody else had the guts to marry them, the way her father was carrying on. Frémont has principles. He refuses to deny being a Catholic."

"That does not make sense."

"To Frémont it does. You know what those God-damned path-finders are like. They breathe so much fresh air that they get light-headed. They see so many mountains that they forget what people are like. Frémont thinks that a denial of Catholicism implies that a Catholic should not run for the Presidency. Let us not think about that, Jim. It is too weighty. As I see it, no Catholic is going to be President and no anti-Catholic is going to make it, either. If my arithmetic is right, that leaves you with a mighty big house in Washington."

"Very well. Where is the key?"

"Ah, my friend, here is the key: Do not let newspapermen or any political group tempt you into that murderous ambush known as 'a statement.' Tell them very coldly that since church and state are separate in this country, you consider the subject improper at election time. Tell them to come talk religion with you at Easter."

"But if I want to be President—"

"Jim, don't you remember that you never wanted to be President? We *prevailed* upon you."

John took another look around the square and left it for the night. He walked toward his house on Royal Street, feeling a sudden curious depression. There was nothing further he could do for

Jim. Now it was all up to the ignorance of the voter. Only God knew how many of them would vote for Frémont just because that brave lad had found a more uncomfortable way to reach California or because his love for beautiful Jessie Benton had been so strong that Frémont had dared to antagonize her powerful father. There was no doubt that Frémont and his high adventures must have a formidable appeal to the drab little fellow who worked at a drab little job all day.

Then there was Fillmore. Who knew what insanity would grip a voter and cause him to choose Fillmore just because this man of humble birth had never been elected President but had simply taken over the office at Zachary Taylor's death? Since Fillmore had not destroyed the country, there were those who would say he had been a damn good President and that the people should show their gratitude. Did anyone care that Jim had been a Congressman, a Senator, Secretary of State, Minister to Russia, Minister to Great Britain and had a fair chance of making the country proud of him?

Chief Justice Thomas Slidell was waiting at the Royal Street house, reminding John of the days long ago when Tom had worked for him. How annoyed he used to be at Tom's habits, the fruit-munching, the scattering of legal papers all over the parlor and dining room.

"I dropped in to have a drink with you," Tom said. "I hope I am not in your way."

"No, I am delighted. I told some fellows at the Saint Louis Hotel that I was tired and wanted to be alone, then, on the walk home, I found I regretted my decision. I was beginning to feel lonely. How does it look for tomorrow?"

Tom shrugged. "It is not easy to tell."

"You did not send an army of questioners from door to door asking how the householder intended to vote?"

They laughed together, remembering. John placed a bottle of brandy on the table and they drank a toast to Buchanan.

"Win or lose, he is our man," Tom said.

"If he loses, he is his own man." John sipped the brandy experimentally. Damn good. A gift from August Belmont. "It is fine having you on our side, Tom."

"What other side could I be on? Once the Whigs merged with

287

the lunatics, I was through with them. And I could not vote for a man just because he did not get lost in Nevada, could I?"

"Judah Benjamin felt just about the same as you. It was a blessing to have him with me at the convention in Cincinnati. He was of great assistance. People who did not like me liked him."

"Didn't anybody hate both of you?" Tom asked.

"Yes, but then they liked Buchanan, so it was a pleasant world. Somebody told me that Cincinnati is a very nice city. I saw nothing of it but hotel rooms and the convention hall. Some of the fellows went to a brothel. They said it was as clean as Grandma's pantry but you know how Benjamin and I are. Anyone would have thought we were attending the Eucharistic Congress instead of the Democratic Convention."

Tom smiled politely and uneasily. John had purposely introduced the mention of a brothel to see if it would shock Tom. It apparently had. Louisiana's Chief Justice was a strait-laced man. Had he always been? John thought back and could remember no time when Tom had been a reckless merrymaker. The short period in which he had kept bachelor quarters with some classmates in New York had been only a dismal gathering of clever children who had somehow wandered away from home. They had sowed their wild oats by quizzing each other on recondite points of law.

"He could not afford to raise hell when he was young," John thought, "so morals became a habit. I wonder if that accounts for most of the morality in the world?"

Jane MacKenzie Slidell's estate had been left to her grandchildren. It did not matter. It was too late for Tom's life to be flavored with spice or even sweetening. He was nearing sixty and he was not young for his years. His hair was white and sparse. His bony body could have belonged to a man twenty years his senior and his protruding eyes were weak and watery. So much for a good life devoted to study. Had he ever had any fun?

John refilled the brandy glasses and they talked of Buchanan, the changes in New Orleans, the law courts.

"You will sleep here tonight, will you not, Tom?"

"Oh, I am just a step from my place."

"I know but it has begun to rain. You might as well turn in here.

288

I'll tell you what—we'll have a hell of a big holiday breakfast and go out and vote together."

Tom yielded smilingly. "It will be the first time we have ever done that."

"Well, we are on the same side now."

Neither cared to remember that in their youth, it had been more than a political schism that had kept them from strolling to the polls together. John had been insufferably overbearing and he had selected his companions for their social value. Tom had been a bitter, unhappy young man conscious of his insignificant position in his brother's office. Long ago. None of it mattered any more.

In the morning, they had their breakfast as planned and walked to Canal Street to cast their votes. As always on Election Day, New Orleans was highly keyed and restless. The streets, even at an early hour, already had been the scene of rowdyism and violence. Drunken ruffians and roustabouts, bloody brawls and unrestrained hoodlumism were the symbols of the day, as unastonishing as carols at Christmas time.

As the Slidells walked, they were occasionally hailed familiarly and not always was the greeting a compliment to John. Once a fat man leaned precariously over an ironwork balcony to ask Tom what he was doing in such company.

"If I was as clean as you, I would not speak to him even if he was my brother."

"You have an outspoken public, Tom, my boy."

"Oh, most of them have only said hello. You must forgive that drunken fool."

"I forgive him. I was never the sensitive sort."

In front of the polling place, there was a small crowd, which parted respectfully at sight of Tom. John was amused at this evidence of how Louisiana graded the relative positions of Chief Justice and Senator. He fell a step behind his brother and as he did so, he heard a strange whizzing sound smite the air. Three things happened simultaneously. A man shouted, "The son of a bitch has a slingshot." A woman on a balcony screamed. Tom moaned and collapsed in John's arms. Gently John lowered him to the street. From somewhere came a shabby coat that was pillowed beneath Tom's head. John, kneeling beside his unconscious brother, was horrified by the sight of blood streaming from a wound at the base of Tom's skull. Yet instinctively he knew that the thin scarlet trickle from the ears was a more dreadful token of the extent of Tom's injury.

"Get a doctor," he said to no one in particular. "Get a doctor quickly."

"They are getting one. He'll be here right away."

A pockmarked youth stood above John with a sharp, jagged object in his hand. "He hit him with this rock and then he run like hell. Had a slingshot, he did, but I didn't see him real good. Can't say who he was."

John, kneeling on the banquette beside Tom, thought soberly that the missile had not been meant for Tom at all. If the assailant proved to be insane and disinterested in what man became his target, that was one thing. But if hostile reasoning had sparked the attack, then Tom had not been the intended victim. And John wiped the blood from his brother's head and remembered the twenty thousand disputed acres in the Houmas tract. The newspapers had shrieked continually at his efforts to clear title on that land. Within the month, they had informed their readers for the dozenth time that here was a bold swindle, a shameless act of greed that would dispossess several hundred people from homes their grandfathers had built. It was ironic if the blasts of the newspapers had caused the death of the most honest man in Louisiana politics. Nothing made much sense. Tom, you did have a little quiet fun somewhere sometime, didn't you, Tom?

The doctor came at last. He was very old and no longer believed in the cheering word, the encouraging smile.

"Looks bad," he said tersely.

"You mean my brother is dying?"

"Well, that is what you have to hope for."

"What the hell are you talking about?"

The doctor aimed a stream of tobacco juice at a passing cat. "Brain injuries. Wicked business. No life and no death. Let us get him out of the street."

They took Tom to John's house and a young man who had been a medical student was brought in to tend him.

290

"Wait a minute," John said. "I want the best of care for my brother."

The old doctor smiled coldly. "Then you had better take care of him yourself."

"I have neither the time nor the skill."

"We don't have many people around here—outside of nuns— who have any more skill than you do. Do you want this young man or don't you?"

"Why is he a *former* medical student?"

"Too stupid to learn much. That's all. He's a fine boy, otherwise. Does not drink or steal."

Tom did not regain consciousness that day or the next or the one after that. Within a week's time, the superficial injury was almost healed. The body of Tom Slidell was sustained by broth and warm milk dripped patiently into his sagging mouth.

"Oh, he will wake up sometime," the doctor said. "He will walk and sit and even feed himself, perhaps, but I doubt that he will ever think or speak. I would say his mind is utterly gone."

John brought a half dozen doctors to the bedside of his brother but none could improve upon the methods of the old man who had been called in an emergency. None could work a miracle or even promise one.

Adrien Deslonde, who had left the sea after the *Somers* tragedy, was in the insurance business in New Orleans. John arranged with him and others to keep a watch on the house on Royal Street, to insist upon good treatment for Tom and to report now and then on the hopeless situation.

He rode back to Washington, thinking that Tom's death would have been a lesser sorrow. What a stupid, horrible, God-damn thing the attack had been. And the police had never caught the bastard with the slingshot. Poor Tom, just quietly going about his business, walking to the polls like any citizen—

John was startled by a sudden extraordinary realization. "Holy God! I never did get to vote for Jim!"

When James Buchanan became President of the United States, he was not so dazzled by the view from the summit that he forgot how he had reached it.

"Slidell," he asked, "how would you like to be Minister to France?"

They were sitting in Buchanan's private parlor after dinner. John and Mathilde had been invited to dine very simply with the President and his niece, Harriet Lane, White House hostess for the bachelor President. John wondered what Mathilde and Harriet, left alone, would find as a possible subject for conversation. Harriet was a spinster, a Protestant and a woman who knew nothing at all about clothes except that they should be nice and clean. To repeat gossip to the White House hostess was socially incorrect and to mention the name of any controversial Washington figure was suicide. Maybe Harriet would be interested in Creole recipes or the best method for raising camellias. Mathilde would somehow fight her way out of the woods. It was not without reason that she was considered the smartest of all Senate wives.

Buchanan said, "Slidell, I asked you a question."

"And it was a very nice question, too, Mr. President. Forgive me. I was thinking." He paused to gather together some thoughts that might have been occupying his mind. A few from yesterday would do. He had known for a week that he would be offered the French post. "I was thinking of Edward Livingston, who was my idol when I was young. Long ago, in the home of my parents, I said that I would like nothing better than to follow in his footsteps. Well, I have been a lawyer, a Congressman, a Senator and now— Rather curious, is it not?"

"Yes, it is. He was an excellent Minister to France. Like to try your hand at it?"

John was heavily conscious of the parlor, with its funereal hangings. Purple velvet. The mahogany furniture was too solid, too massive. The chairs had enormous dignity and uncomfortable seats. Someone had wholeheartedly subscribed to the medieval theory that neither frivolity nor dishonor could flourish in majestic surroundings.

"I wish, Mr. President, that you had not asked me to follow so closely in Edward's footsteps."

Buchanan looked at him in surprise. "You mean you do not want an appointment in France? Would you rather go to Spain?"

John stirred uneasily on the hard chair. "Mr. President, if I had had a chance like this eight years ago or four years ago, I would have jumped at it with delight. It is the sort of thing I have always wanted."

"It is the sort of thing you deserve. I believe you could handle the appointment brilliantly. Why do you hesitate?"

John said, "It will trouble you to know."

"The Presidency is not calculated to relieve a man of troubles. It just entitles him to bear them in public. What is bothering you?"

And suddenly John decided not to tell him. Mr. President was an entirely different person from Jim. To Jim he would have said, "What do you expect me to do? Bet against myself? I have a bloody fortune in Louisiana property. I cannot afford to be stuck in France on a Federal job if Lancaster and New Orleans start calling each other dirty names. I have to stay here, Jim, and watch what is happening."

To the President he said, "To tell the truth, my health is not good."

Buchanan regarded him in silence for a long moment, then said, "I am sorry to hear that, Slidell."

"I knew you would be. That is why I was reluctant to mention it. My heart, you know. I would consider it a great risk to assume so much responsibility and to be so far from my own doctor and—"

"Oh, I understand, Slidell. Don't think for a moment that I do not."

And John was afraid that he did.

"Mr. President, I am very grateful to you. Nothing in the world would delight me more than to be your Minister to France."

That much was true enough. God, how it hurt to refuse so magnificent an appointment. Disheartening to the point of tears. Was it not the kind of thing he had always sought? A position of high honor and historical importance. What a climax to his career it would have been. What a chance to prove his capabilities once and for all. How Mathilde would have sparkled as the wife of the United States Minister to France. When would there be a better opportunity for his daughters to marry so well that by comparison, Creole marriages would seem like unfortunate misalliances?

293

Still, there was no choice. From every corner, north and south, came whispers and gloomy predictions. In the Supreme Court, it had been decided, despite Northern fury, that a Negro whose ancestors were sold as slaves was not entitled to the rights of a Federal citizen and therefore had no standing in court. In the Senate, the aggressive abolitionist Sumner of Massachusetts had been horsewhipped by the nephew of Andrew Butler of South Carolina. In Kansas, a dangerous idiot named John Brown had massacred five proslavery men. Grim warnings. Suppose the worst happened while he was performing a service for the United States in France? In that case, he would be compelled to resign his office, which would cancel any advantages he had hoped to gain from the high position. Or he could continue to serve, declaring his loyalty to the stars and stripes and the Federal government. Louisiana would then seize the property of this Slidell who was an enemy, a traitor and an exceedingly rich man.

Obviously, he would have to cleave to the South and the immense holdings in real estate he had amassed. But he had not yet been forced to a decision. Why could he not take the French post and await developments? No, that was not politically sound, for it would put him out of touch and feel with the atmosphere of his own country. He would not know how to gauge the popularity of a man or an idea. He would not know what or whom to follow. He would return a stranger to a land that had already assigned the leading parts in the drama. He would be permitted to stand in the wings and watch, providing he got in no one's way. The Ministry to France could thus prove to be a passport to oblivion. He must do his watching now and be in a splendid position to be noticed when the roles were cast. Washington was the place for that. Not Paris. Good-by, Paris. Good-by, the opportunity to present his daughters at the Court of France.

"You definitely feel, Slidell, that you cannot accept the post?"

"I am afraid that I cannot, Mr. President."

"Think it over again, Slidell. Consult with your family and friends. And, of course, your doctor." Was there just the faintest tinge of sarcasm in Buchanan's tone?

During the night, John lay wakeful, his mind teeming with bitter resentment. Why were the times so out of tune for him?

Why had it happened this way? Minister to France. What glory, what honor. But, oh, if it were a wrong guess, what consequences. Buchanan had told him to think it over, to consult with family and friends. Perhaps, just perhaps, while he was in New York next week, he would present the matter for August Belmont's inspection.

August was entertaining the first delegation of Japanese officials ever to appear in the Western world. Though they had crossed the ocean on an American warship and were guests of the government, it had been made clear that the State Department would appreciate any diversion provided for them by distinguished citizens. John and Mathilde would be their hosts in Washington.

"Are we being nice to those little brown men for the government or for Cal?" John asked.

Mathilde said, "You are being nice for the government. In my case, it is for Cal. He sent me a huge Chinese vase, a cashmere shawl, the very first arum ever seen in Washington and a dog that will fit in a candy box."

"Personally, I would prefer to find chocolates. And what the hell is an arum?"

"I hope it is a species of lily bulb because I have planted it. What shall we do to make Cal's Japanese happy, John?"

"I don't know. Let us first see what August does with them."

August entertained the seventy Japanese officials for a weekend. In a procession of carriages, he conducted a tour of New York, showing his visitors the city and showing the city his visitors. The most highly placed among the Japanese hierarchy sat like statues, aristocratically calm and indifferent. The subordinates wagged their heads and waved their paper fans at the ladies of New York, and some of the ladies laughingly blew kisses to the strange little men. The evenings were given over to a great banquet at the Metropolitan Hotel and a special performance of opera at the new Academy of Music on Fourteenth Street.

When it was all over, they sat alone, August and John, and talked of the world in general. The Hague had been useful experience but it was not a post one would wish for any extended period.

"Are you going to be Minister to France, John?"

"So you know about that?"

295

"Yes. I know everything."

"Then tell me how I have decided."

August looked surprised. "You have not given a definite answer?"

"Yes and no. I am in a quandary." John fell silent and studied for a moment the understanding, brilliant eyes of his niece's husband. "August, you have never mentioned it but you must be aware that a pretty big storm could be brewing."

August nodded.

"Do you think I should accept the Ministry to France?"

"No. You could not make a more stupid move. Europeans are speaking to Americans on only one subject—slavery. And what would you say to them? You cannot say slavery is a fine thing or you will be recalled by the blended screams of the entire North. You cannot say it is an evil if you ever hope to go home again to your pretty Louisiana. You had better stay in the Senate, John, where you have only Louisiana to please."

"I know you are right, August. By the way, how does the wagering go in Europe? Do they think it is going to rain?"

"They think it is going to pour."

"Do you think any of them will lend anybody any umbrellas?"

August dropped his cigar in a crystal ash tray. "My, we are becoming arch, are we not? I will use plain language, if you do not mind. The Rothschilds have deep admiration for the government of the United States. Is that what you wanted to know, John?"

"Oh, I could have guessed that. Their admiration would naturally stick pretty close to their money, would it not?"

"It would. And if you say that this is a thing you cannot understand, then just leave quietly, without slamming the door."

John laughed. "Hell, August, I understand. I am very realistic. I know that people love money."

August's eyes narrowed. "Some people hate slavery. Did you know that, too?"

"I have heard a rumor to that effect. The Europeans are something like the Northerners, are they not? They believe in using their workers up and flinging them aside when they get old or take sick. It is certainly the simplest and cheapest way of doing things. We take care of our workers throughout their lives, August."

"Of course you do. You place them in the same category as your horses or hunting dogs. You—" August's lips closed firmly, stifling the complete expression of his thought. Then, "John, this is a depressing subject, for it draws people like you and me into sententious mouthings. It finds us repeating the same tired arguments, the same arid clichés that are spoken by every tongue in the country. Worst of all, we have both delivered these somewhat less than original observations as though they had just gushed from freshly tapped springs of wisdom. Let us open a bottle of wine, dear friend, and introduce no subject unless it offers an opportunity for wit and laughter."

"A splendid idea. Have you such a subject in mind?"

"As a matter of fact, I have not, so perhaps we had better just go to bed."

"How dull of you, August. It is not even half past two. I have a beautiful plan. Let us awaken Mathilde and Caroline. Let us drink a great deal of champagne and then the four of us will drive somewhere and watch the sun come up."

August was silent for a time. "John," he said at last, "you have never before voiced your love for us so plainly. Do you really believe it is our last visit together? If I thought that, I would weep. Instead, I shall risk my life. I shall awaken Caroline."

"Tell her it is a madman's idea of a good time. That is what I am going to tell Mathilde, but of course I shall say you thought up this ridiculous outing."

At the top of the stairs, they smiled a little sadly, a little foolishly at each other.

"In case it turns out that it is our last time, John, let us thank God that we are not starry-eyed chauvinists who will regard each other as enemies. If there is anything I can ever do for you—"

"That is understood, August. War is but politics. Between us there is friendship."

"True. And now let us have done with all these vagaries. There may be no war at all. Tell me how you will wake Mathilde at this hour."

John grinned. "Before God, August, this is a hell of a world we live in. I cannot describe this tender and intimate procedure to you without whipping the abolitionists into a new frenzy of hostility."

"What are you talking about?"

"Well, there is a good black woman known as Tia Lula lying on the floor in the hall outside Mathilde's room."

"What!"

"Yes, right on your pink velvet carpet in the passageway between the wardrobe and bath. I will tell her that Master says Mistress must get up and dress right now. If Mathilde's first impulse is to throw things— You perceive the advantages of the system?"

August nodded solemnly. "I do, indeed, and I shall tell the Rothschilds that it has its merits." For a moment, he stared down the corridor toward the suite that had been assigned to the Slidells. "Is there really a Tia Lula, John?"

"Yes, really. In childhood, she was Madame Deslonde's playmate and became Mathilde's nurse. What do you think she would do with freedom, August?"

"I think she would sleep on the floor outside Mathilde's room, John. It is too late for Tia Lula. But for Tia Lula's grandchildren— God damn it, here we are back again hammering away at banalities. Come on, let us wake the girls and go watch the sunrise. The first one who mentions slavery gets no more champagne."

Janie and Cal, sitting before the fire in the New York house, waited for the noonday meal to be announced. Glancing at the clock on the mantel, Janie observed that it had stopped. Odd. Still, many of the articles in this house needed repair. She and Cal had used the house infrequently but now it would be home. She would have to make an inventory of goods and services required to bring them the conveniences they had known at "Moorings."

"Moorings" had been put up for sale when Cal had received the appointment to command the Mediterranean Squadron. None of the Perry children wanted the farmhouse even for holiday jaunts and it irked Janie sorely that not one of them appreciated the beauty and the comfort of "Moorings." She was particularly annoyed with Bill and his wife, who had stated flatly that they would find Tarrytown very lonely. Well, Bill's wife was that kind, of course, thinking of nothing but the next ball. People nowadays had no proper sense of values.

298

"We will keep the New York house," Cal had said. "When I retire, we will want to be in town, close to August and Caroline."

"When you retire? Why, you are entering upon a whole new career with this Mediterranean business. When do you take over?"

"Not till June."

Not till June. It was only March now. She wondered how he would endure the intervening months of leisure. It gave her a feeling of guilt that his extended leave, which irritated him, brought her so much pleasure. To have him constantly at her side was a quiet bliss never known in youth. She turned toward him and smiled.

Aware of her gaze, he abandoned the fascination of the leaping flames and returned her smile. "I was just thinking, Janie. Why don't we spend the month of April at Saratoga Springs? It will be lovely there then."

She said, "When we were young, I could not drag you into hotels. Now you never want to stay home."

"Not true. I have not changed at all but you have settled down so thoroughly that my modest vacation suggestions now seem to you like skylarking. Do you realize I still have not touched the twenty thousand dollars that Congress voted me for my errand to Japan? We ought to do exciting things with that money. Name something you want."

"Very well," she said. "Saratoga Springs for the month of April."

"Good. By the way, if you are figuring on giving any big dinners, please do it within the next few weeks. When we come back from the Springs, I shall be too busy for such things."

"Yes. There are lots of people I am almost ashamed to face. I have been so lazy about entertaining. Julia and Ray had Franklin Buchanan over the other night and Julia said he remarked on not having seen us—" She paused in surprise as Cal's eyes hardened. "What's the matter?"

"I don't care if we never see Franklin Buchanan."

"Why, Cal! What has he done?"

"Nothing yet. Yes, he has, too. In his heart he has committed treason."

"What do you mean?"

"Something he said the last time we met. We were having a drink together and the conversation turned to the way things stand in the country today. He is a Southerner, you know, and he made it pretty clear where his sympathies would lie if hell broke loose."

Janie said, "Now, Cal, it cannot be true that just because he loves his home place the way you love Rhode Island you are vexed with him."

He stared at her. "Janie, do you think that if Rhode Island opposed the Federal government I would stand with Rhode Island? Good God, I am an American first, then a Rhode Islander. These damn Southerners put it the other way around."

"Well, dear, that is not so serious, is it?"

"Of course, it is serious. It means that if it came to it, those people would fire on American ships."

"Oh, no. Franklin Buchanan has given his life to our Navy, the same as you have."

"But he is a Southerner."

"Yes, he is a Southerner and so are many of our friends. I cannot picture any of them firing on American ships. Cal, do you think you could be magnifying this thing a little? Nobody is going to war because some people buy servants instead of hiring them."

"That is not the whole story, by any means. However, it is part of it. It is the part that makes for hatred and I will tell you plainly that I hate slavery and always have."

"I never knew you felt this so strongly."

"I do. In my day, I pursued many a slave ship and I caught quite a few. God help me, I saw what they were carrying. Poor, miserable souls crowded together without room to lie down or—"

"Yes, but you were pursuing them because by that time it was illegal to bring new slaves into the country. The owners of these vessels were criminals to begin with. Decent Southerners did not acquire their slaves from such men or under such circumstances."

"Did they not?"

She looked away from him. "And it all means that you do not want Franklin Buchanan in your home. Because some unfortunate Negroes were mistreated you feel—"

"Oh, Janie, how can you scramble my remarks so thoroughly? When I had Franklin Buchanan as my right-hand man, I knew

300

he was a Southerner. I knew some slaves were abused. I still was friendly with Franklin Buchanan. I ate with him. I drank with him. We had a cordial relationship. Do you understand so far?"

"Naturally, I understand. You do not need to talk to me as though I were a child."

"Oh, don't I?"

"No. I see the thing very plainly. You and a lot of others have let all this discord stir you up beyond all good sense. Franklin Buchanan is not one bit different today than he was a few years ago, only now—"

"Only now I know that he would fire upon American ships. Now I know he could be guilty of treason. That is enough for me. If it is not enough for you, it will still have to do, because Franklin Buchanan is never going to enter my house again."

His mood was not right for further questioning but she would have dearly loved to ask if John and Mathilde were to be avoided in the future. If so, it was certainly going to pose a thorny problem. The John Slidells and the August Belmonts were such warm friends that Janie could see herself in a nasty predicament. She was reasonably certain that in all arguments, John would support the South. Why shouldn't he? He was a Southern Senator and the South had been very kind to him. Of course, in John's case, there was not the question of actually fighting against the Federal government. She had a suspicion, though, that this was one of those situations of which Cal would say, "But, Janie, it is the principle of the thing."

She would not particularly mind John's dropping out of her life. She had never felt a deep affection toward him, and Mathilde was far too perfect, too smooth ever to have been judged on a human basis. She was a beautifully polished machine that turned out the correct reply, the flawless dinner, the wise decision, depending on which button was pressed for the need of the moment.

Janie glanced at Cal. He was scowling. Doubtless, his mind was still on Franklin Buchanan, slavery and the possibility of Southerners firing on ships of the American Navy. He would not welcome conversation. He would growl if his train of thought was derailed. She permitted her mind to return to Mathilde. Mathilde, with the charming shadow of a French accent that lingered on

301

through the years to enchant a listener. Mathilde, whose waist still measured eighteen inches. Mathilde, who had been at the bedside of Jane MacKenzie Slidell when the end had come. She, not Janie, had been there. It was a matter of timing. Nothing for which to reproach oneself but the timing had worked for Mathilde. It would not be Mathilde who was gaily exploring the cities of Europe when she was needed.

"I am mean natured," Janie thought. "I cannot forgive her for being at my mother's deathbed while I was enjoying myself. She was doing the right thing and I did not know that my mother was dying so no one behaved badly. Why am I such a fool?"

She thought of the gifts Cal had sent Mathilde from the Orient. How odd that with the exception of Mathilde's friend Caroline, he had forgotten all his daughters. How odd that Janie's own sister Julia had received no souvenir of the memorable voyage. But Mathilde had been generously remembered.

"Am I sure that it is only for being at my mother's deathbed that I cannot forgive her?"

And Janie, plump and aging, thought back almost a quarter of a century to the time when Mathilde had become her sister-in-law. Mathilde, the quiet little Creole girl who had gone to school with Julia. Incidentally, what had become of that girlhood friendship between Mathilde and Julia? Were Julia and Ray too stuffy for the John Slidells? Too much like the Cal Perrys? Oh, yes, the Cal Perrys. Where on earth had that fetching Mrs. Perry gone? How had it happened that suddenly Mathilde had become the member of the family who drew all the admiring glances?

"It happened because it was a natural thing to happen," Janie told herself. "She was young and I had not yet awakened to the fact that my youth was over. I let her beat me at what had always been my game. Instead of remodeling myself to be an attractive mature woman, I competed with her, lost the contest and became discouraged. I let myself become heavy and dowdy and— Am I sure that it is only for being at my mother's deathbed and receiving gifts from Cal that I cannot forgive her?"

It was no comfort to recall that Mathilde had not known that there had been a game at all and therefore could not know that she had emerged victorious. Mathilde always emerged victorious

302

because she was, as her sister-in-law had long known, a machine geared to explode into a million glittering splinters one moment in advance of the first error.

She glanced toward Cal again. He was still scowling—at least, there were deep vertical lines between his brows. But now she noticed that he was holding his mouth in a hard, tight line and that his eyes were half closed.

"Is something the matter, Cal?"

His voice came in a choked whisper. "Oh, Janie, I have a terrible pain."

She ran to him and saw now the perspiration upon his forehead and heard the difficult breathing. "Can you rise, dearest? Can you walk to the sofa? I will send someone for the doctor. Here, let me help you."

She placed herself so that her arm and shoulder could be leaned upon. He groaned as he bent toward her, then pitched suddenly full length upon the floor.

Janie cried out and the cook and butler came running from the kitchen. "Go quickly. Get the doctor," she directed.

The cook watched as Janie loosened Cal's collar, massaged his hands and stroked his hair. And all the while, the woman kept moaning, "Oh, Mrs. Perry. Oh, Mrs. Perry." And Janie knew what the cook was trying to tell her but she did not want to hear.

She listened when the doctor told her. He represented reality and there was no choice but to listen. She sent for August and Caroline and then went to her room. It was beyond belief. Saratoga Springs for the month of April. Then, in June, he would take command of the Mediterranean Squadron. Things could not happen like this. Not so fast. Life fell away from one gradually, not in a brief, terrible instant. It was not fair that a man should be waiting one moment for his noonday meal to be announced and in the next be felled in agony upon the floor of his sitting room. Yet a similar thing had happened to her father. How had her mother survived the shock? Had she stood transfixed by horror and woe, shivering in the blast of what was known as God's will?

Caroline and August came and after them the other children within reach of August's messengers. Janie sat at the window in her bedroom, staring out at a strange and empty world. She

303

accepted a cup of tea and afterward was aware of discomfort. She looked wonderingly at the cup and realized then that she had mindlessly swallowed the tea before it had fallen far from the boiling point.

August, sympathetic and resourceful, went quietly about the sad business of the day. Matthew Calbraith Perry had been his well-loved father-in-law. He also had been a national hero. August knew how to honor this man in both his identities. August took care of everything. No, not everything. There was one thing that Janie had to do herself.

All through the day, there had been a constant stream of callers entering and leaving. Next week, next month, next year, she thought wearily, she would thank them all for having come. Today she would see no one. She supposed her daughters-in-law were sitting sedately in the reception room and accepting the words of condolence with proper replies. Perhaps they were even serving port and agreeing in hushed voices that the country had lost a great man.

Janie had barely noticed who the callers were, but as one of them stepped briskly toward the front steps, recognition flashed upon her. Swiftly she leaped from her chair and ran from the room. Down the stairs she sped with family, friends and servants gaping at her as, with skirts flying, she raced for the front door. Behind her she heard the frightened questions of her children but she had no time to answer. She must reach the door before any servant.

As the knocker sounded, she was there, opening the door and stepping outside to receive Franklin Buchanan on the front steps.

"Mrs. Perry!"

"I thank you for coming, Captain Buchanan." With her hand behind her, she held fast to the doorknob and lifted her white face to him. "You will forgive me, I know, for not wishing much conversation."

"I have come only to offer my sympathy and to say that if I can serve you, please call on me."

"I thank you, Captain Buchanan. You are very kind. Good day."

Then she went back to her room and to her chair. When August came, a moment later, to gaze questioningly at her, she said, "I

304

know it was an insane performance. Please do not be alarmed and do not ask me to explain."

He shook his head. "You do not have to give explanations—only orders. Have you any?"

She had not and he went away, understanding her need to be alone.

General Winfield Scott, supreme commander of the United States Army, Secretary of the Navy Isaac Toucey, Vice-President John C. Breckinridge, the Senators of New York and Rhode Island and a score of other personages came from Washington for the funeral.

The cortege moved down Fifth Avenue, across Fourteenth Street to Second Avenue. The route was lined with hushed crowds and Captain Adams thought of the Uragans who had gathered to watch the proud procession of the Lord of the Forbidden Interior. And he wept, remembering.

At the Church of St. Mark's in-the-Bouwerie, the Reverend Dr. Francis Hawkes was waiting to receive the boy from Rhode Island who had known the seas of the world, the words in a blue Bible and the respect of his fellow men.

Vault ninety-five. And Janie thought of her father and it gave her comfort to know that Cal would rest beside him. John Slidell's vault, the marker said. And this great man had been John Slidell's son-in-law. And years ago, they had met and sat at a dining-room table together, the midshipman and the prosperous business-man John Slidell, Senior. How strange were the patterns of life and death, for now taps was sounding its heartbreakingly sweet notes at the vault of the prosperous businessman, for his son-in-law was at rest.

And as her mother had once done, Janie turned from vault ninety-five, supported by a son and a son-in-law. Those two had been Alec and Cal, and she wondered if they had seemed the strangers to her mother that Bill and August now seemed to her. She averted her gaze from the curious strangers and permitted herself to be led to the carriage. Beside it stood her brother John.

"Do you want me with you?" he asked her.

She shook her head. She had not questioned Cal but she could hear his answer: No, John would not be literally firing on American shipping, Janie, but it's the principle of the thing.

"Shall I come over later?"

She shook her head again and looked pleadingly at August. Her mother had always claimed that August understood everything.

August was patting John's arm and saying, "Good of you to have come, John. We appreciate it. Good-by."

And now she was in the carriage, driving back to the empty house, the empty life. She knew she would be invited to live with the Belmonts and she knew she would not accept the invitation. From here on, she would live as her mother had lived after her hour at vault ninety-five. Alone and lonely.

Janie turned and looked back once at St. Mark's in-the-Bouwerie. She would not see it again. Foolish to visit with flowers in her arms, for he was not there. He was with Oliver, sailing the seven seas, and if this was not so, then it was only because she knew better than God what would be Heaven for Cal Perry.

I deeply regret the embarrassments which will surround you during the remainder of your term. I see no probability of preserving the Union nor indeed do I consider it desirable to do so if we could—

John looked up from the letter he was writing to James Buchanan. Jim. Jim, who would so soon drift palely into the backwash of history. Only a little while now and he would surrender to Abraham Lincoln the pain and the glory of the Presidency.

Abraham Lincoln. President Abraham Lincoln. And, by God, it need never have happened. The Democratic party had permitted it to happen. Intent on suicide, they had divided themselves into enemy camps while the Republicans had stood firmly united behind the tall man from Illinois.

"August Belmont wanted Stephen Douglas," John thought in anguish. "I wanted John Breckinridge. John Crittenden wanted John Bell. We held so tenaciously to our opinions that we put Abraham Lincoln in office."

John finished his letter to the President and dispatched it. He had thought it a courtesy to commiserate with Buchanan on the difficulty of his position and had also considered it incumbent

306

upon himself to reveal his personal feelings, but he was not surprised when a cool silence was all he received in reply. There had been little cordiality between himself and the President since the time of John Brown's raid on Harpers Ferry.

In the course of conversation with Buchanan, the matter had quite naturally been mentioned. John had spoken hotly and Buchanan with an impatient gesture had said, "The man will doubtless be executed, Slidell. What more do you want?"

"I want this: I want the newspapers to carry a statement to the North that this murdering madman is no hero. Those people are acting as though he was one of God's avenging angels and I think they should be set straight by their Chief Executive."

Buchanan had regarded him with eyes as hard as blue marbles. "Slidell, are you, by any chance, dictating policy?"

"I am making every effort to see that the South gets fair treatment."

So perhaps it was not strange that Buchanan did not reply to his letter.

Pierre Beauregard, on his way to take over the Superintendency of West Point, stopped in Washington to visit the Slidells. The small, slim man with the mournful eyes spoke gravely of conditions in the country. His precise unfolding of all that had occurred and of all that might occur provoked Mathilde, who thought that John Slidell was in a position to know as much about the situation as any Army captain. But this conceited little fellow from St. Bernard Parish was her sister Caroline's husband.

"We are so happy to see you, Pierre, and so anxious to hear all the family news."

Pierre was not concerned with family news. Other things were on his melancholy mind. He had acted heroically in the Mexican War and had never been appreciated. Did not Mathilde and John think he had been badly used? Should he not have had a colonelcy by this time? He had had a splendid letter from General Winfield Scott, hinting that Captain Beauregard's great service to the country would be rewarded, but nothing substantial had resulted.

"You are to be superintendent of West Point," Mathilde said. "Surely that is a great honor."

The drooping eyelids somehow expressed Pierre Beauregard's

disappointment that she should not consider him deserving of a more spirited assignment.

"Is he not tiresome?" Mathilde asked John when they were alone.

"I rather like him."

"Still, he is a bore."

"Just think. He might have been your husband."

Mathilde laughed. "I was too lucky for a thing like that to happen to me. Caroline was always the one who had measles on Christmas or lost her spending money at the fair or had an upset stomach when there was going to be a special feast."

"But he is handsome," John said.

"All Creoles are handsome. We smother the ugly babies."

"By God, come to think of it, I guess you do. But since a kind nurse saved your life by hiding you from view, come sit on my lap and tell me who is coming to our dinner for Mr. Secretary of War Floyd."

"Why, everybody is coming."

"Everybody?"

"Of course."

One of the people who did not come to the dinner was Mr. Secretary of War Floyd. He was feeling very ill, for earlier that afternoon, President Buchanan had requested his resignation. The dinner was a subdued affair. The guests were Southerners. Mr. Floyd was a Southerner. Conversation was quiet. People spoke tensely and there was not a note of laughter throughout the evening.

"John, you are very close to Buchanan," Mason of Virginia said.

"Not any more."

"I was going to ask you why Floyd was ditched."

"That I know without being close to Buchanan. Floyd and he had a disagreement over Major Anderson's moving into Fort Sumter."

Mason's tight slit of a mouth set itself in a grimace of annoyance. His leonine head reared aggressively. "We should have waited upon Mr. Buchanan and informed him that since so little is left of his term, we—"

"It would not have helped Floyd. Buchanan is confused and

unhappy and does not know what to do. He felt that he had to do something so he did it to Floyd. South Carolina has frightened him to death. He is praying that nothing more happens till he can deliver the country to Lincoln."

Mason's light eyes softened. "I suppose the poor devil really is having a few nightmares."

John smiled sourly. "I never feel sorry for Presidents. Not a one of them was ever forced into the job. They all work like demons to get it."

"Who will replace Floyd?"

"I don't know. In a day or two, I suppose Buchanan will send us a name to approve."

But President James Buchanan sent no name to the Senate. Instead, he informed the Senate that the new Secretary of War was Joseph Holt of Kentucky.

There were those who shrugged off this action of Buchanan's. Before the matter could be argued out, they reasoned, Buchanan would be gone from Washington. There were others who were not willing to let his offensive behavior go unchallenged. Their spokesman was John Slidell.

"Mr. Buchanan, in making an appointment of Secretary of War Floyd's substitute without consulting the Senate, exceeded his constitutional authority," John told the newspapers. "If suffered to pass by without expressed dissent, it would establish a precedent alike dangerous to the principles on which our system of government was constructed and in derogation of the rights and privileges of the Senate."

"You are quite correct, of course," Bill Sebastian of Arkansas said. "But with so little of Buchanan's time remaining, nothing will come of our objections."

"I know," John said. "I just wanted to go on record as disapproving his arrogant flouting of the Senate. Holt will scarcely have time to exercise any of the prerogatives of his position before he is yielding it to some crony of Lincoln's."

Holt, however, realizing as well as John that his time was short, wasted not a moment. One of his first official acts was to relieve Pierre Gustave Beauregard of his assignment as Superintendent of West Point.

"I simply cannot credit it," John said to Judah Benjamin. "I will not believe Jim Buchanan is aware of Beauregard's dismissal. It must be all Holt's idea."

Once more, and for the last time, John and Buchanan met. It was on a miserable day in January, when a chill dampness lay upon the city and even penetrated into the offices and hearts of the men charged with the responsibility of government. John's face was flushed with anger as he looked across a desk at the President whom he had created. Buchanan looked back at him. Buchanan pallid and with purple smudges of sleeplessness beneath his eyes. The Union had lost South Carolina, Mississippi, Florida, Alabama and Georgia within the month. Calmly the President awaited whatever it was that Slidell had to say. Nothing could matter now.

"I would just like to know, Mr. President, if Mr. Holt's dismissal of my brother-in-law from West Point met with your approval."

Buchanan said, "I sustain the decision of my Secretary of War. And, Slidell, if nothing else, let us be factual. Beauregard is not married to *your* sister. Legally he is not your brother-in-law."

John said, "And legally Holt is not your Secretary of War. The Senate has not confirmed him, so actually he has no standing at all. He has, however, dealt an insult to a man who has been a loyal and honored defender of his country and it was impossible for me to believe that you endorsed this action."

"Oh, Slidell, stop your nonsense. Louisiana, the state from which you and your 'brother-in-law' come, is only a sword's length from secession right this minute and you know it. Are we to be such fools as to permit a man from a state in rebellion to have charge of West Point?"

"Louisiana has not seceded. You have no right to guess what she is going to do. You have no right to punish Captain Beauregard for a step he has not yet taken."

Buchanan sighed. "Slidell, I find it tiresome to be told by a Southerner what I have no right to do. Why is it that I and all men faithful to the Federal government are constantly charged to uphold constitutional laws, to overstep no bounds, to adhere strictly to each and every convention, while you Southerners flagrantly indulge in breaking every agreement ever made?"

310

"I resent your talking so to me. Louisiana has not seceded."

"Will you be able to say that next week, Slidell?"

"This conversation is taking place today, Mr. President. I came here to discover whether or not you approve of Mr. Holt's removal of Captain Beauregard from the Superintendency of West Point."

"I thoroughly approve."

John turned and walked out of Buchanan's office. Buchanan had forgotten the man who, twenty years earlier, had taken on the job of grooming him for the Presidency.

"Maybe he has not forgotten. Maybe that is what he has against me," John thought drearily.

Needing a drink and an hour of rest, he erased from memory his appointment schedule for the afternoon and went home. There was to be no rest. He had a visitor. In the upstairs sitting room, he was amazed to find Mathilde entertaining August Belmont.

"August!"

They embraced each other warmly and Mathilde slipped away to resume the duties August's arrival had interrupted.

"How is Caroline?"

"In excellent health."

"And the children?"

"Jane and Raymond Rogers, the Second, have sore throats. Frederika has a rash. August, Junior, has a broken arm. Oliver is quite bilious and Perry's teeth refuse to arrive in conventional manner. Are you delighted that you asked?"

"No, and it was very rude of you to tell me. People should always report that everything is fine. What are you doing here, August?"

"Oh, I am not exactly a stranger to Washington, you know."

John gave him a sidewise glance. "I see. Too soon to go into it, eh?"

"Yes. First let us drink and pretend it is a merry world. You will tell me that your beautiful daughters are more beautiful than ever and that your son is doing well in his expensive Massachusetts school. I will tell you of a red-and-gold pleasure sleigh I bought Caroline for Christmas and—"

"We do not have to be that giddy, August. I have just come from

311

a brief—oh, a very brief—meeting with our Chief Executive and I am not in my most carefree mood."

"Was it bad?"

"We do not love each other any more and you know how deadly it is to make conversation once romance has flown."

August laughed. "Poor Buchanan. Romance has flown but you have left him with a parcel of wayward children. That wicked daughter South Carolina is leading her sisters astray, is she not?"

John downed his whisky and said, "So despite your best intentions to chatter of nothing, you have precipitately arrived at the reason for your being here. Very well, let us get to it, August."

August set his drink down and moved with his limping gait to the window. The room behind him was fancifully decorated in white and French blue. It was a gay room but through the sheer curtains, the world beyond showed itself raw and chilling. He turned away and went back to the fireplace and the view of the lovely, ridiculous blue carnations on the material that Mathilde had chosen for draperies and chair covering.

"John, I have come on a family matter. Of course, it hinges on the country's troubles. Everything does today. I believe Louisiana is going to secede. I do not ask you. Perhaps you know. Perhaps you do not. I am only stating what I believe."

He paused as the butler entered with a tray of assorted cheeses and fruits. Both men watched as though nothing so interesting had ever before come within their range of vision. The butler wiped an ash tray, picked up a used glass, made certain he had selected the best possible angle for the tray, and they watched him. Anything was better than meeting each other's eyes. Any interruption was welcome to these two who had laughed together and did not wish to speak of Louisiana. Quietly the butler withdrew. August's glance followed him out of the room, then reluctantly he picked up the burden of his errand.

"Let me say, John, my belief is that within days, Louisiana will leave the Union. In due course, when all the Southern states have gone, there will be war. You know that you will not be permitted to go in peace. War there will be. That is known to every man of good sense."

John studied his boot tips and said nothing.

312

"Please do not hate me for the convictions I will now voice. The South is going to have a hard time. There may be hunger and homelessness before it is over."

John looked up in astonishment. "Now, really, you have not come here to remind me that I was born in New York and that it might be a snug place to be during—"

August waved his hand irritably. "Of course not. You are not the sort of person who is ever hungry and homeless. There are people to whom this just never happens no matter what goes on in their country. You belong to that inside circle of true aristocrats, the people who never get hurt. My interest lies with our helpless relative, John. I am talking about Tom."

"Tom? He is taken care of."

August nodded. "Yes, today he is. What happens to poor Tom if you are not in New Orleans, if his attendants and your friends are scattered? What happens to him if there is a shortage of food and there is pillaging in the houses and perhaps fire and—"

John jumped from his chair. "Jesus, that was a quick war. Louisiana got licked before she even seceded."

August did not smile. "With your permission, John, I am on my way to New Orleans to get Tom and take him North. I have a small, quiet house in Newport where I will settle him with a few servants. He will be safe and well treated. I have never known Tom but I am just the sort of old woman who will fret about him if I think he is alone and neglected."

John sat down and regarded August in dazed disbelief. Here was a man who represented the greatest banking house in the world, a man whose time and thoughts were of the utmost value, a man who employed more than a hundred people to handle the details of his crowded life. Yet he must go himself for Tom. To send an employee, a nurse or even a doctor would strike August as an act so coolly impersonal as to be an insult.

"I guess you are a very nice fellow, August," John said.

"Your niece says that I am a calamity howler."

"And of course you are. Would you take the young man who has been tending Tom all this time?"

"If he wants to go, I will take him. You give your permission, then, for me to look after Tom in the North?"

"Wouldn't I be a bastard to refuse?"

"Yes, I really think you would be."

John placed a sliver of golden cheese upon a small, crisp cracker and handed it to August. "A gift from the Dutch embassy. Do try it. Incidentally, as I figure it, you will be in New Orleans two days. If the Governor is there, have dinner with him one evening."

"Have you forgotten I was fairly well publicized as a Stephen Douglas man?"

"That will make no difference. Louisiana's Governor is a gentleman and knows no way to make a guest uncomfortable." John sighed and said thoughtfully, "Louisiana has not always avoided what may be called sharp politics but every one of us who has represented the state has had style and elegance. Our governors, thank God, always have had the polish to stand at the side of any gentleman in the world. If the Emperor of France visited New Orleans tomorrow, the Governor of Louisiana would make us proud. August, it will not always be so. The world is changing. In time, the trash will triumph and they will elect trash to high office. Their ways will not be more honest than our ways. The only change will be that decent people of the state will be shamed by the ignorance and coarseness of its representatives."

August said, "Of course trash will triumph. There is more trash than anything else. It is simply a matter of mathematics. Now it is time to talk of Caroline's pleasure sleigh."

John picked up the whisky bottle and poured liberally. "To hell with Caroline's pleasure sleigh," he said. "I do not feel all that debonair and sprightly. As a matter of fact, I am sick."

August looked at the vigorous old campaigner—Slidell, very erect, his white hair crowning the straight six feet of still powerful physique. He knew that his wife's uncle had not been referring to any bodily ailment.

"John," he said, "I feel pretty sick myself. It consoles me some to remember that nothing lasts forever. When we meet again, it will be all over. Life will once more be wine and walnuts. Let us think of the future as a time of—"

"August, there is damned little future in being a United States

Senator from Louisiana." Their glances met and locked. John was the first to look away. He said, "Pick up Tom and get out of New Orleans. Stay no more than two days. The climate has always been hard on Northerners."

Mr. William Howard Russell of the London *Times* was a first-rate reporter and he had not made the long voyage from his homeland merely to generalize and editorialize on the American situation. Nor was he content to interview a few Washington celebrities and return to his room to write knowingly of the American picture, North and South.

Mr. Russell's large, fat body would have been more comfortable at Willard's Hotel than on the various river boats and dusty trains he rode in pursuit of the news. His sharp eyes looked everywhere, saw everything, and his luck was of the same high caliber as his reporting. He had just decided that the city of Washington had nothing more to tell him and that he would now journey South, when General Pierre Gustave Beauregard of the Confederate Army fired upon Fort Sumter and initiated war. Mr. Russell was delighted.

He interviewed General Beauregard immediately, then traveled on. Eventually he would reach Montgomery, Alabama, and talk to President Jefferson Davis and to members of the Confederate Cabinet, but Mr. Russell was in no haste. There were interesting people and places along the way.

One night, he rested in New Orleans and visited with Mr. John Slidell, a Senator from Louisiana prior to that state's secession. Mr. Russell sat in a comfortable chair in the parlor of Number 312 Royal Street and beamed at the lovely ladies assembled there. Madame Slidell was the eldest of the group and she was little more than forty-five, Mr. Russell guessed. An appealing, girlish creature in a melon-colored gown with flowers in her hair. An irrelevant thought disturbed Mr. Russell. Had she had a happy life? Slidell was surely old enough to be her father. A remarkable man, however, Mr. Russell noted. Keen gray eyes full of life and wisdom, a still handsome build and an electrifying personality. These things Mr. Russell saw for himself. What he had heard interested him little. Everyone had heard the same thing. Slidell was adroit and subtle, full of device and fond of intrigue. Mr. Russell made it a rule to disregard anything that was already known to all.

He looked at Slidell's blond daughters and wondered if he had the words to describe them to his readers. He was seldom called upon to use the tender phrases that would be required in this particular case. The Slidell girls were almost too beautiful. It would be only justice if they were so ill-natured that no one could stand them. Evidently, this was not the case, for they were surrounded by girls of their own age, who joined them in their gentle war work. All of them sat in the parlor, engaged in the business of carding lint with their fair hands. Cynically Mr. Russell played with the thought that it made a charming and patriotic background for his interview with John Slidell. Could the distinguished ex-Senator possibly have been aware of such a thing?

In any case, the evening would make quite a story, for young Alfred Slidell, a boy in his teens, had just arrived from a Northern school. He had traveled home under an assumed name because Union mobs were stoning relatives of prominent Southerners. At least, that was what the boy said, Mr. Russell properly reminded himself.

Another piquant piece of good fortune was the presence of Madame Beauregard. She was a shy reflection of her lovely sister Madame Slidell, and Mr. Russell's heart went out to her as she questioned him concerning the General. There was a flame of yearning in her eyes and a faint flush upon her cheeks when the hero's name was mentioned.

"Oh, yes, I saw him, Madame Beauregard, and he is in splendid health. He was busy with papers, orderlies, dispatches, and the outer room was crowded with officers, but he was very generous and gave me of his time. I know your husband thinks of you constantly, madame, for he is a romantic man. On his table, flanking his maps and plans, were two vases filled with flowers. He was writing a letter as I came in—perhaps to you—and a little bouquet of roses lay, by way of paperweight, upon the stationery."

The room rang with the pretty, silvery laughter of the young girls.

"He offered me every assistance and facility, relying, of course, on my strict observance of a neutral's duty. He is a very fine person, madame. I was tremendously impressed."

Madame Beauregard, too filled with emotion to speak, clasped Mr. Russell's hand and turned her tearful face from him.

Madame Slidell came to the rescue. "We are so proud of my sister's husband. Not that our pride in him is newly born but now his immortality is guaranteed. History will never forget him."

"That is quite correct," Mr. Russell agreed. "History will not forget General Beauregard. Fort Sumter is not likely to fade from American memory." He turned then to John Slidell, who had quietly allowed his family to rob him of space in the world's greatest newspaper. "Mr. Slidell, what do you think your contribution to the Confederacy will be?"

Mr. Russell marked with surprise that this was a disarming man. When one expected the usual political bombast, the boasting of a dozen offers, the claim of indecision, one received a simple and candid answer.

"I have not the slightest idea, Mr. Russell. So far, no one has indicated a belief that the war cannot be won without my assistance."

Mr. Russell smiled. "You will find yourself assisting, sir. I am quite certain your years of experience, your years of activity in the old government, will be remembered. I understand Judah Benjamin, the other Louisiana ex-Senator, is in President Davis' cabinet."

"Yes, he is. Mr. Benjamin is a genius. I have been only a work horse. Perhaps I have been placed to pasture."

Mr. Russell said, "I will not accept that, sir. My personal conviction is that the Confederate government is as yet too young to be fully aware of its needs."

"You may be right, Mr. Russell."

Benjamin had said just about the same thing. He had been willing to wager a thousand dollars that John would soon be invited to fill some important post. According to Benjamin, the Confederate government, at the moment, was assembling nothing but soldiers and pen nibs.

Mr. Russell took a swallow of the Creole coffee which had been served, gasped slightly but recovered gamely. "Strong, is it not?"

317

"I do hope so," Madame Slidell murmured.

Mr. Russell glanced respectfully toward the cup. Nothing but Irish whisky was supposed to have that effect upon a man. "Mr. Slidell, General Beauregard was the second of your brothers-in-law whom I have met and admired."

"I have been told that General Beauregard is not legally my brother-in-law."

"Perhaps he is not but I should claim him if I were you. There can be no argument about Matthew Calbraith Perry. He certainly was your brother-in-law. On two or three occasions, I had the privilege of being in his company. A very great man."

"Yes, he was. Did you know—this is family pride speaking but it may be of interest to you—Commodore Perry was to have assumed command of the Mediterranean Squadron. At his death, another brother-in-law of mine was appointed to take his place."

"Really?"

"Yes. My sister Julia's husband, Captain Raymond Rogers, was given the command. We were very elated, Mr. Russell, that the American Navy found our family such a natural reservoir for men of superior ability."

Mr. Russell was silent for a moment, weighing the advisability of asking a question which had come to his mind. Did he dare pretend that he was not positive? Did he dare ask if Commander Alexander Slidell MacKenzie had been his host's brother? The reaction might be interesting. It might be too interesting, he decided. The London newspapers had been cruel to Alexander Slidell MacKenzie. Mr. Russell chose a question that also might nettle this white-haired man, but this one was at least an honest question.

"Mr. Slidell, is it not a great sorrow to your family that you have chosen the Confederate side?"

"Of course not. It would be a great shame to them had I done otherwise. For forty years, Louisiana has given me her best. Do you think my family could respect me if I suddenly remembered that I was a New Yorker by birth?"

Mr. Russell took another sip of the dreadful coffee and pulled his fleshy figure out of the deep, soft chair. He thanked everybody for a most memorable evening. "Any message you would like me to deliver in Montgomery?" he asked.

"Thank you, no," John said pleasantly. "I correspond quite regularly with the gentlemen there."

Any message! Suppose he had said, "Why, yes. If it isn't too much trouble, I would like you to tell President Davis that I hope he falls down and breaks his God-damned neck."

Mr. Russell would have been startled but grateful for such a tasty tidbit for the London *Times*.

John had always felt that Jefferson Davis' affection for him was no deeper than his for Davis. Still, he had expected an answer to his letter. He had written, he surmised, as scores of others had written to Davis. The regular job-hunting letter full of flowery phrases and cordiality: "Count on me if there is anything I can do for you or our young government. I assure you, sir, that in serving this bright land which is ours, I would perform with pride and honor any task no matter how small—"

He had worried about those last few words. Davis was a literal-minded country boy with no sense of humor.

"I might wind up being sheriff of Yazoo County, Mississippi," John had thought.

Well, he had not even been offered that much. Davis simply had not replied. Benjamin explained that the President saw little value in those I-will-bear-you-in-mind letters.

"He will send for you when he knows there is something you can and will do."

Mathilde, with no reference to the national crisis or to John's unaccustomed leisure, asked, "Are we going to stay in the town house, dearest?"

"Yes," he said. "I do not want to move to the plantation while future arrangements are still in doubt. When I return from Montgomery, I will know more."

"Oh, are you going to Montgomery?"

He frowned. "Naturally, I am going to Montgomery. That is where the government is."

But presently the government was no longer in Montgomery. It had moved to Richmond, Virginia, and still Jefferson Davis had not replied to John's letter. The months went by. The Confederacy had a magnificent victory at Manassas. Everybody was doing splendidly. Pierre Beauregard was more adored than ever. Jefferson

319

Davis was being hailed as another George Washington. Judah Benjamin was the most powerful man in the Cabinet and John Slidell was reading a lot of books he had never had time for in the past. He wrote a brief note to Benjamin asking if the Confederacy was caught up as yet on pen nibs.

An answer came from the State Department. Could you come to Richmond for discussion of a very important matter?

Secretary of State Robert M. T. Hunter, a man of impressive stature, birth and wealth, received John affably. They had known each other in Washington, though the Virginian had held himself aloof from the deep-South circle. His eyes rested appraisingly upon John for a long moment, then seemingly satisfied, he said, "Little point in talking about this thing unless I know your reply to the essential question. Would you consider accepting an appointment as Confederate Commissioner to France?"

"France?" John asked. "Why, yes, that might be nice."

"I was not sure you would take to the idea. I heard you refused a similar proposition from Buchanan."

John concealed his amusement. The Confederacy's Secretary of State had delusions of grandeur. A similar proposition, indeed!

"I had personal reasons for declining the appointment," John said.

Hunter leaned back in his chair and tapped a pen thoughtfully against his teeth. "We are sending James Mason to London. We think you are the man for Paris. We believe Louis Napoleon will like you and there is no doubt that personalities play a great part in world politics."

"You know, of course, Mr. Secretary, that he is a very different man from his more famous uncle."

"Oh, yes. We know quite a lot about him and his court. Mr. Benjamin tells me that your lovely wife speaks Spanish as well as French and English."

"Yes. Were you thinking of appointing her to Spain?"

Hunter smiled like a man who does not have much time. He said, "I was thinking how Mrs. Slidell will delight the Empress Eugénie by speaking her native language."

John said, "Sir, let us be very sensible. Nobody has yet recognized the Confederacy. Nobody has invited the Confederacy to send representatives. We arrive as upstarts, not as accredited diplomats. It is conceivable that I will be permitted to state our case quite formally to the Foreign Minister and never advance beyond that point. It is within the bounds of reason, you know, that the Empress Eugénie will go through life without ever having heard my wife's fine Spanish."

Hunter bit into the pen handle, winced and patted a front tooth lovingly, as though to assure it that he had meant it no harm. "Slidell, everything is in the lap of the gods, of course, but you and your family are made to order for this assignment. Your wife and your daughters cannot fail to do the Confederacy honor. You yourself are persuasive, brilliant and—"

"You know I will do my best, Mr. Secretary. Some things, however, are difficult to promise. Does Mason think he will gain England's recognition of the Confederacy by just being James Mason of Virginia?"

"No. He is aware, as you are, of the obstacles to recognition. We are sending our best men to the two most important countries. That is all we can do. If England and France recognize us, the world will follow."

John nodded. "Yes. It makes a pretty responsibility for Mason and me."

He and Hunter talked for an hour or so and then John was requested to call at Mr. Davis' office. The President shook his hand and expressed deep satisfaction that John had consented to accept the appointment.

"I believe," he said, "that you will be of as much value to us as a victory in the field."

So Mathilde's Spanish was to become one of the Confederacy's more potent weapons. John smiled to himself as he walked toward the Spotswood Hotel. God, what luck it was to get this second opportunity to present his daughters at the court of France. Of course, this was not, by any means, as good as what Buchanan had had to offer. The United States Minister was a gentleman whose presence was highly desired. The Confederate Commissioner would have to fight for even the narrowest of social footholds. But, by God, the appointment would be all the more exciting for the finesse required. A glow of anticipation gave his step lightness and swiftness as he crossed Main Street. Paris. The court of Louis Napoleon. And who knew? He might even be of some help to the Confederacy.

John and his family were reunited in Charleston, where they lingered for a few days, behaving like any tourist group enjoying a picturesque city. If it was noted that an astonishing number of trunks and packing cases had come along with Mrs. Slidell from New Orleans, there were no comments. Perhaps it was expected that she and her daughters would travel with mountains of luggage. They were famous for their devotion to high fashion and their habit of brightening hotel rooms with luxuries from home.

Charleston was regretful that the Slidells' visit was so short. On an inky black night, during a torrential rainstorm, the family, in what was apparently a capricious decision, departed. Charlestonians were to read within the month that, actually, John Slidell's itinerary had been rather carefully planned and that the next stop had been Cuba.

After two weeks in Havana, the Slidell family and Mr. James Mason were ready to leave. This time there was no secrecy concerning their departure or their destination. They were sailing on the British steam packet *Trent,* which was very different from embarking on a Confederate craft. British ships, being strict neutrals, were in no danger of being sunk or captured by the Federal Navy.

The staterooms aboard the *Trent* were spacious and comfortable. Mathilde and her daughters immediately unpacked to give their fine gowns the benefit of hanging uncrushed during the voyage. The unpacking was rather a lark, for none of them had ever before performed this task. There was great giggling at the thought that somewhere off the coast of England, they would have to find a way to replace all these garments in the trunks. Rosina was certain that never could they do it and young Mathilde thought it would be wise to hire a lady's maid in Southampton to come aboard and pack for them.

"We will do it ourselves, somehow," their mother said. "No maids will be hired till we reach Paris. French maids will be quite wonderful, I understand."

She bustled briskly about, laying out toilet articles and night robes, concealing from the girls her terror at the idea of dealing with white servants. It would be a strange and difficult thing to arrange wages, free time, what she expected of the servants and, appallingly, what they expected of her. She had realized before John had broached the subject that even if France would admit Tia Lula and her superbly competent daughters, it would be the poorest possible diplomacy to bring them.

Alfred, who would try for admittance to Saint-Cyr-l'Ecole, had brought few clothes with him and would not have missed his body servant in any case. His experience in Massachusetts schools had conditioned him to wait on himself. He was concerned only with the hope that meals aboard the *Trent* would be frequent and delicious.

Alfred was not disappointed. The food, if one made allowances for the natural limitations of seagoing menus, was excellent. During luncheon, first day out, John made it a point to congratulate Captain Moir on the high quality of the *Trent*'s service and cuisine.

Captain Moir, a massive, red-faced man with icy British dignity, accepted the compliment to his ship as though it had been an insult. "The British," he said stiffly, "never carry passengers unless the ship is equipped and staffed properly."

"Whereas," John said, "I suppose other nations just do not give a rap how—"

The sentence was never finished, for at that moment, in the Bahama Channel, the *Trent* shuddered and shook, and Captain Moir, racing from the dining salon, knew that his vessel had been attacked. The *Trent* had been fired on.

The passengers, shocked but curious, waited only a moment and as they felt the ship come to a stop, they hurried up the stairs to the main deck. An unbelievable sight met their eyes. There in the hot, sparkling sunlight alongside the *Trent* lay the United States warship *San Jacinto,* plainly marked, proudly flying the American flag, and it was she who had fired two shots across the bow of the British neutral. Three boats filled with American marines and sailors were rowing rapidly toward the packet. It was beyond credibility and now a United States lieutenant was boarding and addressing the furious Captain Moir.

"Lieutenant Fairfax of the United States warship *San Jacinto.* I must ask you, Captain, to furnish me with your list of passengers."

Captain Moir's eyes blazed as he replied. "Sir, I deny your right to make any such demand."

The United States officer consulted a slip of paper. "Information has been given that aboard your ship are Mr. John Slidell, Mr. James Mason and their secretaries, Eustis and MacFarland. I have orders to bring these four men away at all hazards."

As he spoke, a hundred men from the *San Jacinto* were alertly investing the *Trent*. Captain Moir noted them grimly. He said, "I refuse absolutely to hand over to you any passengers or to recognize your authority to interfere in any way with a British ship."

"Then I must take forcible possession of the aforementioned passengers."

"You may regret it, sir," Captain Moir cautioned.

Lieutenant Fairfax suddenly looked pained and uncomfortable. "I have my orders," he said and it was not a lofty statement but simply one sailor's explanation to another.

"How can he identify us?" Mason whispered to John.

"Do not be a fool. We must step forward and declare ourselves," John returned. "Victoria is going to scream bloody murder. We must give her plenty to scream about."

"They will take us to the North. We may be hanged."

"Nonsense. Nobody hangs gentlemen." John, calling Eustis to join him, moved out of the group of bewildered passengers. "Lieutenant," he said, "I am John Slidell. Does your captain have the effrontery to order me taken from a British ship?"

It was not a question that Fairfax could answer with a yes or a no. He said, "Hurry along, Mr. Slidell."

"Hurry along? Really, my good fellow!"

A junior-grade lieutenant stepped forward to aid Fairfax in his unpleasant duty. He placed his hand upon John's arm and drew him toward the rope ladder. As he touched the person of his prisoner, a slim figure with yellow hair rushed at the young lieutenant, delivering a stinging slap upon his cheek.

John smiled gently at his daughter Mathilde. "No, sweetheart, it will not do. Go to your mother."

But young Mathilde stood gazing at the man she had slapped and he, with his face aflame, gazed back at her in wordless anguish.

324

They had danced together in New Orleans one soft spring evening.

Mason, with MacFarland, his secretary, beside him, approached Fairfax. "I am James Mason and, by heaven, you will remove me from this ship only with the use of force."

Wearily Fairfax said, "As you will, sir." He signaled and four seamen hurried to Mason and grasped him firmly.

Mason relented. "Very well," he said hoarsely. "Unhand me. I will go." And he went.

It was not so easy for John. His daughters were clinging to him and weeping. Mathilde's whispered commands to her girls went unheard. Alfred tore Rosina away from her father and prevailed upon young Mathilde by begging her not to make a cowardly show before the Yankees.

John embraced his family, pulled himself to his full height and said to his wife, "Do not worry, my dear. I will join you in Paris shortly." He bowed to Captain Moir. "Thank you for your efforts, sir." Then, with amazing agility, he negotiated the descent of the rope ladder.

Aboard the *San Jacinto,* John turned at once to Lieutenant Fairfax. "I want to see the captain."

"You shall see him, sir. He is awaiting you in his cabin. Will you follow me?" And as Mason fell in behind John, "I am sorry, Mr. Mason. The captain has sent for Mr. Slidell only."

The captain was standing with his back to the door when John entered the cabin. Peering through the porthole at the *Trent,* the broad-shouldered man did not turn, even after the lieutenant had announced John's presence. A full minute went by before the captain and the prisoner faced each other.

"You may go, Lieutenant," the captain said.

It had been many years since they had met, but John recognized him. "Well," he said, "I'll be damned if it is not little Charlie Wilkes."

Captain Charles Wilkes smiled coldly. "Yes," he said. "Sit down, John. You are an old man. Go ahead. Rest yourself."

"Thank you. If you do not mind, I will stand. What is the meaning of this performance, Charlie? You know, of course, that England will be enraged. I am of the opinion that even Abraham Lincoln will be enraged. I doubt that he wants to fight two wars."

Wilkes leaned against his desk and flicked at a patch of dust on his sleeve. "I did not summon you, John, to hear what President Lincoln's reaction might be."

"Very well. You are quite right, as there are more important things on the docket. First of all, I demand that you return me immediately to the *Trent*."

Wilkes shook his head. "No, I am not going to do that, John. You are on your way to prison."

"Is that what you called me in here to say?"

"As a matter of fact, it is."

John looked at Charles Wilkes steadily for a time. Then, "Charlie, this is a very large international riot you have got yourself into."

"Do you feel very sorry for me?"

"Very. I always feel sorry for small-minded people. You have plunged your country into trouble just because one night a long, long time ago, I beat the hell out of you."

Captain Charles Wilkes whitened. "Do you actually think that I boarded the *Trent* and placed you under arrest because of something that happened more than forty years ago?"

"I definitely think that."

"Slidell, you were on your way to undermine the interests of the United States in France. You are guilty of treason and yet you have the almighty gall to suggest that an officer of the American Navy has no more than personal reasons for arresting you."

John shrugged. "Let us consider the evidence. There are many officers of the American Navy but the only one I ever knocked unconscious is the one who has arrested me. Actually, Charlie, the claim that your abhorrence of my possible activities in France motivated your attack on the *Trent* makes a very flimsy case."

Charles Wilkes said, "Jesus, you are a swaggering bastard. You always were. Do you realize that you are my prisoner and that I could put you in irons?"

"I realize these things, Charlie, and I am terribly apologetic that I cannot tremble or faint with fear. That is what you want, is it not?"

"I only want you to recognize the true reason why you have been arrested."

John laughed. "No, Charlie, that is exactly what you do not want. And this conversation is beginning to go in circles. I wonder if I could retire to whatever convenience has been provided for me."

The convenience was adequate, the treatment good. No one thought the Confederate commissioners or their secretaries perilous to the welfare of the U.S.S. *San Jacinto*. They were permitted to walk the deck and to forget for hours on end what lay ahead. John and Captain Charles Wilkes met no more. John knew the newspapers of two continents must be selling very well with a story like this on the front pages. What would England do? He thought of Lincoln's Secretary of State. Seward was a very shrewd man. Too shrewd, John feared, to approve Charlie Wilkes's insane violation of British neutrality.

"I have prepared myself for going to prison," Mason said to John. "But I trust they will act heedfully and mercifully in getting us there. The Northern mobs could be wild, you know."

They were not subjected to the dangers of city streets. They were lodged in Fort Warren in Boston Harbor, a dank, wretched pile of stone, where John contracted a bad case of bronchitis. The doctor was very young, very indifferent.

John said, "I can tell that I am running a fever and after all, sir, I am sixty-eight years old."

"Really, Mr. Slidell? You do not look it."

"That is utterly charming of you to say but this is not a social occasion. I do not need compliments. What I had in mind was some awareness on your part that you have a sick old man on your hands. Do you know of any medicine that might help me? If you do not, please ask your grandmother. She might have some ideas."

It occurred to John as an interesting possibility that he might die in this narrow cell with its sweaty, oozing walls. Well, a man had to die somewhere. If he died here, a soft, sad glory would linger over his memory forever. The Confederate States of America would never forget him. School children would learn of him, would sing of him, perhaps. Of course, before that could happen, somebody had to guarantee that the Confederate States of America remained in business.

"God damn it," he shouted huskily into the gloomy corridor,

where soldiers patrolled night and day. "Let me out of here. Let me out."

No news, no mail was brought to him. A great deal of time, he thought about Mathilde. He had no sentimental image of her as a helpless creature frantic with worry and fright in a strange land where she had no friends or relatives. Mathilde spoke French, had plenty of money and within a day's time would have rallied around her a host of Confederate sympathizers. There was no reason to pity her, no reason to suffer a moment of anxiety for Mathilde. He thought of her because he could not banish her from his mind. He found himself missing her desperately. He had never known that he could long so painfully for the sight of any human being.

"You have finally," he said to himself, "worked John Slidell into that most distressing of all situations. He loves somebody. How long has he loved her? Oh, God, it goes away back. Even before the first baby. Really? How is it he has never known before? Is it because now he is dying?"

In the world outside Fort Warren, the Northerners exulted in the capture of the Confederate commissioners. Editorial writers heaped praise on Captain Charles Wilkes. Secretary of the Navy Gideon Welles hailed this "great public service." Congress rushed through a resolution thanking Wilkes for "brave, adroit and patriotic conduct." There was a grand rally in a New York theatre in honor of the daring Wilkes, and upon the stage, he was presented with a gleaming sword by General Benjamin Butler of the United States Army.

In the White House, through all this excitement, sat a silent, sober-faced man who sent no messages to Captain Charles Wilkes. He was concerned only with the one he himself would receive from Great Britain when the *Trent* reached her home port.

The growl of the angry lion was not long in coming. Eight thousand British troops were dispatched to Canada to stand poised and ready in case the United States Government refused to release men who had been seized while under protection of the British flag. Did the United States commend the behavior of Wilkes? Had Wilkes committed his act of piracy under orders? Or did the United States disavow Wilkes? Would the United States apologize? Would the

328

United States return to a British ship the individuals who had been forcibly taken from the *Trent?*

Abraham Lincoln and Secretary of State Seward felt perspiration cold and unpleasant on their brows. Not yet a victory of any consequence against the Confederacy, and looming upon the horizon, war with England. The two men gazed at each other across a desk on which lay the sizzling protest from Her Majesty's Government. If Gideon Welles and Congress had not made such damn fools of themselves over Wilkes, the fellow would now be standing a court-martial.

The Confederacy held its breath and prayed. England would have to fight, would she not? Surely she would accept no explanation from that vulgar brute Lincoln. Ah, with England on the Confederacy's side . . .

The two lawyers—one from Illinois and one from New York—who saw no virtue in stubbornly defending Wilkes's highhanded conduct, sent a sensible reply to Her Majesty's Government. They disavowed the action of Captain Charles Wilkes. They declared it completely unauthorized. They stated that the prisoners at Fort Warren would be returned promptly to British protection.

And the lion, being as sensible as the two lawyers, said, in effect, "Well, if that is how you feel, let us forget the whole business." The lion had one more thing to say and though it made him feel pretty foolish, he said it, anyhow. "The harbors of Canada are frozen so solidly that our warships are unable to enter. There are eight thousand troops aboard who must be supplied for the return voyage. Would you be so kind as to permit our ships to use a United States harbor?"

On New Year's Day, after more than two months in prison, John Slidell, James Mason and their secretaries were rowed out to a British ship, courteously placed aboard, courteously received. John had lost twenty pounds and was still coughing.

Sumner of Massachusetts had flown into a savage rage at Confederate newspapers' comparing John Slidell to Benjamin Franklin, who long ago had also sought recognition for his country at the court of France. The New York press had printed one of Sumner's comments:

329

The Confederacy is characteristically represented by John Slidell whose great fame is from electioneering frauds.

The London *Times* remarked of the Confederate commissioners:

They need not thank this country for their liberation. It was simply a point of honor with us. It cost us a million pounds sterling but we would have done the same for two Negro slaves.

John had no way of knowing what the world press was saying. He would have cared little. He was on his way to France and France was more appealing, more exciting today than it had ever been. Now Mathilde was there.

And he laughed at John Slidell for finding love in the deep winter of his life. In dreaming romantically of his own wife, he reminded himself of the ferocious old tiger who was being questioned by the police.

"Of course I eat humans," the tiger had admitted. "I am too damned feeble to catch anything else."

At first, they lived at the Hotel du Rhin, but when they discovered that entertaining would be an important part of John's endeavor, the Slidells rented a house at 25 Avenue d'Antin. The satin-covered walls and spectacular pink crystal chandeliers did not particularly please John.

"The house is a bonbon," he said.

"Of course," Mathilde agreed. "This is Paris. Everything is too ornate, too plentiful and too colorful. It was when French taste was toned down by the necessary austerities of early Louisiana that we achieved perfection. It was then our lovely Creole *décor* came into being."

"Yes, darling," John said. "What Paris needs is more Creoles."

"Well, we, at least, are here and Father Lebrun, too."

Mathilde was at peace. She had found a New Orleans priest in Paris. John smiled at her and she walked into his arms, sighing contentedly. "It is a good world," she said. "Your cough has disappeared and I think you have gained back all the pounds of flesh the Yankees extracted from you."

"I am feeling very well," he said. "It is indeed a good world.

Monsieur Cassagnac of *Le Pays* this morning expressed the thought in his admirable newspaper that the United States Government is one of the most barbarous and most inept which has ever been seen."

Mathilde said, "He expressed that thought because Creole food is so delicious. Do you not remember what Monsieur La Gueronnière had to say of the United States after tasting *petits patés aux huîtres?*"

John nodded. No point in mentioning that Cassagnac and La Gueronnière had published fanatically pro-Confederate newspapers before they had ever been exposed to Creole cuisine. He thought about the other newspapers, the ones devoted to the Northern cause. So many of them—*Le Siècle, Le Temps, Le Journal des Debats, La Presse, L'Opinion Nationale.* Mrs. William Dayton, wife of the United States Minister to France, probably believed she was influencing press policy with country-style pickles and ketchup made from Molly Pitcher's recipe. Actually, both Mathilde and Mrs. Dayton were smart enough to know that if a newspaper's good will were for sale, the purchase price came higher than a few tasty dinners, but female minds operated on two levels. On level one was whimsy and girlish nonsense and a maddeningly honest inability to grasp any unwanted fact. On level two there was a very impressive working knowledge of every God-damn thing in the world, complete with a realistic appraisal of men, marriage and machines.

Of course, there were women who had no level two. He would never forget the flighty hostess who had invited the Daytons and the Slidells to the same ball. Actually, it had come off beautifully for the Confederacy.

William Dayton, upon seeing John, had requested in ringing tones that his carriage be called immediately. John had shaken his head at the man he had known in Washington.

"Don't bother, Bill. I saw you first and my carriage is on its way."

Young Mathilde and Rosina had remained at the ball as a courtesy to the hostess, for many of the guests had expressed their intention of following the Slidell family out the door. Hearteningly, too, the hired entertainers had declared themselves Southern sympathizers and unwilling to perform for an all pro-Federal audience. The incident had been very amusing and quite pleasurable. A lovely evening for the girls. They were adding Paris to New Orleans, Washington and New York. The list of cities that had surrendered to their beauty and charm was lengthening.

But then, John thought, he was not doing badly himself. His friend Judah Benjamin had replaced Hunter as Confederate Secretary of State and to him John had written.

It is a pity that Mason is getting nowhere either officially or unofficially with the British. Friends tell me that he has had but one interview with the Foreign Minister and that that was damned brief and freezing.

I have been more fortunate, dear friend, I constantly see de Lhuys and talk very easily and chummily with him. There are a whole pack of delightful fellows who run the government rather like a cigar store. They gather for friendly conversation and card-playing and when, figuratively speaking, the bell over the shop-door rings announcing a customer, one of them walks reluctantly out of the back room to transact the business at hand.

I must say, I seem quite welcome in the back room. Our little circle consists of de Morny who is an illegitimate son of the present emperor's mamma. Also there is Walewski who is the illegitimate son of him who was the very biggest Napoleon. We have besides Persigny, Rouher and Mocquard who I suppose are just plain bastards.

I see His Majesty, Napoleon the Third, Emperor of France. He is extremely cordial and I believe he is with us in his sympathies but he is very loath to move importantly unless England has pointed the way.

I take it as an encouraging sign that I have been presented to the Empress. She conversed with me for thirty minutes. I spoke of Louisiana's traditions and customs, stressing our ancient bonds with France and Spain. To my surprise and delight, the Empress directed me to bring to her my wife and daughters—

The Empress Eugénie, with her sweet, trilling voice and dainty gestures, was a captivating contradiction. Her lovely figure, her smoldering eyes and enveloping warmth suggested that here was a royal lady who could have instructed Pompadour and Du Barry in the art of love. Perhaps she had been a disappointment to Louis Napoleon. Eugénie's passion was for her church and it was said that the court of France, with its casual morals, was for the Empress an ordeal so terrible that she endured it only by remembering the tribulations of the saints. She had a schedule of prayer almost as demanding as a nun's and when official duties compelled her to receive known sinners, she wept afterward in her private chapel.

There were many on both sides of the Atlantic that year who believed that John Slidell with his well-filled bag of tricks had somehow deceived or bewitched the Empress. Cynics thought it only natural that a rascal's wife should make friends with another rascal's wife. Nobody recognized the simple truth, which was that the Empress Eugénie was parched for the exact sort of companionship the ladies of the Slidell family had to offer. Eugénie knew many devout Catholics. None of them was interested in dress materials or the best methods for preserving one's beauty. Eugénie knew many sleekly gowned women, wise in the ways of style and cosmetics, but their love affairs were nauseating to her. In the ladies of John Slidell's family, Eugénie found what she had sought—intimates with whom she could speak of fashion and Catholicism, coiffures and standards of behavior. In the age bracket, Eugénie fell about midway between the elegant Madame Slidell and the lovely, innocent girls. She thought of young Mathilde and Rosina as golden virgins and had let it be known that men who looked upon them with dishonest intent would find they had an empress for an enemy.

Having thus guaranteed that her young friends would be shielded from temptation and their mother from worry, Eugénie welcomed all three wholeheartedly to the life of the French court. The court had taken on a new luster for her. Here at last were ladies with morals as lofty as her own who were yet gay companions and spoke flawless Spanish. She was enthralled by them and insisted that they ride with her on the stag and boar hunts and accompany her to the royal residences at Biarritz, Saint-Cloud and Vichy. As a compliment to her friend Madame Slidell, she even received at court the somewhat dazed little New Orleans priest Father Lebrun.

Presumably, the Emperor's life had not been barren before John's arrival in Paris but there was no denying that he took pleasure in conversing with the tall, white-haired Slidell. They laughed and drank together and the Emperor was pleased with this American who was perfectly at ease in the presence of royalty. The great-chested, short-legged man with the furtive, watchful eyes was rather tired of Americans who, when presented to him, were either too awe-stricken to speak coherently or whose manner plainly said that in good old America, all men were equal. The Emperor of France had spent enough time in New York, during a period when his future had been most unpromising, to know that American equality was not especially noticeable. Never once had John Slidell claimed that back in the States there were no caste lines. He was factual and realistic and he had an endearing trick of pretending that a particular point of discussion would be clearer to him if stated in his native tongue. John's French was at least as good as the Emperor's but it was kind of him to give his host a chance to use the English of which he was very proud.

"If the blockade were broken, Your Majesty, the South would quickly end the war and you would secure a faithful ally bound to you not only by ties of gratitude but by those more reliable—a common interest and congenial habits."

"Yes," said the Emperor pensively. "You have many families of French descent in Louisiana who yet preserve their habits and language. But to open the ports forcibly would be an act of war."

"There is no reason to fear the Yankees. What could their ramshackle navy do against Your Majesty's ships? Why, the *Gloire,* the *Couronne* and the *Normandie* could reduce New York and Boston to ashes."

A slow smile played upon the royal lips. The French Navy leveling cities, winning the South her freedom, suddenly emerging as a power greater than— No, no more dreams. The smile disappeared. He had, after all, an agreement with Great Britain. He could make no unilateral move.

"At this time, Mr. Slidell, France cannot act independently of Great Britain."

"Perhaps not at *this* time," John said. "May I hope we can discuss the matter again?"

"This matter or another, Mr. Slidell. We take pleasure in seeing you. Tomorrow afternoon, perhaps."

Newspapers from America arrived with each ship and were delivered to John's desk in the smart little office on Rue Marignan. In gilt letters on the black walnut door was the information that here operated the representatives of the Confederate States of America.

334

Operations were sometimes very slow and it was then that John occupied himself with the news from New York.

Mrs. Matthew Calbraith Perry, widow of the famous commodore and mother of Mrs. August Belmont, today denied that Franklin Buchanan, Confederate naval officer and commander of the now useless "Merrimac," had been her husband's best friend. "This irresponsible statement," Mrs. Perry said, "was printed in southern newspapers with the obvious intention of giving stature to Franklin Buchanan. It is true that this man was with my husband at the time of the historical mission to Japan but that does not entitle him to a claim of friendship. Franklin Buchanan is a traitor to his country and I know Commodore Perry would resent very hotly any suggestion that this man had ever been his friend."

The New York newspapers all reported that the wife of Commodore Raymond Rogers was convalescing after a serious illness. The item gave scant comfort for it was filled with such phrases as "it is to be hoped" and "in the event that Mrs. Rogers is equal to the journey." Convalescing? Was that a euphemism for dying painlessly? Julia. Little Julia in the swirling pink petticoats. Julia, the baby sister, all breathless wonderment and big-eyed admiration for the stranger from New Orleans who was her eldest brother.

Any day, any paper had news of August Belmont. Week after week, there it was. The Belmonts entertain. The Belmonts donate. The Belmonts dedicate. The Belmonts organize. The Belmonts. The Belmonts. The Belmonts. Most of it was of little interest to the man in the quiet office on Rue Marignan, but sometimes—

August Belmont, National Leader of the Democratic Party, said today—

National Leader of what? With eleven states missing, do you really have a party, August? Perhaps you have. Very well, my friend, if you are a leader, lead. Let me see you convince the lumberman, the farmer and the miner that your problems are exactly the same as theirs. Let me see you lead. Let me see you create a President, August.

Suddenly, August Belmont was in London. Then he was in Paris. And they did not meet because long ago they had known it would be like this. War. And they would fight it bitterly against each other without sentiment and without truce—unless one needed a personal favor from the other.

John walked to the window and looked out at a Paris street and thought that August was perhaps only a block or two away. August, the incomparable companion. August, the most considerate of friends. And John thought of the pleasure it would give him to know that he would be dining tonight with August. And he thought of the laughter and candor and sympathy of their friendship and he thought of August's remembering poor, helpless Tom.

He knew what August had been doing in London. He knew what August was doing in Paris. August was pronouncing very clearly the name of Rothschild. And it was a name that Victoria's ministers and Louis Napoleon had heard before. It was a name they might want to hear again someday. August in his quiet way would tell Louis Napoleon, as he had told Victoria's ministers, that the Rothschilds had deep admiration for the United States of America, that the Rothschilds detested slavery and that the Rothschilds just thought all this ought to be mentioned.

And John pondered on the innocence of soldiers who believed in the surprise attack, the fearless charge, the good fight. Absolutely astonishing that they did not realize they could settle nothing, no matter how gallantly they killed each other. The moment in time when antagonists had ceased to struggle against each other with bare hands, the moment the first crude weapon had been wielded, that was the moment when victory through courage had been lost to man forever. After that, it had all become a question of supplies.

And once that was true, then a war could be won by two blond girls giggling with an empress or by a man from the House of Rothschild.

In the house at 25 Avenue d'Antin, there was always a flurry of excitement; on the horizon, an imperial ball, a garden party or a state dinner.

"The clothes that are needed, darling!" Mathilde whispered. "Do you hate your whole family?"

"No," John said. "I adore Alfred. His Saint-Cyr uniforms are completely paid for."

336

"The girls and I are costing you a fortune."

"Have I complained? Who is to be Rosina's escort at the De Ronier ball?"

"The Count de St. Roman."

"What does she intend to wear?"

Mathilde stared at him. "Why, you have never before asked such a question."

"I have never before cared."

"She is wearing black lace and do not tell me that is incorrect for a young girl. She will be the most striking creature there. With her hair and her skin—"

"You do not have to convince me. It sounds like a lovely idea. Young girls in pale pinks and blues are rather plentiful." He reached for a cigar and examined it closely. "Has the Empress expressed any opinion on the Count de St. Roman?"

"Yes. She is deeply fond of him. His mother, it seems, wanted to be a nun but God told her she owed it to her parents to marry. The issue of this marriage naturally seems to the Empress a gift from heaven."

"He might be, at that. He might really be." Ruefully John replaced the cigar in its box. He had had his quota for the day. Doctors were unreasonable fellows.

"John."

"Yes, dear?"

"Young Mathilde must really stay home tomorrow evening?"

"I wish she would."

"When we give dinners for your business associates, it has never been expected of her to—"

"Oh, blast it, Mathilde, the Baron d'Erlanger is bringing his son. Now, you know that. Don't make me spell things out."

Mathilde looked at him stonily. "Wherever we have gone," she said, "our daughters have always surpassed other young ladies. They can marry into the finest families of Louisiana any time—"

"Mathilde, my love, have you not yet realized that we have traveled beyond the finest families of Louisiana?" She gasped and he knew that for the first time in all their years together, he had hurt her deeply. He took her hand and fondly kissed her slim white fingers. "Mathilde, the fact that you and the girls can know a comfortable friendship with an empress illustrates clearly enough that Creole breeding is as royal as any in the world. A Louisiana marriage is a wonderful thing. I would be the first to sing its praises and yet—"

"And yet you want something quite different for your daughters."

"Dearest, did you never think it might be pleasant to have a certain distinguishing mark affixed to one's name so that all might know that one was not the wife of a coachman or a grocer or a day laborer?"

Mathilde said haughtily, "By their behavior, the ladies of my family have always conveyed the information that they were not of common stock."

"Yes, of course. I remember that your poor mother actually shimmered with regality. I used to say to myself, 'A crime that she is not a titled lady so that—' "

Mathilde said, "And now you have spelled it out for me, have you not? Let us see if I can spell a word or two for you. It is true that Frederic d'Erlanger is not engaged to marry and it is true that his family is almost as wealthy as the Belmonts. Frederic will of course become a baron one day but he still will not be a Catholic."

"And have you a quarrel with such a marriage? I thought ours had worked out splendidly."

"But you permitted me to raise the children in my church."

John howled with laughter. "Whereas that selfish son of a bitch Frederic d'Erlanger has absolutely refused to hear of such a thing. Ah, Mathilde, you are a joy to me. The two young people have not yet met and already Frederic has barred Father Lebrun from the house and the innocent babe is unchristened. I tell you what, my dear. I shall give Frederic a good dressing-down for the misery he has caused us. Only, do have young Mathilde stay home tomorrow evening so she can meet this wretch."

Against her will, Mathilde smiled.

Emile d'Erlanger, of the great French banking house of D'Erlanger et Cie., was outspokenly pro-Confederate. He was a round little man with a bland expression and a soft voice. All his life, he had been in what he frankly termed the money business. It had not left him with either the time or the energy for other interests.

The Baroness, a sullen-eyed, stout woman, who had received no notice from the Empress beyond a heavily formal presentation at court, had come to the Slidells' unwillingly. Why had the Empress found it necessary to choose an American friend? It made the Baroness no happier to see that the American was a woman almost her own age but slim as a knife. Mathilde caught the quick flash of the Baroness' resentment in the first second of their meeting. I must attend to that, she thought, and turned to look at Frederic—Frederic, curiously aristocratic in bearing, as though Nature had cast a new d'Erlanger mold when Emile had been created a baron. The young man was fair-skinned, with shadowy dark eyes and an enchanting smile.

After dinner, young Mathilde and Frederic walked within the glass walls of the conservatory. He admired the tender plants and exotic flowers and asked questions about America.

"You are homesick, mademoiselle?"

"Not a bit."

"Does that mean there is no one you especially miss?"

She said, "Oh, I miss dozens of people."

He smiled. "That is so much less painful than missing one."

In the parlor, Mathilde asked the Baroness for the address of a good doctor. "I have such pains in my joints. The stiffening one must expect with age, but I thought perhaps there could be some relief. Please do not mention this to my husband or daughters. I tell them nothing of my trials."

The Baroness said, "But you ride horseback with the court. How can you, if you are in pain?"

"Oh, you are a mother. You understand, surely, the things one does for one's children. If I could but sit back with my sewing, how happy I would be. The girls cannot be left to themselves. I must accompany them. You cannot guess how tired, how ill I grow with fatigue. Baroness, when you reach my age, you will know what I am going through."

Well, there was a surprise. Mrs. Slidell was really a very nice woman.

In John's private sitting room, he and Emile d'Erlanger discoursed in quiet tones on the subject of twenty-five million dollars.

"I believe in your Confederacy, Mr. Slidell, but, as I have said, she will need money."

"It is well known that she needs it now."

"She would get it now from my company." The Baron examined his small white hands and beautifully tended nails. "Of course, the terms might seem harsh but then your country is not yet a going concern. D'Erlanger et Cie. must protect itself."

John lit a cigar. He promised himself that he would smoke one less tomorrow. "I have not the authority to arrange the loan, Baron."

"You can recommend it, however, can you not?"

"I shall certainly recommend it."

"Good. By the way, do call me Emile."

New Orleans fell to the Yankees that month. Mathilde fainted when the news came and John carried her to her bed. He could not stay to comfort her. The Emperor had sent for him. John drove away, deeply disturbed at leaving Mathilde with no one to watch over her but a blank-faced French maid. If Tia Lula were there . . . And suddenly, the fall of New Orleans was not the loss of the house on Royal Street and three and a half blocks of damned valuable real estate in the Garden District but the numbing realization that security, as represented by the sure hands of Tia Lula, was part of the past.

The Emperor said, "We are unhappy for you, Mr. Slidell. It is a terrible day in your life."

"Your Majesty, I will not pretend that I am untouched by the fall of my city but I am not dejected. I have faith in the Confederate Army and I believe we will regain New Orleans."

The watchful eyes blinked once and then no more. Steadily they bored into John. "We wish you to explain what the loss means. This was a great harbor, was it not? How does the rest of Louisiana survive without it? How great a blow will this be to the confidence of the common people? Will a feeling of discouragement sweep the South? Tell us how it happened and what you think will be the result."

John gazed back at the Emperor of France. Why, this is a very

340

cruel man. He knows damned well that I am bleeding but he demands a performance just the same. By God, he shall have it.

"Your Majesty, the loss of the city means little. The United States once lost the city of Washington and won the war. The South has other harbors. The rest of Louisiana will survive without New Orleans and the people of the Confederacy are not fainthearted. They will fight on and they will win their freedom. Those who did not help them will be embarrassed. Those who did will feel as your beautiful France felt, Your Majesty, in the days when France helped another infant country to live."

The Emperor smiled. "But, Mr. Slidell, if this infant should die . . ."

"This infant cannot die if France wishes her to live."

"France wishes her well but the loss of New Orleans . . ." The Emperor paused and shook his head.

Son of a bitch. Behaving as though he had been on the verge of recognizing the Confederacy, behaving as though this Yankee victory had sent all wheels spinning in reverse. John lowered his eyes to conceal his emotions. Someday you will be of no more use to me and I may tell you then what I think of this game you are playing with me today. I never knew before how much you royal little boys missed your court jesters. Pity that they went out of style. Oh, yes, someday I shall definitely tell you what I think.

Louis Napoleon said, "We are heartened to see that you are not depressed."

We! Why, there is not enough man in you to count for one. The royal "we" sits more ridiculously on you than on any other crowned head in the world. Yes, including the King of the Zulus. And I may mention that someday, too.

John returned to his house at 25 Avenue d'Antin. He felt a cold rage as the thought came to him that Yankee officers were probably making themselves at home at 312 Royal Street. He could picture them with their feet on Mathilde's exquisite tables and he could picture the blowzy women of Gallatin Street in the stately beds. What would they have done with Tom?

The girls were with Mathilde. She was leaning against her pillows, looking wan, but she smiled at him. "I was saying that it is only a matter of time and we will again have New Orleans."

Rosina had been crying. Her handkerchief was a small, damp ball clutched savagely in her hand. "I want to go home," she said. "I have not thought of home before. Now when I cannot go, when they have taken New Orleans from us, I want it more than anything in the world." She threw herself into John's arms. "Oh, please, I want to go home."

He said very soberly, "Very well. If that is what you want, I will arrange it."

She drew away and looked up at him, startled. "How? How can you?"

"Dear child, I am not helpless. I am not without friends, ideas or means. As long as I live, I will try to save you all from unhappiness. If you want New Orleans, you shall have it, my sweet. By the middle of next month, you will be home."

Rosina hugged him wildly and smiled again.

"Ever since they were babies," Mathilde said when she and John were alone, "I have been begging you not to lie to them."

"Yes, and I am getting pretty tired of it. Why don't you stop? I have never told them a single lie that did not improve a situation. What in hell good is truth when it hurts? All she needs is the *feeling* that she can go home. I think I would be awfully cold-blooded to give her the facts."

"But when the middle of next month comes—"

"By then, she will have forgotten the whole thing or will be taking pleasure in the romance of being a homeless wanderer. If not, I will simply change her sailing date."

Mathilde lay motionless and silent for a minute. Then she said, "John, sit down. No, no, over here. New Orleans has fallen and I find I am no Spartan woman. Come closer, John, and please lie a little to me."

John had exchanged all American investments, with the exception of real estate, for French securities. The loss of New Orleans had sharply reduced his income but not to the disastrous level where there need be any readjustment of his living standards.

"At my age, it is no longer necessary to worry about the future," he thought. "As long as the Marseilles bonds lie untouched for Mathilde's use when I am gone, then that is enough. We will just go on as always. Economizing and retrenching are for the young."

Besides, he acknowledged with a pang of regret, his two greatest expenses were about to be assumed by others. Frederic d'Erlanger and the Count de St. Roman seemed eager to dedicate their lives to the buying of gowns and bonnets for young Mathilde and Rosina. To be sure, the cost of the weddings would equal a five-year dressmaker's bill, but that was to be expected. The happiest men at fashionable weddings were always the florists, wine merchants and caterers.

Young Mathilde was married first since she was the elder. The wedding was what was known publicly as "important," for added to its costliness, it was said to have the blessing of the Empress Eugénie. Frederic d'Erlanger had become a Catholic convert.

"Frederic has made me the happiest mother-in-law alive," Mathilde said.

John was silent, reflecting on how unreasonable humans were. The gentle Frederic d'Erlanger would have been a kind and loving husband had he been a worshiper of cross-eyed cats. As a matter of fact, his adoration of young Mathilde and his good-humored acceptance of her whims made his conversion, in John's eyes, extremely suspect. Still, if it brought joy to the two Mathildes—

The young D'Erlangers honeymooned on the Mediterranean aboard a private yacht which Emile d'Erlanger had recently purchased. He had thought it would be the ideal possession for a man who wanted to travel without encountering bad cooks, uncomfortable beds and indifferent service.

"We can go away and still stay home," he had said to his wife. They had used the yacht once. At home, Emile d'Erlanger did not get seasick.

When young Mathilde and Frederic returned from their honeymoon, Rosina's wedding took place. This one also had the Empress' blessing and the most expensive caterer in Paris. John, as he looked at Mathilde, was once again moved to thoughts on the subject of the unreasonableness of humans. Mathilde, though radiant at Rosina's happiness, showed none of the unearthly rapture that had glowed in her eyes at the earlier wedding. The Count de St. Roman had always been a devout practicing Catholic and in all good sense, this should have admitted him to a very special compartment in the heart of his mother-in-law. But no. Installed in that compartment was Frederic d'Erlanger, the brand-new convert.

The Slidells' popularity at court continued undiminished. Louis Napoleon had dropped into the habit of saying to John, "We are following the Empress out of Paris this evening. It is our understanding that Madame Slidell will be in the party. Would you care to accompany us?"

And so it happened that the Slidells were sitting in a palace whose windows opened wide upon glittering fountains and a fairy-tale forest when they heard of the Seven Days' Battles. They were reclining on soft lounges in a terraced garden where avenues of flowering trees led to waterfalls and tiny lakes when a courier brought the newspapers that told of Second Bull Run. They were at a hunt breakfast in the east wing of an ancient château when they learned that Lee, outnumbered two to one, had held Mc-Clellan to a draw at Antietam.

"Your men fight a hard war, Mr. Slidell," the Emperor said on each occasion, and the watchful eyes were hidden beneath heavy lids.

"Of course they fight a hard war, Your Majesty. As I have often remarked, they fight a winning war."

And at Saint-Cloud, when the news came of the Battle of Fredericksburg, the Emperor raised his eyelids and said, "My sympathies are entirely with the South. My only desire is to know how to give them effect."

John cautioned his suddenly pounding heart to remember that the Emperor was a cruel man, a man who could amuse himself by stirring futile hopes.

"If the Confederacy had just one ship like the *Gloire*," John said, "the Federal blockade could be destroyed and the success of the South assured."

"Really, Mr. Slidell?"

"But the Confederacy has no shipyards, no experienced workmen for such a project and no materials. As you know, Your Majesty, British shipyards have played a merry game with us, wasted our time and left us still without warships."

Louis Napoleon considered the marmalade, rejected it and chose

344

strawberry preserves. He said, "Why could we not build warships in France supposedly for the Italian Government? I do not think it would be difficult. I will consult the Minister of Marine about it."

It was the pleasant card-playing companions, Persigny and De Morny, who brought the news to John within a week that two ships of heavy armament would be built for the Confederate Government. Emile d'Erlanger acted as financial agent, receiving a commission of fifty thousand dollars.

From the capital of the Confederacy, which seemed as far away as the valleys of Saturn, came a letter from the Secretary of State. It was filled with joy and congratulations but there was a stinging postscript.

Could we not have done without the services of Monsieur d'Erlanger? I have a feeling that his rather stunning profits on the loan his company made to us should have animated him to act in this matter at no cost at all. He could very well have afforded the friendly gesture. Best wishes to your daughter, Madame d'Erlanger.

The office on Rue Marignan was a busy place these days. All at once, everyone in Paris knew that the Confederacy was going to win the war. Newspapermen and bankers, visiting Americans and self-styled diplomats, soldiers of fortune and inventors thronged the reception rooms. Manufacturers of boots and broadcloth, of weapons and knapsacks, of blankets and canteens all experienced an overwhelming urge to do something really fine for the Confederate States of America. Guaranteed delivery. Pay on the day of victory. Not one penny above what it costs us. With Dixieland we take our stand.

There were the battles of Chancellorsville and Second Winchester and suddenly August Belmont was in Europe again. He had raised his second German regiment in New York City and was grooming George B. McClellan for the Presidency.

August did not linger long with Victoria's ministers. John knew he had not come to see them. He had come to speak very quietly to Louis Napoleon concerning what the House of Rothschild thought about those warships that were being constructed for—was it the Italian Government? And very quietly, too, August would mention that the string of Confederate victories were without meaning since, in the end, the war would be won by the United

States. August would smile gently and beg the Emperor's forgiveness for having remarked on what His Majesty knew without any American telling him—that the Confederacy could not even afford her victories, while the United States had yet to feel the slightest pinch. Then August would depart and the Emperor would call frantically for the boys to come out of the back room and comfort him.

The end of July brought bad news. Earlier in the month, there had been a great battle in Pennsylvania. John, sitting in the formal little garden behind the house on Avenue d'Antin, glanced back at his newspaper. Gettysburg, Pennsylvania. Gettysburg was the name of the town. He had never heard of it but evidently it had been the scene of one hell of a bloody encounter. It was illogical to expect the South to win every battle and yet he felt a boiling resentment against this General Lee for having lost. There was no point in marching into enemy country unless one could win there. Without assurance that you could beat the enemy in his own backyard, you ought to stay home.

Mathilde, sipping lemonade from a tall, sugar-rimmed glass, looked at him questioningly. "Shall I cancel the dinner?"

"Why? This battle was fought weeks ago. We have probably had a tremendous victory since then."

She stared into the depths of her cool drink and he knew she did not believe there had been a tremendous victory since Gettysburg. She had read, no doubt, that there had been seventeen miles of wagons carrying the wounded away from Pennsylvania. Had she read, too, of the other disaster? Vicksburg fallen to the Yankees, and the Mississippi River now a Federal waterway, from an icy blue lake in Minnesota to the tepid Mexican Gulf.

A servant was standing beside him with a note upon a silver tray. It was not really necessary to read it. He had known the Emperor would want to speak of Gettysburg. The tired old arguments would have to be dusted off and made to serve again. The fall of a city, the loss of a battle—these things are inconsequential and as everyone knows, Your Majesty—

As he drove toward his meeting with Louis Napoleon, he felt an advance surge of anger for what he knew would pass between them. The Emperor would shake his head and look worried and

346

express fear that France was building warships for a country that did not have the look of victory about it. And John would want to shout that the Confederacy would God-damned well have the look of victory if Louis Napoleon had given help when help had first been requested.

The dinner party that evening had a certain similarity to the conversation with the Emperor. There were many guests and though their sympathy was genuine, they, too, wanted to know if seventeen miles of wagons filled with wounded was a horror the Confederacy could survive.

It was interesting to note that young Mathilde and Rosina, of all the people present, asked no questions, sighed no sighs nor carried in their clear eyes the faintest shadow of sadness. A year ago, the smallest skirmish lost by the Confederates had been a reason for tears and renewed prayer. Now within their lovely young bodies, each of John's daughters nourished a future loyal subject of France. The war which was being discussed in the parlor at 25 Avenue d'Antin might have been between eastern and western Tibetans for all these adorable little French wives cared. That is as it should be, John thought, but he suffered a minor bruise at the sight of Rosina smiling with her husband over some secret joke, not even listening to Monsieur Cassagnac's tribute to the bravery of the Confederate soldier.

John had told Louis Napoleon that Gettysburg would not be the last battle and of course it was not, but the office on Rue Marignan became very quiet again after the news from that Pennsylvania town. John did not follow James Mason's example and close his headquarters but many a day he read the newspapers in the garden of his home and felt no need for the services of a secretary.

And there was an afternoon on which the Empress Eugénie did not laugh with Mathilde but looked at her with sorrowful eyes. In parting, she wept and clung to Mathilde's hand and as the carriage drove away, Mathilde looked back and saw the Empress standing at the window, still weeping.

It was on that day that John was told the two warships which had been intended for the Confederacy had been disposed of to Prussia and Denmark. De Morny gave John the news. The Emperor was rather busy. He could see no one. Perhaps when his

347

sudden press of duties subsided, he would have time to see Mr. Slidell again but at the moment, it was out of the question.

The Tuileries and the Villa Eugénie at Biarritz welcomed the Slidells no more. An invitation to the Imperial Autumn Ball did not arrive. Foreign Minister de Lhuys was as busy as the Emperor. He had not a moment for the Confederate commissioner and apparently all card-playing had ceased.

When the *Alabama* appeared in the harbor of Cherbourg, she was driven to her death. The Federal warship *Kearsarge* was waiting for her with mysteriously gained knowledge that France would refuse to shelter the *Alabama*. The *Rappahannock,* an unarmed Confederate vessel, was interned at Calais and the Daytons danced at the Imperial Autumn Ball.

"The Empress Eugénie," said John, "has disappointed me. She called you her friend but she has turned out to be more empress than woman."

Mathilde smiled at him. "My love, she has turned out to be all woman. Her husband has told her what must be done and she is doing it. If that is wrong, then I have been in error all my life."

In newspapers that were three weeks old, Mathilde read of the death of her sister Madame Beauregard. Poor little Caroline, who had always lost her spending money at the fair. Shattered by the news, Mathilde sobbed unrestrainedly. To die alone in an occupied city from which all friends and relatives had fled. Beauregard unable to enter New Orleans. God alone knew when Caroline had last seen the man she loved. Why had such a terror of loneliness been the gentle Caroline's to bear? Too ill to join her husband, she had waited in solitude for death, waited in a city that had been taken from those whose ancestors had willed it into being.

Ten thousand people had attended the funeral of this shy woman. Ten thousand people had gone to stand for Beauregard at the casket of his wife. Sullenly defiant of the ready Federal bayonets, they had prayed and gone their way in silent dignity.

John held Mathilde close and found that he was weeping with her. They had not needed this grief to remind them that every day they lost something that had belonged to a warm and wonderful yesterday.

"When the war is over, when Pierre can return to New Orleans,"

Mathilde said, "I will write and ask him to please place her beside my parents."

And he saw that Mathilde understood that along with a great many other things, in all likelihood, they had lost the right to go home to Louisiana.

August and Caroline Belmont walked into the Slidells' parlor at 25 Avenue d'Antin and for a moment not one of the four could utter a sound. Tears wet their cheeks as they searched each other's faces for changes and samenesses. They embraced, holding each other fast, stepping back to look again at a friend who had been snatched away and was now restored, then joyously renewing the embrace.

"Oh, it has been so long. So terribly long."

It had been too long. For four years, they had hoped for this reunion and within an hour they knew that they had forgotten how to laugh together.

"Talk," John said. "Do not stop talking. What is the news?"

"There is no news. But you are grandparents. Tell us of the children."

No news? The United States had won a war but it would be rude to mention this in the parlor of 25 Avenue d'Antin. Grandchildren were nice safe subjects. God help the friendship that sought for nice safe subjects. God help four civilized people who now must watch the precious thing that had been perfect communication bleed to death before their eyes. There would be a flutter of words that would not really break the painful silence.

"Young Mathilde had a boy. Rosina had a girl. We are grandparents to tiny French creatures who live like tropical flowers. Very elegant nurseries, you understand, with special visiting hours —even for the parents. If the nurses take a liking to you, you may get a look at the babies. How are your children? Tell us everything."

August thought that John at last was showing his age and that Mathilde looked pale and frightfully fatigued. The Slidells, studying the Belmonts, observed that the climate on the winning side was evidently fine for one's health.

John had dreamed that one day he and August would compare

notes on the Emperor, ask questions of each other concerning the campaigns waged across desks and dinner tables. August did not mention his wartime visits to Europe. John did not speak of the ships that had been sold to Prussia and Denmark. How could it happen that the agonized screams of men who had died in the peach orchard at Gettysburg had made it impossible for two couples in a Paris parlor to meet in easy intimacy?

"It does not work," John thought with a sick feeling. "Even among worldly-wise people, it does not work. You cannot fight a friend and, at the end, find the old friendship waiting untouched, unbloodied. If we had never known each other, if we had not met till now, it would all be simpler."

And after a week of mimicking the thing they had once had together, they said good-by. The Slidells spoke of how kind it had been of the Belmonts to come. The Belmonts spoke of how thrilling it had been to see the Slidells' grandchildren.

"There will be no more long separations," August said.

The truth, of course. August would come to Europe at least twice a year and he would not forget to give an evening to his wife's uncle. He was such a considerate, such a warmhearted man. He would decline the most enticing invitation for the sake of family loyalty. I am sorry but tonight I must dine with Caroline's old uncle and his wife. Perhaps I could join you later, unless they seem lonely and cling to me.

Caroline and Mathilde kissed good-by. Their eyes brimmed over with the sad knowledge that they did not mind parting. They said foolish things. Take care of yourself. It has been wonderful being with you. Do write.

The men said foolish things, too. Visit us in New York when you are tired of Paris. Perhaps on my next trip, we will all go back together. A nice idea, if we can tear ourselves away from those little tropical flowers.

August and John did not look at each other as they spoke. It would take more than a steamship ticket to get John to the United States and they both knew it. It was indicative of the abyss that yawned between them that John had been unable to tell August of the letter he had written to President Andrew Johnson and the answer he had received. August must have heard of that exchange but the time was no more when he would frankly say, "John, my friend, it is too bad that the little tailor will not let you come home. But then, Paris is not exactly hell on earth and you have your family with you."

And so the Belmonts' visit was over and much had been learned from it. It had been a hard lesson and a worthless one. To what use, John asked himself, could such bitter wisdom be put when the end of the road was in view?

"We are not having the fun we should be having," he said to Mathilde. "We have as much money as we will ever need and the leisure to enjoy it. We should be having a glorious time. Let us go to the opera tonight."

After that, they went to the opera often and to the theatre as well. They went too often. John remembered that for forty years he had been contemptuous of those who had seen all the season's plays and had heard all its great voices. Such people plainly had nothing worth while to do and were not invited to many important dinners.

It was a shock to read of Tom's death. He had almost forgotten Tom. Tom had died years ago in the street outside a New Orleans polling place but his body had stayed warm, so only now was his obituary printed in the New Orleans *Times*.

—at Newport, Rhode Island. Deceased was the brother of ex-Senator John Slidell but altogether different from him in character and inclinations. He was kind, pure-minded and just. By the Bar of this state he was loved, honored and respected. Thomas Slidell will be remembered for—

John rattled the newspaper angrily. For Christ's sake, what do you want of me? Can you not report my brother's death without spitting venom at me? Yes, yes, yes, Tom was altogether different. He was kind, pure-minded and just. But you are rid of me. You are rid of me forever so leave me alone. That is all you have to do. Leave me alone.

He found himself suddenly deathly sick and walked dizzily to his bed. Had the rage that had risen within him at the newspaper item caused— No, he remembered that at breakfast he had eaten little, that he had felt indisposed. Mathilde came to him and with white and worried face hovered over him throughout the day.

351

"I will be better tomorrow," he said.

But he was not better and Mathilde sent for the doctor. He could hear their solemn whispering in the corridor. He was aware of pain and of curious dawns and twilights that were indistinguishable one from the other. There were rows of medicine bottles on the table beside him and at the foot of his bed, sometimes, he saw his daughters and once when his wavering vision pierced the dimness, there was Father Lebrun.

"Go away," he whispered. He saw the stricken look in Mathilde's eyes but he managed to say again to the priest, "Go away." And when Father Lebrun had gone, John beckoned Mathilde close to him and he tried to tell her what was in his mind. He wanted to say that he could answer Father Lebrun only with lies and that it was too late for lies. And he wanted to say, too, that he was sorry he had not told those lies years ago so she could have been married in St. Louis Cathedral.

"I could have done it then, I would have done it then, but I was too arrogant to make concessions to your family. I wanted them to make the concessions. That is the truth and I am ashamed of it but that is the way I was, that is the man you married."

And he did not know whether he said all this or only thought it but Mathilde smiled gently and placed her cool cheek close to his and he felt her tears upon his face. Then he was back in that murky dawn world where everything was silent and colorless.

When he awakened, the doctor was there and in the doorway, Mathilde, looking more tired than he had ever seen her.

"You are an amazing man, Mr. Slidell," the doctor said.

"What have I done now?" And as he spoke, John realized that his voice sounded somewhat stronger in his own ears.

"You must lie quietly, Mr. Slidell, and try to eat well. I really think now that we will see you up and about again."

John lay quietly as he had been told and thought about being up and about again. By God, there would be no more stagnation. He and Mathilde had had enough of the theatre and the opera. They would travel. They would take a trip to Spain. Why not? Travel would be a fine thing for them. He ate an extra piece of toast at dinner, thinking of Spain.

The next morning, when his tray was brought to him, he observed there were two eggs and he tried to eat them both. He was filled now with desire to get away from this bed, from this house, from this country. The second egg was surprisingly revolting. How could one egg be so different from another? To make matters worse, he was unnerved by the sounds that always accompanied the stupid accidents of the upstairs maid. This time, she had apparently taken a fall in the corridor outside his room. The rush of three or four other servants to her assistance, the whispering and milling about was very disturbing. She was such a clumsy girl. So inept. He was amazed when after a long delay, she appeared and took his tray.

"I am glad you are not hurt," he said. "It *was* you who fell?"

She shook her head. "No, sir."

"Oh, I took that for granted."

She burst into tears and ran from the room. Well, perhaps he should have phrased his remark another way. She was probably sensitive about her awkwardness. He was still too ill to be tactful. He closed his eyes and slept. The second egg had been very tiring.

When he awakened, his daughters were in the room. Rosina sitting on the edge of his bed. Young Mathilde on the floor beside him. They did not look beautiful. Their faces were puffy, their eyes red with weeping.

Rosina, seeing that he was awake, flung herself on the pillow and sobbed desperately. He was annoyed. He had his rights as an invalid. "Please," he said, "I am very weak. Go somewhere else with your troubles, child."

Young Mathilde took his hand and kissed it, wetting it with her tears. "We know how weak you are, how sick, but we have to tell you. There is no way to keep it from you. Oh, dear God, I cannot say it. Rosina, can you—" Young Mathilde lowered her head and wept stormily.

He lay motionless for a time, listening to the sobs of his daughters. Then he crawled from the bed and left them to weep. It was not easy to walk. Even when he clung to chairs and bureaus and clawed at the wall for support, it was not easy. Trembling and gasping for breath, he found his way to Mathilde's room.

They had placed her upon the pink silk lounge where she had liked to rest in the afternoons. Someone had closed her eyes and

353

had crossed her arms upon her bosom. Father Lebrun sat beside her.

John fitted his shoulders into the corner of the room so that in this terrible moment he might stand like a man.

"It was too fast," Father Lebrun said. "Nothing could be done. She walked upstairs as usual. She was on her way to you and in the corridor her heart ceased beating. That was all. It was the end."

John tried to reply. He tried to go to Mathilde. He tried to hang onto the small measure of strength that had brought him to Mathilde's side. But the room reeled before his swimming eyes. He could hear himself whimpering. Black waves of misery surged over him and he fainted.

It was pride that kept him erect as he walked through Paris on small errands which he invented for himself. Pride that made him the bête noire of tailors and shirtmakers. A man could not be a pathetic figure, could he, if nothing concerned him but a poorly cut sleeve or an ill-fitting collar?

He made it a point to laugh when the Confederacy was mentioned. "Ancient history, my friend. What is the news of today?" But why had the Confederacy been mentioned? Did people think it was the only subject that could possibly interest him? Did he belong so entirely to the leftover odds and ends of yesterday? He could remember the ridiculous old man Pierre de Landais, who in outmoded clothes had wandered the streets of New York City speaking of the Revolution. The memory would send him to his bootmaker to order two or three pairs of extremely stylish dress pumps.

The house on Avenue d'Antin had been given up after Mathilde's death. He lived in an apartment now, and in the evenings he sat with a brandy bottle at his side. He would think of the past. He would think that long ago he had castigated himself for losing a city. He had punched Charlie Wilkes, had shot Steve Price and lost New York. He was doing better now. He no longer simply lost a city. He had found a way to lose a country. James Mason had gone to live in a Canadian town where there was quite a settlement of ex-Confederates. A colony of Pierre de Landaises, John thought scornfully. He would remember Fifth Avenue and he would remember Royal Street and after a while, he would walk to his desk, taking with him the brandy bottle.

Dear Mr. President:

I solicit permission to visit the state of Louisiana and respectfully ask to be informed on what condition, if on any, I may be allowed—

If a President turned a deaf ear, would an ex-President be more likely to listen? Surely Buchanan had some memories of him that were touched with a mellow affection.

Dear Jim:

We did not part as friends but the war is over now and I know you are big enough to forgive and forget. As a former president of the United States you certainly are an influential and honored citizen. I wonder if you would do me a favor. Would you find out what I must do to gain permission to visit Louisiana? Of course I realize—

Perhaps when Johnson was no longer in office, the whole thing would be easier. Perhaps with the next President, it would be only a matter of packing a trunk and buying a ticket. Still, why wait for a change in administrations?

Dear Bill:

Here is a voice from out of the past which I hope will not ring unpleasantly in your ears. I am happy that President Johnson retained you as Secretary of State after Mr. Lincoln's death for, in my opinion, the country never had one to equal you. Permit me, too, to congratulate you on the purchase of Alaska. The newspapers say that in some quarters the deal is being derisively called "Seward's Folly." Do not let such gibes trouble you. It was a brilliant move on your part.

Now, Bill, I would like to ask on what grounds I am being barred from the United States. Knowing you to be always on the side of good sense and justice—

There were never any replies. He stopped writing letters. One day, he called on John Dix, the new United States Minister to France, who had been Buchanan's Secretary of the Treasury. Dix was cool but he had made time for John without an appointment. He addressed his visitor formally, giving straightforward answers without either gloating or hypocritical expressions of regret.

"Mr. Slidell, my information is that there are no conditions under which you will be permitted to re-enter the United States."

355

"Is that not a harsh decision when one considers that my activities were no more inimical to the country than those of many another man?"

"It is a decision," Dix said. "And, as I understand it, one that leaves no room for discussion."

"I have heard that James Mason will be allowed, in due course, to return to Virginia."

Dix said, "Mr. Slidell, if James Mason returns to Virginia, it will be as a quiet, private individual. He has had his fill of politics and intrigue."

"Do I look strong enough to fight my way back to a position of importance?"

John Dix stared down at a stack of letters upon his desk. He said, "Reconstruction is a complex business. The United States is in no need of additional problems. I think your record, prior to the war, suggests to some that your unusual approach to political issues might not be altogether helpful."

"You are saying that the edict against my return is aimed not at a Confederate commissioner but directly at John Slidell."

"Yes, that is what I am saying, for it is my belief."

"And John Slidell, of all Southerners, is singled out to be the one man who can never again return to the United States?"

Dix said, "That is exactly true."

John stood up. "I thank you for seeing me and I thank you for your honesty. I have been dangling in midair, not knowing how to plan my last years. Now I know."

What rubbish that now he knew how to plan his last years. He had not the slightest notion what to do with them. This much was established: his home was Paris. Very well. Was that not fine? He had children and grandchildren here. What more could an old man ask? Ah, but to accept with gratitude an old man's lot, one must look at life through the eyes of an old man. And he could find within himself only the John Slidell energetic and imaginative enough to have shaped the political thinking of a state and a nation. There was no place for that John Slidell any more and grandchildren could delight a man only when he was so busy that he fitted them in on special occasions or when his mind had slowed to a toddler's pace.

He took his trip to Spain. And one to Italy and several to England. The traveling became like the theatregoing. Something to do. Somewhere to go. Dinners, of course, at the homes of his daughters. He was touched and frightened by their desire to make conversation which would entertain him. Did he strike them as pitiable? He, who had been their hero? By God, Rosina must be subscribing to a New Orleans newspaper in her anxiety to throw him morsels of interest that he might be able to understand.

"I am so sad, Father. The Théâtre d'Orleans has been destroyed by fire."

"Do tell."

"And the New York-New Orleans steamer *Evening Star* sank with a loss of two hundred and fifty lives."

"Really, sweetheart?" Could he tell her that he knew what was happening in Paris on this very day? Could he tell her that he was not yet ready to sit in the chimney corner, drooling in repulsive senility? Though, come to think of it, who had offered him a chimney corner?

Young Mathilde did not concentrate on New Orleans. Out of respect, no doubt, to Rosina, who had staked out that conversational territory. Young Mathilde asked him if he remembered the terrible trip it had been from New York to Brooklyn that time when they had visited Aunt Janie and Uncle Cal. Well, there was going to be a bridge built. Fantastic but true, she said. A bridge from New York to Brooklyn. Did he remember Niblo's Garden? Well, they had remodeled the stage at a cost of twenty-five thousand dollars!

"My, my," he said and went on a trip to Greece.

When he came back, his daughters were ready to entertain him again. There was a great deal of new building going on in New Orleans, Rosina told him. Young Mathilde had news for him of the development of Central Park on Manhattan Island. And did he remember the talk of St. Patrick's Cathedral that would be so enormous and so magnificent? Well, the construction was coming right along and did he remember—

He said, "Bismarck is skillfully propagating fear of France in order to provoke a war. Have you thought of leaving Paris? It may not be pleasant to be here if the Prussians arrive."

There was war and the Prussians arrived. John's daughters fled with their children. When the war was over, they returned to a republic. Louis Napoleon had lost his throne and France was cheering new symbols, new sound and fury. Neither Rosina nor young Mathilde remembered from whom they had first heard the name of Bismarck. Poor Father, he had been in Paris throughout the war. Perhaps they should have warned him that things looked threatening. Perhaps they should have taken him with them. He must come to dinner now that they were home again. They must have a good talk. Did he remember Leonard Jerome, that friend of the Belmonts who drove the four-in-hand so wildly? Well, Leonard's daughter, Jennie Jerome, was going to marry Lord Randolph Churchill. It would be a very important London wedding. Did he remember—

The Franco-Prussian War had meant nothing to John Slidell except for the visit of Colonel Von Borcke. Von Borcke, a handsome blond giant who had served heroically in the Confederate cavalry simply because he loved war, was one of the conquering Prussians who arrived in Paris. Very drunk, very sentimental, weeping for his dead chief, Jeb Stuart, he had found his way to the apartment of another ex-Confederate.

Von Borcke's French was dreadful and John spoke no German. So in a sitting room in occupied Paris, a New Yorker and a Prussian drank together and, with faint traces of Southern accent, conversed in English.

"How did you find me, Colonel?"

"I was in a bar. We were drinking toasts to William the First of Prussia, to Bismarck and to Von Moltke. All at once, I want to drink a toast to General Jeb Stuart and the Confederacy. When I mention the Confederacy, I am told by the barman that there is here in Paris someone else, so I find out where and come."

"You are very welcome, sir."

"Thank you. Now we talk of the Confederacy. Ah, that Jeb Stuart. You recall what a man he was? With you I can talk of that beautiful war."

The huge Von Borcke lay back in a chair and stretched his booted legs in massive comfort and spoke of Malvern Hill and

Martinsburg and Cunningham's Ford. John had seen none of those places, had barely heard of them. He had never met Jeb Stuart. He had not known of Von Borcke till this very evening.

Von Borcke told of a day when his death had been reported in Richmond and the government had telegraphed General Lee to send Von Borcke's body there.

"I cannot spare it," Lee had responded. "It is in pursuit of the Federal cavalry."

John opened another bottle of brandy. The sky grew pale and Colonel Von Borcke's rumbling voice and lusty laughter fell silent and he slept. But John could not sleep. He sat gazing at the Prussian colonel who had brought him the news that he was even more anchorless than he had guessed. A Confederate with no thrilling memories of the Stars and Bars. A Confederate who had not known the date or the sorrow of Jeb Stuart's death. A Confederate totally unable to talk of the Confederacy. De Landais, my friend, you, at least, knew what happened in the Revolution.

John visited England again that autumn. In an art gallery as he was drifting indifferently from one painting to the next, he became aware of a slight figure in dull, deep black. From beneath the jet-trimmed bonnet, two sad eyes rested upon him.

"Mr. Slidell."

"Madame!" He bowed before the woman who had been the Empress Eugénie.

Tears glittered upon her lashes. "We are in exile," she said, as though the loss of the French throne might have escaped notice. "Life is cruel but, sir, you know that. Your lovely Mathilde." She crossed herself and the tears rolled down her cheeks as she stood with eyes closed, her body held in rigid despair. "How you must miss her."

There were no words for that anguish. He resented her thinking that there were, that any conventional compassionate phrase would fit the measure of his heartache.

He said, "You have suffered much, madame."

"Not so much as my poor husband. Will you come to us for tea, Mr. Slidell? Tomorrow afternoon?"

John remembered that he had once planned to tell Louis Napoleon that a crown set awkwardly upon his head but when they met, they clasped hands wordlessly and searched each other's eyes for sympathy.

They sat in the private parlor of an imposing house on a tree-lined street. The room was crowded with treasures that had not yet been assigned to permanent locations. Escritoires, portraits, tables, fire screens huddled in disorganized, undecided groups like—yes, like exiles, John thought. He sat holding a teacup, listening to the soft, distressed voices of deposed royalty telling him, between sighs, that they prayed for the people of France. Tragic innocents who would be the main sufferers. The curtains rustled eerily, the servants walked on silent feet and the soft voices droned on and on, talking of defeat and treachery.

John left them, bowing deeply and backing away as though departing from the presence of the Emperor and Empress of France. The man and woman in the cluttered room shed tears at this kind gesture.

He walked back to the heart of the city through a steely-gray drizzle. He went to the taproom of one of the fine hotels. It was a place where sometimes he saw someone he knew. Now there was no one but himself in the dark oak drinking place. Oh, the barman, of course. Well, was not the barman a person? Had he not a tongue and feelings and opinions?

"Rather quiet, is it not?" John asked.

"A little early, I think, sir."

"Did you just come on duty?"

"No. Actually, I shall be leaving when my relief comes. This week, I have my evenings free."

"Have you?" John downed his whisky and looked at the aging but brisk fellow on the other side of the bar. In his way, he represented comfort, changelessness and security as unmistakably as the Bank of England. "Have a drink with me," John invited.

"Don't mind if I do, sir. Thank you."

As the barman filled the glasses, John said, "Do you like your evenings free?"

"Very much, sir."

"Don't you ever—" John paused and began again. "Don't you ever wonder what in hell to do with them?"

360

The barman smiled. "Oh, no, sir," he said. "That is never a problem. I come from a big family."

John picked up his drink, then pushed the empty glass back toward the barman. "Fill it again," he said. "And leave the bottle right here."

IV

The Calendar

They lived at Neuilly in an exquisite house with a peaceful garden. There were more servants than two elderly widows really needed but as Mathilde, the Baroness d'Erlanger, often said, she and her sister were accustomed to many servants.

The Baroness thought they were obligated to do some entertaining and she would plan the menu, settle on the date and decide what flowers to use for table decoration. But then she could not think to whom they were obligated. Guests were such a problem. Who was still alive?

When Madame Jean Baptiste Marchand, wife of the famous general, came on her visits to the house in Neuilly, it was sometimes difficult for the Baroness d'Erlanger to remember who she was.

"Sister dear," the Countess de St. Roman would murmur, "Please try to remember that she is my daughter. Do I forget your son?"

"No, but then you are smarter, Rosina. You are younger."

Rosina was not much younger but it was she who learned to talk on the telephone, she who was not frightened by the little mother-of-pearl push buttons that lighted the chandeliers.

Sometimes in the night, the Baroness could be heard calling like a lonely child, "Sister, I must get up. Will you come touch that thing in the wall?"

They were sweet old ladies, the servants said. They said it smilingly as though to beg the listener not to judge the sisters by their overuse of cosmetics or their curious habit of going hungry at times to keep their slim figures.

"They were very beautiful. You can tell by the portraits. So much must have been said of their beauty, it is no wonder they still think of it. Besides, you know"—and here the servants would lower their voices to mention a thing that was explanatory but not thought to be very complimentary—"they are originally Americans."

It was difficult for the Baroness and the Countess to remember that this was true. They never had any occasion to speak the English language. It slipped from them. They could no longer form sentences with facility or recall words and meanings swiftly enough for speech. Reading was different. They subscribed to New York and London newspapers, sometimes looking up from an item with haunted puzzlement in their eyes.

"Why is the name of Gansevoort familiar?"

"I do not know."

"Nor I. Yet it troubles me, for once I must have heard it. No matter. He was a very old man and he is dead. He had been an American admiral."

"You do not mean Charles Wilkes, do you?"

"Of course I do not mean Charles Wilkes. He was an American admiral and he is also dead but I know who he was. Do you?"

"Yes, yes. He was—he was—who was he, Rosina? Not that I really care. The name you asked about was Gansevoort, was it not?"

"Yes, and you must have known the name yourself at one time, for I spoke it but once and you were able to repeat it."

In a wardrobe in her room, the Baroness d'Erlanger saved the newspapers which she thought she had not yet read. She would pull one at random from the enormous stacks and say to her sister, "Your son-in-law is in grave trouble, my dear. Is his name not Marchand? He has established a French post somewhere in Africa and he should not have done so. Lord Kitchener is furious. France and England stand at the brink of war because your son-in-law has—"

"My God, Mathilde, you are taking papers from that left-hand stack again. You will be discovering tomorrow that my son-in-law has been wounded. Do not tell me about it. That was in the Boxer Rebellion, which is now some time ago. Dear, this week's papers are on the table beside my bed."

366

"I will get to them, Rosina, but here— Listen to this. This is not the same paper. This is news. There has been a great celebration in Japan. A superb monolith has been unveiled in Perry Park in the presence of Commodore Frederick Rodgers. The newspaper says that he is the grandson of Matthew Calbraith Perry. He must be a relative of ours."

Rosina nodded. "Of course, dear."

"There were American vessels and Japanese vessels and fireworks and speeches honoring the memory of Uncle Cal."

"Yes, Mathilde, you are quite right. All that actually happened —but not recently. Begin taking from the stack on the extreme right-hand side of the wardrobe, will you?"

But the Baroness still preferred her own method of getting the news. A front page that was pink was irresistible. Once when she had reached for a newspaper to use as a weapon against a buzzing fly, she had quite forgotten the insect in her delight at having selected a London daily made entirely of green pages. Immediately, she had seated herself and begun to read the news.

"I forget so much," she said dreamily, "but I will always remember the fountains, one spurting champagne, the other perfume."

"Now, how on earth did you come to think of that?"

Mathilde was amazed at the stupidity of her sister. "Why, it is very natural that I should think of it. That was in the spectacular home of Leonard Jerome."

"Yes, it was, Mathilde."

"And his daughter, Jennie, married Lord Randolph Churchill and right here in the paper it says that her son, Winston, has been elected to Parliament."

Rosina smiled. "He is First Lord of the Admiralty now."

"The paper does not say that."

"If you keep looking, you will find one that does." Rosina's glance wandered to the garden, where she could see the luncheon table being set beneath the trees. Beguiled by the thought of soft breezes and flower fragrances, she moved through the open casement windows to the bright beauty of outdoors. Mathilde followed. Poor Mathilde. Her legs were troubling her. She walked with difficulty. Stiff and graceless as a marionette.

They lunched on delicately flavored fish, a crisp salad and the small heart-shaped strawberries from the French woods, which they smothered deliciously beneath thick cream.

"Do you remember Tangipahoa strawberries, Mathilde?"

"No. What were they?"

"Part of our childhood, sister."

"Can we have them for our dinner party? I think we should give one."

"Very well. Whom shall we invite?"

"I will consult with my son. He knows distinguished people and August Belmont may be in Paris soon."

"August Belmont is dead," Rosina said gently.

"I thought so, too, but he is not. In a very new paper, one I took directly from the right-hand stack, there was a reference to him. August Belmont, head of August Belmont and Company, representing the Rothschilds and—"

"Yes, dear. That is his son. He is also head of things called Rapid Transit Subway Construction Company and Interborough Consolidated Corporation. He has arranged for trains to travel under New York City."

"But why? One can not observe the scenery if one travels so."

"It is very swift and practical and perhaps the scenery is no longer attractive. Perry Belmont has engaged in pursuits you will understand. Congressman, Minister to Spain and—"

Mathilde said, "Now it comes to me. I have been meaning to ask you of a name I saw. Who can a lady possibly be who is referred to as Mrs. O. H. P. Belmont, the former Alva Vanderbilt?"

Rosina's lips curled in distaste. "The wife, I assume, of August, Senior's, son Oliver Hazard Perry Belmont. She is very fashionable and has been a society leader of great note but there are no ladylike qualities in this creature. She is a suffragette."

"A what?"

"A woman who wants to vote!"

Mathilde stared at her sister. "Rosina, women cannot vote."

"I know that, dear, but Mrs. O. H. P. Belmont does not see why they cannot. She has led a parade down Fifth Avenue, a parade of hundreds of insane females all dressed in white, all carrying banners demanding the vote. It is disgraceful."

"And on Fifth Avenue, too! It is perhaps well that August is dead. How shamed he would have been. In which stack will I find news of this frightful occurrence?"

After luncheon, they took their naps and when they awakened, Mathilde's son was waiting in the garden for them. He was always a shock to Rosina. A fat little middle-aged man, as mild and humdrum as a mountain of soapsuds.

"I had forgotten it was Sunday," Mathilde said.

He was startled and displeased.

"Did you not go to mass!"

Rosina buried her smile in a bouquet of yellow roses. Really, this man resembled too closely his grandfather, the banker D'Erlanger, for his Catholic piety not to be amusing.

"Yes, I went to mass but it is now so many hours ago that I had forgotten it was Sunday," Mathilde said.

"You would have remembered, had I failed to appear."

But how nice, Rosina thought, if only once young Emile did something unexpected. Every Sunday, world without end, there was Emile, turning resolutely from the worshiping, the polishing and cataloguing of his collection of topazes and amethysts to drive to Neuilly to see his mother. On alternating Sundays, he brought his wife, a light-haired Italian who wore eyeglasses.

"It does not matter how a woman sees," Rosina had told Emile's wife. "It is how she looks." But only Mathilde had agreed that eyeglasses were hideous and quite unsuitable for a lady to use in public.

Emile invited them for a ride in his motorcar as he always did. Today, they preferred the quiet of the garden. Perhaps next time.

"Then I shall send word to the chauffeur to go rest in your kitchen and have a cold drink."

"Do that," Mathilde said. "How are the children? When will you bring them? It has been so long—"

Emile said, "Mother, you are not thinking. Louise is married and living in England. Robert is—"

"Yes, yes, I remember. He is at Saint-Cyr."

"No, darling. He is many years out of Saint-Cyr. He is with the army in Indochina."

Mathilde shook her head. "I keep forgetting. Your Uncle Alfred was at Saint-Cyr, you know."

"Yes, Mother, I know."

"But he is dead now."

"Yes, Mother."

Tears came to Mathilde's eyes. "He was so young."

No one called Mathilde's attention to the fact that Alfred had been past sixty at the time of his death.

Rosina said, "Dear, you were going to ask Emile about our guest list."

"Guest list?" asked Emile. "Now, that sounds interesting." He glanced at Rosina, smiling. It was a game they played quite regularly.

It was on such a Sunday that Emile spoke softly and hesitantly of a terrible possibility. If war should come, if France should be swept into it, then perhaps the garden at Neuilly would not be such a pleasant place to be.

Mathilde smiled. "I was not afraid of Germans in the last war. I would not be afraid of them now."

Emile patted his mother's hand. He knew she was convinced that she had remained in Paris throughout the Prussian occupation.

"Last time, you took care of me," he said. "This time, you must let me take care of you. If there is a war, you must promise to do as I say. You must go where I tell you to go."

But Mathilde, Baroness d'Erlanger, did not live to need her son's protection, and this time Paris remained the unattained goal of the old enemy. Rosina stayed in the house at Neuilly in company with her daughter. Together they prayed for General Marchand, who was fighting the Boche, and they prayed that the United States would realize that German ambition was threatening the whole civilized world.

Rosina saw the Americans when they came, the boys from New York, Philadelphia, San Francisco and from New Orleans. So young and strong, so fresh-faced. Shyly, because it was an old lady's whim, she asked her daughter to find a way to bring a dozen boys from New Orleans to the house at Neuilly.

"Nothing could be simpler, darling. Through the Salvation Army or the Knights of Columbus, this can be arranged in no time at all."

Rosina wished Mathilde could have lived, for at last there were guests and there could be a dinner party. In an old trunk, Rosina found her mother's Creole recipes and turned them over to the cook.

"There are ingredients we cannot get," the cook protested.

"My mother always got them, no matter where she was."

In the end, it did not matter, for the boys from New Orleans ate heartily and happily without guessing the origin of the foods on the Countess' table. She had expected their eyes to glow in surprised recognition. She had expected to still their homesickness. Not a one of them had ever seen or tasted Creole delicacies. Not a one of them spoke French.

"The chow was great, Countess. *Comprenez-vous* 'great'? *Merci*. Many thanks. It was real *bon* of you."

"Are you sure they were from New Orleans?" Rosina asked her daughter.

And though in trivial matters the soldiers had disappointed her, she thought much about them and the country from which they had come, the country from which she had come. Her son-in-law, Jean Baptiste Marchand, and her nephew, Emile d'Erlanger, were alarmed when she told them of her plans.

"When peace returns, I am going to visit the United States."

"But you cannot think of it. Such a voyage at your age?"

She laughed. "It can do no more than kill me and time is doing that. Truly I should love to see the country that once was mine."

"You will take your maid?"

"I will take two maids and if it will lessen your anxiety, the nurse who tends me when I am ill."

She was more than eighty years old. Patiently she waited for peace and then for passenger service to be resumed on the French ships. The thought troubled her that delay might rob her of the last thing she would ever want from life.

But Rosina, Countess de St. Roman, was not robbed. She, who had been born during the administration of Martin Van Buren, lived to see President Woodrow Wilson's America.

"I am glad he is a Democrat," she said. "My father was a Democrat, you know. Unpack the blue trunk first. It has my wine. Here one cannot buy wine. There is an odd sort of law. So fortunate

371

that my son-in-law has a friend who helped me through customs. Must I really rest? There is so much to see."

So much, indeed. Almost sixty years had gone since her last glimpse of New York. A dozen buildings for which she sought, she failed to find. She saw the corner of Eighteenth Street and Fifth Avenue but the marble mansion that had belonged to August Belmont was not there. It had been demolished. She had not bargained for that. It brought a sadness to the bright, exciting day. The home of August Belmont—

"Belmont?" asked the chauffeur, happy to hear a word he understood. "Of course, madame."

And that is how it happened that Rosina, Countess de St. Roman, saw the great horse Man o' War run a mile and a quarter in two minutes, three seconds flat. The Countess and her nurse laughed all the way back to the Waldorf. Tomorrow she must really tell the hotel people to send her a chauffeur who spoke French.

"How August would have roared," she thought, "if he knew that in seeking his home, I was taken to a race track." And she dismissed the sudden thought that came to her mind, for she disliked those who could twist an ordinary experience into a marvelous brush with the supernatural.

Still, as she drove through the city, there was no denying that she felt close to her father. That, too, was easily explained but it almost seemed that he was beside her when on the following morning she walked a block or two upon Fifth Avenue. Had Fifth Avenue meant anything special to him? She did not know but now at the end of her life, if she wished to be a fool, she supposed no harm could come of it. So she turned from her nurse and spoke to the wind.

"We will go to Washington. Yes, and to New Orleans, too, and we will walk on Royal Street. Will you like that?"

For answer, a gentleman walked past and the wind brought to Rosina the aroma of a very fine cigar.

And that afternoon she drove to St. Mark's in-the-Bouwerie and stood at vault ninety-five. John Slidell's vault. Her grandfather's grave. How cold-blooded of her to have come without a flower. She had a French-speaking chauffeur now and he told her

372

that Matthew Calbraith Perry, an American naval hero, had once rested here but had been removed to his birthplace in Rhode Island.

"I did not know," she said.

"Sometimes even Americans do not know such things, madame. I happen to like history. I could show you much in this city that might interest you. Is this your first visit to America?"

She thought it ironic that only in French could she find the words to say, "I was born and raised here."

"Oh, in that case, you probably know more American history than I do."

She smiled at the earnest young man. "No. Actually, I know no history at all, either French or American." After a moment of silence, she spoke again. "Of course," she said, "at my age, one remembers conversations and happenings from the past, but as for history—"

FOR THE RECORD

John Slidell married Jane MacKenzie in 1790.

They were the parents of: Ellen, 1791; John, Jr., 1793; Janie, 1797; Thomas, 1798; Alexander, 1800; Julia, 1814. Two others died in childhood.

Ellen married but bore no children.

John, Jr., and his wife were the parents of two daughters and a son.

Janie was wed to Matthew Calbraith Perry and had twelve children, four of whom died as babies.

Thomas does not appear to have taken a wife.

Alexander married Catherine Robinson and fathered two sons.

Julia married Raymond Rogers. Records vary as to the size of this family. There were four or five children.

LAST WORD

So much glamour, drama, and importance surrounded the Slidells, Perrys, and Belmonts that it may be of interest to know precisely what in this chronicle has been manufactured.

The events dealing with the marriage of Jane and John, the progenitors, are outright fiction. Since no one has left a clear picture of how a humble soap-boiler managed to marry a wealthy-young lady of fine Scottish ancestry, it was necessary to imagine how this may have come about. Several lengths of whole cloth have been cut to cover the entire situation.

Historically, only one incident rests on a shaky foundation. There is nothing to substantiate that John, upon learning that he would be defeated in his first attempt to win a seat in Congress, then cleverly devoted himself to Andrew Jackson's cause. However, it is true that after the election Jackson rewarded him with the position of United States District Attorney at New Orleans.

There is little inventiveness required in writing of a family who lived more melodrama than Steve Price produced at the Park Theatre. Perhaps the audience at the Park would have hooted unbelievingly when the junior-grade lieutenant whom young Mathilde slapped was recognized as a former beau. And what would the critical New York theatregoers have said when the captain of the *San Jacinto* turned out to be Charles Wilkes?

The last section of the book, which is called "The Calendar," is as fictitious as the first section, "The Progenitors." It is definitely known that Rosina Slidell lived at least till 1925, and it is said that in her old age she visited the United States. Since her visit is not, by any means, an established fact, naturally all things concerned with it are inventions.